"About two-thirds of the way through this finely tuned first novel, Michael Cummings describes a phenomenon exclusive to Norway called a 'super bloom.' It's also an apt description of this story—a beautiful adventure into the mysteries and miracles of life."

—TODD GOLD, *New York Times* best-selling author

"*Bergen Spring* is a beautifully written story about grief, love, guilt, and the artist's journey as he explores his ancestral past in a search for personal identity."

—MATT GOLDMAN, *New York Times* best-selling author and Emmy Award–winning television writer

"*Bergen Spring* recreates that magical time in the 1970s when we all wished to backpack across Europe, making the transition from youth to adult. Cummings's understanding of the art world, theater, and literature—and his personal travel experiences—add to the credibility of the material. If you want to imagine yourself as young, free, and easing into adulthood, join Erik on his journey of personal, spiritual, and professional discovery."

—JOHN NABER, Olympic champion, network broadcaster, author, and speaker

"Erik Hellberg's grief-laden, solo journey through Europe affirms that we never truly travel alone, even when we feel alone. Our lives are filled with people who teach us something along the way. For Erik's journey of self-discovery, the people who weave in and out of his life give him the courage to love, lose, and let go."

—SHERRY ROBINSON, author of *Shadows Hold Their Breath*

"Written with style and poignant grace, Michael Cummings's *Bergen Spring* is part love story, part travelogue—a timeless tale that transports you to a foreign land with such vivid description and profound accuracy as to make you feel like you are truly along for the epic journey. Along the way, a haunting tragedy lingers until, at last, the birth of spring brings renewal, hope, and even forgiveness. Highly recommended!"

—Rusty Fischer, author of *Zombies Don't Cry*

"Priceless—something very meaningful for everyone who is lucky enough to read it. Michael Cummings has captured lightning in a bottle. Rarely am I that taken with something I've read. The narrative and the language are so powerful, I could not put it down. I could feel and smell the Norwegian taverns and flats Erik visited; I felt I was on those long walks with him. It was captivating and did what a book should—I forgot about everything that had been on my mind that day."

—Reinhard Denke, screenwriter of *Sex, Greed, Money, Murder, and Chicken Fried Steak*

"In Erik, I saw glimpses of my younger self: wide-eyed, full of wanderlust, eager to take center stage and find true love. Michael Cummings has crafted a rich and nuanced coming-of-age story that is all at once universal because of its specificity and attention to detail. Erik embarks on a European journey of a lifetime, and we're lucky enough to be on the *tog* bound for Bergen."

—Cullen Douglas, actor and screenwriter

BERGEN SPRING

BERGEN SPRING

A NOVEL - MICHAEL CUMMINGS

Shadelandhouse
MODERN PRESS

LEXINGTON, KENTUCKY

A Shadelandhouse Modern Press book

Bergen Spring
a novel

Copyright © 2025 Michael Cummings
All rights reserved.

Without in any way limiting the author's and publisher's exclusive rights under copyright, any use of this publication to "train" generative artificial intelligence (AI) technologies to generate text is expressly prohibited. The author reserves all rights to license uses of this work for generative AI training and development of machine learning language models.

For information about permission to reproduce selections from this book, please direct written inquiries to Permissions, Shadelandhouse Modern Press, LLC,
P.O. Box 910913, Lexington, KY 40591, or email permissions@smpbooks.com.

Bergen Spring is a work of fiction. Any references to historical events, or real locales are used fictitiously. Other names, characters, places, and incidents are products of the author's imagination or are used fictitiously, and any resemblance to actual events, locales, or persons, living or dead, is entirely coincidental. To the extent any trademarks, service marks, product names, or named features are used in this work of fiction, all are assumed to be the property of their respective owners and are used only for reference. Use of these terms does not imply endorsement.

Printed and manufactured in the United States of America.
Published in the United States of America by:
Shadelandhouse Modern Press, LLC
Lexington, Kentucky
smpbooks.com
First edition 2025

Shadelandhouse, Shadelandhouse Modern Press, and the colophon
are trademarks of Shadelandhouse Modern Press, LLC.

ISBN: 978-1-945049-49-1 (paperback), 978-1-945049-58-3 (epub)
Library of Congress Control Number: 2024951828

Cover art: *Train Smoke*. Found in the Collection of Munch Museum, Oslo.
Munch, Edvard (1863–1944) ©ARS, NY
©2024 Artists Rights Society (ARS), New York
©2024 photograph of art, Art Resource, NY

Author photograph: Jonas Mohr
Cover and book design: iota books

to Maureen and Natalie

Chad,
  I love you and your family so much.

Every man is guilty of all the good he did not do.

—Voltaire

THE FLOWER

The brief Bergen sunshine season was spent, and now a light rain accompanied Erik on his walk to the train station. He'd made this trip down Mount Fløyen to the city at least a hundred times over the past months and then made the same walk up the mountain to his basement apartment—nearly two hours each way.

Everything he owned was crammed into his backpack. He carried his friend's guitar by hand, wrapped in plastic against the incessant drizzle. All other accumulations had either been given, shipped, or thrown away.

Erik should have been elated starting his journey home. Instead, he was miserable. He'd hurt someone who didn't deserve to be hurt. Someone who had been kind, whose attentions had permitted others to view him as something other than an outsider. She'd been open and vulnerable. She'd been honest. She'd invested herself in him. *Could he say the same?*

She said she wouldn't see him off. He was painfully aware that she'd opened her world to him and now he was leaving. *Was he betraying her?* She may have been in touch with her feelings about him, but he was confused as hell. He felt like a kid around her, and by any measure he was.

Erik removed his gray tweed cap and tilted his face skyward so that the wetness of Bergen caressed his face—as if rain had the power to assuage guilt. The other passengers sheltered under the platform's canopy with characteristic Norwegian reserve.

Rain was a daily occurrence in Bergen, usually just a misty, steady drizzle. Rain had greeted his first footstep in this tiny seaside town on the western coast of Norway and nearly every step since, save for a few glorious weeks in spring when the flowers of Bergen exploded in a kaleidoscope of color and fragrance.

The rains he faced upon his arrival and the rains he faced today couldn't have been more different. He was no longer a boy, but he didn't feel like a man either. He felt like the shell of a man. Erik took off his pack, leaned it against one of the platform pillars, and then looked through empty eyes down the tracks.

A woman's hand reached around from behind him and pressed against his chest. He tried to turn, but the hand would countenance no movement. Her soft body pulled insistently into his back and her warm whisper penetrated his inner ear, triggering tingling sensations throughout his body.

"Don't turn around."

A familiar perfume ignited silken memories. The two figures stood there for a frozen moment. Erik staring stupidly ahead, unable to move, while the woman hugged him as if he was the only living person on earth.

Her delicate fingers slowly unbuttoned his raincoat and then reached up under his sweater and shirt. Erik inhaled a quick breath at the cool touch of her hand against his skin. Her fingernails lightly scratched him as they slid down his chest, leaving something moist and fragile in its wake. *A søstermarihand*—her favorite. The fragrant yellow orchid appears only when the sun shines during the short spring season. Except today there was only rain in Bergen.

She whispered again in his ear. "Don't turn around, and don't look." He felt her hands leave him and her body pull away. He stood for a moment, stunned and dumb—finally turning and looking out into the rain.

She was gone. Not a trace of her anywhere. *Was she just a figment of my beleaguered imagination?* He reached inside his shirt and pulled out the yellow orchid. The flower's aroma conjugated with the scent of her perfume and clung stubbornly to him, refusing to be washed away by the rain.

How long did he stand there, staring uselessly into the darkening countryside as day silently acquiesced to night? He couldn't say. And he was only obliquely aware of the train pulling into the station. Was this moment real, or was it a dream? Was he about to leave, or was he looking down at the station from the heights above Bergen and watching someone else grab his pack and board the train?

As the locomotive climbed through mountain passes cloaked in burnt sienna skies, he found himself in the dining car staring at the first page of his weatherworn journal. He looked at what a boy had written while bound for London on that first day during the beginning of his journey nearly a year ago. A carousel of memories flooded his mind.

The Journey
By Erik Torsen Hellberg
September 15, 1973

I have just witnessed the most beautiful sunrise in the history of sunrises. Let it be an omen for my journey. Below us, vast white fields that billow and undulate like an agitated ocean. To the east, knifing its way into the horizon, a scarlet red streak topped by an orange brighter than Van Gogh's imagination.

Today my life begins. As the seeds of discontent compelled Siddhartha to enter the world and seek his path, I too will seek my path. The tools I take with me are identical to those Siddhartha possessed: I can think, I can fast, I can pray.

I have no Govinda to accompany me, and that's as it should be. Charlie will be my sole companion, my "secret Govinda." I'm putting it in writing, here and now, that I'll make it up to you, Charlie. Somehow, somewhere, before this journey is over. I swear I will. God made a mistake. It should have been me. It never should have been you, Charlie. If there truly was justice in this universe, I wouldn't be on this plane. You would, Charlie.

A man from Yugoslavia is seated next to me. I wanted to talk with him about his country, but he can't speak a word of English and, of course, I don't know his language. How frustrating! The day is coming when I shall be a citizen of the world and can speak a dozen tongues and I will understand the insanity of an unjust world.

The plane will soon land and when next I write, I shall be somewhere else. In a foreign country with a new life. I don't care where the night finds me, so long as I'm free.

I love DD

"*I love DD*" *Ha!* He had to laugh at himself.

DD. He only wrote her initials. What, was he afraid someone would find his journal and know his secrets? *Ha! That's rich!*

Diana Dresden. She had been his muse. His inspiration. A patch of light in a universe of darkness, an oasis within a hellish jungle. He closed his journal.

That was a lifetime ago and a different universe.

The porter entered the car and Erik signaled him. He spoke to the porter in Norwegian.

"*Unnskyld, en kopp kaffe?*"

The porter nodded and left to bring Erik his coffee.

Not many people in the dining car at this hour. This was the night train, and the sleeper cabins are intoxicatingly comfortable—one might say a relic from the Old World. Normally, Erik would have been bunked down by now and the sounds of the rails would be lulling him to sleep. But he couldn't sleep even if he had wanted to. The *søstermarihand* burned where it had touched his skin. Yet he didn't want the stinging to stop. He needed the catharsis of pain.

At this time of year, the night skies between Bergen and Oslo are graced with a perpetual nautical twilight. The terrain seems to change shapes and colors as the train races in and around the mountains. Mysterious formations ebb and flow, like water crashing against a rocky coastline. An azure blue might become cerulean blue or midnight green in the span of twenty kilometers. A menacing troll-shaped creature might suddenly appear mere meters from the train window, only to quietly morph into a goat-willow tree.

The porter entered the dining car with the coffee. Erik pulled out his briar, scratched a *fyrstikk* to life, and held the flame against his perfectly packed plug of Mac Baren Mixture. The rich, aromatic tobacco always had an ataractic effect on him. Between the coffee, the Mac Baren Mixture, and the mountains, Erik's mind flashed through all the events of the past year, crystallizing on his state of mind at the dawn of his sojourn.

Looking at that first page in his journal, he remembered the cocktail of emotions he had ingested in the skies over England as the plane had prepared for descent just last September. The memory of his brother's burial six months before the start of his journey was still raw and had sat like maror in his gut. He couldn't stop thinking about it. *Must keep moving. Must leave Minnesota. Leave the States. Escape.* Escape, or he would surely go insane.

ONE

LONDON

Mandolin winds blew warm and gently across the Northern Hemisphere during the autumn of 1973. Seeds planted during the Summer of Love matured, were harvested, and then cured, replanted, and reinvested in the younger brothers and sisters of the Woodstock generation.

Erik's brother was old enough to have been part of that generation, but temperamentally, he didn't qualify. There was nothing about Woodstock that held the least appeal for Charlie. On the other hand, if Erik had been Charlie's age, he might have been one of the half-million who attended that legendary "Aquarian Exposition of Peace and Music" on Max Yasgur's dairy farm in upstate New York.

On the heels of the British Invasion of the sixties, an infestation of young Americans traveled abroad. They spoke a language that shared universal concepts, like distrust of anyone over thirty, questioning authority, and advocating sexual freedom, music, drugs, turning on, tuning in, and dropping out.

September clung to August's warmth, and summer continued to blossom across Europe in a brilliant show of color and temperament. As most of the itinerants headed back stateside to finish school or start careers or otherwise pay the piper for their dalliances abroad, an eastbound Boeing 747, glistening in the morning sun, began preparations for its descent into London's Heathrow Airport.

Erik hadn't slept a wink all night. How could he? He'd been planning this trip for a year, and now the day had arrived. Outside his oval window, the sun turned the clouds into a billowing orange sea. Initially, he'd been in a race with himself to reach European soil before the final ticks on his boyhood clock ran out. Now that no longer seemed important.

If only you'd been able to make it until March 20, Charlie—just eight days! You could have returned home with all the other soldiers, and maybe you'd be on the plane with me right now, and we'd be going to Europe together. We could have gotten to know each other all over again, seen how each of us had grown over the last two years.

Charlie's death changed everything. For a while, Erik even thought about abandoning his trip; he would just stay in the United States and be there for his parents and his sister. But that was stupid. What would it accomplish? How could he comfort anyone else when he himself had no peace and no answers?

If anything, the trip was more imperative now than ever. He had a one-way plane ticket, and he wasn't coming back until he had some answers. But what were his questions? That was the problem—there were too many. There were too many even before Charlie was killed. Now he didn't even know where to begin. The only thing he knew was that he wasn't going to find the answers in Minnesota. He needed to be out there, out in the world, among the citizens of the world.

Minnesota was an indelible part of him. He loved his home state. So did Charlie. Their mom had always said, "Bloom where you're planted," and both boys did just that. Charlie was into radio and electronics. He worked hard on his paper route, eventually becoming territory route manager. When he turned sixteen, he bought a VW bug with the money he had earned and saved. At seventeen, he built a radio station by hand in the basement and broadcast weekend programs to the neighborhood.

For Erik, it was theater, music, and sports. When he wasn't acting in school plays, doing community theater, or playing his guitar or harmonica, he was outside enjoying Minnesota's boundless natural resources. The winters meant skiing, snowshoeing, ice fishing, skating, bonfires, girls with red cheeks from the cold air, and hot drinks around the fireplace in the ski lodges.

In the spring, there was green everywhere, the sweet petrichor smell of wet forests, rushing rivers, swelling creeks, inner-tubing, picnics, and the fragrance of flowers thick enough to cut with a knife.

In the summer, there was fishing, swimming, camping, tennis, the lakes, the cabin, and canoe trips in the Boundary Waters of Northern Minnesota and Southern Ontario, where one might encounter a spectacular display of the aurora borealis in the night skies.

And in the fall, the forest colors were so bright that when you closed your eyes, you could still see them. There was the smell of musty leaves, the sound of muffled shoes on woodland paths during a cross-country run. Finally, in that briefest and most beautiful of all seasonal moments when autumn pauses just long enough to relive the warm breezes of summer rustling though silver-dollar leaves, the trees sing in a magnificent chorus before the advent of winter.

Yet, without Charlie, everything wonderful about Minnesota just exposed the emptiness it held for Erik. Something integral to life was missing, something was wrong with the world. Erik knew he had to leave not only Minnesota but also the United States. He needed to understand. He needed to find…what?

He didn't know. He had been to St. Cloud State College in Central Minnesota for two years and felt like he was dumber now than when he entered. He felt like he couldn't learn anything. Nothing stuck. There seemed to be a hundred theories and no facts. Death was the only certainty in life, and he had a burning urge to discover who he was before that final note played for him.

He needed the world to stop spinning for a season so he could climb off and just stand still for a moment. This was going to be that moment. When he set foot in London, he would start the process of reimagining himself, becoming a citizen of the world. Everything about him would be different except for his name.

When he first conceived the idea of going to Scandinavia—before Charlie had been killed—it was about figuring out who he was, which of his multiple heritages was dominant: Norwegian, Swedish, Sámi, or possibly even Jewish. Then, in an unexpected twist of fate, during his second year at St. Cloud College, a visiting interim theater department chairman from Belgium offered to write a letter of introduction to a Norwegian director friend of his—maybe this friend could find a job for Erik.

When the Norwegian director wrote back saying that she would see what she could do, that—to Erik—was tantamount to a job. It was like gasoline had been poured into the fire that burned in his soul. Finally, an opening, a crack in the universe, a sunspot in a distant land. Now maybe, once he got a toehold in Norway, he could gain some perspective and begin to understand why he felt he was different from everyone else he knew. He could see how his mettle would measure up against the teeming masses in the great unknown.

Then word came of Charlie when his discharge was less than two weeks away. There hadn't been any fighting for a long time near Phu Bai where he was stationed. He was heading back to the barracks after recording voice patches for the wounded soldiers at the hospital so they could talk with their loved ones back home. The M151 MUTT jeep Charlie was traveling in had veered off the main road to avoid hitting a stray dog. The jeep hit a landmine and blew into the air. Charlie was killed instantly.

Finding out who he was in this incomprehensible universe was no longer Erik's primary objective. Now it was a matter of survival. Something had gone terribly wrong on a cosmic level. Maybe it had always been wrong and he only recognized it now in the vacuum of Charlie's death.

Charlie should never had been drafted. I should have been the one to go. I could have handled it; I could have survived. Charlie was too trusting, too innocent. *How in God's name did he pull a fifteen? The lottery system is too arbitrary, too rife for interference. It's based on the day you were born for crying out loud! The lower your number the greater the chance you'll be drafted. What control do you have over the day you were born? Born a day too soon or a day too late and you're screwed. It's the difference between going to Vietnam and having a life.*

It made no sense. *Where was the justice?* Erik had gone over every detail of the damned lottery system a hundred times, and it always led to the same conclusion: injustice. If there was one thing Erik couldn't stand, it was injustice.

Preoccupied with these thoughts, almost providentially, Diana slipped back into his mind. She was omnipresent. As the plane began its final descent, the thought occurred to Erik that he finally understood what *omnipresent* meant.

Until this moment, it was only a two-dimensional concept on a piece of paper. Now the word gave him the power to describe how his thoughts about her clung to him like the fragrance of her perfume. Thoughts which could literally be heard, tasted, seen, smelled, and felt—blankets he could wrap himself in.

Erik had met Diana shortly before Charlie was killed. Had she not been there, Erik might never have made it through the school year. Her presence alone was enough to pull him out of the self-made abyss he fell into time and again. She did this unknowingly and effortlessly.

It's not that Erik didn't want to share his feelings about Charlie's death—it was that he couldn't. It wasn't in his nature. He was never one to talk about his emotions. How peculiar it was then, given this intransigence, that the profession of acting held such a calling on his life. Or maybe that was the cause of his compulsion for acting.

Diana never tried forcing her way into those emotional lockboxes he kept tucked away deep inside himself; she just accepted him the way he was, without pressing or pressuring him to talk about his anger, his grief. For this, he was grateful to Diana and had clung to her even more. She was there for him, she believed in him. When he told her about his plan to postpone school and leave the United States for an unspecified period, she loved the idea. No recriminations. No guilt trips imposed on him about how long he would be gone. No thoughts about how this would put her outside of his world.

"Erik, you HAVE to go. This is the perfect trip for you."

Unlike any other girl he'd ever known, Diana wanted him to do the very things that he wanted to do. This selflessness was nectar he'd never tasted before, and he hungered for more of it. At times, Erik felt as though he could glimpse the world through her eyes. Her world was a playground of amazing and magical perspectives, a parallel wonderland he traversed while negotiating his own world of dreams, ambitions, and perplexities.

The pilot announced final landing preparations. Erik put his seat upright, released himself to his memories, and breathed deeply. The memory of Diana's gardenia perfume was strong enough for her to have been sitting in the seat next to him instead of the man from eastern Europe, whose pungent cologne stunk. Her dark, silky hair, azure eyes, sparkling white teeth, and playful laughter washed over him like a wave as the plane landed.

Lost in the tranquility of the moment, his hands loosened their grip on the armrests as the plane taxied down the tarmac. His journey had now begun. In a few short minutes, he would step on foreign soil and the adventure, his search for his Holy Grail, would begin.

Stepping inside Heathrow Airport was like emerging into the hub of the universe. Instructions blurted over the loudspeakers in multiple languages. An endless stream of various nationalities and accents tumbled by like a cacophony on all sides of him.

Delirious with excitement at having escaped the homogeneity of Minnesota, with its pedestrian and provincial mindset, he had at last crossed the threshold of his new life. He drank in this moment; this was part of his work, part of his assignment, part of his training for a life that he hoped would be guided by an allegiance to truth.

Slowly he turned 360 degrees, taking in the whole vast cavernous space. He relished the thought that he was a stranger in a strange land and that there were no parents, cousins, uncles, or friends. He was on equal footing with everyone around him—no favorites and no favors. No quarter asked and none granted. Every step forward from here on was up to him—just the way he wanted it.

For maybe the first time in his life, he was truly and completely alone. He quelled an urge to spin around to see if anyone was following him—and then savored his escape. He was free—physically, emotionally, mentally, and spiritually.

From this moment forward, he told himself, *I will not tie myself down to American customs, values, and prejudices. I will have a clean slate and start all over, fresh and unbiased. I will observe the nuances of life going on about me and will record all of them in the depths of my soul—grist for the mill.*

Two businessmen in raincoats crossed in front of him. The edge of one of their briefcases struck his knee as they hurried by, sending a jolt of pain up his leg and jerking him out of his reverie. The thousand nameless faces in a torrential blur around him came into focus. The businessmen were in a hurry to get wherever they were going.

Erik had nowhere to go in London. The entire initial phase of his trip hinged on reconnecting with Diana in Denmark, where she was spending a school year abroad studying at a place called Pro Pace. That could be two or even three weeks away. Prior to reaching Denmark, nothing was set in stone.

Suddenly black shadows crept into his newfound freedom while ice water flowed through his veins, as though he were standing in the arctic tundra instead of in the throbbing heart of London. Being alone, which just a moment ago had meant freedom, now was a terrible ogre looming in front of him. What was he supposed to do now? He had never thought about this stage of the trip, in all the planning he had done. London was a blur.

A moment of raw panic set in. An old fear returned. Films like *A Clockwork Orange*, *If,* and *O Lucky Man!* colored his concept of London. Dickensian slums and androgynous English roughnecks popped into mind and jostled for position among his thoughts.

At this moment, he knew he was not an international citizen—he was a twenty-year-old American kid who didn't have a clue about life. His panic was like an old enemy showing up in a strange neighborhood, like the three bullies who had accosted Charlie and Erik on Ottawa Avenue when they were little kids. Here, now, all alone, he had once again come face to face with that feeling of helplessness, of being in too deep.

Are you watchin' mate? Are you getting this down? Are you recording how you feel? He leaned his weight onto the frame of his backpack. *This is it, Erik. Are you just a knee waiting to have the briefcases of the world jammed into it? Where are you going to stay tonight? What will you do if you run into some droogs in Soho?*

Perhaps he had thought about this. Perhaps he was directionless by design. He reached over the top of his pack and, with slightly shaking hands, undid the top section, from which he pulled out a leather pouch. Opening it, he extracted his pipe, popped the lid on a tin of Mac Baren Mixture, and scooped a moist plug of tobacco between his thumb and middle finger.

Relishing the ceremony of the ritual, he tamped the plug into the briar bowl, fired the head of an Ohio Blue Tip match, and cupped the flame over the mouth of the pipe. The tobacco tasted meaty and rich. He exhaled slowly toward the vaulted ceiling rising five stories above. The familiarity of the routine, the bold statement he was making with his smoke rings fortified him. Renewed, he calmly resumed his survey of the room.

A group of four Americans about his age, two guys and two girls—obviously students—clustered together on the other side of the terminal. Their looks of bewilderment and intimidation echoed his own fears. He had observed them earlier in the back section of the plane and, disdaining their herding activities, had avoided them in a self-imposed nonfraternization injunction.

Now, having crossed the starting line, he could render his injunction null and void. Erik permitted himself to contemplate a bridge from his old life into the unknown, one last footstep on the ledge before diving into his new life. Their confusion gave him courage, but he had to act quickly or they would evaporate into the teeming mass of travelers flowing on all sides of them.

He hoisted his fifty-six-pound backpack to his shoulder, and an ice pick of pain stabbed him in the lower back. So far, the pack hadn't been the burden he feared. In an instant, that all changed. A lightning bolt of pain shot through him like an electrical storm, igniting every single neuron in his body. He grunted in agony and winced through clenched teeth. With his feet frozen to the floor, the crowds shifted around him like water circumventing an obtrusive log in the middle of a river.

Oh my God, did I really damage my spinal cord in that idiotic dive at the quarries? Is my back choosing this minute to unleash the pain? Is my trip ruined before it's even started? Am I going to end up phoning home from some London hospital bed? He cursed himself for thinking he'd been invincible before the dive.

Just weeks before Erik was to board the plane to start his new life, he wanted to squeeze in a final goodbye to the quarries. The quarries had cast a spell on him, and he had become as addicted to them as any junkie was to drugs.

If Minnesota had an equivalent to the ancient world's Seven Wonders, the quarries of St. Cloud would rank high on that list. There were over a dozen of them, all with different monikers: "Beer Quarries," "Camping Quarries," "Stoner Quarries," "Nude Quarries," and Erik's favorite, "Diving Quarries."

Erik had pledged to himself that this time he would not jump, but would *dive*, off the highest ledge—which rose sixty granite feet above a majestic reservoir filled with cool, clear groundwater. Diving Quarries was rumored to be a hundred feet deep. Preparing to dive, Erik could see a long, narrow drill bit protruding from the water's surface, directly beneath his toes. The drill bit angled away underwater—about ten or fifteen feet visible below the surface. A fuzz of algae covered the exposed bit.

A dozen college kids were mashing it up around the cliffs. Intoxication was in the air and on their breaths. Erik, too, was intoxicated but not on drugs or alcohol. He sensed that in this pinnacle moment, he was standing on the precipice between boyhood and manhood. Naked except for a pair of cutoff jeans, he surveyed the landscape.

Erik, you're facing a test. A test that will determine how the rest of your life will go. Are you the type that takes life by the horns and lives it at full throttle? Or are you the type who is content to let others risk it all and to live in the shadows of their dreams, their sacrifices?

"C'mon Hellberg! Either jump or get off the damned rock!" a voice taunted.

"Yeah, 'Erik the Auburn!' Remember Valhalla!" mocked another voice.

Ignore those ignoramuses. You're not contemplating another jump; you're mustering up the nerve to dive.

Earlier in the day, Dale Skarsgaard, an acidhead from Stearns Hall, the most debauched of all the dormitories on the campus, had performed a perfect swan dive from this same granite ledge.

If a hippie like Skarsgaard can execute a perfect swan dive, so can you.

He sensed this was a defining moment. Somehow it would determine his fate—not just for his trip to Norway but also for the rest of his life.

"Braack, braack, braack... C'mon chicken! Jump!"

Erik tried to concentrate. *They're drunk. You're not. You're stone cold sober. That's why you can do this. If Charlie was here, he would have said, "You can do it, Erik," and he would have meant it. God, I miss you, Charlie.*

With that thought, Erik crouched into position, leaned forward onto the balls of his feet, raised his arms behind him, and coiled his muscles for an explosion into a perfect swan dive.

Only that isn't what happened. His bold swan formation contorted into a crablike posture as he hurled toward the water. When he slammed into it neck first, he felt two simultaneous pops—one in his neck, the other at the base of his spine.

Erik's submerged body slowly floated to the surface like a stunned catfish. *Was he alive or dead?* Clawing forward, he lay prostrate on a rock slimy with algae. Immobilized, he assessed the state and condition of his body, eventually concluding that he was still alive.

For a moment, the universe came to a standstill. There was no one else at the quarries. Even his tormentors had disappeared. There was no one else on the entire planet. *Where had they all gone?* He slowly inched away from the quarries and gingerly climbed into his rusted 1954 Chevy Bel Air and drove back to campus as if he were carrying nitro glycerin under his seat. For the next two weeks, he walked around with extreme caution, afraid that one wrong step could unleash a debilitating pain. Unbelievably, aside from an annoying tingling in his extremities, his neck and back were not in pain. He was even able to lift his backpack.

He feared that the long transatlantic flight might be too much for his back, but that hadn't proved to be the case. In fact, up until this specific moment at Heathrow Airport, he hadn't experienced any pain or disability whatsoever. Now, it seems, he had damaged his back after all. Maybe severely. *Would he ever walk again? Was his life, as he knew it, over? What was it like for Charlie in his final moment of life? What did he know? Charlie, I wish you were here right now.*

As he contemplated the termination of his journey and a life confined to a wheelchair, he experienced an odd sensation. As suddenly as the pain had come upon him, it evaporated. In its place, a warm liquid-like current emanated from his coccyx and spread like a balm across his nervous system. Other than a tingling sensation in his fingers and toes, he felt unbelievably whole.

He moved his body slowly, afraid that the pain would attack again. This new warmth he felt encouraged him to try lifting his pack again.

Inch by inch, he raised the pack and carefully threaded his arms through the shoulder straps. No pain. Not even a little discomfort. It was miraculous.

How can this be? How can I go from excruciating pain in one moment to this warmth throughout my body in the next? Is this God toying with my mind, tormenting me, reminding me that my health and strength can be taken away in a flash without any warning—just like he did with Charlie?

He didn't know, and in any case, he had no time to contemplate the riddle. He must move quickly, or the lost American students would be gone. He moved toward them, mindful that at any second a new lightning bolt of pain might strike him again.

As he approached, he discerned from the confused and directionless looks on their faces that they didn't have prearranged lodging for tonight. Neither did Erik, so he figured they already had a lot in common. He stepped right into the middle of the group, interrupting what appeared to be an inconclusive and divisive debate.

"So," he offered casually to the strangers, as though returning to his compadres after a brief visit to the john, "where are we all staying tonight then?"

The group scrutinized the young man confronting them. A tweed cap too small to contain his unruly hair. Not yet twenty-one years old, exactly six feet tall. The muscular frame of a gymnast concealed under a JCPenney houndstooth jacket—purchased specifically because it looked British.

In high school, his nickname was "Erik the Auburn," partially because of his hair color but also because of his penchant for rallying his fellow gymnasts to "remember Valhalla" during competitions. A reference to the spirit of his Nordic forebearers (as in, "Erik the Red") who believed that to ascend into the hall of slain warriors (Valhalla) one had to die in battle.

He had no idea what these Americans were thinking. This could be an embarrassing denouement or a triumphal entrance into the city of London with a new group of friends. He doubted that he was threatening to them—he was smiling inside. He took a pull on his briar as he awaited their verdict.

None of them gave any response, just dumb stares. Finally, Erik simply said, "C'mon, let's go," and he walked toward the exit. Without ceremony, the four Americans silently acquiesced and followed him.

He led them out of the international terminal to destinations unknown. With a confident, nonchalant gait, he pushed his way into the main terminal, where an information kiosk materialized, as though by an unseen hand pulling back a curtain. They were given information about Kent Hall—a nearby youth hostel—and they set out in the direction of the Manor House tube station.

Erik felt no further pain that day and wondered if he had been given a sign, or maybe a warning, that something far bigger than himself was present and watching.

By the time the group reached Kent Hall, Erik knew their names, that they were all from Philadelphia, what they were doing in London, and how long they'd be here. Conversely, all they learned about Erik was that his itinerary was fluid. He hadn't yet decided how long he would be in London.

Erik's only immediate hard and fast goal was to get to Fredericia in Denmark and reconnect with Diana by September 26—the date of his actual birthday. Everything hinged on that reunion. Before leaving England, he wanted to visit his ex-roommate Bob Keefendorf up in Durham, but not if it meant being late to Denmark.

Long after Erik was well into planning his trip to Norway, Diana learned that St. Cloud College was putting together a year-long study abroad program for the following school year based out of Denmark. She immediately signed on board along with a hundred other St. Cloud College students and actually ended up leaving the United States for Denmark six weeks before Erik started his trip. The last couple of postcards he had received from Diana made him unsure how their meeting would go. He had invited her to go with him to Sweden to visit his friend Anders Lundström whom he hadn't seen since they were both fifteen and had met on a camper exchange program in Sweden. She hadn't responded to that idea.

If the Swedish trip was off the rails, what did that say about their prospects for spending time together in Norway? It's not like Erik had a rock-solid plan. He had no assured lodging once he got to Norway. Sure, his Norwegian friend from high school, Jens, would put him up for a few days, but after that? And what about employment? No guarantees there. All he had was a referral—a referral written by the theater department chairman to an acquaintance on the other side of the Atlantic Ocean at a theater in the town of Bergen, Norway. And, as Erik kept reminding himself, he didn't speak Norwegian.

The youth hostel overflowed with a crosscurrent of young people from all over the globe. Multiple languages could be detected, as the five of them walked up to the reception desk to register. It felt like they had stepped into the beating heart of London.

"Terribly sorry," the desk clerk attendant said. "I'm afraid that we only have three bunks left. If you want to all stay together, you'll have to find other lodgings."

Erik leaned into the counter and spoke quietly with the desk clerk. "Look, these four are traveling together. I don't care about me. I can sleep anywhere; hell, I'll sleep on the floor. But there must be a way to scrounge up one more bunk—"

"I'm afraid we have exactly three bunks left. If you want to reserve them, you'll have to do so now as I can assure you that they'll be gone within the hour, if not sooner."

David, the tallest of Erik's new friends, leaned in, shoulder to shoulder with Erik, and declared to the clerk, "We'll take the three bunks and two of us will sleep on the floor."

"I don't think our regulations permit sleeping on the floor—"

Sensing wiggle room, Erik jumped in. "I completely understand. You have your rules, and we respect that. Look, we're not rowdy tourists. We're students studying engineering, biology, art history, and theater." Erik nodded toward each of his new companions as he rattled off whatever subjects popped into his head. It wasn't exactly a lie, it was improvisation.

"Well…I'm not sure…"

"Tell you what," announced Erik. "We'll pay you for five bunks and take the three. Then tonight, two of us will throw our sleeping bags down over there on the other side of the pillar where we'll be out of the way. No one will be any the wiser, and you can donate the extra funds to your favorite charity." It wasn't exactly cheating, it was facilitating.

"Well, I suppose we could make an exception if you're paying in cash. But mind, the manager is here by half eight every morning. If he finds people sleeping on the floor, he'll throw a wobbly."

"No problem," said Erik as he pulled out a traveler's check. "We'll be long gone by then. Got a lot of activities planned here in your beautiful city."

The others quickly pulled out their wallets and the three bunks and two floor spots were paid for before the attendant could object further.

As the travelers stowed their gear and headed out into the busiest city in Europe, Erik said to David, "What the hell time is 'half eight'?"

"Beats me," David said. "Should we risk a 'wobbly' and find out?"

Erik entered notes in his journal as time allowed:

Saying England is "old" is to exercise the English penchant for understatement.

How were the Brits able to build Westminster Abbey in the thirteenth century?! Or St. Paul's Cathedral? How are such buildings even possible?? They didn't have cranes or any modern equipment! And where did this architecture come from? Who invented it?

Who decided that Greenwich would be the Prime Meridian? Was this because the sun never set on the British Empire?

Charlie would want to hear the stories that the walls of the Tower could undoubtedly tell.

Can't believe I'm walking without pain! Promise to self: no more cliff diving!

London was experiencing unusually pleasant weather for this time of year. Erik was grateful for the temperatures but even more so for the company of his new friends. The foursome accepted him as one of them—probably because he didn't interfere with their vigorous debates over their London itinerary. In fact, he was content to let them take the lead and just go with the flow. This left his mind free to think about his own goals for London and about what was ahead in Denmark.

The names of Erik's new friends were Linda, David, Gus, and Corrie. Linda and David were a couple; Gus and Corrie were unattached. David was the leader of the group. He was tall with shoulder-length hair, sideburns, and a handlebar mustache. Linda was shy and cautious. Gus was a goofball, with a haircut like Moe of the Three Stooges, and Corrie was flirtatious.

"I think I like this guy," Corrie said to Linda.

"He's cute, but we don't really know anything about him."

"Cute? He's gorgeous and sexy. What's to know?"

"He said he has a girlfriend in Denmark," reminded Linda.

"So. We're in London."

"Corrie, you're bad. What is that one-track mind of yours cooking up now?"

"Well, whatever it is," mused Corrie, "it will have to happen soon. Erik said he needs to leave in a few days if he's gonna have time to visit his old college roommate up in Durham before going to Denmark. Apparently, Erik promised his girlfriend that he would 'set foot on Danish soil' by the time he turns twenty-one. That's like less than two weeks away. Anyhow," she said conspiratorially, "I don't think things are going to go exactly the way he plans."

After a busy first day in London, the gang tried a few different pubs and sampled each specialty brew. London pubs were busy; each had a distinctly different milieu. Erik liked the Coach & Horses best because of its wide diversity of patrons. They came from all strata of society and seemed to leave their divisions behind as they stood elbow to elbow at the bar or shared the tables throughout the pub.

It was late when they got to back to Kent Hall. Erik rolled out his sleeping bag behind the pillar and fought to stay awake as he wrote a final entry into his journal. Corrie suddenly appeared on Erik's side of the pillar, wearing a mini-nightshirt and holding a sleeping bag in her arms.

"I drew the short straw," she said with a smile. Erik smiled back but continued to focus on his journal as she rolled out her bag next to his.

September 16, 1973

Stayed in a hostel called Kent Hall in North London on Seven Sisters Road. Pubs and theaters everywhere. Hooked up with a group of American students who are traveling during their fall semester. Good group, but not really on my wavelength. Glad I could share the day with them, but tomorrow I need to break out on my own. They're not interested in seeing any plays or spending time visiting art museums.

We saw the Tower of London today. Damn! I wish Charlie was with me to experience this. He would have loved the Tower! Such incredible history! Will write more about it later, so tired right now. Went to a couple of pubs and had kidney pie and overall, got properly sloshed. My favorite pub was the Coach & Horses. It was packed.

Everyone goes to the pubs here, including all the actors from the theaters, and everyone mixes. So much better than anything I expected. So tired right now, I can hardly keep my eyes open. Charlie, I miss you. Wish you were here. You're in my prayers, brother.

Unlike "Clockwork Orange" I see no milk bars or any droogs, although there does appear to be a malenky cheena here who is getting a tad too cozy...

While Erik wrote, Corrie chatted about her day and her impressions of London.

"Oh, that shower felt sooooo good!" Her hair was slightly damp; a hint of lavender filled the space between them.

"Ugh. No hair dryer. I had to towel-dry. Life on the road, right?" Corrie sighed and then continued. "Linda is waiting to shower until morning, but I couldn't wait another second." Corrie watched Erik write for a moment and then changed the subject.

"I can't believe we just arrived in London this morning and look at how much we've done already!" She pulled out an emery board and began filing her nails. "What do you want to do tomorrow? I hear there's a music festival at Trafalgar Square. Wouldn't that be groovy? Everyone in the group wants to go. You could bring your harmonica."

Kent Hall had become blissfully silent. The muted city sounds of London just outside the hostel had ceased altogether. The temperature inside the building was enervatingly warm; the floor where Corrie and Erik had spread out their bags was refreshingly cool.

"Seeing the Tower was my favorite part of the day. What was yours?"

Corrie turned to look at Erik, but the only response she saw was the slow raising and lowering of his body as he breathed. Wrapped in his sleeping bag, the room as silent as a medieval forest, he appeared for all the world like a hibernating bear.

Corrie smiled inwardly and as she continued filing her nails she whispered, "This is going to be a challenge."

The following morning, Erik was up early. He showered and had his bag rolled and stowed by the time the others were just groggily sitting up. There was just too much to see. As he headed out, Erik waived goodbye to the others and said, "I'm going to grab some coffee and then take in a museum or two." He kept it vague. Covered his trail. He didn't want to do the National Gallery with anyone else. He wanted the freedom to roam or linger as he felt inspired.

Once clear of Kent Hall, he exhaled a sigh of relief. Escaped just in time. *They'll spend an hour rolling out of bed, trying to decide what to do. Then they'll spend the next hour eating breakfast at some tourist trap and probably wait in a long line for the privilege.*

He found a small coffee shop off the beaten path and bought a British newspaper. Over a stoup of coffee, Erik planned out his day.

Mentally converting pounds to dollars, he estimated a budget for seeing two plays. If an acting career was to be his lot in life, and of this he was as certain as anything he had ever been, he wanted to see how the Brits did it. Erik had high expectations.

There were some promising plays in the paper, and he went to see what the ticketing game was. Maybe there were some last-minute seats at a discounted rate.

Good writing and great acting. London, is that too much to ask?

After he secured tickets for two promising plays, he went to the National Gallery. Hopefully, he wouldn't run into any of his mates there. He craved some quiet time with the geniuses who hung out there permanently, especially Da Vinci, Rembrandt, Michelangelo, and Monet, among others. Erik himself had no talent for painting, but he was fascinated by the those who had the gift for it.

These painters were real people. With flaws and frustrations. They had problems and dreams of their own. Brushstroke by brushstroke, they poured themselves onto these canvases. They must have spent countless hours staring at their paintings, struggling to get them precisely the way they wanted them.

Anyone standing in front of these works couldn't help but be amazed and inspired to do the best they could in whatever their field of endeavor. Holbein's *The Ambassadors* had a peculiarly shaped object drawn just above the floor in the middle of the painting that made no sense until you viewed it from the correct angle. Then you could tell it was a skull—the symbol of death.

Van Gogh's *A Wheatfield, with Cypresses* was so familiar that he could scarcely believe he was looking at the original; da Vinci's *The Burlington House Cartoon*, eerily, could only be viewed in a darkened room.

Painting after painting, it was like drinking water from a hydrant. He easily passed half an hour in front of Rembrandt's *Belshazzar's Feast*. As he sat on the polished wooden bench in front of the painting, Erik remembered one of his dad's favorite little quotes, "That which is worth doing is worth doing well."

How is creating a painting any different from creating a character? They both require great effort and patience. Great art, if done well, lives on. It lasts for century upon century. Theater, on the other hand, is ephemeral. Once it's done, it's gone. Not so with films and TV. That lives on—good or bad. So it damn well better be good.

Admittedly, he was just at the beginning of his career and had a long way to go. Moreover, as stunning and significant as London may be in the grand blueprint for his life, he was anxious to get on with his trip. Not having to carry his pack around everywhere had been nice. He had made some new friends and had some new experiences, but it would soon be time to move on.

"Fancy running into you here."

The familiar voice jarred Erik from his thoughts. He pivoted on the bench seat to face the speaker.

"Corrie. What are the odds?"

"Imagine my surprise this morning when I woke up next to an empty floor," she said with a playful pout.

"Ah, well, got to make hay while the sun shines, right? The good news is I'll be seeing two plays before leaving London."

"How exciting. What are we seeing?"

"*I* am seeing *Sleuth* and *Habeas Corpus*."

"Hmm, I saw the movie version of *Sleuth*," she said. "Michael Caine was great in it. I must have missed the other one."

"Alec Guinness plays the lead."

"Guinness," Corrie teased. "Isn't that what we were drinking last night?"

"Ha! Pretty sure that's a different Guinness," Erik laughed.

"Oh, I think I know who you're talking about. He was in *Dr. Zhivago*."

"And *Kind Hearts and Coronets*, *The Bridge on the River Kwai*, *Lawrence of Arabia*, and twenty or thirty other movies."

"You're serious about this *acting* thing, aren't you?"

Erik didn't answer immediately. It wasn't the first time he had been asked this type of question.

"Ever notice how all these Brits keep coming to the States and getting roles in our movies? Except for maybe Richard Chamberlain, we never reciprocate. Thought I might check out the scene while I'm here and see what the fuss is all about."

It was afternoon when Erik and Corrie left the National Gallery. Together they stopped at a sidewalk restaurant near the museum, and they both ordered fish and chips. Afterward they went back to Kent Hall, where they found the rest of the gang hanging out.

Erik left the group and headed for the Garrick Theatre to see *Sleuth*, the first of the two plays for which he had purchased tickets. Just standing in the foyer of the theater gave him goosebumps. The Garrick was built in 1889—the roster of productions mounted here and the actors who have graced the boards were awe-inspiring.

Erik was not disappointed with the production. The acting and staging were first rate. As good as anything he had seen anywhere. When the production concluded, Erik was slow to leave the theater or even the vicinity. It was too soon to end the night; he wanted to absorb the atmosphere.

He lingered in the Charing Cross Road area absorbing the atmosphere. Seeing a group of theater patrons disappear into an upscale pub, he ventured in. The crowd here wasn't quite as rowdy as those at the Coach & Horses, but the pub was nearly full. He saw an open spot at the bar and eased in. A young couple standing next to him were discussing *Sleuth*, and Erik took the liberty of joining in on the conversation. Their names were Ben and Sarah, and they were theater aficionados. This was Sarah's second time seeing the play. She had seen a previous production at the St.

Martin's Theatre last year. This was Ben's first time seeing the play. They both loved it.

"Have you seen the movie version?" Erik asked.

"Actually, I'm not keen on seeing the picture," said Sarah. "Not that I've got anything against Michael Caine, but I just can't fancy this play as a movie."

"No, the movie is very good," said Erik, "but this was better. I knew what was coming at the end, and it still caught me off guard." That comment brought a good laugh from both Ben and Sarah.

Their conversation ranged from movies and theater to the recent IRA bombings at King's Cross and Euston railway stations where multiple people were injured. While both Ben and Sarah were concerned about the bombings, they said it would not affect their going to the theater to see plays. Erik told them he had tickets to see Alec Guinness in *Habeas Corpus*. They both had seen the production and said it was simply first rate.

When Erik finally got back to Kent Hall, he was surprised to see that his friends still hadn't returned. He pulled out his journal and wrote.

September 17, 1973

Saw "Sleuth" tonight! After having seen Laurence Olivier and Michael Caine in the movie, I didn't know how it could possibly be done on stage. But they pulled it off! They didn't spoil the surprise at the end—if you didn't know what was coming, you never would have guessed! Had a great time with a young London couple at a pub afterward. So friendly! We exchanged addresses.

London was just the first stop of what he hoped would be an epic journey. He was loving London and planned to make the most of it for as long as he was here, but he was also itching to get moving.

Two more days until "Habeas Corpus" starring Sir Alec Guinness. It's at the Lyric Theatre. Don't know anything about the play, but it must be good if Guinness is in it.

After Sir Alec, I'll need to make it to Durham in no more than two days if I want to have any time with Keefendorf before catching the overnight ferry to Denmark. Bottom line, I promised Diana I would be in Denmark by my 21st birthday and I'm damn well going to make it. I'll budget about a week or so to get to Durham and spend time with Keefendorf. Then it's off to Harwich to catch a ferry across the channel to Denmark. Hope to do a little traveling with Diana once I get to Fredericia.

As Erik walked toward the Lyric Theatre on the night of the performance, he found it hard to believe that he would soon be sitting in the same theater where Alec Guinness would be performing. And that Alec himself would be walking onto the stage and performing—live and in person. Alec Guinness, the legend! It seemed impossible.

How is it possible that I got a ticket in the eleventh hour? Such a momentous event should have been sold out for months. Not only that, but the cheapest tickets are the ones in the front row! Who doesn't want to sit as close as possible to the actors so you can see all the nuances of their performances? Londoners have the concept backward, but I'm not complaining.

As Erik took his seat in the front row and listened to the accented buzz of the patrons sitting around him, he thought about this special moment. *There's a magical, transcendent quality about live theater. True, the actors speak the same words with each performance. Yet, because the audiences are different each night, every performance is unique. That perceptible current that passes between actor and audience anew each night is what creates the magic, the juice.*

The chatter immediately abated as the house lights faded. When the curtain rose, the man himself strode out onto the stage. Immediate applause broke out.

Guinness appeared oblivious to the audience's approval as he focused on an obstinate prop. At precisely the appropriate second, when the audience's ardor had settled to a level detectible only to an artist of infinite perceptibilities, the legend spoke.

His timing is impeccable.

Enamored as he was with Guinness, Erik quickly became consumed with Arthur Wicksteed, the character he played, rather than the actor. Not until intermission did Erik realize how complete the transformation had been.

The man is good. You can't fool a live audience.

The atmosphere of the Lyric, the milieu of London itself, all seemed to work toward informing the action that was taking place on the stage. In that moment, Erik felt like he was part of this world. That there was a place for him. He hadn't found it yet, but he was on the right track. He just needed to trust his instincts and keep going.

He wished his brother was here. Charlie would have loved this play, this theater, this town. Erik lingered in the theater. It was like being part of the history of London. Here he wasn't sightseeing with a bunch of tourists. Here he was mingling with Londoners, listening to their adamantly stated opinions in a multiplicity of nuanced accents.

When he stepped outside of the Lyric, it was a glorious, drizzly London night. Guinness had been magnificent. Erik himself was feeling magnificent, like his soul had been ignited. He couldn't go back to the hostel. He needed to be where the Londoners go after the theater. He wanted to be where the action was and where the actors were.

The Coach & Horses was packed and noisy. Joe Cocker's "Feeling Alright" was playing over the sound system. The pub was littered with a cross section of London flotsam and jetsam—locals, foreigners, the well-heeled, the well-intended, businessmen, actors, and actors-in-training.

His four American friends from Philly were there and well into their pints—especially Gus. They hovered around a small circular table near the bar. Gus was rocking out to the music, imitating the antics of Joe Cocker. "Jeez, Gus, can't take you anywhere," David said as he rolled his eyes.

"Man, I love this song," enthused Gus. "It's from the *Mad Dogs and Englishmen* album."

Erik shook the rain off his poncho. The Coach & Horses felt like a home away from home. He reveled in the atmosphere. *This is right where I want to be at this moment in my life.* He navigated his way to the bar and ordered a pint of Guinness. Then he worked his way over to the small table to join his friends.

"Well, look what the rain blew in," teased Corrie.

"Welcome, Erik!" said David. "Glad you found us. Cheers!" The five Americans raised their glasses in unison, and they all said, "Cheers!"

"Man, you missed a great music festival today," said Gus. Then he immediately resumed playing his air guitar and imitating the manic mannerisms of Joe Cocker.

"How was the play?" asked Linda.

"Sir Guinness was amazing, what can I say? It was worth every shilling."

A raucous burst of laughter erupted somewhere in the back section of the pub.

"I sat two feet away from him. His performance was perfect. The play was a riot. The house was packed. Londoners are a great audience. They love their theater and their actors."

"You'll never guess who was here tonight," said David. "Michael York. You just missed him."

"Ah, you're kidding," Erik said. "I would have loved to have met him. Tybalt in *Romeo and Juliet*, D'Artagnan in *The Three Musketeers…*"

"I said hi to him," bragged Corrie.

"That calls for another toast. This place is amazing," announced Erik. "To England, to London, to the Coach & Horses, to all the Mad Dogs and Englishmen, especially Michael York and Sir Alec Guinness, and to new friends."

They raised and clinked their bumpers again and shouted, "Cheers!"

Another loud outburst of laughter and shouts from the back of the pub. "Sounds like someone's having a friendly game of darts," observed David. "You guys want to check it out?"

They made their way to the section of the pub where the dartboards were mounted along the wall. One board was open and available—at least partially. There were two Brits who were looking for a couple more players to join them. David, Erik, and Gus were up for it, but by now it was clear that Gus was completely snockered. Throwing a dart, let alone hitting a dartboard, was beyond his present abilities. Linda volunteered to take him back to Kent Hall.

In June the age of majority in Minnesota had been lowered from twenty-one to eighteen, enabling Erik to visit St. Cloud's public houses legally. Prior to that, in contravention to the law, Erik had managed to establish a rapport with the gatekeepers of the Olde Brick House on Sixth Avenue South during his sophomore year, where he developed a reputation as having a supple dart wrist. He was pretty sure the game of *501* was played the same way everywhere. In fact, he'd read somewhere that the game was invented in France and came to England during WWI, before eventually making its way to the United States. Erik and David ponied up to take on the Brits. Corrie got another beer and took a seat to watch the action.

Here in this blurry haze of smoke, alcohol, laughter, music, and humanity, Erik recognized himself. He was in the right spot, the right place, but this wasn't his time yet. He needed to learn his craft first. Thoroughly and deeply learn the craft so that he could stand toe to toe with anyone in the profession. He had his path ahead of him. He needed to keep moving, to get on the road and experience whatever *it* was that lie ahead for him.

Yet he had a reluctance to leave this moment. A desire to connect with these Londoners. Ever since an inspiring teacher in junior high got Erik to read *The Canterbury Tales*, a book he thought he was going to hate but ended up loving, he'd been an avid reader.

Drink this moment in, Erik. This is a mile marker. Take a mental picture. Record this moment in your soul.

The Hermann Hesse novel, *Narcissus and Goldmund*, had been on his mind since boarding the plane to England. Erik and his friends in school would argue whether they identified as Goldmund or as Narcissus.

Erik was unequivocally Goldmund—the wanderer, the artist. He needed to experience life. He wasn't content to sit back while others jumped off the cliff. It didn't matter whether you won or lost, but you had to play. His brother Charlie was more of the Narcissus character—not one to throw caution to the wind. He would have stood on the cliff alongside Erik, but he wouldn't have attempted to jump, let alone to dive. But he would have been there to pick up the pieces if Erik had broken his neck. Maybe that was why the brothers were so connected. One's *yin* to the other's *yang*.

The pub used high-quality sisal fiber dartboards that looked new. It was clear to David and Erik from comments they picked up that these two Brits were matadors. In other words, they hit a lot of bull's-eyes. And they were playing on their home turf. David and Erik started out slow, but gradually, they both warmed to the game and held their own. Dave was a deft player, and Erik was on such a high from experiencing London, seeing Alec Guinness, and being here at the Coach & Horses with friends, that at times his darts seemed to float to the target.

While one of the Brits was lining up a shot, Erik sat down next to Corrie and took another pull on his Guinness.

"I think you're going to do okay," Corrie said.

Surprised at the comment, Erik said, "Thanks. To be honest, it's not my first game of darts."

"No, dummy. At whatever it is you're looking for."

"What makes you say that?"

"You've got focus."

Erik eyed Corrie closely. He appreciated that this was a comment she had given some consideration to. "Are you telling me that I'm one of the Mad Dogs?"

"I think you are whatever you want to be."

An hour later, after losing a close game, David and Erik said goodnight to their new English friends. Together, Corrie, David, and Erik walked out into the drizzle and headed toward Kent Hall. The slap of wet and wild on their faces was invigorating.

In moments like this, Erik felt as though he had been given a few extra hall passes in life. He could think of a half dozen crazy, impulsive acts he had done in his life, right up to that dive at the quarries. He was lucky to be walking, let alone carrying a backpack across England.

Erik's stomach felt pleasantly full of Guinness, and his head was floating a couple of feet above him. As they zigzagged their way back to Kent Hall, *Belshazzar's Feast* popped into his mind. He pictured the hand of God writing on the wall in the painting—the hand and writing which had so terrified Belshazzar. The young Babylonian king knew that he had been weighed in the balance and found wanting. "That very night Belshazzar lost his life."

What if I was "weighed in the balance"? Would I be found wanting?

Of course, God would find me wanting. Charlie, who didn't have a mean bone in his body, who was honest and told the truth even when it made him look bad, pulls a fifteen in the lottery and goes to the hellhole known as the Vietnam War. I pulled an even lower number, a five, and should have gone, but I fought to convince the draft board that my real number was three hundred and forty-four. It wasn't exactly cheating. It was self-preservation. Now, Charlie's dead and I'm alive. And what am I doing? I'm bumming around England, footloose and fancy free, a vagabond keeping an open mind and leaving all options on the table.

The trio arrived at the hostel and went inside. Linda was in the lobby waiting for David. Erik made a beeline for the pillar, opened his bag, and poured himself in. There was no hiding. Not from himself and certainly not from God. The best he could hope for was a few hours of sleep. The last sound he heard was Big Ben letting London know it was now three o'clock in the morning.

DURHAM

Morning came fast and hard. Erik said goodbye to his friends and wished them happy trails. Corrie said she would be looking for him on the big screen. Erik laughed and told her not to hold her breath. Despite the sledgehammer pounding inside his brain, it felt good to strap himself into his backpack once again. Still no recurrent back pains.

The green army-surplus rain poncho had kept him dry last night on the walk home from the pub. He covered himself with it again now. The drizzle continued, painting the streets and buildings with a glossy shimmer. Traces of diesel oil in the roads glowed with an iridescent blue, and Erik wondered if Charles Dickens had ever walked on these same streets.

He had one pair of shoes that he'd carefully selected. Rugged, sturdy, and comfortable for walking. Not stylish, but the thick soles would keep his feet relatively dry in all but a heavy downpour. Acceptable both for back roads and for museums.

The sojourn continued! Erik Torsen Hellberg was on the road again. The drizzle revived him, and the sledgehammer ceased its pounding.

Thank you, London. I needed a proper rain and you've given it to me.

His pace quickened as he studied the map of London. He was eager to leave the city and get out into the countryside. The whole of Britannia would soon be stretched out before him, Merlin's magnificent Isle of Gramarye. His immediate goal was the M1, the highway to Northern England.

Would he make Durham tonight? Doubtful. It depended on how many rides he could get. Despite the map, he had to stop and ask for directions along the way. Cresting the final hill to the entrance point of the M1, he was stunned by what he saw: a long, long line stretching into infinity, filled with hitchhiking Londoners, all hoping for rides.

His trip came to a screeching halt. Looking at this line, he could easily be waiting all day for a ride. It was brutally sobering, and there wasn't a damned thing he could do about it but join the line and wait his turn. He walked up, stood behind the last person, and assessed the situation. Erik watched as cars swooped in and picked up riders indiscriminately. Might be from the front of the line or somewhere in the middle. Someone joined the line behind Erik and said something unintelligible.

Erik turned around and saw a tall man with long, greasy hair, dripping wet from the drizzle. The man had a four-day beard and blue, bloodshot eyes. Erik was probably a mirror image of him except with brown, bloodshot eyes, but he still didn't understand what the guy had said.

The man spoke again, "Fag?"

"Excuse me?"

"Av yer got a fag, mate?"

"What?" Honest to God, Erik didn't have a clue what the bloke was talking about. "I'm sorry, I don't—"

The man spoke louder and slower as if that would make the difference.

"Av. You. Got. A. Fag? A tab? A smoke, yer know? A ciggie???"

"Oh. Sorry, man. No, I don't have any smokes."

Annoyed, the Brit moved on and muttered under his breath, "Fuggen' foreigners!"

The guy in front of him turned around and smiled, "Where ar' yer from, mate?"

"The States."

"What part?"

"Minnesota."

"Ah, right. I've a cousin in Boston. Have yer been there?"

"Naw. They don't speak English in Boston."

"Huh?"

"Never mind. Bad joke. How long do you think we'll be waiting for a ride?"

"It's hard to say. Could be an hour, could be 'alf a day."

"You're kidding. At this rate, it'll take me a week to get to Durham."

"Durham! You're in the wrong line. You should be over to the A1."

"The A1?"

"The A1 is the ald highway. This 'ere is the M1, the superhighway. Most of us are commuters and only goin' a short distance."

"I don't know. How far away is it and how long is the A1 line?"

"It's not far, just a few kilometers. Won't take more than ten er fifteen minutes, mate. An' I don't think you'll finds much of a line there. Like aye said, most of us are just goin' a short distance."

"Naw, what if I get over there and that line is longer than this line? I'll have to come back here and start all over again."

"Well look, mate, if the line there is too long, just come back. I'll saves yer place in line."

The guy seemed honest. "Oh, what the hell, I'll give it a shot. Thanks. If that line is longer, I'll see you in a bit."

Twenty minutes later, Erik came to what looked like the entrance to a highway. No signage though. There was no one standing at the entrance. Not a single hitchhiker. Even a short line would have been reassuring, but Erik was the only hitchhiker in sight.

This can't be right. I knew it. What a mistake. I never should have trusted that guy.

Just then, a truck approached. An old beat-up lorry, something out of the fifties, with a gated bed, hauling a mound of wet dirt. Erik stuck out his thumb. The driver saw Erik and pulled over. He rolled down the window and called out, "War yer headin', laddie?"

"Durham."

"Ach, I ain'ts goin' 'at far, but I kin brings ye a wee bit farther on yer way. Hop in."

Erik opened the passenger door and stepped up on the running board. The inside of the cab was cramped. In the States, it would euphemistically have been labeled a vintage cab. A large dog took up nearly the entire passenger seat. The mutt could have been a cross between a Saint Bernard and an Irish Wolfhound.

The driver flashed a wide Cheshire Cat grin, while the dog, tongue drooling continually, panted loudly. "You'll 'av'ter put yer sack in the lorry bed."

Erik stepped back to the side of the vehicle. The unmistakable odor told Erik that the lorry was hauling manure, not dirt. He hesitated, wondering if he would have been better off on the M1. Finally, he shrugged, *What the hell, a ride's a ride.* He gingerly set his pack into the bed, trying to avoid the wetter areas, and then squeezed up into the passenger seat, forcing the dog to yield a few inches of space.

"Welcome, laddie. This 'ere's Churchill. 'E doesn't bite." Churchill was as big as Erik's pack and as soon as Erik shut the door, Churchill leaned into Erik and licked his face with his massive tongue.

"Look at that, 'e likes you!" said the driver. "'At's a right, proper omen. So, me good man, an' where ye fram?"

"Uh, the United States."

"Yer don't say, eh? Which part?"

"Minnesota." Churchill licked Erik again, as if Minnesota was his favorite state.

"Minnesota, eh? Right smack in der middle av yer country! Way up in ther northern border next to Ontario."

"You know Minnesota?" Erik was surprised.

"Oh sure. Never been thar, of course, but we do have maps 'ere, ya know. An' what's it likes? America? It's a big coontry, ain't it?"

"Yes, it is—"

"Ye 'erd abouts all the bombin's har in London by the IRA, right? What'cha thinks 'bout that?"

"Yeah, I've heard—"

"Yep, she's a bloody mess. Been goin' on far a loong time. No end in sight… Corse, yer got yer own troubles," the driver continued. "What does yer think abouts Vietnam? So many yoong lads have lost their lives… We keeps 'earing about 'Watergate' an' Nixon. Nasty business it is. What does yer think about it all?"

The driver had hit a nerve with his comment about lads losing their lives in Vietnam and then just rattled on, as if he had a litany of events that had been bottled up inside him with no one to talk to except for Churchill. Erik let it pass. Besides, it was hard to get a word in edgewise with this guy. It was as though Erik was doing the driver a favor by climbing in his cab. Like he wanted company. The driver kept firing statements at Erik on a range of topics. He knew a lot about not just British affairs but also international affairs in the far corners of the world.

Here is yet another example of how little you know about the nations of the world, Erik. Even the lorry drivers know more than you do! This is one of the reasons why you need to be traveling. You need to learn this shit, and you can't learn it from books, and you can't learn it sitting in a classroom in the middle of nowhere. You must get out and live life.

The lorry driver asked Erik's opinion about everything under the sun. Erik began to feel like he didn't have an opinion about a damned thing. *What have you been doing your entire life, Erik?*

Erik shifted the conversation and began asking the driver questions about England and his personal background, his family, where he grew up, and what *he* thought about the IRA bombings. The lorry driver was delighted with the questions and talked nonstop. He loved reading everything—newspapers, magazines, novels, biographies, history, Shakespeare—whatever he could get his hands on whenever he wasn't behind the wheel.

Erik was currently reading *The Return of the King*, the final book of *The Lord of the Rings* trilogy by J.R.R. Tolkien. The lorry driver said he loved J.R.R. Tolkien.

"Most a' Middle-earth is set in what we calls West Midlands. You'd have ridden right through it, had yer stayed on the M1 highway."

Time flew as they drove through the lush, green landscape billowing out on all sides of the A1.

The topic of Tolkien led to a conversation about Chaucer and *The Canterbury Tales*, which led to Shakespeare, to Rudyard Kipling, and then to Robert Service, and finally to Oscar Wilde.

"'Ow 'bouts a cup o' tea?" the driver asked.

Almost before Erik could answer, they pulled into a roadside café filled with truckers. The driver let Churchill do his business, and then the two men walked into the café. Seemed like the driver knew everyone in that watering hole.

"'Ello, mates," the driver said to the other drivers. "Got one of our 'American coosins' with us today." It was like the driver had won a prize and he was showing it off.

Erik and the driver continued their conversation over a cup of tea as other truckers joined in, eager to opine about local or global events.

That was Erik's first of several rides that day. All were lorry drivers, all tea lovers.

Hitchhiking is a great way to travel, Erik concluded. *You see the best of the world. The good people stop and pick you up; the bad ones just pass you by.*

It was early evening when the last lorry driver dropped Erik off somewhere north of Peterborough. It had been raining off and on all day, but the sky was trying hard to rid itself of clouds and Erik felt optimistic about a clear night. He looked for a patch of ground where he could make his bivouac and get some shut-eye.

Even though it wasn't raining now, this was England and Erik knew the rain could start again at any moment. He was on a limited budget, and he really didn't want to squander his hard-earned dough on a hotel for the night. The temperature was still relatively warm. Besides, he was in the countryside and he had no idea where a hotel might be. Erik might walk for hours and not find a place to stay.

He found a secluded spot that had a good cover of foliage. He spread out his ground tarp, laid his sleeping bag on top of the tarp, and covered the bag with his rain poncho. Erik prayed that there wouldn't be any rain tonight and then tried to close his eyes.

Usually when he hit the pillow—or, in this case, his sweater rolled up inside of his T-shirt—he was out, especially when he was as tired as he was at this moment. Instead, Erik looked up into the night sky, which was vacillating between clear and beautiful and then filled with ominous, fast-moving thunderclouds.

Even though he was exhausted, he couldn't fall asleep. He was too excited about this day and the incredible journey so far. Only a week had passed, and yet it seemed like he'd been gone for a month.

Making this trip was the right thing to do. Charlie would have approved. The last thing Erik did every night was to throw a quick prayer Charlie's way. *For sure he is okay "up there"—it's inconceivable that he's anywhere else.*

Tomorrow Erik would be in Durham and would see his old pal, Bob Keefendorf. After that, a quick overnight ferry ride to Denmark, and he would be with Diana.

From the first second Erik laid eyes on her at St. Cloud, he had trouble thinking about anything else. It was like there was an aura emanating from her. It was the way she looked at things. She seemed to find the beauty and humor in everything around her—the way a child notices butterflies or balloons or caterpillars.

He knew she was an artist. He didn't know how he knew this, but he would have staked his life on it. Where she came from, what year she was in school, what she was studying, or whether she had a boyfriend—he didn't have a clue. All Erik knew was that he had to meet her.

One day he saw her talking with Eddie Henson. Erik and Eddie had gone to the same high school, and Eddie played a mean guitar. Eric Clapton was his idol. Anytime there was a dance at the school, Eddie Henson would be the guy playing lead guitar. He was like Schroeder, the Beethoven-obsessed character in *Peanuts*.

So here they were, both at St. Cloud State College, and Eddie Henson knew Diana. They were clowning around, but it seemed like they were just friends. The girl always seemed to be up and happy. Such joy about her. Mesmerizing. At the first opportunity, Erik cornered Eddie.

"Oh, we're just friends," Eddie said, "and I don't think she's going steady with anyone. I met her in art class. She's fun to hang out with."

"I think she's amazing," Erik confessed.

The next time Eddie saw her, he said, "Hey Diana, guess what? EH loves you!"

She thought for a second and then laughed. "Yes, Eddie Henson, I love you too!"

Of course, she had no idea who Erik Hellberg was, but his instincts about her had been right. She was an artist. Seemingly all objects she touched transformed to art in her hands. A stone would get painted, an apple would get carved, a piece of string would get tied to resemble a ladybug. He was mesmerized by her. He saw no flaws, only perfection.

Diana was self-effacing, and she didn't think she was particularly attractive. She was. She was beautiful and quirky and different. Her unwillingness to think of herself as desirable only made her more attractive to Erik.

"When I was a little girl, up until I was about eight, I cried all the time. Every day. The whole world made me sad," she said. "I wondered how people could be happy in this life. The world was a strange and cruel place. People got hurt. Puppies and birds and snails died. There are thunderstorms and blizzards and car accidents, and there are people who drink and people who yell at each other."

"Then, one day," she continued, "my mother got so frustrated with me crying all the time that she slapped me. That slap stopped me in my tracks. Something inside of me woke up, and I started to see the world in a different way. The world seemed not to be so much about the way things were but about the way we perceive them to be."

And from that young age, Diana looked at the world differently. It seemed to Erik that she now saw the world as a continual stream of curiosities which didn't require a preoccupation with the inevitability of death but rather a reverence for the life force that fought against death. Every living creature, each in their own way spoke of the beauty and humor in all the life that surrounded her.

Her fascination with life was intoxicating. She saw beneath the surface of objects. It didn't matter whether it was animals, plants, people, or clouds. Whatever she saw somehow ended up tumbling out of her like a fountain of reimagined colors and shapes and impressions. The entire natural world was her playground.

When Charlie's death fractured Erik's world, Diana's inexhaustible fascination with life served as a bulwark against succumbing to the guilt and anger he felt. *Charlie is gone? How is that possible? If Charlie isn't good enough for this world, who is? Certainly not me. What might I have done, had she not been in my life during those wretched first months?*

Diana had kept him sane, kept him from going off the deep end over the regret he felt for not being a bigger part of Charlie's life. For not being more interested in the things that Charlie was interested in and for being so self-absorbed. Maybe he wasn't an island after all. Maybe he did need other people. Well, he wasn't going to take Diana for granted. He missed her, and yes, he could admit that he needed her.

Her postcards said she was traveling all over Europe from her base in Denmark. She was taking "side trips" and "weekend getaways." In her postcard to Erik she wrote, "I like traveling with a guy, because it's safer."

The postcards confused him. *Did she mean she liked to travel with guys in general because it was safer or that she liked traveling with a particular guy?* He had to admit, the postcards had gotten under his skin and made him feel a bit insecure.

You've got to stop thinking about it. She's your one in a billion, just like... He picked out one of the stars overhead. *That one!* The brightest star in the Gemini constellation had an orange hue; he picked it because it would be easy to find again.

His eyelids grew heavy as he watched Diana's star pop in and out between the ominous gray clouds that glided across the heavens. *Maybe she's looking up at the stars right now too...* He got drowsier and drowsier... *The same stars Shakespeare looked at...* His eyes finally closed completely...*and all those painters in the National Gallery...*

The next sensation he had was the stars falling and lightly hitting him in the face. He was so deep in sleep that the raindrops merged into whatever dream he was dreaming. That ended abruptly.

Erik scrambled out of his bag and cursed his stupidity. Or maybe he had just been lazy. He should have asked the driver to drop him off where there was a motel. In all actuality, he could afford it, but he didn't want to spend the money. *Who knows how long my funds will last?*

The decision not to bring a tent had been a strategic one. In anticipating his needs for this trip, he had weighed the pros and cons. In the Boundary Waters, mosquitoes were ubiquitous, rain was continuously a debilitating possibility. The absence of an adequate tent meant misery. Or worse. In Europe, how bad could the mosquitoes be? And the extra weight of a tent could be a loathsome burden, given the possibility of access to hotels, youth hostels, or even lodging with good people he hoped he might meet along the route.

The flaw in Erik's thinking was now painfully clear. He stuffed his wet sleeping bag into its cover, attached it to his backpack, and started walking. Although he was soaking wet and muddy, he was optimistic that he would survive what was left of the night.

After twenty miserable minutes, he noticed a small wooden structure set back from the road. Stepping cautiously through the brush, Erik discovered it was an old, three-sided woodshed, probably long out of use. He explored the interior with the flashlight he always carried. The shed was probably filled with spiders and mice, but it was dry. He moved around some logs and fashioned a space where he could wedge in his backpack. Not near enough room to stretch out, but by leaning back on his pack, he was just recumbent enough to be quasi-comfortable. Sleep came within moments.

When he awoke, the rain had stopped, and waterdrops on the leaves sparkled like diamonds all around him. What a beautiful morning! Erik was soaking wet, but his spirit was soaring and he was eager to get his adventure back on the road.

It took Erik two more rides to reach Durham. The last ride let him off right at Durham University. In fact, the driver was a student there and he pointed to the building that Keefendorf was supposedly staying in—the old Durham Castle. Keef's dorm was literally a castle built in the eleventh century!

Erik found Keef's room and, sure enough, he was in there studying. Keef was a little surprised to see him because he hadn't been sure Erik was going to make it.

Bob Keefendorf was an unlikely friend. They had gone to the same high school, but Bob was an *A* student who took honors classes and they didn't hang in the same circles. In the one class they had together, Keefendorf sat up front, while Erik sat in the back. Keefendorf dressed on the preppy side, and no one would ever take him for a hippie, as usually happened with Erik.

As luck would have it, Bob and Erik became friends on the first night of freshman orientation weekend at St. Cloud. Erik had noticed Bob and his posse from high school hanging around outside one of the many liquor stores in town and arguing about something.

He was surprised that this honor student had chosen St. Cloud over the Ivy League schools he would undoubtedly have qualified for. None of Erik's high school chums had chosen to go to St. Cloud, so he would need to make new friends. He waved to Keef and walked over.

Although he recognized most of the guys with Keef, he didn't know any of them well. In Minnesota you had to be twenty-one to buy beer. None of these guys, including Erik, were over nineteen. You didn't have to be an anthropologist to recognize what the big problem of the night was.

"Hey, what about Hellberg? He's the actor!" The one named Deuce came up with that brilliant piece of reasoning, and everyone else quickly piled on.

"Yeah, he's the newbie. He's got to do it." *Newbie!?* Erik thought. *I'm not part of this group.*

He wasn't friends with any of these guys, and furthermore, he didn't want to be the one to get the beer. *Why should I do their dirty work just because I'm an actor? They should get their own damned beer!*

On the other hand, Erik saw the look on their faces. These guys were hell-bent on scoring beer. To refuse the challenge would be disastrous for his reputation. He ran through all the different scenarios in his mind if he didn't at least make the attempt. All of them had catastrophically antisocial endings.

The boys congregated in the alley behind the store. With a tremulous hand, Erik pulled open the rear door, activating a bell that loudly announced his entrance. His heart pounded in his chest like a bass drum. Affecting a nonchalance that he didn't feel, he sauntered up and down each aisle, trying to work up his courage. *The clerk is watching your every step, Erik.* He passed the glass door coolers where the beer was kept, without grabbing a case. *What are you waiting for?* He walked by the coolers a second time. *Stop stalling. What's the worst they can do to you?* The third time he reached the cooler area, he opened the glass door, reached past the Hamm's beer, and lifted out a case of Miller High Life. *If you're going to get busted, it might as well be for the good stuff.*

Still stalling for courage, he pretended to search for some crucial item as he circled the store once more. Out of desperation, he finally grabbed a six-pack of Coca-Cola and set it along with the case of Miller High Life on the counter in front of the clerk—or maybe the guy was the manager. He just hoped that the man wasn't the owner.

Erik manufactured a look that said, *nothing unusual here—I buy a case of beer and a six-pack of soda every weekend.*

The man snubbed out his cigarette in the ashtray next to Erik's merchandise and let the smoke slowly filter out of his nostrils as he sized up the long-haired freshman facing him.

Erik thought the guy looked like Lee Van Cleef having a bad day.

There was a speck of toilet paper stuck to his chin where he must have cut himself shaving. When the man asked Erik, "Is that it?" the piece of toilet paper came off, floated down to the counter, and landed on top of the case of beer.

It was a leading question. Undoubtedly he meant, Isn't there something missing, kid—like your driver's license?

"No," Erik said as he grabbed a pack of yellow highlighter pens that were on display next to the register. He put them on top of the case of beer and said, "These too."

God, why did I do that!? Erik thought. *If I wanted to telegraph that I'm a college student, nothing says it louder than beer and highlighter pens.*

Too late. The deed had been done.

The clerk had to know he was underage. This was orientation weekend. All the merchants in town were undoubtedly on high alert for the new crop of freshmen kids arriving in town, trying to get away with everything they possibly could.

The clerk rang up the case of beer, the six-pack of soda, and the highlighter pens and then gave Erik a price.

Erik paused, waiting for the clerk to ask for an ID. He waited for two minutes. Well, it seemed like two minutes. It was probably less than two seconds.

Erik reached in his jeans and pulled out the wad of bills that the guys had given him. *Until you pay for the liquor, you haven't broken the law.* Erik handed the entire wad to him and told him to keep the change.

Another dumb move! Who gives a tip to a liquor store clerk? Erik internally kicked himself.

Without waiting for a reply, Erik picked up the beer, soda, and highlighter pens and then turned and walked rapidly toward the back door, the hairs on the back of his neck tingled as he waited for the clerk to yell, "Stop!" *Technically they can't arrest you until you pay for the liquor and take possession of it.*

Erik held his breath as he reached for the door. He opened the door. The bell rang. He stepped through. He shut the door behind him. Silence.

A breath-holding pause. Then the guys started whooping and hollering, just like the dumbass college kids they were.

And Erik joined right in.

The gang of freshmen ran to Deuce's car, and they squealed out of the parking lot. The look on the faces of Erik's new best friends was a mixture of disbelief and euphoria.

Erik's reputation was sealed. They all got freshman drunk that night, and Erik did not darken the door of a single orientation event the entire weekend.

Keefendorf was an odd mixture of studious conservatism and raucous behavior. Whenever he drank, he was like Dr. Jekyll and Mr. Hyde. He would be the guy at the party with a lampshade on his head or the one dancing on top of the table. But when he wasn't drinking, he was studying.

Now, two years later, Bob Keefendorf was part of a group called the Institute of European Studies (IES) and was spending a semester abroad at Durham University.

Keef took Erik on a tour of the grounds. In every way imaginable, the vintage British campus was like being time-warped into the past. Just one more mind-expanding journey into world history for Erik; he couldn't help but envy Keef for this incredible opportunity he was experiencing.

An old wood-and-stone bridge arched over the River Wear. Several racing shells flashed under the bridge, while a large group of men in kilts and full Scottish garb came out of nowhere, playing "Amazing Grace" on the bagpipes.

Later, back in the castle, they ate dinner in the commons and Bob introduced Erik to some of his pals. That night they frequented a few of the pubs off campus. Like Erik, Keefendorf was a junior. His curriculum consisted of English lit, archeology, economics, and Latin.

Keef's roomie was kind enough to give up his bunk for Erik. This was the first time since leaving Minnesota that Erik didn't sleep on the floor or on the ground somewhere. Hell, this was the only time he'd ever slept in a castle.

Bob's archeology class had a scheduled field trip to Hadrian's Wall on the following day. The excursion was only for class members, but Erik was intrigued about the wall and curious to see what the country looked like in that area. The next morning, there were about twenty students plus one stowaway piled on a bus heading for Hadrian's Wall.

The stunningly beautiful English countryside made Erik's heart ache that his brother wasn't alive to experience this with him. He remembered when his parents made a big deal out of Charlie being able to read *The Canterbury Tales* in its original Middle English while still in high school. The bus was taking them through the middle of Canterbury Tales country right now. Erik stared out the bus windows, lamenting that he'd been jealous of the praise that Charlie got from their parents. But that was Charlie, so acute in some ways and so obtuse in others.

The centuries had eroded much of Hadrian's Wall, and it was fascinating to hear the professor resurrect gory details about the blood that went into building and defending the wall. Hadrian was one of only five good emperors of Rome, and he supposedly built the wall to keep those nasty northern barbarians out of Latin Britannia.

When they got back to the campus, a student dance at a local venue in town was in progress. Several of the IES students were going. Erik thought a dance would be great fun and would do the both of them some good. He noticed that Bob had become withdrawn; he'd seen this happen before.

"Come on, pal. Let's get out of this stuffy old castle and go to the dance."

"Naw, you go," Keef said. "I've got homework."

"Homework? You've been doing homework every night since you first arrived! You're in England, man! You need to put on your kilt, grab some bagpipes, and blow off a little steam!"

"That damned bus ride gave me a headache. You go and have fun."

Erik knew he wasn't going to be able to get Keef to change his mind. There were many times when, as roomies back in St. Cloud, Bob would be morose for days. Then he'd ace a test, and that night he'd be the first one to the kegger and the last to leave. Often Erik had to help him back to the dorm. Now, here in England, Bob seemed to be especially morose. Erik didn't know what was causing Bob's pain, but he understood what it felt like to hurt.

Erik went to the dance. Hanging around people his own age and hearing some old-time rock n' roll was soothing. The dance reminded him of the time he was about seventeen and drove down to Rochester, Minnesota, where Charlie was going to college. Charlie had gone to great pains to set up a double date for the two of them. This was completely uncharacteristic of him. Charlie liked girls but he was shy and unsure of himself around them. He rarely dated. Somehow though, he'd worked up the courage to ask a classmate if she wanted to go to the school dance and if she had a friend for his younger brother who was coming to town for a visit. Miraculously she said yes.

When Erik arrived in Rochester, Charlie told him that his friend had just called saying she had to cancel—something had come up. Erik had a hunch that she'd only said yes to Charlie in the first place because she didn't have the guts to tell him no to his face. *People are always taking advantage of Charlie, and it ticks me off.*

Erik asked for the girl's number. When she came on the line, he told her that he'd heard so many wonderful things about her and that he and Charlie were super disappointed because they were both so looking forward to tonight. Erik kept talking and finding positive things to say about her. He wasn't exactly lying—more like exaggerating. Eventually, the girl changed her mind. The two couples ended up going to the dance and having a great time.

Erik stood alone, leaning against one of the brick walls of the Durham University recreation center, thinking about his brother's innocence, when one of the female IES students approached.

"Notice how all of the Brits are preoccupied with PDA?" she asked.

"PDA?"

"Yeah, public display of affection."

He hadn't noticed, but now that she mentioned it, he had to agree. Most of the kids in the room were British, and the plain truth was that many of them were hanging all over their partners.

The young woman was attractive. She joined Erik in leaning against the wall, their arms folded across their chests, watching the crowd as though they were somehow above the amorous antics of the Brits.

As they stood there, Erik wondered how she knew that he wasn't British.

Was it my clothes? My demeanor? Erik didn't want to stand out. He wanted to blend in. He never wanted to be mistaken for a tourist. This was his life now. The road was his home. Erik would have sworn that his tweed cap shouted, "I'm a Brit!"

"How do you know Bob Keefendorf?" she asked.

So that's it. She saw me with Keef. Where, I wonder? I think I would have remembered seeing her...

Erik's puzzled expression elicited a response from the coed. "Saw you at The Dun Cow last night." She paused and then said, "You stood out."

The Dun Cow? "Oh, right," he said. "Yeah, that place was packed. We couldn't find anywhere to sit so we didn't stay. Ended up going over to The Shakespeare."

"You should have joined us. Me and some of my mates had a nice table. We could have squeezed you in."

She was tall, almost as tall as Erik. Now that they were talking, he could see that she was more than just attractive, she was gorgeous. Her eyes were green, and she wore a cable-knit sweater that fit her like a birthday suit. What's more, she had approached Erik and was talking about PDA.

How different it is for girls. It's easy for them, by comparison. If they see someone they like, they can just walk over and start talking. The guy never gets offended or put off. He's always flattered and happy to talk.

"Keef and I roomed together last year. I tried to get him to come tonight, but—"

"We all know Bob's story," she said, cutting him off. "He's mooning over his girl back in the States."

Clearly the Americans here were a small, tight-knit community and knew each other well. She was eager to talk and pivoted the conversation back to her observations of the Brits. There was a mini-pub in one section of the room, and he noticed her noticing it. He offered to buy her a beer.

They sat on pub stools and watched Brits entwining. "Have you noticed how much better dressed these British kids are than American kids?" she asked.

"Yeah, they're obsessed with fashion. When I was in London, they were selling tickets for a Bowie concert on Canal Street and there were dozens of kids all looking like Ziggy Stardust recreations."

"I love Bowie." The beer was a strong ale, and her eyes glistened.

"Yeah, Bowie's cool," Erik said. "Although I have to admit that I'm more into Cat Stevens, the Eagles, and Jackson Browne."

"I love Jackson Browne."

She was so damned agreeable and open. Two American expats in a tiny pub at a dance in Durham. They had so much in common. If his heart hadn't already been given to someone else… If the circumstances had been different…

Impulsively, he said, "Tomorrow I'm hitchin' to Harwich to catch a ferry to Denmark. My girlfriend's there doing a year abroad study program."

She smiled, "My boyfriend's back in Indiana. He didn't want me to go, but he said I should, otherwise I'd regret missing this opportunity for the rest of my life. He's such a good guy. I miss him."

Erik managed an enigmatic grin. "You don't know what you have 'til it's gone."

A bond was forming between them. A vulnerability set free from the parameters voluntarily established. A safety shield in which to share their loneliness with a sympathetic listener.

Erik bought another round. Their voices grew softer as the subject grew more intimate. The Brits coiled themselves more tightly into their PDA postures. When next she spoke, her voice was low and had a natural sultriness.

"So you haven't seen her in about three months, you've been getting postcards from all over Europe, telling you how much fun she's having with some traveling buddies who happen to be male, and you're not worried. That about sum it up?"

Her pithy summary stung. "Yeah, that about sums it up."

She smiled again. "Should be an interesting reunion."

Just then, the loudspeakers, which had been playing British songs all night, played "Take It Easy" by the Eagles. *Take It Easy*. She looked at him with a wry smile, pregnant with meaning that he didn't fail to notice. He offered her his hand, and they walked out onto the dance floor. The transition felt organic.

After "Take It Easy," Roberta Flack's voice filled the room with "Killing Me Softly." The DJ announced this would be the last dance. The two of them shifted from free-form to Erik having one arm around her waist and then two arms around her waist. Their embrace gradually tightened as the dance went on. Increasingly, they resembled their British counterparts. Then the dance was over.

He offered to walk her to wherever she was rooming. The strong English ale made them both lightheaded and giddy as they stepped out into the cool night air. They didn't hurry. They were enjoying the night, the fresh air, the ale buzz, and the intoxication of not knowing exactly where this was heading.

When they came to the bridge that crossed over the River Wear, her foot tripped slightly on one of the wooden planks. He reached out and caught her; she laughed. They continued to walk, now hand in hand. At the center of the bridge, they stopped to admire the moonlight shimmering silently on the river. The night was achingly beautiful.

Slowly, seamlessly, they turned and faced one another. Her eyes appeared almost iridescently green. Her lips were full and inviting, and suddenly he wanted to kiss them. The night breeze picked up and blew gently between them, wrapping the scent of her perfume around him like a scarf of the softest gossamer. He could see goose bumps forming at the base of her neck where it merged into her chest.

The only sound was the river slapping the smooth, centuries-old stones under the bridge as it journeyed eastward from the Pennines to where the waters poured into the North Sea at Sunderland. He was vaguely aware of a faint voice somewhere deep inside his subconscious telling him to stop. He pushed the voice back down into his subterranean muck, as if trying to drown it.

This is the new you, the free you, Erik. The one that's not going to tie himself down to American customs and values. The one that's going to have a clean slate and to start fresh.

He placed his hands on her shoulders and gently pulled her body into his. She eased her hands around his waist and tilted her head back slightly so that the moonlight reflected off the glossiness of her lips. Any resistance he felt disappeared into those bottomless beacons of emerald green—

Erik, what the hell are you doing?

The voice leapt up from deep inside him.

The voice was right. *What was he doing?* He loved Diana. He couldn't do this. He knew himself. Once he heard the voice, he knew that was the end of it. He couldn't do what his body was aching to do. Instead of kissing her lips, as he almost had, he leaned in and kissed her on the cheek. Then he pulled back and gave her a smile filled with regret.

She returned his smile, matching his regret. Neither spoke for a long time. Finally, she reached up and placed her hand on the side of his face and said, "She's a lucky girl. I hope you find what you're looking for."

Bob Keefendorf was sleeping when Erik got back to the dorm room. He saw a letter that Bob had written to his sweetie back in the States. He shouldn't have read it, but he did. The letter was touching, a side of Bob that Erik hadn't really seen very often. Bob and his girlfriend had been going steady throughout high school, and apparently, they were still going strong. According to his letter, Bob was coming apart at the seams without her.

Bob still had a couple more months left to go here in England. No wonder he was so morose all the time. As Erik looked at him curled up in his bunk, he had to admit that he could relate to what Bob was going through.

HARWICH

The long stretches between rides gave him too much time to think about Diana and her guy traveling companion. Erik's desire to get to Denmark was now almost manic. He said goodbye to Keef early in the morning, with the goal of arriving in Harwich in plenty of time for the ferry to Esbjerg, Denmark.

Getting rides today was like watching sap run down a pine tree. *Damn! Nothin's going anywhere.* Maybe that's just the way it seemed because he had set a hard and fast goal for himself. He wanted desperately to turn twenty-one while in Denmark and if he missed the ferry, that goal was ashes.

No girl had ever given him the freedom to pursue his interests the way Diana had. His interests were not a threat to her. At least that's what he had always thought.

We're a perfect fit. She has her world, which I respect, and she supports me doing what I feel I was born to do.

Not that there weren't plenty of naysayers, especially after Erik's second semester in college. He'd been cast in a main stage production—something that never happens for a freshman. The part wasn't huge, but it was integral to the play.

During the first read-through, the director, Dr. Cervante, the toughest, most badass director and professor in the entire college, who reportedly had been a drill sergeant in the army and suffered no fools, said, "Okay, we're going to cut the next four pages and start at the top of the following page."

Those four pages were most of Erik's part. There went his Tony Award. He counted the lines he had left. *Three. So much for my brilliant career.*

I know, I know, he told himself. *There are no small parts, only small actors.*

For the next week, the cast practiced what the drill sergeant called "exploration and discovery." This consisted of character development exercises, such as finding some small space in a corner of the theater and shouting out whatever phrases came to their minds or acting out which animal best represented their characters.

Erik chose a fly, which he felt was roughly commensurate with the size of his part.

As pointless as he thought all the exploration and discovery exercises were, what made them untenable was that he was woefully behind on homework assignments. Four hours imitating flies every night instead of doing homework made achieving sophomore status seem like the impossible dream.

After rehearsal one night, Erik approached the sergeant.

"Dr. Cervante, may I speak with you?"

"Yes?"

"Ah, I'm falling behind in my studies, and I was wondering if on some nights I could leave a little early—just on the nights when my character isn't needed…"

Dr. Cervante didn't say a word. He just looked at Erik with his black, penetrating eyes—eyes that would have made Charles Manson shudder—and held out his hand. He motioned for Erik to hand him the script.

Erik protested—he wasn't telling him that he wanted to quit the play, he just wanted Dr. Cervante to cut him a break on the rehearsal schedule. But there was no arguing with the eyes. Cervante was done with him and that was final. There was no room for half-assed commitments. An actor was either all in or all out.

The next day, Erik was the gossip of the entire theater department. Everyone knew he'd been kicked out of the play, and more than one upperclassman pulled him aside and said he'd made a huge mistake. They said he'd never again be in a main stage production at St. Cloud State College.

The blackballing didn't break him though. Erik was relieved. He desperately needed to catch up in his classes and get some sleep. He was certain of what he knew about himself. This was just a minor setback—nothing that would derail his eventual career. They could kick him out of a play, but they couldn't take away his love of acting and the theater.

A Volkswagen bus painted with psychedelic colors and peace signs pulled over, and a hippie couple offered Erik a ride and a toke. He declined the toke but took the ride, which brought him to the outskirts of Harwich. The couple told him how to get to the ferry, but their instructions were a little hazy and he had to stop and ask a couple more people for directions.

Why can't the Brits just give simple, straightforward directions? Must every explanation be a topographical history lesson?

Erik could smell the fumes before he could see the ferry. Fortunately, the boat was still docked. He rushed into the office to get a ticket.

"Terribly sorry, sonny, but yer've missed the Esbjerg ferry for today. Next one'll be leav'n tomorraw at the same time."

"*Tomorrow?!*"

Erik pointed to the clock on the wall.

"It's not five o'clock yet. There's still another eight minutes!"

The clerk gestured toward the dock and said, "Wal, yer might make it, young fella, since the gate hasn't closed yet. But ya'd better make haste. Once the gate closes, thar'll be no boarding the ferry."

Erik bought the ticket and took off running with his fifty-six-pound pack. As he got closer, he could see the gate starting to close. He broke into a full sprint. This was going to be a close call. He pushed as hard as he could and as he transferred the pack from his back to his arms, a searing pain shot up his spinal cord as though a large hypodermic needle had just been thrust up the middle of it.

Screaming in pain, he slammed against the wire fence bordering the exterior of the entrance gate and collapsed to the ground. Erik watched helplessly as the gate finished closing. The ferry sounded its horn while a couple of the ship's sailors tossed anchor lines onto the dock. As the ferry pulled away from the dock, the sailors watched Erik dispassionately while he writhed in agony.

The excruciating pain he had endured at Heathrow Airport had returned. He had almost forgotten about it. Erik threaded his fingers through the lattice mesh of the fence and slowly pulled himself up to his feet. The motion relieved some of the weight pushing down on his spine and the pain settled into a dull ache.

He was angry. Angry for not getting more and better rides, angry at the Brits for not knowing how to give good directions, angry at himself for not leaving for Harwich sooner, angry for not jogging that last mile, angry at the ferry for leaving the dock at 4:59 p.m., and angry at God for giving Charlie a fifteen.

Erik stood on that decrepit dock for a long time, struggling against the reality that he had missed the ferry and that there was no way he could will himself onto it. As he watched the ferry slowly sail farther away, he fought his urge to utter a cry of frustration.

Where did this primal urge to be on Danish soil by my twenty-first birthday come from? And what difference does it make? It's as if by achieving my self-imposed deadline, I could prevent Diana from decoupling herself from me. That she wouldn't be train-hopping across the continent with a smorgasbord of companions seeing the seven wonders of the world without me. Really, is this what I am trying to do?

He slowly and carefully sat down on his pack. Although the pain was now a dull ache, it was devastating to think that the searing pain could return without warning. This was not good. His heart kept pounding, but no longer from the exertion of trying to catch the ferry.

The pounding now was from his life imploding. *Maybe you will never arrive in Fredericia now and maybe she doesn't care if you ever do.*

"Erik, don't even go there. You're just upset because you missed the lousy ferry. There'll be another one tomorrow. It's not a big deal."

The voice shocked Erik. It was Charlie. Erik sat bolt upright. "Charlie?" he shouted.

His brother's voice had been as clear to Erik as if he were sitting on the dock right next to him.

Erik scrambled to his feet and spun around. No one there. He was alone on the dock. He glanced back at the ferry station and then seaward—out towards the ferry.

"Oh my God, I thought you were here, Charlie!"

As soon as he realized that Charlie wasn't there and that he was on the dock alone, Erik suddenly became aware that his back pain was gone. Completely. There wasn't even a hint of it. In its place was a surging warmth. It was just like Heathrow all over again.

He watched the ferry churn farther and farther away. It was like his brother was on that ferry and he was losing him all over again. Erik wanted to scream "Charlie!" at the top of his lungs—to yell until he couldn't yell anymore. Instead, a fog of loneliness engulfed him, and a helplessness he hadn't known since he and Charlie were little kids on Ottawa Avenue, when they were cornered by those three bullies.

Charlie's right. It's not the end of the world. I need to get my head back in the game and I need to do it right now. There are other pressing issues. Since I'm sure as hell not going to be sleeping on the ferry tonight, I'd better find someplace to stay in this godforsaken country.

Just as he had done at Heathrow, Erik slowly threaded his arms into his backpack. Amazingly, he felt no pain. This was just like before. It was crazy and made no sense. *What is going on? Is it possible that Charlie is watching over me? Or is it God?* He could understand if somehow it was Charlie, but why would God care?

Erik didn't want to sleep outside again, certain that with his current string of luck, rain would be a foregone conclusion. On the other hand, he had already blown past his daily budget, and he didn't want to spend any more money today. Sleeping outside would be just punishment for missing the ferry.

What do I care if it rains?

Erik walked back toward town. He hadn't eaten since noon when he devoured three small apples picked from a lone apple tree. Two more apples were still nestled in the pocket of his pack. He ate one as he walked, deep in a thundercloud of thought.

Before reaching the main section of town, he veered off onto an old gravel road, partially lined by a dilapidated stone wall. He looked for a secluded spot with any kind of overhead shelter. No rain at present, but an earlier downpour had left the ground wet. A forlorn wooded area loomed up ahead.

He spotted a large evergreen with a wide umbrella shape. *Who could object to me throwing down here?* Erik casually stepped into the cover of the foliage and took off his pack. He kept the ground tarp in the top section of his pack for quick and easy access. The tarp blended perfectly with the gravel and grass beneath his feet.

As he prepared his bivouac, a large mastiff jumped through the thicket and, with ear-splitting ferocity, barked at Erik as if he were a creature from the black lagoon. She scared the living hell out of him.

Immediately, he crammed the ground tarp back into his pack. Ignoring the dog's barking was futile. Any ears within a one-mile radius would surely be aware of his trespassing. Erik's face turned beat red, and his skin tingled as though he had rolled naked in poison ivy.

The beast unleashed her full rancor in punishing this criminal vagrant. She hounded Erik with her gnarled teeth bared, foaming at the mouth and making hideous growling sounds. Fortunately, her bark was not followed with a bite.

"Shut up, you mongrel!" Erik barked back at her.

He didn't want to run, but he sure wanted to get the heck out of there. The mutt followed him for the longest time, barking constantly, but now keeping a respectful distance. The dog was obviously pleased that she had managed to rout this intruder from her master's property. Erik endured the humiliation in silence until eventually the cur tired of being ignored and let him walk on.

Erik kept moving. He now wanted to get as far away from civilization as he could so that he could turn off the day in peace and not worry about any more dog attacks.

The farther Erik walked, the more remote the country road became. He looked for another spot where he could just put an end to this interminable day. He found the place next to a big tree—not too far from the path but just far enough to be concealed.

He knew he needed to make an attitude adjustment. *Erik, you can't let circumstances control your mood.*

Surveying the area for any sign of a dog or other prying eyes, he slowly started to relax. He saw another evergreen with spreading branches and pulled his pack up against the tree trunk. Although it wasn't raining, the sky was partly cloudy. Even so, he continued unpacking. In a short while, he had his green army-surplus tarp and his sleeping bag laid out. He leaned against his backpack and pulled out a harmonica. He always carried two—a G harp and a C harp. He'd picked up the habit a couple of years ago during a Boundary Waters canoe trip. Playing them always soothed and comforted him. He began by playing a soft and slow version of *Bobby McGee.* He quickly lost himself in the music and was startled when he felt raindrops.

He stopped playing and looked up through the branches at a sky that was swiftly getting darker and darker. He shook his head and said, "You win."

With that, he put away his harmonicas and stuffed the tarp and his sleeping bag back into the pack. Strapping himself in, he turned and walked back toward the town of Harwich.

Erik had passed a pub earlier in the day on his way to the ferry wharf. Pubs often had rooms for rent. A thundercloud cracked, and the skies above opened their spigots for the pouring rain.

What would be so terrible about finding a warm and dry lodging for the night? To hell with how much it costs. Whatever the cost, it will be worth it.

He was drenched when he finally found the pub after nearly an hour of miserable walking. The orange light above the door emitted a welcoming beam with a faint, cautionary undertone. He stepped inside. A moment passed before his eyes could adjust to the dim room. The rain rolled off him and puddled on the wooden planks under his feet.

The pub patrons all stopped whatever they'd been doing and looked at Erik as if he were a mythical creature in from the woods, dog-dirty and loaded for bear.

Erik took his poncho off and laid it over his pack. Even the clothes underneath his poncho were wet. He stepped up to the barkeep and asked if he had any rooms to let.

The man turned his head and shouted, "Tilly!"

A woman came limping out of the back room. She waddled up to Erik, looked him up and down, and said, "The B&B is £2. Paid in advance."

B&B! Erik grimaced. This was a pub. He doubted that they had anything here remotely resembling a bed and breakfast. Still, what choice did he have?

"Alright, I'll take it."

Erik gave her the money and followed her as she limped up the stairs, mumbling under her breath about a bad hip. She opened a door.

"'Ere's yer room."

Room? This is a closet minus the clothes' pole.

There was just enough space for a small cot and a nightstand. Barely room to set down his backpack.

"The washroom's down the 'all. It'll cost yer a pound extra fer a bath if yu'd like one."

She left, and Erik sat on the cot for a while. This is not how he had anticipated spending the eve of his twenty-first birthday. He got up and walked down the hall to the washroom. There was an open door into a room where a young man wearing thick glasses was sitting on a bed reading what appeared to be a large Bible.

When Erik came out of the washroom, the man was watching him as he passed by in the hallway. Erik nodded as he walked past. The man called after him, "Are you American?"

Erik stopped. *He'd better not try preaching at me.* Erik was tired, pissed off at the world, and frustrated that everyone seemed to know he was an American.

"What's it to ya?"

"Rather none of my business, of course," said the stranger, "but what the deuce is an American doing in Harwich in a hole like this?"

What's this guy's angle? And how does being an American exempt me from staying in "holes"? Erik felt no obligation to explain how this dump was a step up from some of his previous lodgings. Instead, he gave the man a condensed version of his little saga about missing the ferry.

The stranger listened politely and finally said, "You don't belong in a place like this. You should be staying in a proper B&B."

"Yeah, well, I don't know how I would find one at this time of night. Besides, I've already paid for the closet."

"There's a B&B just down the road. If I was you, I wouldn't stay in this dump. I'd demands me money back from Tilly and get the 'ell out of here. Go stay in a B&B."

Erik went back to the tiny room and sat down on the cot, thinking about what the bloke had said.

It's risky. The easiest thing to do would be to just stay here. Sure, it's not the Taj Mahal, but it's warm and dry.

Still, the more he thought about this situation, the angrier he got.

I shouldn't be here. I should be on a ferry on my way to Denmark. It's my fault, I know, but I'll be damned if I spend my last night in

England in this dump. Charlie would have expected me to take my chances.

He went back downstairs and told Tilly that he wanted his money back.

"This 'ere's the best ye'll do in this town at this time o' night."

"I'll take my chances." Erik's tone left no room for equivocation, and Tilly grudgingly gave him his money back, muttering all the while.

Once more, Erik strapped himself into his pack and put on his wet poncho. The rain hadn't abated in the least. He walked in the direction the young man with thick glasses had instructed.

Now that he was outside in the rain and perambulating again, his temper cooled and he turned the situation over in his head. I wonder what makes that dump good enough for the guy with glasses, but not good enough for me? *What if I don't find the B&B? Or what if I do find it and it's occupied? Shit, why didn't I think of that before I left the pub!?*

He cringed at the thought of going back to Tilly and begging her to give him back the closet. The harridan would probably like nothing better than to say, "Sorry, laddie, but yer suite's been let."

Erik saw a house with a rectangular sign above the door but owing to the rain and darkness of the night, the sign was illegible. No lights on the house. He walked to the front door. Now he could read the *Bed & Breakfast* sign, but there was no indication whether they had a vacancy or were even open for business.

Erik knocked anyway because that's what you do when you're cold, wet, and hungry. Presently, a matronly woman came to the door.

"Gracious," she said. "What a night to be out! Come in, you'll catch yer death."

Erik stepped inside their tidy entryway, as she called out to her husband. "Aiden, we've got a guest! *Tch, tch*, it's not a fit night ut fer man ner beast. Come in, dearie, and let's get yer wet things off."

Aiden came in from the other room. Erik could hear a TV in the background.

"For the love of God, lad, what ar yer doin' ut on a night like this?"

"Oh, hush up, Aiden. Don't be botherin' the lad with a lot of questions. 'Ee's soaked to the skin." The good woman continued, "I'll bet you'd like a nice, hot bath now, wouldn't you, sonny? And I bet yer hungry too. 'Ow would yer like me to warm up a little something for yer to eat?"

That bath was the closest damned thing to heaven that Erik could honestly remember. When he was finished, there remained a massively dirty ring in the tub. Knowing what his mother would have said and having become aware of the strong anti-American sentiment in England, he cleaned the tub until it sparkled.

When Erik came downstairs, Aiden invited him into the living room where the BBC could be heard on the "telly."

"Well now, yer lookin' a tad site better, laddie. An' what brings yer ta 'Arwich on such a fine night as this?"

"Trying to catch the ferry to Esbjerg. I came too late."

"Ahh, right," Aiden said. "The tides wait fer no man."

The newscaster in the background could be heard saying, "The Senate reversed an amendment to begin US troop reductions overseas…"

Erik turned his attention to the television, while Aiden said, "Where's yer final destination? I'm thinkin' it's not Esbjerg."

"Senate Majority Leader Mike Mansfield had hoped for the reduction…," continued the newscaster.

"What's that?" Erik turned back toward Aiden. "No, not Esbjerg. My girlfriend is doing a study program abroad this year—in Fredericia."

"Ah, a girlfriend, is it? *'Cherchez la femme,'* as they say. Nothin' like a woman to make a man wander around 'utside in the middle of a staurmy night."

Erik's attention was drawn back to the TV. "Senator Baker asked E. Howard Hunt if the CIA was involved in domestic activities…"

Aiden too turned his attention to the TV. "Hunt agreed that they were and added that they may have always been involved. Hunt stated that he believed the orders he received had the highest sanction and such orders were not meant to be questioned…"

"*Tch*, there's no good news on the telly anymore," mused Aiden. "Vietnam. Watergate. IRA bombings. The world is so divided now. It's a shame, laddie…"

Harriet poked her head in the room. "Well, they'll be no division in this house. You boys come on into the kitchen now while the tea's hot."

Aiden and Erik took seats at the table, and Harriet placed a large bowl of steaming cauliflower in front of Erik. He was stunned by the size of the bowl but proceeded to devour every morsel gratefully. Never had he tasted a meal more delicious. He hadn't expected that he would be eating anything tonight except for the one small apple he still had left in his pack.

When he finished the bowl, Harriet asked if he wanted more. *Was she kidding?* Harriet saw his grateful smile. She laughed and brought out a second bowl of steaming cauliflower.

By the time Erik finished that second bowl, he was full. His stomach must have shrunk since leaving the States. He hadn't expected such warmth and generosity. *On my birthday eve, no less!*

Harriet returned and set a plate of mutton, potatoes, and peas in front of Erik. He was stunned. Had he known that the cauliflower was just an appetizer, he never would have had that second bowl. How was he going to eat all this food?

Erik shook his head, *I guess this is what they call a "happy problem."* He forked a tender slice of mutton into his mouth and murmured with satisfaction at each succulent bite.

"Before I came here tonight," he confessed through a mouthful of food, "I booked a room at the pub down the road. I was all set to stay there—paid for the room and everything—when one of the other lodgers said that I should come here."

"Harrumph," interjected Harriet, "'At would 'a been Tilly's place. Bless 'er 'art, she's not a happy woman. Got a bad hip along with two and twenty other troubles. Yer say there was another lodger? 'At's strange, she's only got but one room to let."

"Wasn't much of a room, more like a converted closet."

"No doubt that's exactly what it tis," ventured Aiden. "The 'ol gal is trying ter squeeze every quid she can outa that spare room above the pub."

"Be that as it may, y'ar here now, an' we're tickled ta have yer," said Harriet. "Now Erik, tell us about yar girlfriend, what's she like an' 'ow long 'as it been since yer've seen 'er?"

"She left for Denmark two and a half months ago. She's… like an artist. Not a specific kind of artist, she's just artistic in her life. Like, the way she sees things, and how those things end up getting expressed in everything she does."

"I'll bet she's pretty," prodded Harriet.

"She doesn't think so, but believe me, she is. You know, it's strange sometimes the way things work out. A few hours ago, I was miserable. I had missed the ferry which meant I couldn't keep the promise I made to Diana to be with her on my birthday. I had wrenched my back and was in a lot of pain. I was drenched from the rain and about to spend a night in that dismal pub. Then that other lodger insisted I should come here. How weird is that? Now I'm glad I missed the lousy ferry, and I don't care that I won't be with her on my birthday. My back pain is completely gone. Being here with you two in your beautiful English home beats everything else."

After Erik had finished his meal, Harriet invited him into their cozy English living room for a spot of tea where they continued the spirited discussion about affairs of the heart and the vicissitudes of life. Aiden entered carrying a bottle of Blanton's Single Barrel Bourbon and three brandy snifters. "I've been savin' this bottle fer a special occasion, and by God, a lad tarns twenty-one but once."

Aiden poured them each a generous amount, raised his glass, and proposed a toast. "To the ties that bind, whether they be heart to heart or between two great nations; may the path before our young friend Erik be clear and sunny; may our families be safe from the damned

IRA bombs and from foreign wars—to the many good lads who have already given their lives..."

Aiden surely meant the toast to be uplifting and positive, but his words found their way to the inner recesses of Erik's heart where he was trying desperately to prevent the memory of Charlie's death from subsuming him.

Erik froze and couldn't move. It was as though Charlie's spirit had entered the room. Erik had planned to make some clever toast in response, but suddenly he couldn't speak. Emotions overtook him and clogged up in his throat. Whether it was his full belly, the presence of these good, kind people who had welcomed him with open arms, or being out of the storm and having escaped that decrepit pub, he couldn't say. Maybe it was just that he was alive and breathing while Charlie was dead and buried.

Erik stood with his glass raised, unable to speak as a memory washed over him—a fragment from one of the many tapes Charlie had sent home. In this tape, Charlie was interviewing a fellow soldier, a guy who had lived in England and had a slight British accent.

Charlie and the guy were laughing. Charlie was trying to imitate the guy's accent, but it kept sounding Irish or Scottish—definitely not British English. They both thought it was hilarious. Two soldiers finding something to laugh about in Vietnam. That always stuck with Erik.

Charlie, you told us you were safe. You were in a DMZ. The area had been cleared for months. No danger you said.

Harriet and Aiden gaped at Erik in astonishment as he stood like a statue with outstretched arm, eyes filling with tears. Harriet crossed to him and gently placed her hand on his shoulder.

"There, there, son. It's alright. Y'ar among friends."

Ashamed of his inability to prevent these memories from overtaking him—especially in front of these good people—he tried to speak but was unable to utter a word. Harriet's kindness only made it worse. He sat down on the couch and worked to hold in the painful sadness that begged to be released. Harriet and Aiden looked at each other, not knowing what to do.

Stillness filled the room as minutes ticked by, marked only by the steady *ticktock* emanating from the Black Forest cuckoo clock that had been in Harriet's family for five generations. Finally, as Erik felt the ebbing away of the grip his emotions had held over him, he wiped his eyes on his sleeve and said, "I'm sorry, I didn't mean for that to happen."

Harriet sat down next to Erik on the couch and placed her hand on his shoulder again. "Yer've nothin' to apologize far, dearie. It's alright. Take all the time yer need."

"You folks have been so good to me. I… I wasn't expecting to meet such kind people. I… my brother," Erik struggled to keep his eyes from filling with tears again. "In March. His tour was up in two weeks. He never made it back."

Harriet reached out and hugged Erik. "Oh, Erik, we ar so sorry…" She hugged him as if he were her own son.

"You know," Erik said after Harriet released him, "we weren't anything alike. Different as night and day. But I loved him. He was such a good man. Much better than I'll ever be."

Aiden crossed over to Erik and placed a hand on his shoulder. "I'm sorry, Erik. War is a terrible thing. We've all seen too much of what war can do. We ar honored to have yer in our home tonight."

The kindness of this British couple, and the generosity they showed Erik in their quaint, modest home in the English countryside, was almost too much. Erik struggled to find the right words. Finally, he simply said, "Thank you Aiden and thank you Harriet. I think it was fate that I ended up knocking on your door tonight. This is a birthday that I shall never forget."

Aiden seized the moment and proclaimed, "Aye, Erik, it's a night that we, too, shalln't forget. You have honored us by knocking on our door and sharing our table. Now then, I think it's high time far that drink."

With that, the three of them let out a laugh of relief and raised their snifters. Aiden simply said, "God save the Queen," and Harriet, Aiden, and Erik swallowed their shots of Blanton's Single Barrel.

Harwich, England—September 25, 1973

The day before I <u>actually</u> turn 21.

I'm lying on a huge, soft bed in an English B&B on the outskirts of Harwich, writing a few lines as I fight to stay awake on a full belly. I almost missed this enchanting experience. I took a chance because of what that guy at the pub said to me. It was so weird.

Even though I was bummed out when I missed the ferry, I can see now that the story isn't over until it's over. Even when bad things happen, it's good to look for the good and always be optimistic.

Drank bourbon tonight with the hosts of this B&B. I told them about Charlie, and I broke down in front of them. I couldn't help myself. So strange how the night just evolved, but it felt like these people were family.

Going to make damn sure I don't miss the ferry tomorrow.

FREDERICIA

A twenty-one-year-old Erik was at the ferry dock three hours before the departure time. Once boarded, he explored the entire ship. Since he was early, he was able to check out all the guest cabins. His was the smallest. *So what? I'm happy. The cabin has a bunk and a washbasin—what more does one need? I can roam anywhere I want, make new friends, begin my real life...*

The top floor of the ship boasted a magnificent mahogany lounge, commanding a three-sided view of the ocean. As the ferry powered out of the harbor and into the open sea, Erik took a seat at the circular bar in the center of the lounge and ordered a beer. A half dozen people were already comfortably seated, their beverages of choice in front of them.

Erik was easily the youngest one in the room. There was one man sitting by himself, on the other side of the bar, who may have been just five or six years older. He was wearing a peacoat, similar to what sailors wear, only this one was olive green and beautifully tailored. Everyone else was middle-aged.

A mix of English and Danish emanated from his fellow patrons, making Erik long to be bilingual. When his beer arrived, he took a drink and turned to the Danish man sitting next to him, "Have you taken this ferry before?"

"Ja, many times. You are sitting in ze best room to spend entire trip."

Erik was eager to converse with the Dane, but as the ship stretched out into the open waters, it lurched methodically from side to side. The motion made Erik lose his equilibrium, as though his brain was sloshing around inside his skull.

When he felt the room begin to spin, Erik asked the Dane, "How long does it take to get to Esbjerg?"

"Ja ja, about fourteen hours. Best to have drink and enjoy trip. Skoal!"

The man raised his glass and Erik clinked it with his, but the room had become claustrophobic; he felt nausea rising rapidly. As much as Erik wanted to continue the conversation, he couldn't. The nausea became so insistent that if he closed his eyes even for a few seconds, he feared he would vomit. No way could he take another swallow of beer. It was all he could do to hold down the first gulp. A sickening taste rose through his esophagus, and vomit gushed into his mouth.

"Ye look a bit green," said the Dane. Erik forced his mouth shut and dashed out of the lounge into the fresh air. He ran to the railing and purged the contents of his mouth into the sea.

For the next twenty minutes, Erik hung over the railing, nauseous and green. It was cold on deck and getting colder, but he was afraid to leave the railing for fear he might vomit again. The smell of the ship's diesel added to his nausea. Never having been on a ship before, Erik had arrogantly assumed he would be immune to seasickness.

"Y'all don't look too good," said a voice behind him. Erik turned to see the man in the peacoat staring at him with a grin on his face. "I get seasick too. Every damned time I'm on a ship. Here, take this." The man held out his hand, which contained two tiny brown tabs. "Motion sickness tablets. Take one now, the other in the morning." With his other hand, he pulled an unopened can of soda out of his jacket pocket. "Wash it down with this."

Erik's eyes were glassy, his face was bleachy white. Sweat beaded on his forehead. He reached out, weakly grabbing the tabs and the soda can. "Thank you," he managed a hoarse whisper. Erik could tell the man was American. He had a slight southern accent—Texas, maybe, or perhaps Georgia or Alabama.

"As soon as y'all feel up to it, I recommend hitting your bunk and getting horizontal. You'll feel like a new man in the morning. Well, take care." With that, the man turned and walked toward the upper bow deck, but before he got too far, Erik said, "Hey, wait! What's your name?"

The man turned, "Coleman," he said. "Jim Coleman."

"Thanks again, Jim, I appreciate it. By the way, your accent, where are you from?"

"Tennessee. Franklin, Tennessee. It's a small town near Nashville, the home of the Grand Ole Opry."

Erik wanted to talk with the man, but nature demanded that he lean over the railing once again. By the time Erik had finished, Jim was gone.

Coleman had been right—the next morning, Erik was like a new man. But he was dry as desert sand and the cactus it felt like he had swallowed was stuck in the back of his throat. After drinking a glass of water, he ordered a coffee from the ship's bar and brought it out onto the deck. The coffee, the tablets, and the fresh air chased away any lingering seasickness.

Erik settled into a comfortable deck chair with a book, his journal, and the ever-changing views. He looked for Jim Coleman but didn't see him anywhere. While his jacket and sweater kept him warm on the outside, his briar of Mac Baren Mixture and the coffee kept his insides warm. He felt like the reincarnation of Ernest Hemingway.

The ship docked in Esbjerg around noon. When he stepped on Danish soil, he felt as though he had entered a new world and crossed another one of life's major boundaries. Here they spoke a different language. He couldn't wait to be immersed in the Danish language and culture. He hung around the ship awhile, hoping in vain to see Coleman again.

Eventually, he hoisted on his backpack and began walking. The scents and aromas of Denmark were markedly different than those of

Harwich. A diesel odor was prevalent in the air. More industries? More diesel-fueled trucks? If Harwich was a town, then Esbjerg was a city.

As Erik walked through the streets, he heard snippets of Danish. *The language of the realm! You're going to have to develop a facility for languages, Erik. Starting now!*

He wanted to learn a foreign language in the worst way. Before he left the United States, his great-aunt had given him some phonograph records, *Spoken Norwegian*. In some small, perhaps significant way, listening to them before embarking had helped.

Great-Aunt Lucy traveled to Norway as a young professional woman and had purchased the records prior to her trip. Her grandparents spoke Norwegian in the home, but to her regret, she retained little of it. Lucy was delighted that Erik had an interest in the old country and the old language.

In fact, Lucile Torsen had played a major role in his decision to go to Norway in the first place. She had a good job throughout the Depression and well into the 1960s. Lucy had many friends, and they were all well-traveled.

All of them had lived through two world wars and appreciated the life and opportunity that America had provided them. Erik came along too late to catch the immediate post–World War II optimism and euphoria that America was experiencing, but during the 1960s he was aware of the travels of Lucy and her friends and occasionally he was invited to attend their slideshows.

As soon as it was logistically feasible, Erik stuck out his thumb. The first ride was from two Danish students driving a British Leyland Mini 850. He was eager to try out some of the Norwegian he had learned from Lucy's records, but that turned out to be a bad idea.

In the first place, he barely knew a dozen words. Second, why speak Norwegian to Danes? The languages are similar but only to native speakers. The two exchanged a look that seemed to say, *Why the hell did we pick up this clueless American?*

After they dropped him off, he kicked himself as he thought about something his dad used to say: "Better to keep your mouth shut and be thought a fool than to open it and remove all doubt."

Erik caught some luck hitchhiking along the E20 highway, which cuts across the midsection of Denmark. By early afternoon, he arrived at the outskirts of Fredericia. The letters and postcards he had received from Diana said she was staying with a family somewhere in town, and upon arrival, he should go to Pro Pace.

By mid-afternoon, Erik was standing at the front door of *Pro Pace Armatus*—meaning "armed for peace." The building was constructed in the mid-1940s, and whatever its original intent, Pro Pace was now a youth hostel. Young people, barely discernable from Erik sans backpack, were milling about like bees in and out of a hive.

Through arrangements with the local university, the organizers of the St. Cloud College group had booked the entire youth hostel for the school year. Some of the group, like Diana, had found lodging with local families.

To Erik's surprise, he saw Eddie Henson, the guy who had introduced him to Diana. Erik had had no idea that Eddie Henson was also part of this student exchange trip. Eddie offered to drive Erik to Diana's in his borrowed car.

When Eddie dropped him off at the house, Diana came out to greet him. Immediately he could tell something was different. Of course, they hugged and kissed, but that old, comfortable, familiar relationship just wasn't the same. One of her girlfriends was by her side every minute. They all went into the house and sat around and talked.

She told him how much she LOVED Denmark and that this trip was the BEST experience she had ever had in her entire life. The family she was staying with was "the most wonderful family she had ever met."

She was like a built-in babysitter for the family's children, whom she ADORED. The kids were four, five, and seven years old. They were in the room hanging all over Diana like she was the queen bee.

The youngsters cautiously surveyed Erik with great curiosity and protective skepticism.

She asked if he was hungry and, of course, he was. She left the children and her girlfriend with him while she disappeared to make some sandwiches. Erik horsed around with the kids, while Diana's friend told him about all the side trips they'd been taking to other parts of Europe. Diana returned with some food, and they talked for several more hours.

Erik assumed that he'd be invited to stay in this family's home. Sleeping on the floor in the basement would have been fine with him, but Diana said that wouldn't be possible. This family was poor, and there simply wasn't enough room. He was disappointed, but he understood.

They talked about taking a trip—just the two of them—maybe this weekend. There were a lot of interesting places in Denmark. They thought Copenhagen would be perfect. They could take a local bus and be there in a few hours. The plans all sounded great, but at this point, it was just talk. Nothing definite was set.

Erik hiked back to Pro Pace, where he joined the students who were living there. This was a tight community, and most everyone there already knew who he was. He gathered that he was viewed as an anomaly since he was traveling solo and since his trip was undefined and open-ended. There was an empty bunk at Pro Pace and Erik was invited to stay.

The students in this program had bonded. They traveled in pairs or small groups and studied together and, other than learning token Danish phrases—stuck to English.

Eddie Henson was going crazy because of his decision to leave his guitar behind in the States. His folks thought that being without his guitar would be good for him. "Experience life without it for a season," they had told him. "Develop some new talents and interests and take advantage of being in Europe."

From the second Eddie boarded the plane, he knew this was a mistake. He missed his guitar terribly and was going through major withdrawals. He wrote his parents that he couldn't live without his guitar and that they had to ship it to him, or he would have to leave Denmark.

The next day, Erik went back out to the house where Diana was living, but she was away at school. He stayed at the house and talked with Solveig, the woman of the house. She was warm and welcoming. He ended up playing with the kids most of the day. Even though they didn't speak much English and he didn't speak any Danish, they were able to communicate without difficulty.

Erik picked up some of the children's books written in Danish and was able to read through them. They were surprisingly helpful, a useful icebreaker for learning the language. Written Danish is similar to written Norwegian.

When Diana returned, her girlfriend was with her and so was a guy named Benny. She said Benny was "a friend" and "a traveling companion." They had taken several trips together.

"It's good for a girl to travel with a guy," she said. "European men are much more forward than American men. There was this guy in Munich who cupped his hand between my legs and lifted me off the ground."

Erik was not comfortable with the direction this whole conversation was taking and tried to get alone with Diana. Alas, this was not to be. Not yet anyway. There was just too much going on with the children, the family, school, Benny, and her friends.

He returned to Pro Pace feeling anything but comfortable. Being at Pro Pace was only marginally better than being at the house where Diana was staying. Honestly, he felt like a cuckold, even though he may not have been able to technically lay claim to that title.

He spent another torturous night there. Everyone knew what was going on between Diana and him; no one said anything. It was like everyone spoke a different language from the one he was speaking. Erik was getting the old go-around, the whispers, the furtive eyes, the manufactured laughs and smiles.

Somehow a spare room materialized at one of the homes in this close-knit community of Fredericia. Erik's relief was palpable. He could not have spent another night at Pro Pace. It was a vexing conundrum—he couldn't stay and he couldn't leave. Erik couldn't remember ever being so uncomfortable in his life.

Diana was in classes and didn't have a lot of time to spend with him. All the other students were wrapped up in their lives and studies too. Even if they hadn't been busy, it was painful being around anyone. Erik was the five-hundred-pound gorilla in Fredericia.

The family that had so graciously put him up for a few days couldn't have been kinder. Of course, they knew everything about the "situation" and talked about everything and anything else. They were generous with their meals and their house, but Erik ate as little of their food as possible without being impolite.

He mostly wandered around town like a ghost, eating fruit from the apple trees, along with half-price pastries, which are available at every Danish bakery after four o'clock in the afternoon.

Erik made the following entry in his journal:

October 3, 1973

I've been in Denmark for a week. Am staying with a nice family. They couldn't be more generous, but the truth is they just feel sorry for me. I hate that. Everyone here loves Diana and they're all circling the wagons.

The only reason I'm in Denmark at all is to see Diana, and that seems to be the only thing I can't do. If I could just get some one-on-one time with her. If we could get away from this community and be by ourselves for a few days, I think we could reconnect. This is not what I expected. I need to talk with her. I don't think I can write about this situation just now. I'm not up to it. Besides, I don't understand the situation anyway.

Diana and Erik finally got a chance to go for a walk, just the two of them.

"I have to tell you Di, this isn't how I had pictured the way things would be."

"What do you mean?"

"I mean, everything seems different. You. Us. I thought things between us would be the same, and now I'm not so sure."

"Well, our circumstances have changed," she said. "We're not in St. Cloud anymore. I'm living in Denmark and having the best time of my life. You're on your way to Norway and having the best time of your life. Right?"

"Ah… right, but I mean I've been thinking a lot about you and a lot about us. I've never thought so much about anyone in my life ever. You're different than anyone I've ever known. I'm having trouble thinking about my life in the future without you in it."

Now she seemed like the one who was uncomfortable. This was a different conversation, a difficult one. The more they talked, the more Erik perceived that this distance between them hadn't started when she got to Fredericia but had, in fact, begun sooner.

In their relationship, Erik had always been the guy with big plans. His trip to Norway was already baked into the cake before he met her. She accepted his plans as part of the Erik package. That was so freeing, so liberating. Then, when Charlie was killed, Erik's world changed. The new world was uncertain, less safe. The security Erik had always known vanished. What could be counted on in this world? The Erik package changed. A vital piece was missing.

Diana had been a safe harbor. She had a way of drawing out all his plans and dreams like water from a well. Her level of enthusiasm seemed to match Erik's, beat for beat. Even this trip to Denmark was something that he thought she was doing to create a kind of parallel journey with his journey. He saw them as a team.

Now he wasn't so sure. Erik's feelings for her had deepened, but he didn't know what she was feeling. He sensed that she was struggling with her feelings and hadn't made up her mind. Or maybe she had.

In any case, this was not the place to talk. He felt they needed to get away from Fredericia, away from all her friends and her surrogate family.

Erik knew she was happy here and she was having a great time traveling and seeing Europe and making new friends. Those were all good things and he truly was happy for her, but he just didn't know where in that picture he fit.

The sun was getting low in the sky, and they agreed to get away for a few days or even for just one night. The weekend was almost here, and they agreed that they would catch a bus on Friday afternoon and go to a nearby town—Århus or Copenhagen or someplace not too far away. They needed to talk and clearly that couldn't happen here.

That night, lying on a bed, Erik pulled out his journal:

October 4, 1973

I don't mean to write about one problem so much, but perhaps I should, considering the importance of the situation. After all, I've been thinking about Diana every day since I first met her. And I've been thinking seriously about her. I love who I am when I'm with her. She makes me a better man. But in this damned Fredericia fog that surrounds us here, it's impossible to breathe. We must get away and find out what we have.

On Friday afternoon, as they'd arranged, Erik went back to the house where she was staying. When he got there, she came down in a bathrobe and said she was sick. Erik was pretty sure she wasn't faking it.

Whatever could be said about Diana, she was honest. At any rate, she wouldn't be going anywhere this weekend. He decided then and there he needed to get the hell out of Fredericia for a few days. Get his mind clear. At this moment, in this place, he couldn't think clearly about anything.

ÅRHUS

Erik wished her a speedy recovery, went to the nearest road, and stuck out his thumb. He was on autopilot and didn't care where he went. Whoever picked him up, and wherever they were going, would be good enough for him. He took his small pack.

Several hours later and as many rides, he arrived in Århus, a college town. Beautiful buildings and lots of young people. His bones told him he had arrived in the right town.

This is as good a place as any to spend a few mind-clearing days. It'll be good to be around a bunch of people my own age who don't know me or any of the actors in my little drama.

At first, Erik walked around the campus to get a feel for it—the size, the vibe. Eventually, though, he found himself walking away from the campus. He needed exercise. Too much sitting around doing nothing but fretting and feeling sorry for himself.

The days were getting colder and that felt great. Invigorating. Crisp. They were at the back end of fall now. He could just as easily have been in St. Cloud, Minnesota. There were apple trees everywhere; he filled his pack.

At one point, he meandered into a deserted stone amphitheater. He sat down to eat an apple and enjoy the solitude of this special place. The amphitheater seemed almost providential. He belonged here, surrounded by an audience of stones.

What a great place to practice my monologues.

He walked to the grassy stage and recited the Saint Crispin's Day speech from *Henry V.* He began quietly, but clearly there was no one around to hear him.

In the speech, King Henry's army is outnumbered five to one and his men are scared and grumbling. If only they had more men to stand with them and fight. As Henry walks among his men, he overhears their fears.

"*What's he that wishes so? My cousin Westmoreland? No, my fair cousin. If we are marked to die, we are enough to do our country loss; and if to live, the fewer men the greater share of honor. God's will! I pray thee, wish not one man more.*"

It's an inspirational speech chronicling Henry rousing his men. The young king feeds off the rising enthusiasm of the men to fight the upcoming battle and win glory for themselves.

Erik got louder and louder, letting the moment take him, infusing his own frustrations into the immortal words of Shakespeare. By the time he got to the end of the speech, he was full-throated.

"*But we in it shall be remembered—we few, we happy few, we band of brothers; for he today that sheds his blood with me shall be my brother; be he ne'er so vile, this day shall gentle his condition; and gentlemen in England now-a-bed shall think themselves accursed they were not here and hold their manhoods cheap whiles any speaks that fought with us upon Saint Crispin's day.*"

Erik recalled stories of Richard Burton going off into the Welsh countryside, filling his mouth with pebbles and shouting at the top of his lungs with his considerable vocal prowess.

Then Erik launched into Marc Antony's speech from *Julius Caesar*—how Marc came to bury Caesar, not to praise him. Both monologues were masterful pieces of writing.

Erik lost any inhibitions he might have harbored. Initially concerned that someone might hear him, and then relishing the thought that he might be heard. These speeches each reached a crescendo and when they did, he belted them out in a fashion such that Burton himself would have been impressed.

The expulsion was a way of working out the pain he was feeling. Catharsis. But the feeling didn't last. When he became hoarse, he recited Romeo's balcony soliloquy to Juliet. These words did not require volume—simply youthful passion. In his mind, he gave the speech the best interpretation it ever had, but who would know?

Erik was spent as he walked back toward campus. The grounds surrounding the campus were picturesque, and he realized that the ground upon which he walked was Hamlet's country.

Ha! Hamlet the Danish Prince. How ironic. I'm like Hamlet. I can see all sides of the issue, but that also gives me paralysis of action. If I were more like Laertes, I would stake my claim to Diana. I would challenge Benny to a duel.

Benny, the "traveling companion," Erik thought derisively. *The guy who was good to travel with because European men are different and lift you up by the crotch.*

Erik would casually take off his gauntlet and throw it down at Benny's feet. Erik would let him choose the weapon—foil or épée. Erik was skilled in both.

It would be so one-sided.

Erik wasn't carrying his full pack. His backpack could be downsized. He could take the frame out so that his full backpack became more like a day pack. He left most of his stuff at Pro Pace. Regrettably, his sleeping bag was one of the items he left behind. Inexplicably, he felt he wouldn't be needing a sleeping bag on this little side trip.

After his monologues, the long hitchhike from Fredericia to Århus, and his mental fatigue, he was exhausted by the time he arrived back on the main campus.

Also left behind were his traveler's checks, and he only had a small amount of cash on him. He would need to take care how he spent it. He found the student cafeteria and ordered a cup of tea and some Danish pastry. The Danes have the best pastry he'd ever tasted.

No wonder they call it Danish.

He meandered over to the student library and looked at their cinema and theater sections. They had quite a few books in English.

I wonder how many books and movies in the St. Cloud student library are in Danish? Not many, I'll bet.

When he left the library, the sun was low in the sky. He went back to the student cafeteria and ordered more hot water for the tea bag he had saved and a pastry. He ate the last of his apples.

Erik watched students studying, goofing around, flirting with each other, basically all the stuff that American students do. He was carrying a burden for Diana that was heavier than his pack. As soon as he recognized that he was feeling sorry for himself, he got up and moved. He needed to stay in motion. He hated self-pity but couldn't shake it off this time.

He heard music and moved in that direction. There was a dance going on. The music sounded inviting, and he ambled over. Erik stood outside for a long time, trying to decide if he should fork over part of his rapidly dwindling stock of kroners and go in.

Charlie wouldn't have done it, but then Charlie would never be in this predicament. Erik paid the entrance fee and went in. Once inside, he felt even more disconnected than he had been on the outside. Erik didn't belong here, but he didn't belong back in Fredericia either.

Where the hell do you belong, Hamlet?

He didn't have the answer. Erik thought back to his freshman year at St. Cloud College, and it seemed like every weekend half the student body was inebriated. It was easy to make new friends and have the choice of crashing at any number of places. He left the dance.

What a waste of money that was!

It was getting cold, and his sweater was not up to the task. He worried about spending another night in the cold, especially without a sleeping bag for warmth. He wandered around the campus. He saw a young couple walking together, and he approached them.

"Hey, do you think you guys could help me out? I need a place to crash tonight—"

The guy shook his head no, and the couple hurried on. The sun was setting. Erik continued wandering aimlessly. He approached two guys that were sitting on a park bench, having a conversation.

"Hi, guys. Hey, I don't have a place to crash tonight, and I left my traveler's checks in Fredericia."

Both guys said no and went back to their conversation.

He couldn't bring himself to ask anyone else. The rejection hurt like hell. It was humiliating. He found himself back at the dance. He didn't want to go inside again; it just reinforced his sense of isolation. He sat down on the steps of the building and pondered his situation. This was the most rejected he'd ever felt in his entire life.

What's wrong with you, Erik? You're not a kid anymore. What are you doing walking up to strangers, asking for a place to crash? If you were harebrained enough to leave your checks behind and you can't afford to stay in a hotel, it's your own damned fault. Suck it up.

It occurred to him that he had been struggling against the realization that Diana had rejected him. It was over. Erik knew it in his bones. The world was in motion, and he was not controlling it. He was an observer to the cavalcade of events going on all around him.

As Hamlet said, *"All the world's a stage and all the men and women merely players."*

That's it, Hamlet. You're just an actor on a giant, cosmic stage.

This realization was like a personal turning point for him. *Okay, I give up trying to be the author of my destiny. Whatever happens next is out of my hands.*

At that moment, a college-aged Danish kid with John Lennon–type glasses and a wispy beard came and sat down next to Erik. The Dane was smoking a cigarette and was well into his cups. He spoke to Erik in Danish. *"Hej. Kender du det engelske band,* The Byrds?"

"Sorry, I don't speak Danish," Erik said.

"Ah," he said. He thought for a minute and then in English he asked, "Are yoou familiar vis Ze Byrds?"

"The birds?"

"Ya. Ze Byrds. Ze singing group."

"Oh, The Byrds. Sure, I'm familiar with them. Who isn't? They did the song *Turn! Turn! Turn! There is a reason or season*—something like that."

"Ya. Did yoou know ze lyrics vas based on Ecclesiastes?"

"Uh, yeah. So?"

The Danish kid started reciting the verses from Ecclesiastes. He was drunk but lucid:

For everyzing der is en season,
und a time for every matter oonder heaven:

En time to be born und en time to die,
En time to plant und en time to pluck up vat es planted,
En time to keel und en time to heal,
En time to break down und en time to build up…

Erik stared at the Dane. *Is this kid off his rocker, or is he just drunk? Who memorizes Ecclesiastes? And he knows the whole damned thing…*

En time to weeps und en time to laufs,
En time to mourn und en time to dance…

Just then, a woman came and sat down on Erik's other side. She had light blonde hair that curled inward toward her neck just below her chin, and she had hazel eyes that exuded sophistication. She was maybe five or six years older than Erik. She lit a cigarette and said hi. Erik said hi and wondered how she knew to speak English to him. They listened while the drunk kid rambled on:

En time to cast avay stones und en time to gather stones together,
En time to embrace und en time to refrain from embracing,
En time to zeek und a time to lose…

"He a freand of yours?" the woman asked Erik as she blew out a smoke ring.

"No, I've never met him before," Erik said. "He just came and sat down. Apparently he's a Byrds fan."

En time to keeps und en time to srow away,
En time to tear und en time to sew…

"Danes are beeg drinkers," she said, "but not as beeg as the Svedes."

En time to keep silent und en time to speak,
En time to love und en time to hate,
En time for vaar un en time for peace…

The inebriated Dane stopped, raised his hand in a gesture for silence as if he were waiting for word from his muse, and then repeated the last line like an incantation, *"En time for vaar und en time for peace."*

Finally, turning and facing Erik and the woman, he lamented, "I vonder eef it's too late?" With that, the kid stood up, said he needed another drink, and went back inside the building.

"Teepical Dane," the woman said. "Zhey work hard all week, and on tze weekends zey get properly sloshed."

"Aren't you Danish?" asked Erik.

"Half Danish." She didn't expound.

"Vhere are you from?" she asked.

"America." Erik said.

"I knew zat much, but from vhere?"

"Minnesota," he answered. *Why does everyone seem to know I'm an American as soon as they lay eyes on me?*

"Ah," she said. "I visited New York vonce."

She had just been a kid, but the United States had left a lasting impression on her. She wanted to go back some day but needed to finish University first and then get a job as a designer. She was relaxed and talkative. She was friendly, but maybe she was just bored with the college dance scene.

Erik didn't feel like making small talk. *"A time to keep silent and a time to speak." I guess now's a time to keep silent.*

He was cold and hungry and had already resigned himself to whatever it was that fate had in store for him. He wasn't going to ask anyone for any more favors. He'd already made up his mind to just sit on the steps for the rest of the night or maybe curl up in the building's alcove after everyone had left.

"My boyfriend es Svedish," she said.

Erik waited for her to say something else, but she didn't. She just pulled out another cigarette and took a deep drag. *Maybe she's letting me know she has a boyfriend, so I won't get any ideas. Or, more likely, this is how she knows that Swedes are bigger drinkers than Danes.*

"Yoou don't 'ave any place to stay tonight, do you?" she asked.

Erik shook his head.

"Vell, yoou can stay en our flat. Ve don't have mooch room, and yoou'll 'ave to sleep on ze floor."

Erik simply nodded. The two sat silently while she finished her cigarette. Then she stood and crushed out the stub with her shoe.

"C'mon. Leet's go," she said.

Her flat was a third-floor walk-up. The apartment door opened into the living room, which had a glass-covered coffee table and a large, colorful oriental rug. There was a drafting table against one wall and bookshelves on the other. A poster of Édith Piaf hung on one of the walls.

"Make yourself at home, the loo is srooh zat door. I vill get you en pellow und en blanket. Yoou can sleep on ze carpeting," she said and then disappeared through the other door, which led presumably to the bedroom where she and the Swede slept.

Later that night, as Erik lay on the carpet, covered with the blanket the woman had brought him, he mulled over the events of the day. *How odd that this woman should take me in, just when I had given myself over to the fates. And how strange it is that that Danish kid with John Lennon glasses quoted those lines from Ecclesiastes—what's up with that?*

Erik kept thinking about the phrase "A time for war and a time for peace."

If only Charlie had been born a day sooner or a day later, he would have missed the time for war and made it to the time for peace.

There was a bowl of fruit on a glass coffee table, and Erik ate all of it. In the morning, he woke early and wrote the woman a thank-you note and placed a few *kroner* in the empty fruit bowl. Then he quietly slipped out of her building and hitchhiked back to Fredericia.

Erik went directly to the house where Diana was staying. She wasn't there. Apparently, she had made a quick recovery from her cold. The family invited Erik in and asked him to join them for a meal. They were kind and sympathetic people. After eating, he played games with the children while they taught him some Danish.

Diana came home in the late afternoon and joined him with the kids. After a while, she asked if he wanted to go for a walk.

They walked in silence for several blocks. As they approached a neighborhood park, Diana's fingers reached for Erik's. They held hands as they entered the park.

"Erik, you're at the beginning of an amazing adventure. You're the most courageous person I know. I could never do what you're doing. I don't think there's another person in our entire group who could do what you're doing. You're setting your own course. You're following your own destiny. You have huge dreams, and you must follow them. I'm so proud of you. Everyone here is amazed at you and what you're doing."

Erik was silent as her words slowly penetrated him. After a pause, she continued, "Where you're going, you have to go alone. You have worlds to see. Unknown worlds. New worlds that no one else has experienced. You're like a poet, and you must absorb all the life that you can. I'd only be in your way. If you're carrying me in your heart, you'll miss out on what you must do. And you must do those things for your soul. I'd be like an anchor, holding you back."

There was a noiseless space between them for the longest time. An owl's distant hoot pierced the encroaching twilight, followed in due course by a plaintive response.

She's right. He knew she spoke the truth. He just hadn't been able to admit this to himself. She was the courageous one. She didn't mince words; she didn't dance around reality. She just brought out the unvarnished truth and fired. *Bang.* A reality bullet went straight into his heart.

Funny, the bullet didn't hurt as much as he thought it would. Undoubtedly because she was right. As usual. She was releasing him in her own unique way. He was being dumped, but she made him feel as though this was the right thing to do and the only thing to be done.

Oddly, Erik's respect for her grew. As they walked back to the house, they continued to hold hands. Erik said goodbye to the family. The parents knew what was going on; he could see this in their eyes. He was sure that even the children knew. Some situations transcend language and age barriers.

"Erik the Rejected" went back to the Pro Pace building, empty and hollow. Yet, in a strange way, being dumped was a relief. He had survived, and there was a lot of sense in what she'd said. Everyone at Pro Pace seemed to already know what happened.

The room that night was eerily quiet and somber. Perhaps this was nothing more than Erik projecting his own melancholy.

Eddie's guitar had arrived that day, and he'd been polishing, tuning, and loving on it like a girlfriend. Eddie hooked his guitar up to an amp and played softly. The sound was soothing. The room was dark. No one bothered to turn the lights on.

Jeff Nelson drummed gently and rhythmically on the dresser, adding an earthy quality to Eddie's melodic strumming. Eddie and Jeff were close friends and when one signed up for the Denmark trip, the other followed suit. Erik felt and appreciated an empathy coming from both of these friends during this whole vexing week.

Another Pro Pace student pulled an acoustic guitar out of its case, adding a third dimension to the sounds that quickly filled the room.

Damn, thought Erik. *This is exactly what I needed.*

Erik pulled out his G harmonica and softly mingled his sound with the others. Pro Pace was having an old-fashioned, impromptu jam session.

The music meandered around the room like a soothing scent. Everyone in the room, whether they were playing an instrument or not, sank into the sounds and the moment. Eddie caressed his notes like a lover home from across the ocean.

Erik lost all concept of time and place. Strains of the Allman Brothers, Jimi Hendrix, and Carlos Santana flowed from Eddie's guitar and lifted the soul of everyone in the room.

Then, without warning, a Pro Pace student burst into the room and flipped on the lights.

"Hey, Nelson! Are you packed for tomorrow? We've got to leave here by five if we're gonna catch that damned train."

So much for the jam session. It was nice while it lasted.

Erik sighed. *What lasts forever?* He needed to get his head back into his journey now anyway. He too would be leaving in the morning and getting on with his "destiny," as Diana had put it.

Ironically Erik was now sad to be leaving this insular community. Yet that was how matters should be—he didn't belong here; he belonged out there.

The moment had been an important and transformational one, the jam session was like a gift from Eddie and Jeff to Erik. Everyone at Pro Pace knew and loved Diana. Eddie and Jeff were the only ones who knew Erik—they'd known him since high school. Even though no one was taking sides, there was comfort in knowing that at least two people here were aware of and understood Erik's side of the story.

You're still at the beginning of your trip.

Erik consoled himself with the thought. He'd been planning this long before he met Diana. He had to let her go, or he would never move forward. She was right about that. This was a moment when Erik's heart needed to yield to his head.

Hang on to the memories, Erik. They're good, but you have no claim to her now. Get used to it. Be happy for her, for her experiences here in Fredericia and wherever else she may travel. Release her to her future. Just like she's released you.

It was the wise action. Besides, there really was no other choice. He had a long road ahead of him, and the great unknown was patiently waiting for him to arrive.

COPENHAGEN

While waiting for a ride, Erik pulled out his journal:

On my way to Copenhagen—

Said goodbye to Diana yesterday. It's over. She's an incredible woman. Once again, she said and did the exact right thing. She knows me better than I know myself. It never would have worked out anyway to have her travel with me to meet Anders in Sweden. I don't know what I was thinking.

As he traveled, even though he'd released Diana, he felt as though she was with him. He thought about what she would be thinking and saying to this person or that and how certain situations would make her laugh.

This is good, Erik. There's nothing wrong in thinking about Diana in this way. After all, she has impacted your life. You're better off now because of her. You can see many more colors in the rainbow. She is unique, and she has made you a better man.

This type of thinking was natural, even healthy.

When all this is done, when I'm back from my Norway trip and we're back at St. Cloud, I'm going to take her to the Camping Quarries and—

He caught himself and stopped in mid thought.

No. That ain't gonna happen, and you can't think like that. It's over. She gave you a great gift, Erik—she released you. You must remember that. You're free. You can dive into your life and let it take you wherever you're destined to go.

On a magnificent day like this, Erik relished his mode of travel. Being a hitchhiker grants one access to the private sanctuary of a person's automobile. Denmark is a picturesque country, and her people are equally colorful—as well as industrious and generous. Erik recognized, as he had in England, that accepting such generosity from strangers will teach one more in a few hours than any amount of time spent in a classroom ever would.

Erik was having great luck getting rides on the E20 highway, and he grew more excited the closer he came to Copenhagen. Erik heard so much about this town from the people who gave him rides. Moreover, as a young boy, Erik had heard and read the stories of Hans Christian Andersen—and here he was about to enter Andersen's birthplace.

The last ride left him off on the outskirts of Copenhagen, next to a manicured park, hemmed in with a wide border of deciduous and coniferous trees. The driver said the downtown area of Copenhagen was straight ahead.

Wouldn't it be great to walk unencumbered through town?

The park was basically deserted, and the manicured grounds were surrounded by a wooded area. Lots of bright fall leaves on the ground—perfect camouflage for his orange pack.

There ain't a cloud in the sky, and no chance of rain. Why not ditch the pack for a few hours? Stroll into town, grab some lunch, take some pictures of your favorite mermaid…

After finding the ideal spot and burying his pack, Erik memorized the surroundings. Once he was certain that he could find it again—and that no one else could—he walked backward while leaving the wooded area so he would see the scene exactly the way it would look when returning.

Out of the woods and into the park, Erik headed out in the direction the driver had indicated. Without his backpack, he was like a tortoise released from its shell. He felt an inch taller and pounds lighter, and he was able to set a brisk pace. Except for the separation anxiety he felt without his pack, life was perfect.

After walking nearly an hour and not seeing anything remotely resembling a town, Erik became worried. *What the hell? I should have been in town a long time ago!*

There were plenty of houses and buildings but nothing like what he was expecting. What he was walking through was more akin to a suburb, not a town. This was like an endless suburb.

I think I've just made a bad decision. He approached someone walking in the opposite direction.

"Excuse me, sir, how far is it to the town center?"

"Ze town zenter?"

The man had a heavy Danish accent and for some reason was stumped by the question.

"You know, where the *Little Mermaid* is and where I can get a bite to eat?"

"Oh, you vant to zee za mermaid. I should zink it es seeks maybee zeven kilometers."

Erik cursed himself. *Six or seven kilometers! That's four miles. At least another hour away!*

Even if he were to hitchhike now and get a ride right away, it would be dark soon. He would have to eat quickly and then hitchhike immediately back to his pack. He would only experience the town in a blurred rush!

If you hadn't been so lazy, if you had just carried your damned pack, you wouldn't be worried about where you'll spend the night. You could have even splurged and stayed at a B&B somewhere in town. Now you're separated from your pack—everything of value in your life.

The potential enormity of his folly began to sink in, and he realized that he'd better turn around immediately and go back to his pack.

Dammit! You just wasted precious, valuable hours. Yet there was no other choice. It would be evening soon and, if he didn't turn around now, he might never find his pack.

Then the panic set in.

What if you can't find it? What if someone else has discovered your pack? Hellberg, you idiot! What were you thinking? How could you leave your pack in a public park?

He broke into a run. Being separated from his pack was unimaginable. Unacceptable. Cataclysmic. Everything he owned in the world was in that pack.

Ha! What a joke to think that wisdom was going to be your companion going forward! How could you be so reckless, Erik?

When he got back to the wooded area, there was no sign of it anywhere. The pack was gone! Where exactly had he left it? His heart pounded against his ribs like a large rubber mallet. His legs trembled and the woods began to blur.

Some clever bastard found my backpack and is long gone by now. How could that have happened so fast? Was someone watching me? Erik, you idiot, you weren't paying close enough attention.

The universe stopped turning and looked directly at him. Erik was so small, so vulnerable. *I'm lost without that pack. Charlie, what would you do if you were in my shoes right now?*

In his mind's eye, Erik could hear Charlie's calm voice say, "Well, for starters, I would take a deep breath and then let it out slowly."

That's exactly what Erik did, and as he was exhaling, he noticed an incongruity in the leaves. A discordant orange peeking out of the multicolored collage of leaves. *Is it still there? Had he done too good of a job of camouflaging it?*

Erik ran over and yanked his pack out of its hiding place.

"Thank God. Thank God. Thank! God!"

A loss of this enormity would have been almost incalculable. *Would this have ended my trip?* He sat down on his pack and tried to get ahold of his emotions. He took a mental inventory and assessment.

It would have been dire. My clothes, my sleeping bag, my tarp, raingear, journal, address book. Thankfully, I was carrying my camera, passport, and traveler's checks. Everything else is replaceable.

His heart continued to pound as he contemplated the various scenarios of life without his pack. He vowed in that moment, sitting on his orange pack and surrounded by this wooded parkland on the outskirts of Copenhagen, that from now on, he had to do a better job of thinking every situation through completely. He had to be more aware of his surroundings and less careless.

You're not a kid anymore, Erik! You have to be an adult every day. You're responsible for everything that happens to you. To be honest, you deserved to lose your pack.

As his heart rate slowed to normal and a calm settled in, he recalled the previous promises he had made to be less careless. There had been many in his twenty-one years—the most recent and egregious was the ill-fated dive at the quarries. It didn't take long to break that vow!

He knew he had to learn how to live his life in such a way that he either stopped taking reckless chances or…or he could look forward to a life full of trouble.

How will your vow this time be any different from previous vows? It was a good question, but night would be falling fast and he had a decision to make.

It would be crazy to walk to the town center now. It would be late when I got there, and where would I stay? I'm better off staying here and getting an early start in the morning.

So what if you're hungry? You've been hungry before. Besides, you have no one to blame but yourself. Bunking down hungry will serve you right.

The days had gradually been getting colder, and now, as the sun disappeared, it was downright chilly. He went deeper into the park, the part that wasn't groomed, where it morphed into a forest. He scooped leaves to make his bed, releasing imprisoned odors of dead and rotted leaves. He laid out his poncho and put his sleeping bag on top of it.

Erik fell into an uneasy sleep that didn't last. His eyes opened to a gloomy, freezing forest. He got up and gathered armloads of leaves and twigs, laid them over his sleeping bag to create a kind of natural blanket, and then climbed back in his bag.

He still couldn't get warm. The condensation of his breath told him the temperature was in the low 30s or high 20s Fahrenheit. Erik pulled all the clothes out of his pack and put them on. He climbed back in his bag and laid there shivering. He couldn't fall asleep. It was too damn cold.

He was used to dealing with cold, but this time its icy fingers burrowed in deep. The cold demanded his attention and fatigued his brain.

He tried to take his mind off the cold and prayed for the morning to come. He forced himself to think of any situation he had experienced that was worse than this one.

That time on Saganaga Lake in Ontario, Canada. When the rains created a Victoria Falls–like deluge. We thought the tents were going to get swept out from under us and we would all end up in the lake. Couldn't get warm, couldn't get dry. Rained all the next day. Couldn't build a fire. What a miserable experience that was.

Thinking about it seemed to help; he laughed out loud.

"At least it's not raining now," he said to himself.

God! Why did I say that? Now it probably will rain!

He burrowed as deep as possible into the cocoon he had created, imagining that it was a chrysalis, that he would survive the night and emerge reinvigorated and warm in the morning. As he lay still and silent in the blackness, a loud snapping noise—the sound of a branch being stepped on—not twenty feet away pierced the night. Whatever or whoever was out there had to be large.

"Erik!" A whispered and urgent voice cut through the stillness.

Was that the wind? Erik clearly heard his name being called from somewhere out in the night.

"Erik. It's me. *Shhh*, don't make a sound."

"Charlie? Charlie, what are you doing here? I thought that was an animal."

"*Shhh*. Be quiet. I've got to get you out of here. C'mon, we have to move—now!"

"Wait a minute. How did you find me? How did you get here?"

"Don't worry about that now. The important thing is to get away from this awful place."

"Wait a minute. I thought you were safe. I thought you were a rear echelon radio teletype operator and that you were outside of the war zones."

"Ha, you have no idea. Look, just follow me. Walk exactly where I walk. Exactly. Do you hear me?"

"Yes, I hear you. Don't worry, I promise I'll follow you exactly. But Charlie, I've got to tell you, I went to the draft board. I told them… I—"

"It's okay, Erik. None of that stuff matters. All that matters right now is that you do exactly as I say. Now, c'mon."

Charlie turned and took three steps. Erik heard a click and then the earth exploded in front of him. Charlie's body blew up into the air.

"Charlie!" Erik screamed his name. He sat bolt upright in his sleeping bag. A sweat covered his face and soaked through his shirt despite the cold. The woods surrounding him were silent, while gray streaks of morning slashed across the sky. It took a moment for Erik to realize where he was, that he wasn't in a snake-infested swamp jungle with his brother, that he was in the middle of the woods in a park outside of Copenhagen. That it was just a dream. A horrible dream that seemed all too real.

As terrifying as it had been, he had survived the night. The dream weighed heavy on him as he broke his bivouac and set off on a brisk pace for Copenhagen. With each step, his body warmed. It took just over an hour to get to the downtown area. By the time he reached the cobblestoned courtyard of Langelinie promenade in a waterfront section of Copenhagen, he was completely thawed out and exceedingly hungry.

Erik found an empty table outside of a restaurant called Det Lillie Apotek, said to be the oldest restaurant in Copenhagen, supposedly frequented by Hans Christian Andersen. He treated himself to eggs, potatoes, Danish, and coffee. While he ate, he noticed a group of people buzzing around an attraction next to the shore across the promenade. After he finished his meal, he walked over and joined them at the water's edge. It was the *Little Mermaid*. Memories returned of his mother reading Hans Christian Andersen stories to him, his sister, and his brother—everyone all together in their pajamas on Mom and Dad's huge bed.

He hated to admit it, but he was…disappointed. *The image of the mermaid I've carried in my mind all these years doesn't jibe with this diminutive statue... Another childhood fantasy bites the dust.*

Erik turned to the man standing next to him and said, "This is the mermaid? She's so small."

"Funny, I was thinking the same thing," responded the man.

Astonishingly, the man facing Erik was unquestionably the man in the peacoat from the ferry. "Jim Coleman? Oh my God, I can't believe it. I looked for you when we docked in Esbjerg, but you'd vanished. I wanted to thank you for the motion sickness tablets. How are you?"

"I'm fine. The question is, how are *you* feeling?"

"Oh, I'm doing great. Yeah, the tablets were perfect, just what I needed. That would have been a miserable trip if you hadn't helped me. I can't believe I've run into you again. What are you doing in Copenhagen?"

"I work for a Danish company. Its headquarters are here in Copenhagen. How about you?"

"I'm about to hitchhike to Gothenburg to meet with a friend and then I'm on my way to Oslo, Norway. How long are you going to be in Copenhagen?"

"I'm done here. Had meetings all day yesterday. About to leave for the airport. Heading to Brussels."

"Oh well, that's a shame. I would have loved to chat…"

Jim looked at Erik for a moment and then out over the harbor, apparently making some mental calculations. Then he said, "I imagine you're crossing the channel at Helsingør. I can give you a lift to the E47.

That'll at least get you through the worst of Copenhagen."

"Really? Oh man, that would be great."

Jim Coleman had a soft-spoken southern accent, but it belied a harder reality lurking just below the surface. He had an intense, steely stare that reminded Erik of Dr. Cervante's penetrating eyes—Dr. Cervante, the dreaded acting coach who had formerly been a drill sergeant in the army and who had kicked Erik out of his play in college.

As they climbed into Jim's rental car, Erik did most of the talking. He felt comfortable with Jim, almost a kinship with him. He told Jim about his pal Anders Lundström in Gothenburg, Sweden, and how they had met at a camper exchange program five years ago. Then about how he was going to meet his Norwegian friend Jens in Oslo, whom he had met in Minnesota during their junior year in high school.

Erik was eager to switch the subject and learn more about this mysterious man in the peacoat. He said, "You're lucky you've got a job that pays you to travel."

"I could do without the quotas, but I do enjoy experiencing new places."

"You mentioned you were from a small town in Tennessee. How did you manage to land a job with this Danish company?"

"One of the guys in my platoon hooked me up."

"Really? That's interesting. Which branch of the service were you in?"

"Infantry."

"Infantry? So was my brother. Where did you serve?"

"Vietnam. Bravo company. Part of the 9th Infantry Division. I was a rifle platoon leader. How about your brother?"

"He was a radio operator—in the MARS program. He was with the 8th Radio Research Field Station in Phu Bai."

"Doing phone patches for the soldiers?"

"Yes."

"God, I loved those guys. I used them once to talk with my folks back in Franklin. I was in from March of '67 to March of '68. When was your brother in?"

Erik wanted to answer, but the words didn't come. It was like they were stuck inside of him and refused to leave. Jim turned toward Erik with his knowing eyes, which seemed to penetrate inside of the younger man's soul. Erik tried to stop tears from filling his eyes but couldn't. He didn't want to lose it in front of this battle-hardened soldier. Looking away from Jim, Erik said, "He didn't make it back."

As Jim digested Erik's statement, his mind seemed to leave not just the car but also the entire civilized world. A silence filled the rented vehicle as Jim maneuvered through the streets of Copenhagen.

Finally, Jim broke the silence, "I'm sorry, Erik. I'm grieving with you, man. It was hell over there, no other way to put it. I lost too many friends. Too many brothers. The truth is, we all died over there. Some of us made it back, some didn't, but a part of each and every one of us died. If you don't mind me askin', what happened to your brother?"

Erik didn't mind talking about what happened to his brother—at least not with Jim. In fact, he wanted to tell him because he knew Jim would understand.

"When Charlie told us he got into the MARS program and he'd be out of the fighting areas, we all were grateful and so relieved. We all thought he was safe. Relatively safe, anyway. His tour was up on March 20 of this year. On March 12, the jeep he was riding in hit a land mine. Charlie was killed instantly when the jeep fell on top of him. The other two guys in the jeep survived; one of them lost both his legs."

"Oh man. That's tough. He was eight days from getting out? Shit, that's just...that's just... I'm so sorry Erik."

Most of the rest of the ride was passed in silence. There really wasn't anything either one of them could say that would make the pain go away or make the world a better place. When the car reached the entrance to E47, Jim pulled over to the side of the road and parked.

"Let me give you a hand with your gear." Jim pulled Erik's backpack out of the rear seat and leaned it against the car. Erik reached out to shake hands with Jim. Instead, Jim grabbed Erik's outstretched hand

and pulled him into a bear hug. Jim's understanding and compassion over Charlie's death comforted and sustained Erik for the next several days of hitchhiking—ever northward through the rain, snow, and ice of Sweden.

GOTHENBURG

Anders Lundström's home was in Gothenburg, Sweden, but he was now living in Stockholm and going to medical school at the Karolinska Institutet. Erik hadn't seen or spoken with Anders in nearly six years. At that time, they were both campers at YMCA Camp Sparreviken in Sweden.

In the summer of 1968, as an exchange camper from Minnesota, Erik was the sole American in a cabin called Celsius.

There was probably only one camper in the entire camp who knew that Celsius was named after the famed Swedish astronomer and physicist who invented the international temperature standard. That camper was Anders Lundström, a force of nature inhabiting the body of a fifteen-year-old Swedish kid.

All the Swedish kids spoke English, to a degree, but Anders's command of the language made Erik wish he'd carried a dictionary. More than anything though, Anders's willingness to participate in pranks is what bonded their friendship. Just silly stuff, like disconnecting the wires to the intercom of a rival cabin so that they missed assembly call and had to suffer the indignity of a demerit.

Five years later, Anders received a letter from Erik saying he was planning a trip to Norway and would be passing through Sweden. Could they meet up somewhere?

The friendship thus rekindled, they stayed in touch via letters as plans developed, eventually leading up to Erik calling Anders from a pay phone before leaving Copenhagen. Erik was traveling by thumb, so it was impossible to name an exact arrival time. Erik offered Anders his best guess and resumed hitchhiking.

Almost from the moment Erik entered Sweden, the weather turned nasty. He had a Student Rail Pass, but he wanted to refrain from using it for as long as possible, since it was only valid for three months from its first usage.

As far as Norway went, he planned to visit all the major theaters in all the major cities, but he didn't yet know where his base of operations would be once he got to Norway. From Jens's letters Erik got the impression that Jens had a rough time adjusting after the family moved back to Norway. While living in Minnesota, Jens had developed a taste for marijuana and some other recreational drugs—activities that were viewed very differently by Norwegian society.

Erik had no idea what the situation would be like when he got to Oslo. He could probably count on staying with Jens and his family for a few days, maybe a few weeks, but everything was uncertain. There was no guarantee.

Best to keep the pass in reserve for when I really need it.

Getting the Student Rail Pass hadn't been easy. Criteria included being a current student in good standing at a recognized institute of higher learning. Setting aside the question of whether St. Cloud College qualified as an institute of higher learning, technically speaking, Erik wasn't a student.

If a student doesn't show up for classes and doesn't turn in assignments, the school considers them persona non grata, essentially no longer an enrolled student.

Instead, to circumvent this arcane restriction, Erik enrolled in three classes for fall semester 1973 and showed up before classes started to meet personally with each of the instructors. His goal: convince the professors to allow him to set his own curriculum for the courses and then allow him to turn in the assignments late—most likely *very* late.

Of course, Erik had no idea of how long he was going to be gone. Three months or three years? He was enrolled and paid up for just the fall semester classes—but what would he do for all semesters thereafter? This was a fair question, and he anticipated that they would confront him with it.

The first professor taught Photography 201. Erik loved taking pictures. His dad had given him his old Pentax camera and Erik had become adept at adjusting shutter speed, aperture setting and focusing almost without thinking. The professor was young, iconoclastic, and laid back. Erik was sure this professor would be a slam dunk. That's not quite the way the interview went.

"Okay, look, Erik, I don't mind that you want to take a year to do a semester's worth of work. I'm cool with that. Go ahead and travel," the professor said. "See the world; it's good for the soul. But simply taking pictures of all the theaters in Norway isn't my definition of challenging.

"Instead," he countered, "here's what I'd like to see you do: First, choose a subject that reflects an aspect of your life that's unique to the culture you'll be living in and that represents your role in this culture.

"Next, I want to see a progression of thought or personal growth depicted in a series of photos. Your pictures should be numbered and dated. And finally, all photos must be personally developed by you in a lab where you can demonstrate the principles that you learned in Photography 101."

Damn, thought Erik. *That's all well and good, but I didn't learn anything in Photography 101. I barely passed.*

That was in his freshman year, when it could be said that he failed to set any personal scholastic high-water marks. Erik did manage to set a few consumption records at several keggers. Of course, he also had the distinction of being the only freshman in memory to have been blackballed by the theater department.

Notwithstanding the ignominies of these distinctions, Erik became adept at using the chemicals supplied by the photography department and earned a reputation for creating psychedelic-like pictures in the darkroom, even if many of them were not suitable for classroom submission.

Where he would find chemicals and a darkroom in Europe were details that he could worry about later. The prof and Erik shook hands on the deal, and Erik set off to speak with the second professor—the one for English 301.

He felt a little more prepared for this interview and informed the professor that Scandinavia had a strong literary tradition with writers like August Strindberg, Ludvig Holberg, Henrik Ibsen, and Hans Christian Andersen. The professor agreed and asked what he intended to do with these Scandinavian titans of the literary world.

"Okay, here's my concept, Dr. Maxwell," said Erik. "I propose to write a paper illustrating the influences that these Scandinavian authors have had on some of our most prominent American authors, like Arthur Miller, John Steinbeck, and Tennessee Williams." Erik continued, "I contend that there are commonalities within the Scandinavian block of writers that differ from the commonalities shared by the American authors."

He hoped that the names of these heavyweight writers would indicate that he was serious and that this project would be a worthy topic for a third-level English curriculum. The name he chose for his project was "Creating a Literary Bridge to Scandinavia."

The English professor demurred. She wasn't any more enthusiastic about his ideas than the photography professor had been.

"That paper could be written while sitting in a library at St. Cloud State," she said. "No, I'd rather see you do something that requires a little more research and investigation. I'd like to see something that could only be done from where you're living and out of what you're experiencing. What else do you have in mind?"

Erik had nothing else in mind. There was no plan B. After listening to him sputter for a few minutes, she suggested, "While you're living in Norway, why don't you read some of the current Scandinavian authors that might be less familiar to Americans, such as Pär Lagerkvist, Sigrid Undset, or Knut Hamsun. You might discuss how stylistically these writers represent a culture that is uniquely different from ours and perhaps what similarities might exist.

"You should also discover two or three new Scandinavian authors who have been recently published and are popular in Scandinavian culture but not yet in ours. Once you've discovered these authors," she continued, "write an essay on each one, followed by a book review on one or more of each of their works, and explain why they're resonating with that culture and whether they would resonate with ours."

Erik left her office with a page full of notes and the feeling that this might turn out to be a lot of work.

The final class was Theater History. Erik was optimistic he could get his idea for this class approved. He knew the professor, Jack Addison, and respected him. Dr. Addison had even tried to get Erik to enroll at Theatre L'Home Dieu, a summer theater company in Northern Minnesota run by the school. But that wasn't the reason that Erik was confident in getting an approval. The real reason was because of an accidental meeting Erik had had with Dr. Walter Van Langenhove, the new chairman of the theater department.

Earlier in the year, Erik had bumped into the chairman on campus. "Erik, what's this I hear about you leaving school and moving to Norway?"

What? Erik was stunned the department chairman knew of his plans.

Not that his plans were a big secret, but at the same time, he wasn't going around telling everyone that he was dropping out of school until he could figure out who the hell he was. What was more surprising was that Dr. Van Langenhove even knew who he was. After all, Erik had been blackballed from the theater department the previous year, when he was a lowly freshman with a big ego.

"Yes. I haven't worked out all the details yet, but that's the plan."

"What are you planning on doing there?"

"Well, like I said, I haven't worked out all of the details yet, but I've written to all of the major theaters and I'm hoping to get some work."

"I see," said Dr. Van Langenhove. "Why Norway?"

"It's one of my heritages, and I have a friend who lives there. I have Jewish and Sámi heritage too, but no connections. I also have some Swedish heritage and a friend who lives there." Then Erik grinned and said, "I'm waiting to hear back from the letter I sent to Ingmar Bergman."

Dr. Van Langenhove laughed. "Well, don't hold your breath on that one."

Van Langenhove hadn't been around last year for Erik's degradation. Maybe he'd heard of it, maybe he hadn't. He was from Belgium and brought an international flavor to St. Cloud.

"When I heard you were going to Norway, I thought of a friend of mine who's a director there. She's rather influential and well-connected and so forth. If you'd like, I can write to her and make an introduction."

If I liked? Was he kidding? The chairman of the theater department walks up to me, a blackballed sophomore, offers to make an introduction to a director in Norway—where I'm about to cast my lot in the great lottery of life—and the question is, Would I like to accept his offer?

No, Erik mused to himself. *I'd rather wander around aimlessly, hitchhiking from pillar to post, waiting for the mythological Thor, God of thunder, to throw the lightning bolt of theatrical employment at me.*

In fact, being struck by a mythologic lightning bolt was exactly what he felt like had just happened.

It was a light bulb moment for Erik. *Maybe the reason one goes to college is not so much to get an education but rather to make connections that can be used as you enter your chosen profession.*

The long and short of Dr. Van Langenhove's intervention was that his Norwegian director friend, Fru Greta Gullestad, wrote him back. In her letter, she said there was to be a major production of Bertolt Brecht's

Arturo Ui at Den Nationale Scene (The National Stage) in Bergen the following year.

"True, the production wouldn't be in Oslo," she wrote, "but Bergen is a charming little town and the theater there is rather good. In any case, there's a clever young director named Wolfgang Pintzka coming in from the Berliner Ensemble. There should be lots of roles, and your student might be able to get one."

Fru Gullestad. Her name in English literally means "place of gold." No name could have been more apt because to Erik, she was like gold.

He was on cloud nine and saw only blue skies ahead. A few short months ago he had been stuck in a rut—he had a black mark against his name in the theater department, he was lost and didn't know who he was, he was dizzy and desperate to step off the merry-go-round, he faced major obstacles about the upcoming trip, and he'd lost his brother on the other side of the world and there wasn't a damned thing he could do about it.

Now he had the prospect of a job in Norway. And the job was in Bergen, no less. He didn't know squat about Bergen, except that it was a "charming little town." The job was in the theater, and this would undoubtedly mean he'd have to learn to speak Norwegian. And it was a professional gig, so he'd be getting paid!

His prospects were starting to look up.

So Erik met with the third professor, Dr. Jack Addison. Erik described a workbook he would create, detailing his entry into the world of Norwegian theater.

It would describe what he was learning about the inner workings of the theatre system there. He would highlight the similarities and differences with the American system, the kind of training their actors undergo, the involvement of the community, the impact on Norwegian society, governmental and private sponsorship of the theater, salary for the actors and crew, and any other aspect of the Norwegian theater system that Erik finds of significant interest.

After finishing his pitch to Dr. Addison, Erik held his breath. Addison had an inscrutable face and a reputation of being demanding and tough. Erik needed all three teachers to be on board for his plan to work.

"Erik, I heard about your trip, and I admire what you're doing. Takes guts," admitted Dr. Addison.

In all likelihood, Dr. Addison was probably thinking that the chances of this job ever materializing was next to nil. Still, why be the one to rain on his parade? Let the kid learn the hard way what the real world is all about.

"You'll have setbacks, but don't get discouraged," Dr. Addison said. "I've watched you grow over these past two years. You're a fighter and you have talent. I remember when you came to St. Cloud. You were sure that the Minnesota State acting award you won in high school would open doors here. You got knocked down a bit, and deservedly so. But you didn't let it stop you. So just keep fighting and, no matter what, remember to believe in yourself."

Dr. Addison then offered Erik his hand said, "We'll see you when you get back, Erik. Break a leg!"

The Swedish word for Gothenburg is Göteborg. Two full days of hard thumb work to get there. Hitchhiking in Denmark was spotty, but in Sweden the practice may as well have been illegal.

Erik had the worst luck in getting rides. He had to stop at a pay phone more than once to give Anders an update on his progress. Eventually, a realistic rendezvous was set, and Erik worked diligently toward hitting the goal. The destination was a sorority house in Göteborg.

Sorority house?

The icy Swedish wind cut through his clothes like driven nails, while flurries of snow dusted his face with a white sawdust powder. Slushy streets penetrated and befouled his shoes.

The only rides he got after crossing the border from Denmark into Sweden were from non-Swedes. A shared kinship from fellow outsiders. Fortunately for Erik, the past decade had seen several waves of emigrants to Sweden and enough of these newcomers took pity on the slush-soddened young man that he arrived at the prearranged meeting place only a few hours late.

Pajama-clad coeds chattered throughout the three-story sorority house where Anders waited impatiently for his mysterious American friend to arrive. He let out a shout when he saw Erik, unmistakable with his backpack, lumbering up the street.

At the same time, Erik noticed Anders's large frame in an open second-story window, peering out into the night. Anders's school in Stockholm was on break, and he'd returned to Göteborg for the rendezvous. After an exhausting day of hitchhiking in the slush and cold, Erik was bone-tired yet thrilled to be reunited with his old friend.

Five years had passed since the two had seen each other at Camp Sparreviken. Now Erik was in his junior year of college and had his sights set on a career in acting. Anders was studying to be a doctor and had his sights set on gynecology.

During the year that Erik had spent ruminating on and planning this Norwegian odyssey, he'd considered making Sweden his destination. Erik had almost as much Swedish ancestry as he did Norwegian.

He wrote to nearly every major theater in both Sweden and Norway. He wrote a letter to anyone and any institution he thought relevant. Had any of these theaters or institutions or personages written him back, such a response might have swayed the direction of his travel.

Fru Gullestad and Anders Lundström were the only significant responses he received, and Fru Gullestad's letter was the one that had the scent of employment.

The essence of what Erik recalled about Anders was still evident. Big personality, friendly, inquisitive, fun-loving, adventurous. No wonder he had made such a positive impression on him. The young men looked forward to unpacking the years since Sparreviken.

Anders had some adventures planned for the night and invited Erik to make himself at home in the sorority while he went to make a phone call. Freed from his backpack, Erik floated through the house.

He poked his head through the open door of one bedroom, where a half dozen girls laid like a patchwork quilt across the bed and onto the floor. They invited him to join them. The room was blissfully warm, and Erik felt as though he could melt into oblivion among these sorority sisters.

There was a vigorous discussion going on in the room, and Erik learned his first Swedish phrase: *En svensk flicka behöver inte å vara vacker.* (A Swedish girl does not have to be beautiful.)

After getting dumped by Diana and having to leave the comradery of the students at Pro Pace, after thinking he'd lost his pack and then nearly freezing in the park outside of Copenhagen, and after two days of hitchhiking in the Swedish sleet, Erik was quite content to sit here in this warm house with these Svenska *flickas*—whether or not they were beautiful.

Anders was not of the same mind. He'd been waiting patiently for hours for Erik's arrival. Days, actually. Anders was restless and wanted to paint the town and show off his American friend.

Erik would eventually learn that Anders had spent far more time in sorority houses than he ever had in a fraternity house. He knew all the girls in this sorority and was looking for greener pastures. Anders's itinerary was all planned, and he and Erik were hours behind schedule.

Also, for Anders, *En Svensk flick måste vara vacker!* (A Swedish girl does have to be beautiful!)

Anders was persuasive and his enthusiasm was infectious. Erik reluctantly left the warmth of the sorority house and joined Anders for a night on the town.

First stop on Anders's itinerary was a discotheque in the center of Gothenburg. The music was loud and the place was packed. Tons of young people. Lots of girls.

Anders was like a fox in a henhouse. He was eager to jump into the mix and see where the night might lead. Erik was resolved to just listen to the music and absorb the atmosphere. Anders wasted no time and in short order he was dancing with one girl after another. Erik distinctly got the impression that Anders was expecting Erik to do the same.

Truthfully, Erik didn't feel like it. He was tired after carrying his pack for two days in the cold. He was grateful to have a friend, happy to be around other people his age, and loved not having to make all the decisions about where he would find food and shelter for the night. He was relishing the shielding anonymity of the disco lights and blaring music.

Even if he hadn't been tired, at this juncture in his journey, this wasn't his scene. He had no intentions of asking a girl to dance or even scoping out the girls that were there. After losing Diana, after hitching all these miles in the slush and sleet, he simply would rather be someplace quiet and warm. Erik would have much preferred to go to Anders's parents' house, where Anders said they would be crashing when they were done clubbing.

As Erik sat mutely watching the crowd and seeing Anders pop up here and there with this girl or that girl, his eye was drawn to a quiet spot in the room. A girl was sitting serenely at a table next to the DJ's booth. She looked completely out of place—not into the music or the party scene. She was simply silently observing the activity swirling around her. Her presence was incongruous with the disco.

The DJ's spotlight spilled over onto the girl, illuminating her sharp features. Her presence was alluring, even mesmerizing. Erik immediately called to mind the painting, *A Young Girl Defending Herself against Love* by William-Adolphe Bouguereau. The same irresistible pull that the painting always elicited beckoned him now. The two of them were completely out of sync with the room. As if both existed in another dimension.

The thought occurred to him that she was not here by choice. That her presence was involuntary. That was the only way the tableau made sense. But how could that be? It was a mystery. She was a mystery.

Her hair appeared iridescent as the disco lights flashed over her. Jet black and shiny. Such features served to further differentiate her from the blondes that predominated the room. When the disco light stroked her face, her eyes were illuminated for a brief second. Impossible to tell their color. They could have been violet, blue, or green. Erik was unable to look elsewhere. He was unable to see anything else. Like a magnetic trance. *What was happening?*

He heard a soft but insistent voice. Somewhere not outside of him—but not altogether inside of him either.

"Erik, this is not normal. This is not a chance encounter. There's something that you must do. You must stand. Now. I know you're afraid, but that doesn't matter. There's nothing wrong with being afraid, but you must stand up."

Erik stood, but he didn't move. He just stared at her across the room.

I don't think she sees me, but I think she knows someone is looking at her. I can tell she senses a pair of eyes focused on her.

"Walk over there. Go up to her."

He was powerless. He walked toward the girl but then he stopped in the middle of the dance floor. The pounding, pulsating music permeated every inch of the room, yet Erik was oblivious to anything other than the light on the girl and the voice in his brain.

He began moving again and, as he got closer, he sensed a familiarity. Perhaps they had met and been separated long ago. Maybe before either of them was born. That made no sense. None of this did. An aura surrounded her, not dissimilar to that which surrounded Diana.

Erik froze. Unlike the circumstances in which he had met Diana, this wasn't a college campus. Erik would never see this girl again if he didn't go over to her table now. Who knew where he or she would be tomorrow, let alone in an hour?

"Move!" the voice commanded. The pulsing light seemed to open a pathway on the disco floor. He navigated the dance floor quickly, never taking his eyes off her. She never looked at him.

Now what?

She looked up. She was young. Probably younger than Erik. Her eyes sparkled as the light from the disco ball danced off them. She did not smile at him, but she was not unfriendly. He was scared but committed to the moment.

"Yes?" she asked in English.

Erik hadn't anticipated that she would ask him a question; he didn't know what to say. His brain froze. He was not the cool, calm, collected, smooth, debonair international traveler who had just stopped in to scope out the local scene before jetting off to Saratoga to check in on his racehorse.

Then it dawned on him that he had to respond. His mouth became intensely dry, yet he managed to say, "Vil du dansa med mig?"

Anders had taught him the phrase. Erik never thought he would need it since he hadn't anticipated asking anyone to dance. She looked at him and said in English, "No, I really don't think so."

He understood. *Why should she? Who was he? She clearly was not here to dance or make new friends.* This was not a person who was on the prowl. She was here for some other more noble reason, no doubt.

Erik nodded that he understood but he didn't leave. He tried to move but he couldn't. He had violated her space; he had interrupted her thoughts. He was an unwanted intrusion, and that was the last thing in the world that he wanted to be. Her space was sacred, as were her thoughts, and yet he seemed to be incapable of gracefully turning around and walking back to his little universe.

Strangely, his mind was functioning enough to realize that she saw through his charade of being a Swede. Was his Swedish really that bad? Unlike Charlie, Erik was good with accents, and he thought he had pronounced the phrase exactly like Anders had. While he was thinking about that and fighting the embarrassment he was feeling, she looked up at him again.

She studied him for a moment. Maybe she knew that he didn't belong here and somehow that correlated to her situation. He couldn't tell what was going on behind those eyes but whatever she was thinking, she said, "Well, I suppose I could, if you really want to."

She stood up and together they eased into the center of the swirling mass of bodies. Erik was not sure their movements could be called dancing, but they shuffled into whatever spaces emerged as the crowd, music, and lights allowed. Because disco music never stops—one song just morphs into another—they didn't have the luxury of a break in the music signaling them to stop.

Eventually, though, the inanity of searching for open spaces amid the pulsing movement made retreating to her table the only viable and sane option. An exchanged glance between them confirmed they were both ready to quit the floor. Thankfully, mercifully, they fought their way to her table next to the DJ's booth.

She hadn't invited him to sit at her table, yet Erik sensed that if he did, she wouldn't chastise him. He was almost certain now that her eyes were deep violet. If there was the slightest hint that he was trespassing, Erik would leave. He wasn't going to force himself into her private sphere, no matter what the damned voice might say. This had to be mutual.

After sitting at her table for a few minutes, he was prepared to pop up and dive back into the crowd if necessary. Then she offered a quick but sincere smile and lightly touched her hand on top of his for the briefest moment. That was all the reassurance he needed to keep him from evaporating.

Despite her tacit approval, and happy as he was to be sitting at her table, conversation was difficult. First there was the blaring music, which made conversation all but impossible. Then there was the significant language barrier. She was uncomfortable in English, yet there was no other option. The only Swedish he knew, besides how to ask someone to dance, was, *"En svensk flicka behöver inte å vara vacker."* Fortunately, he had the presence of mind not to say that.

After learning that her name was Mette, that she was a student, and that her brother was one of the bartenders at this club, he had run out of his store of small talk. After several moments, he bluntly asked the question that had been on his mind from the first second he saw her, "Are you an artist?"

"How did you know?" she asked with a pleased expression.

How could I not know? he thought. *She exudes it. It's just obvious with some people.*

At that exact moment Anders materialized at their table. He was all smiles as he sat down and joined them. This was only one of the discos that he had planned to visit on this night. He had already cased the entire joint and in his estimation, there wasn't a single female worth hanging around for, present company excepted.

Anders had been on the verge of telling Erik that the time had come to blow this watering hole and move on to the next one, but when he saw Erik sitting with this beautiful girl, he effortlessly adjusted his plans.

They stayed until closing. Anders proved himself to be quite charming and a good conversationalist. In fact, he did most of the talking and Erik was glad for his presence. Anders was adept at drawing Mette out, despite her natural shyness. Thanks to Anders's savoir faire, Mette's intriguing aura and beguiling beauty, and Erik's internal voices, the evening coalesced into an enjoyable event with enticing possibilities.

As they left the disco, Erik asked Mette if he could see her again. Her brother was standing close by, and Erik was curious to see how he would react to this stranger asking out his younger sister. If anything, her brother seemed pleased—almost proud of Mette when she smiled and handed Erik her phone number. This probably had less to do with any trustworthiness that Erik engendered than with the way Swedish society in general responded to such encounters.

The Swedes were more open and accepting of human interaction between sexes. Erik had noticed this during his previous visit to Sweden as a camper exchange student. He had observed profound differences in the way that the Swedes dealt with sexuality versus the way that Americans did. At the outset of this journey, Erik's intentions were to leave these invisible shackles at the border and to liberate himself from any such American constrictions—now and forever.

Anders and Erik walked through the deserted streets of Göteborg until they found a taxi. As they rode back to his parents' house, Anders filled him in on some details about Mette that he had learned while speaking with her in Swedish.

She was a senior in *gymnasieskola*, the Swedish equivalent of the American high school system. She was studying art but hadn't yet decided on a career path. She lived at home with her dad, about a thirty-minute train ride out of Göteborg. Her brother lived with friends in the city.

Anders had to get back to med school in Stockholm. The original plan was for Erik to go with him, but they decided that he would stay with Anders's parents in Göteborg for another couple of days so that he would be able to see Mette again.

So Mette had messed up Anders's original plan, but then, with Anders, the original plan was always to have plans messed up by women. For Anders, accommodating friends when women entered the orbit was sacrosanct.

Anders's parents were asleep when the boys arrived at the apartment. Anders's sister was away at school, so Erik slept in her room.

As he lay in bed, Erik realized that he hadn't thought about Diana for more than a second since leaving Denmark. His meeting with Jim Coleman and their discussion about Charlie and Vietnam, the cold, the rigors of the road, the sorority house, the whirlwind life force of Anders, the disco, the music, and finally, Mette—all these things had completely preoccupied him.

What would Diana think of Mette? Would she be jealous? No. Probably not. She probably would say that Mette was incredible and gifted and exciting, and that Erik had to pursue her fully.

It made him sad to realize this, but yep, that was exactly what she would have said. The realization that Diana had fully dismissed him from her heart felt like a massive hole in his chest.

Fru Lundström was a housewife, a mother, and the heart of the Lundström family. Colonel Lundström was a career military man who had served in the Swedish Calvary, eventually rising to the rank of *överste* (colonel). Their lives had been heavily shaped by World War II. Although Sweden maintained neutrality during the entire war, many Swedes, including the Lundströms, were strongly supportive of the Western Allies.

The Lundströms had been unable to have children biologically and were already in their fifties when they adopted Anders and his sister. Anders was deeply grateful that his adoptive parents wanted not just him but also his sister. He was fiercely protective of his parents and had developed a paternal outlook toward them.

His parents, in turn, were extremely proud of Anders. The fact that he was in medical school and on the path to becoming a doctor was the pride of their lives.

Fru Lundström was a phenomenal cook. Her English was nearly nonexistent, but somehow she and Erik had no difficulty in communicating. The colonel's English was functional.

Colonel Lundström was now retired, and his daily "constitutional" consisted of a rigorous ten-kilometer walk. During his time with the family, Erik joined the colonel on several of these walks and profited from an exposure to aspects of Göteborg that few others experience. Having been a habitual walker for many years, the colonel was acquainted with many unorthodox paths throughout the city which boasted incredible vistas, as well as earthy underground tunnels, some of which were used by the Swedish Resistance during the war.

Colonel Lundström's back was ramrod straight, and he set a pace that one would expect of a younger man. He didn't talk a lot, but when he did, it was usually to impart some useful tidbit of information. This generation was one that Erik understood well. The colonel shared many traits he had noticed in his own father and his father's army buddies.

Erik called Mette. As he had noticed at the disco, she was less comfortable speaking English than other people he'd encountered so far in Sweden and before that in Denmark. It was becoming increasingly frustrating to Erik that he was constrained by his inability to speak in any language other than English.

Having gone through the entertainment section of the newspaper, Erik had seen that the film *Blue Hawaii* was playing in town. The film was not new—released in 1961—but it was the only film in the paper that he recognized. And the film would be in English with Swedish subtitles. They would both be able to follow whatever miniscule plot might exist. Moreover, how can you go wrong with Elvis Presley?

He asked Mette if he could take her to see the film. When she said yes, the Lundströms supplied Erik with a map and directions on how to take the train to downtown Göteborg for the rendezvous.

For Anders, the Holy Grail was women—the more beautiful, the more holy. Again, for Anders, *en Svensk flicka måste vara vacker*! Anders was no Elvis, but he had a magnetic charm that had more to do with his intelligence, his focus, and the sheer force of his personality, which enabled him to cover remarkable distances in pursuit of his Holy Grail.

Mette looked beautiful in the afternoon sun, even more than she had appeared in the shimmering light of the disco ball. She was a radiant counterpoint to the myth that all Swedish women were blondes. They walked to the movie theater, Erik bought the tickets and popcorn, and they watched Elvis charm girls in English, while Erik studied the Swedish subtitles.

After the movie Erik suggested they find a place to eat, and they started walking. There was no shortage of restaurants near the theater, but without saying it, Erik was looking for something he would be able to afford. Mette divined his dilemma and led them down a few streets until they came to a modest eatery.

Conversation didn't flow easily, but Erik felt it was due to the language barrier. He asked Mette to teach him how to say things in Swedish, how to order from the menu or to pronounce the Swedish word for everything around them. He asked her what she thought of the movie and then asked her to translate what she had said into Swedish. It was a start, a way to begin peeling off the easiest layers for their disparate worlds. The only item they had in common was his absolute certainty that she was an artist and he was…well, he was someone who had a destiny. The kind of destiny he had was unknown, but he had confidence that there was a force guiding him.

That was it. There was something guiding him. Surely others had this too. This was not unique to him. Still, like a secret guardian, this was the true voice that was guiding him and watching over him. It was what gave him the courage to travel to Norway and to walk across the disco floor and stand before Mette and ask if she would dance with him.

The evening had grown late, and Mette told Erik she needed to catch the next train home. She couldn't miss it because it was the last train of the day. Truthfully, he didn't want this moment to be over.

"Would you like me to come with you on the train?" Erik asked. "I can make sure you get home safely."

She got quiet. She turned her eyes away from his. *Was she upset? Did I say too much? Have I crossed over a line?* He wasn't sure how much she understood in English. Was his offer to see her home interpreted as something more than that? *Was it something more than that?*

Erik didn't stop to consider that if it was the last train going to her area, there might not be a train running back to Göteborg. What would he do then? His brain must have ceased functioning altogether.

Even though Erik was older than Mette, he recognized that in some ways she was older than him. She appeared centered, mature, and focused. That merry-go-round that he wanted so desperately to step off had suddenly turned into a roller coaster. Right now, he felt like it was going down fast.

"Walk me to the train," she said and smiled.

They walked to the station in a cloud of silence. She turned before climbing on the train and fixed him in her stare. He felt transparent and vulnerable in her gaze. The violet eyes he had observed in the club were now a midnight blue. They were probing into Erik's eyes for any hint of insincerity—a sin in any culture, in any language.

Erik's eyes stated flatly what his intentions were—that he was subservient to this inner belief that he was being guided toward a destiny which he must follow. He had no choice. He could no more have refused to ask her to dance than he could have refused the call that he felt to go to Norway. She was part of his journey now. That is, she was part of it only if she wanted to be.

In this moment, being in Sweden was the most natural place for him to be. Somehow he belonged here. Had his dad's Swedish ancestors not emigrated to America, Göteborg might have been his home and he might be speaking Swedish with Mette this very minute. Instead, they were speaking English, he was American, and she was Swedish.

Erik wished her a safe train ride home and thanked her for the evening. She smiled, turned, and vanished into the train.

STOCKHOLM

"Du kan inte lämna förrän du har haft några av mina lingonberry pannkakor."

He knew what Fru Lundström meant without needing a translation. She was not about to let him leave for Stockholm until he had some of her Swedish pancakes. These were nothing like pancakes he'd ever eaten before. These pancakes were paper thin and bursting with a buttery flavor, drenched in lingonberry jam and finely whipped cream. Erik deliberately ate as slowly as possible so he could savor every morsel.

Stockholm was to Göteborg what New York City was to Minneapolis. It was the Big Apple with a Swedish accent. Anders was quintessentially at home in Stockholm and during his two years of medical school there, he had gathered an eclectic group of friends. Anders reveled in these friendships, and he was eager to introduce an international flavor to the group. Although Anders had a heavy class load, he'd planned a few adventures for them all.

A young Björn Borg was all the rage in Sweden at the time, causing a surge in tennis mania. Anders and Erik met up with the rest of Anders's gang at an indoor/outdoor tennis club. The club was a large, tony facility, which housed multiple tennis courts. Players displayed a wide range of abilities. Half of the guests were on the courts; the other half populated the lounge areas, sipping strawberry daiquiris and mint juleps, and showing off their fashionable attire.

Erik knew his way around a tennis court and had played competitively for a year in high school. For the first time since leaving English soil, he felt like he was not at a disadvantage because of language. That was one of the best aspects of sports—they're truly international. The language barrier having no consequence here, Erik could let his borrowed racquet do the talking.

There were some hard-won singles battles and some well-matched doubles games. At the end of the day, no one could remember who lost or who won the most games. A side benefit of sports was the banter. Sports jargon and razzing opponents were great ways to pick up idioms quickly. Erik tucked away a few choice phrases for future use.

The Swedish language is beautiful—it's a musical language that can be modulated in a way that the English language simply cannot replicate. Erik was envious. The cadences, the alveolar trill, the lyrical qualities are all absent in his native tongue. Moreover, there's a slight, whispery inhalation sound that Swedes make when they are agreeing with someone during a conversation. This sound thrilled Erik every time he heard it.

Danish, by contrast, was more like German, with many of the vowels emanating from the back of the throat. He was curious to hear how Norwegian would stack up alongside of Swedish.

The following day, Anders brought Erik to his medical school. He couldn't leave Erik behind at the dorm but bringing him to the lectures didn't make sense either. Even if Erik could understand a lecture in Swedish, he wouldn't have been able to decipher the lexicon of medical terminology.

Erik was willing to sit through the classes, but Anders said he wouldn't do that to his worst enemy. Instead, Erik spent the morning catching up on some correspondence while rummaging through the campus bookstore and library.

When the boys reconnected after Anders's morning classes, they went to the student cafeteria for lunch. Erik's willingness to sit through a lecture, combined with a remembrance of the pranks they used to pull at camp, had given Anders an idea. He handed Erik a white lab coat and a clipboard.

"I have an anatomy lab this afternoon, which I think you'll find interesting," Anders said. "It's a closed lab, and only students who are registered for this class are allowed. But as a doctor, you'll be able to walk right in."

"What?" Erik protested. "I don't know anything about being a doctor, and in case you forgot, I don't speak Swedish!"

"Don't worry. If anyone asks, I'll say you're a physician colleague visiting me from the United States. Just look stern and authoritative. No one will question you."

"Anders, I can't do that. Nobody's going to believe I'm a doctor."

"I thought you were an actor. Being a doctor should be a breeze for you. Besides, you told me earlier that you wanted to see a cadaver. Now's your chance."

"That's what your anatomy lab is? Cadavers?"

"What, did you think we would be dissecting frogs?" Anders laughed.

Erik's initial reticence vanished as soon as they entered the lab. There were a half dozen naked corpses lying on lab tables throughout the room. Anders was enjoying the clandestine aspect of their little charade. Any activity that was illegal, risky, or rebellious was an appetency to Anders.

The room was quiet as a library. The only sound was a hum that came from the HVAC system. A pervasive odor of formaldehyde infused the room. Flood lights situated directly above each examination table were reminiscent of a billiards hall Erik used to frequent in Minneapolis. Instead of students playing hooky from school though, this room was filled with med students dissecting cadavers.

It was hard to believe that these were real dead people. Erik affected a nonchalant attitude as he followed Anders to one of the examination tables. Green cloths covered the faces and genital areas of the cadavers.

In preparation for the anatomy lab, the arteries of the cadavers had been flushed of their blood and their skin and organs had been sprayed with chemicals as a preservative. The skin of most of the cadavers was either gray or a jaundiced white.

Anders and his physician friend from America, "Dr. Hellberg," casually strolled around the room as if comparing the efficacy of Swedish anatomical procedures with those of American procedures. As Anders had predicted—the students, holding forceps, scalpels, and scissors—were so engrossed in their work that they didn't pay any attention to Erik.

"Dr. Hellberg" bent over one of the bodies for a close-up inspection. He boldly lifted the green cloth off the cadaver's face. The man looked like he might have been fifty years of age. He had a week's worth of beard. Anders explained that fingernails and facial hair continue to grow postmortem.

Not too long ago, this cadaver had been a living person with an entire life history, just as Charlie had been such a short time ago. Now this poor soul was lying inertly, face up on a table, providing endless educational opportunities for these eager, inquisitive medical students. Erik peered inside the cadaver's body and identified his lungs, heart, liver, stomach, and large and small intestines.

As he examined these inner workings of the human body, inexplicably Erik's own body began to rebel. The smell of formaldehyde was overwhelming. He felt the blood drain from his head as though a trap door in his neck had opened. Drained of blood, his brain began to shut down. The room began to spin, slowly at first and then rapidly. He fought against it—he didn't want to faint—but he no longer had control.

As his body went limp, a strong arm grabbed him around his torso and walked him briskly out of the room. Once outside in the fresh air, he slowly felt himself reviving.

"Are you okay?" Anders asked.

"Yeah. Wow! I don't know what happened. I was fine one minute, and the next I just felt all the blood drain out of my head. I couldn't control it."

"Don't worry," Anders said. "Your reaction is quite common."

So much for Erik's performance as a doctor. Still, the experience had been fascinating and enriching. Up to this point, Erik had seriously contemplated officially donating his body to science in case he should ever die prematurely. The anatomy lab experience gave him pause. He shuddered to think that one day his body might be picked apart by a bunch of third-year med students, or heaven forbid, some foreign kid posing as a doctor.

The experience gave Erik a new perspective on his friend Anders. For the first time, Erik could picture Anders as a doctor, rather than just as a fellow student or as an amorous party animal. He had no doubt that Anders would one day turn out to be a fabulous gynecologist.

And Anders was impressed that Erik and Mette had hit it off so well, but he ribbed Erik for not going home with her.

"I don't know how you found her—she was the best-looking girl there. I could tell she was crazy about you. You should have gone home with her."

"I'm crazy about her too, but we're just getting to know each other."

"That's nuts. Look, you have a great connection with Mette," Anders said. "You're overthinking it. Just go with the flow, man!"

For Anders, it was all physical, biological. For Erik, there needed to be the metaphysical and spiritual aspect. *Two different worlds*, Erik thought. Yet he had to admit that Anders's singular pursuit of the physical challenged him to define what his principles were. After all, wasn't this part of the reason he was making this trip—to discover the extent of his boundaries?

Erik remembered his frame of mind when he arrived in England and stood inside of Heathrow Airport. *I'm free—not just physically, but free in every other way—emotionally, mentally, and spiritually. I will not tie myself down to American customs, values, and prejudices. I will have a clean slate and will start fresh and unbiased.*

Maybe it's good that Anders is challenging me. Maybe I should just pursue Mette to whatever extent possible instead of endlessly dissecting every situation…

What exactly is this carousel that I'm jumping off anyway? Isn't it the carousel of society, of those invisible barriers that constrict natural human behavior?

It's not that he wasn't physical; it's just that he needed something more. This was part of the concept he was struggling with, what he was trying to figure out. This was part of why he had to leave Minnesota and America. How much of himself was uniquely self and not merely inherited traits from his family, his lineage, his state, and his country? Who was he if he stripped it all away?

Every time Erik got to the point of asking these questions, he felt as though Charlie was suddenly standing next to him. Not that Charlie was judging him—he wasn't like that. His brother just had this inner calmness, like a conviction, even though there was no earthly reason for it. He wasn't physically strong, he wasn't some brainiac, he wasn't even particularly popular—he was just this quiet, peaceful guy with a head full of ideas and plans, a man who marched to the beat of his own drum.

That's what made Charlie getting drafted so damned incongruous and unjust—even diabolical. Charlie must have been terrified when he learned that he would be going to Vietnam. Yet he never complained. He just accepted it like it was fate. And, if it was fate, he would just have to go.

Erik and Charlie had never discussed Vietnam—at least not before Charlie was drafted. The brothers lived in different parts of the state prior to Charlie's departure, so they really hadn't spent much time together during that period. Did Charlie think it was a good or a bad idea that the United States got involved in Vietnam? He assumed that Charlie was against the war in Vietnam, but he probably thought that war, at times, was necessary. Their father had fought in World War II. That war was clearly necessary. Nazism was evil. Well, what about Communism? How many innocent people had Mao Zedong and Stalin killed?

The letters and tapes Charlie sent home to the family never discussed what he thought about the war; they were more about what he was doing and seeing. Once he got into the MARS program, he mostly wrote about the process of the communications he was involved in and the challenges of the equipment (or lack thereof) that he had to work with. That was Charlie—making the best of a bad situation.

There was one observation about Charlie's time in the service that Erik noticed: a new and unfamiliar hardness that had taken hold. It showed itself over time in lots of little ways. For example, he wrote about a friend of his who had been shot and killed by a sniper one night while on guard duty. The only thing Charlie had to say about it was that his friend "bought the farm."

Charlie never would have said something like that before he went in. Erik had been bedeviled by the war in Vietnam ever since Charlie's conscription. It was madness that Charlie had gotten sucked into that quagmire of death. *It makes no sense. If I were God, Charlie would be the last person in the world I would have sent. I would have sent me instead. It doesn't take the Almighty to see that Mrs. Hellberg's youngest son was the reprobate of the family. Why is it that the innocent one had to be sacrificed?*

He never talked with Anders about this stuff, but it occupied Erik's mind for his remaining days in Stockholm. Besides, he was now fixated on reaching Norway. Rather than trying to hitchhike the final leg of his journey, he decided to pull the trigger on his Student Rail Pass.

Why not start it now? Now that I know Mette and have reconnected with Anders, I'll probably be doing a lot of traveling between Sweden and Norway over the next three months. And I must visit all the theaters in Norway. I might as well start doing that as soon as possible.

He was tired of hitchhiking, and it was getting too damn cold to do it now anyway. Besides, hitchhiking in Sweden sucked. Erik's internal compass pointed west, toward the Land of the Midnight Sun, and specifically toward Oslo.

At long last, I'll be in Norway tonight. What will it be like? Will Norway be markedly different from Sweden and Denmark? What will Jens be like, with all the drugs and crap he's been through? Will his family put me up until I can make other arrangements? How will I even ask them? Will I be able to get a part in Arturo Ui?

So many unknowns. This was the end of the line and the beginning of the line. The dawn of his new life was about to begin.

October 23, 1973

Sitting on a "tog" bound for Oslo. Decided to start the Student Rail Pass. It's good for three months. This will bring me through the Christmas season and beyond. Will take advantage of it and see as much of Norway as I can.

At long last, the final leg of my journey to Norway! Each passing mile, the terrain seems to grow colder—this could be Minnesota! I'm finally about to reconnect with Jens and his family. Can't wait!

So much has happened already! Traveling through England and Denmark and Sweden. Losing Diana and wandering like a lost and drunken sailor in Århus. Finding Jim Coleman in Copenhagen and confiding in him about Charlie. Reconnecting with Anders and finding in him a friend for life. Meeting his parents, walking with his dad, and learning that respect and communication is not dependent on words. Then, meeting Mette and having my soul reignited and rescued from the downward spiral of rejection.

Life is so full of conflicting emotions. I ache as I sit on this train, watching the frozen ground flash by, knowing that Charlie will never walk this earth again. While at the same time, I'm living my life, excited about all the possibilities that lay ahead.

How can I be happy, Charlie? How can I be happy, angry, and sad at the same time? I'm so confused Charlie, and I'm no closer to the answers I promised you.

Erik put away his journal and stared out the train's window. He watched as the early winds of winter layered trees and fields with a fine, white dusting of snow. The landscape began to blur as mental dreamscapes beaconed him to rest in the realms of his nocturnal imaginings. He pulled out his rain poncho, fashioned it into a pillow, and then released himself to the somniferous humming of the train as its wheels strummed rhythmically against the smooth iron rails.

TWO

OSLO

Jens Christian Åstergard was waiting at the train station in Oslo for Erik. The kid Erik had met during their junior year in high school four years ago was nowhere to be seen. Instead, there was a tall, Nordic hippie with hair down to his waist, a Fu Manchu mustache, and buckskins festooned with American Indian beads and bright colors. Clearly, the smiling man standing before him had weathered some major storms. Worry emanated from his eyes, yet they still shone brightly with intelligence. His smile—infectious. His embrace—warm and sincere.

This was a joyous reunion. His good old friend Jens. Erik knew that Jens had had a rough go at life after leaving the States. He'd heard that when Jens got back to Norway, he couldn't adjust to the culture, even though he'd only been away for a year. As they drove to his parents' house in the suburbs of Oslo, Jens provided a patchwork overview of the craters in his life since he returned. Erik sat in sobered silence.

The boys had met the first week of the eleventh grade, which was destined to be a pivotal year for both. Although they had no classes together, it was hard to miss this tall Norway pine amid a forest of birch trees. During lunch, the friendless foreigner sat alone at a large, empty table in the cafeteria. Erik took the seat next to him.

By the time they had eaten their way to dessert, Erik learned that Jens was the eldest of four kids in the family. His dad was a doctor and was taking a sabbatical year to teach pediatrics at the University of Minnesota and his mother was an attorney and taking a year off. They were renting a house on the street one over from Erik's. Most importantly, Erik had a gut feeling they were going to be lifelong friends.

Jens was intelligent, inquisitive, humorous, fun-loving, and adventurous, yet at the same time, there was a reserved nature about him—not so much a shyness as a requirement to draw him out, like he needed a kind of prodding to peel back the layers and get to the core.

One evening early in their friendship back in Minnesota, Erik invited Jens to the local bowling alley to hang out with some of his pals. There was a little café in the bowling alley, and they sat down for burgers and soda. When the waiter came to take their order, Jens spoke up for the group and said they would have burgers and beer all around.

The legal drinking age in Minnesota was 21 at the time, and without forethought, without a plan, without any hesitation, Jens had calmly ordered beer as casually as one would order a Dr Pepper. His moxie was impressive. Erik was even more impressed when the waiter brought them the beers.

That was an epochal moment in Erik's universe, cementing Jens's place in the firmament of that universe. A second lesson learned from this incident was that *how* one asked for something was often more important than *what* one asked for—in this case, beer. Six months later, however, they were no longer asking for beer; the object they craved had evolved.

Neither Erik nor Jens had ever smoked marijuana. The year was 1969—the same year as the Woodstock Music Festival, Neil Armstrong's walk on the moon, and Nixon's election as the nation's thirty-seventh president. The war in Vietnam was raging, a draft lottery system was being implemented, and the Troubles in Northern Ireland were escalating. This was also the same year that Ted Kennedy drove his car into the waters off Chappaquiddick Island, gas was thirty-five cents per gallon, and the followers of Charles Manson murdered actress Sharon

Tate and four other people. Plus, the same year, the movie *Easy Rider* debuted, and a little-known singer/songwriter named John Denver, while visiting his parents in Minneapolis, sang "Leaving on a Jet Plane" in the auditorium of Erik's school.

And so, as the country was undergoing a massive political and cultural upheaval, this change came also to Erik's high school. One night that winter, Erik and his friend Barney had agreed to give Barney's older brother a ride to a party. His brother had just returned from his tour of duty in Vietnam.

"You guys mind if I light up?" Barney's brother asked, not waiting for a reply.

The smoke quickly filled Barney's tiny 1960 Corvair. Barney and Erik looked at each other. That wasn't tobacco they were smelling. A moment of silence passed as the brother took several hits off the joint. That wasn't the way you smoke an ordinary cigarette either. Barney and Erik looked at each other again.

"Is that marijuana?" Erik asked as casually as he could muster, as though these sorts of occurrences routinely happened to him.

"Oh yeah."

He said this in such a way as to let them know that there could be no mistaking that this was not just marijuana—this was the finest kind of marijuana available at any price.

"What's it like?" Erik asked.

He really wanted to know. He had heard so much about "the evil weed." He had seen the movie *Reefer Madness*. He knew there were more than a few kids in his grade that had used the stuff, but he had never witnessed marijuana use firsthand. Erik had even researched *Cannabis sativa*, the plant from which marijuana is derived, and had written a report for one of his classes on the drug.

Barney's brother proceeded to describe the experience of being high, in lucid, concrete terms. His explanation had the effect of demystifying the physiological impact the drug might have on a person's mind. This all sounded fascinating and enticing, but Erik wasn't convinced that marijuana was for him. He was concerned that he might not personally respond well to the effects of the drug. Images from the movie *Reefer Madness* flashed across his brain—people jumping off of buildings and women tearing off their clothes.

"How long before you're high?"

Barney's brother looked at Erik like he was loco. "What do you mean? I'm higher than shit right now!"

"Right now?" Erik asked. "You're high right now?"

Erik couldn't believe that Barney's brother was experiencing all those enticing things he'd just told him about, and yet he was still able to maintain his composure. He wasn't shouting and yelling or being batshit crazy like Erik had described in his report or what he'd seen in *Reefer Madness*.

With the revelations that Barney's brother was high and that there was no detectably crazy behavior coming from him, Erik simply said, "Can I try that?"

That was it. Both Barney and Erik took a few puffs of the brother's joint, and down the rabbit hole they went.

While Erik was discovering the highs of hemp, Jens, within his own crowd at school, had also developed a cannabis habit. As Erik learned from Jens on the drive to his parents' house, the almighty weed was still significantly higher on Jens's priority list than it had been on Erik's.

Jens and Erik had intersected with each other several times over that junior year in high school, and Erik recalled getting high with him once at a party somewhere. Other than that, their schedules and separate interests had kept them apart much of the school year.

Toward the end of that year, and shortly before Jens returned to Norway with his family, Erik invited Jens up to his family's cabin in northern Minnesota. Just the two of them up in the great Northwoods, with a cabin, the lake, and a forest at their disposal. For some reason, either poverty or propriety, they were weedless.

Regretting the deficiency, they experimented smoking the leaves of every plant they found growing in the woods. Nothing got them high, but they both got headaches and cases of poison ivy. That was the last time Erik had seen Jens before being picked up by him at the train station in Oslo, three and a half years later.

Jens's family lived in Bærum, at the end of the rail line from Oslo. The Åstergards' house consisted of four children and a dog. Jens's dad, Øystein, was Norwegian. His mother, Tove, was Danish. The children spoke Norwegian to their dad and Danish to their mother. The house swirled with activity.

Jens and Erik were the same age. Jens's sister, Ingegerd, was next in line and two years younger than Jens, then Anders, and then young Morten. They were a close family, and Jens's troubles were painful for all of them, especially his mother, Tove. Erik could feel her pain.

Since Jens was no longer living in his parents' home, he offered his old bedroom to Erik until other arrangements could be made. Both Øystein and Tove Åstergard readily agreed to let Erik stay and immediately made him feel at home. They insisted on Erik calling them by their first names.

The awareness that he wasn't able to provide for himself weighed constantly on Erik. This lack of self-sufficiency was another reminder that he was still a kid and not a man. He was dependent on the generosity of Jens and the kindness of Jens's parents, even though he had done nothing to deserve this kindness.

There wasn't even the promise of a job—merely the promise to submit his name for a job. No formal arrangements. Such was the stuff upon which he was building his edifice.

Tonight, however, Jens had made plans for them. They'd stay and have dinner with the family, and afterward Jens would drive the two of them to his *hytte*—the small cabin in the nearby mountains where he lived. In the early morning, they'd climb the mountain to watch the sunrise.

During dinner, Erik picked up on the tension in the family over Jens. The gist of the tension seemed to be that Jens had fallen in with the wrong crowd when he got back from America. They were concerned with the direction his life had taken, and they were afraid he was never going to find his footing again.

Jens was not exaggerating when he said "small" cabin—it was approximately fourteen by sixteen feet. There was a narrow bed, a table with a wooden chair, a second chair that was padded, a space heater, a cupboard, and a closet. In the corner was a sitar. One hundred yards from the *hytte* was a one-seater outhouse. That was it.

The space heater kept the *hytte* snuggly warm. Snow had been falling steadily since before he arrived in Oslo, and up here in the mountains the air was crisp and cold. Snow was already waist-deep in some areas. Jens and Erik talked long into the night.

"Society here in Norway is different than in the United States," Jens explained. "Here marijuana is not only illegal but also taboo. And difficult to get. You must go to certain places and work with certain people to get it. And anyone using drugs of any kind here is looked upon as a deviant and immediately ostracized from society."

Jens's drug habit had put him at odds not only with his parents but also with his entire community. He was no longer accepted by his old friends, and he formed new friendships that his parents and family didn't like. Eventually, he dropped out of school and drifted from job to job.

Before Erik arrived, Jens had discovered meditation and Eastern philosophy, which further isolated him from his family and friends. Erik perceived that his drug use had tapered off, but once trust is broken, all communication becomes strained and onerous. Rebuilding trust takes time, effort, and sacrifice.

On the plus side, he was getting good on the sitar and made the best damned Norwegian bread Erik was ever likely to taste. Jens sat cross-legged on the floor of his *hytte* and played the sitar for him. It sounded good, but what did Erik know about sitar music? As far as he knew,

George Harrison and Ravi Shankar were the only two people in the world who played it.

Erik was fighting to stay awake when Jens said if they wanted to see the sun rise, they had to start climbing now. This time of year, the sun rose at about eight thirty in the morning and set at about four thirty in the afternoon—never fully reaching a solar zenith in the sky.

The snow was deep, and their progress up the mountain was laboriously slow. Finally, they reached an outcropping that offered a breathtaking view of the valley below. They sat down on the large rock and waited. When the sun came up, the boys had what could almost be described as a religious experience.

The warm, crepuscular rays illuminated first the mountain tops, and then the tallest trees, and finally the snow dust, which was being agitated by a gentle but persistent wind. Slowly, the blue snow surrounding them turned orange in ever-increasing intensity, indescribably beautiful and well worth the climb. Jens may have temporarily lost his footing in the world of mankind, but he hadn't lost sight of the grandeur of the universe.

When they got back to Jens's *hytte*, Erik was exhausted. He sat down in the padded chair without even taking his jacket or boots off and fell into a deep sleep. When he awoke, he looked over at Jens stretched out on his tiny cot. Jens opened his eyes just then. Suddenly, they both started laughing.

Erik couldn't explain why they laughed, nor did he really care. It just felt good to be reunited with his old friend. Erik sensed that somehow life was going to work out okay for Jens. And Erik knew he was going to need help from Jens beyond his parents providing him a place to live until he could lock in employment in Bergen. Maybe the fact that Jens was able to play a crucial role in helping Erik get situated was a net positive in Jens's life. Sometimes helping others was the best way to help oneself.

It was good to have climbed the mountain. To have been in such deep snow. To have arrived in time to watch the sunrise. The shared experience. The effort. The uniqueness and the solitude. Being with his old friend Jens again and being invited into his sanctum sanctorum, this was so deeply satisfying.

That experience gave Erik a glimmer of the connection with life that he was longing for. When Jens drove Erik back to Jens's parents' house later that day, Erik felt like he had come to understand some of the isolation that Jens felt and the dynamics at play in the Åstergard family. Erik hoped that he would be able to play a positive role in helping Jens find a path back into society and into his family again.

Erik's first task, however, was to get enrolled in a Norwegian language class somewhere. In this endeavor, Jens proved to be indispensable. Jens made multiple calls and learned that there was a beginner's class that would start in a couple of weeks at the University of Oslo. The class was free if you had a job. Government policy was to help visitors and immigrants learn the language, thus enabling them to get better jobs, thereby contributing to the betterment of the overall economy.

At city hall, Jens argued on Erik's behalf that since Erik had the promise of a job, he should be allowed to have the government pay for his class. The clerk listened respectfully but rejected his argument out of hand. If he wanted the government to pay for his tuition, he had to prove that he currently had a job—not just the promise of a job. That meant Erik had to fork over the *kroner*. The clerk agreed to refund the money once Erik showed them proof that he was gainfully employed.

Erik's coffers were getting low, even though he'd been frugal with the funds he'd worked hard to put together. He was so eager to jump into classes that he soon stopped fretting over the sting of having to sign three big traveler's checks. Now he had yet one more reason to focus on locking up that promise of employment.

Next on his list was to connect with Fru Gullestad, the director friend of Dr. Walter Van Langenhove. Erik had written to Fru Gullestad, letting her know approximately when he expected to arrive in Norway. She wrote him back saying that as soon as he was able, he should come and visit her in Bergen. Now, with his Student Rail Pass, he could travel anywhere in Europe and the train trip was already paid for.

November 1, 1973

> Sitting at the railway station in Oslo, waiting for my train to Bergen. I hear the countryside is beautiful, and the train ride to Bergen is rapturous. Unfortunately, I shall not see it. I shall be on the night train. Amazingly, the sleeper berths are only an extra $4 USD, which fits my budget perfectly, and the bonus is I don't lose a day.

Erik had plenty of time before his train left the station. He ordered a coffee and sat down at one of the tables in the station café. He packed a plug of tobacco in his pipe, relishing the ritual of the process. He wasn't addicted to smoking, at least not in the physical or physiological way. It was more of a social or an ideological addiction. A tobacco pipe always seemed to compliment and prolong a good conversation, or, for that matter, a good book.

On each table there were metal ashtrays. He picked one of them up and studied it. These weren't the cheap, throwaway ashtrays he was used to seeing in America. These were heavy, quality ashtrays with the name of the café and the national railway insignia stamped on them.

This is part of an old-world ethos that has become increasingly rare. Why don't businesses in America openly display quality goods like this? The answer, he knew, was that people would steal them. He once read a magazine article while waiting in a dental office about a "virtue test" that some organization had conducted. The test involved leaving a wallet with a hundred dollars cash in various major cities throughout Europe and the Americas. The test was to see which city, state, or country had the greatest number of wallets returned with cash intact. Norway and Denmark were the only nations that had a 100 percent return rate.

On the train now. It's late and I'm on the upper bunk. I'm grateful that there's another passenger that I share the sleeper car with—keeps me from dwelling on Charlie not being here. This man is a doctor. When I mentioned I was staying with the Åstergards, he said that when he was in med school, he attended a lecture given by Dr. Åstergard. What a small world!

The Åstergard family couldn't be nicer to me, and I don't know what I would have done had they not taken me in. They've made me part of their family!

I hope the idiots at St. Cloud State follow through and send my transcript to the University of Oslo. I won't get credited for the Norsk class if they don't.

I haven't thought that much about Diana since meeting Mette. Only just now has she popped into my mind. I would like to write her and tell her about some of the stuff I've been through. Can't though. That would be bad form. Nope. The ball is in her court.

Bergen ducked in and out of view as the train followed a final obstacle course of hills and trees prior to docking. A steady symphony of snowflakes and hail drummed upon the oversized train windows, melting into rivulets of rain, which raced horizontally toward the caboose. The city of Oslo had won his heart, but he was intrigued and eager to explore this "charming little town," as Fru Gullestad had described it.

Bergen was waking to the day as Erik walked from the train station down Kaigaten Street, which ran alongside an expansive and beautiful park. The park featured a large pond edged with carved stones and surrounded by tall and neatly trimmed evergreen bushes. A large water fountain sat in the middle of the pond.

He continued walking as Kaigaten Street became Markeveien Street. People were emerging from or entering buildings and alleys as they prepared for the day's work. The merchants and workers were wearing rubber boots, raincoats, and hats, yet oddly, few carried umbrellas.

There was a strange sensation he had been here before. A dream? When he reached Veiten, Den Nationale Scene came into view. The austere and imposing building dominated a small park known simply as *Teaterparken*. Erik was hours early for his appointment with Fru Gullestad.

He turned and walked back to a café that he'd passed earlier. The rich aroma of coffee and freshly baked *skillingsboller* and *solskinnskringle* seductively enticed him to splurge on these Norwegian delicacies. Rather than cloistering himself inside the café, he took his breakfast outside where he could inhale the sights and sounds of the city. An awning cantilevered over the patio, providing protection from the pluvial thumping all around him.

As he ate, he heard rubber boots slapping cobblestones whenever people walked by, gulls caviling, horns from the fishing schooners in the harbor proclaiming their presence—it was all wonderful. And the language! From the woman who served him coffee to the patrons in the café—he immediately discerned a distinctive Bergen accent. They spoke more slowly than their Oslo neighbors on the eastern coast and spent more time enjoying the singsong cadence associated with an older version of their native tongue.

As he lit his pipe, he thought about the differences in the two Norwegian cities he'd seen so far. Oslo was the capital and the largest city in Norway, yet compared to other metropolises, it was small. Oslo didn't have the feel of a major city. It was friendly, clean, knowable, yet unexpectedly diverse. It was like combining aspects of both Minneapolis and St. Paul. Of course, then one would have to add some mountains and a harbor.

In contrast, Bergen was even smaller, quainter, and more picturesque, had more cobblestones and narrower streets, and was more open to the sea. There were mountains on all sides of the city except where the fjord and open ports interjected themselves into the city. In a word, Bergen was beautiful; it was just the right size for Erik at this juncture in his life.

He pulled his journal from the top of his pack.

November 2, 1973

Bergen is amazing! My kind of town. It's quaint and small and old and picturesque. A lot of the streets are cobblestone, the roads in the residential areas surrounding the main town are narrow, and the buildings all seem like they're straight out of a European movie. Bergen is called "Byen mellom syv fjell"—the town between seven mountains. I think that's an understatement.

I feel more comfortable here than in Oslo. Oslo is larger and more businesslike by contrast. It was raining a few minutes ago, but it's snowing now! The sky can't make up its mind! They say it rains every day in Bergen except for a few weeks in the spring when all the rain magically disappears. The combination of snow and rain on the ground is called "sludd"—in Minnesota, we call it "slush." Breakfast is over, and I need to start walking to Den Nationale Scene.

His instructions were to meet Fru Gullestad inside the main foyer of Den Nationale Scene. He stood outside the building and studied the architecture for a moment. Although built in the mid-nineteenth century, the building had a majestic, almost Gothic appearance. It was as if the architects wanted to stress that in this theater only important and worthy productions would be produced.

Erik stepped through the doors of the main entrance, and the exterior austerity morphed into a warm and inviting interior atmosphere. Norway had great hope for its native writers and artists and wanted a building that would encourage and foster their gifts.

Fru Gullestad came walking briskly into the foyer. She had a ruddy complexion, reddish-brown hair, a slight British accent, and an impressive efficiency about her. They shook hands as she greeted him warmly.

Erik said, "I can feel the spirit of Henrik Ibsen just standing here in the foyer."

Fru Gullestad laughed appreciatively. "Yes, we're quite proud of our national hero. He was the first playwright in residence here, as well as stage manager, and eventually artistic director."

She gave him a brief tour of the building, reiterating the role that this theater played in developing the young Ibsen into a world-class dramatist. After the tour, she introduced Erik to Dr. Harold Thomassen, the artistic director of DNS. Dr. Thomassen invited him to see all the plays currently running at the theater.

Now that Erik was here, the dynamics changed. That easy promise made to an old friend suddenly had to be confronted. Fru Gullestad looked him up and down. Was Erik someone she could pitch to Wolfgang Pintzka, the mercurial director of *Arturo Ui*? Pintzka, too, was a foreigner, and that might work to Erik's advantage.

Sure, there were any number of small parts, but these were highly prized perks for the stable of actors who are fixtures at the theater. Was Erik worth expending her political capital on? She had less influence with a foreign company and director than she did with her fellow Norwegian directors. Erik didn't need to be fluent in Norwegian to understand that he was being sized up by both Fru Gullestad and Dr. Thomassen.

Arturo Ui had been like a distant star. Something to aim for but not something that had hardened into a reality that he could depend upon. Now, having arrived in Bergen, standing in the theater made famous by Ibsen, the reality that his trip had been fueled by vapor became abundantly clear.

A promise made an ocean away and a couple of months ago to a college student was an easy punt, with scant downside. There were so many variables, not the least of which was that the student could easily flake out on the trip and simply never materialize.

> On a night train to Oslo—some good news and some maybe not-so-great news. The good news is that there may be a small part for me in an upcoming production of "The Wild Duck"—a play by Ibsen. The not-so-great news is that getting a part in "Arturo Ui" looks like a long shot.
>
> Disappointed, but I guess it really doesn't matter—if I get in <u>something</u>. Fru Gullestad is really going to bat for me. I don't know what I've done to deserve her helping me like this. I'm struggling to express my gratitude. I can't get a "read" on Fru Gullestad but she seems genuinely happy to help me. I'm really touched by this. Dr. Walter Van Langenhove was as good as his word.

The train back to Oslo allowed Erik time to reflect on the genesis of today's meeting. It was mind-boggling to think that all those months ago, when Dr. Van Langenhove offered to make an introduction, Erik would be here meeting with Fru Gullestad face to face and that she was going to help him.

What a roller coaster life could be. To be confronted with the fact of how truly unlikely the prospect of getting a part in *Arturo Ui* was, and then to be told that there was a possibility that there might be a role for him in *The Wild Duck*. It was astounding and humbling in the same moment. These people didn't know him. Fru Gullestad certainly didn't know whether Erik was worthy of her going out on a limb. They owed him nothing.

The Wild Duck was an interesting and unexpected development. Fru Gullestad was friends with the director, and she was cautiously optimistic he would get a part. Naturally, any such part would be rather small.

Who cares? It's an Ibsen play! Ibsen, the "Father of Modern Drama." The man who changed dramaturgy—the way plays are written. No playwright wrote the same way again after Ibsen. Every first-year theater student knows who Ibsen was. Both Eleanora Duse and Sarah Bernhardt, the great actresses of the late nineteenth century idolized Ibsen because he wrote deep and wonderful roles for women. And Den Nationale Scene was the theater where Ibsen started his career! Erik's head was spinning.

Back in Oslo, his stock had risen a notch. At least that's the way it felt. He wanted to prove to the Åstergard family that his being here was legitimate. He was more hopeful now than ever that this might happen. In his mind, getting a job, having a success in Norway would in some way be a recompense for the faith they had placed in him by putting him up. He needed to give them something.

Did the Åstergard family hope that Erik's presence would be a positive influence on Jens? He wanted that to be the case. Erik believed wholeheartedly in Jens. He knew Jens was remarkable in many ways—he was sensitive, intelligent, and creative. Jens had just picked up a bad habit while in the States.

It was understandable. Jens had arrived in America just when the culture was undergoing a major generational shift. He'd been at an age when acceptance by his peers was paramount, and he was old enough to make decisions that had the potential for unseen, serious consequences. Once back in Norway, he'd found it difficult to extricate himself from the path that he'd started down while living in America.

Erik doubted Jens was still using drugs; he hadn't detected any telltale signs. Perhaps the stigma was all that remained, or a mindset that refused to acquiesce or bend to societal pressure. He certainly understood that the cultural adjustment could be difficult.

Erik vowed that he would look for ways he could be a bridge between Jens and his family. He felt that in some ways, that was beginning to happen now. Jens had proved himself to be invaluable in helping Erik as he was trying to integrate himself into Norwegian society. In a sense, that was what both he and Jens were doing.

Erik's most pressing task now was getting ready for what potentially lay ahead in Bergen. That meant learning Norwegian and getting prepared for *The Wild Duck*. Fru Gullestad said she would contact Gustaf Husman, the director, but closing the deal was up to Erik.

She gave him the director's contact information and wished him success. Gustaf Husman, as director, would have complete say as to who would be in his play. Erik immediately sat down and wrote a letter to Director Husman. He was so excited he could hardly stand it.

Norway looked a lot like Minnesota, and Erik felt like he was in his element. Snow everywhere. The difference was, here there were mountains. The Åstergards had mountain access directly across the street from their house. The mountain was called Kolsås, and consequently, so was their suburb. Erik looked longingly at that beautiful mountain and vowed to hike to the top at his first opportunity.

For now, he wanted to acquaint himself with the local area and he decided to take a nice, long walk down to the town at the bottom of the hill to mail his letter to Director Husman. As Erik walked outside, he saw Tinka, the family dog.

Wouldn't it be fun to take Tinka with me on the walk? Erik went back inside and got her leash.

Erik had known some great dogs, and he liked to think he had an affinity with all dogs. *Well, except for that wretched mastiff back in Harwich.* He'd been keeping an eye on Tinka; she was different from other dogs. She was aloof and didn't like to play. And it wasn't because she was old and tired. She was two. Tinka was a Siberian Husky and maybe part something else. Wolf? Who knows? She had one blue eye and one gray eye.

Erik was sure that he could get along with any dog, given enough time. Tinka was not going to be easy. She stared at him like she might go wild at any second, like Buck in *The Call of the Wild*.

No one in the Åstergard family had ever had a problem with her, and she was gentle with the kids. But Erik she viewed warily. Despite his acceptance by the rest of the family, it appeared Tinka was reluctant to admit Erik into the family pack.

Erik tried putting the leash on her, but she was having none of it. He tried to coax her into coming with him. He called to her, clapped his hands and thighs, and pantomimed how much fun a hike would be, but she just stood still, silently staring at him through her gray eye.

"Fine. I'll do the walk by myself," Erik finally said. "You don't know what you're missing, ya stubborn mutt!" *What do I have to do to prove to her I'm trustworthy?*

And with that, he headed down the long, switch-backing road that led to the little local shopping area. Before he had reached the end of the first street, he noticed that he wasn't alone. Tinka had decided to follow him after all. Erik still had the leash and he called her to come to him. She kept her distance.

Happy as he was that she had decided to join him, he was concerned that she wasn't on a leash. This meant he had virtually no control over her. Erik continued to try and coax Tinka into the leash, but she always stayed just out of his reach. One time when he got a little too close, she gave him a low, throaty growl.

He gave up. "All right, have it your way."

Erik continued, hoping that she would stay close and not go running off.

The road went back and forth in a series of tight switchbacks. Erik grew increasingly concerned that something might happen to her—there were not too many cars, but the turns all had blind spots.

Tinka kept wandering off, and much of the time he didn't know where she was. Halfway down the mountain road, he heard a loud car horn and the sound of screeching tires. He froze, praying that Tinka wasn't the cause of the ruckus. He ran toward the sound, his heart in his throat.

Rounding the corner, he saw Tinka laid out on the side of the road and a young man standing by his car in near hysteria. Erik ran up to Tinka and saw that her leg was bent grotesquely, clearly broken. She had been hit. He crouched down by her and reached out his hand to comfort her. She growled and snapped at him.

In English, Erik asked the man to please call the police or an ambulance. The man understood and took off in his car. Erik cautiously sat down near Tinka, speaking gently to her, trying again to pet her. She snapped at him even more fiercely.

What the hell! It's like she's blaming me for getting hit! She doesn't need to do that—I already blame myself.

Erik agonized through the longest twenty minutes that he could ever remember, feeling intense remorse. The smell of burnt rubber lingered longer and more acridly than he deemed necessary. At long last, an ambulance arrived, and two paramedics stepped out with a stretcher. Erik watched in utter uselessness as Tinka was lifted without complaint onto the stretcher.

Clearly, Tinka has it in for me. Not sure what I did—or didn't do—but dogs are supposed to be able to tell the good guys from the bad guys. They're supposed to have a sixth sense. I'm just going to have to be patient and hope that she comes to realize that I'm not the enemy. In the meantime, what the heck am I going to say to the Åstergards?

The Åstergard parents didn't appear to be overly concerned about Tinka and were more worried about Erik. Mr. Åstergard, being a doctor, was used to broken bones and knew that Tinka would be all right. The kids took it hard, especially Morten, the youngest.

Overall, the family couldn't have been more gracious to him. They were letting him stay, they were feeding him, and they didn't ask for a dime. In return, Erik took Tinka for a walk and got her leg broken.

Now that the three-month period of his Student Rail Pass had begun, he wanted to squeeze as much mileage out of the pass as possible. Erik let Fru Gullestad know that it was his intention to visit all the major theaters in Norway for his college report. His next trip, he told her, would be to the Trøndelag Teater in Trondheim.

Fru Gullestad responded by offering to contact Kjell Sørhegge, who was an old friend and the artistic director at the Trøndelag Teater.

November 20, 1973

Tomorrow is the 21st and it's the first day of my Norwegian class. This week, I'm going to Trondheim to see their regional theater, "The Trøndelag Teater"— that is the way they spell theater—"Teater."

I've been trying to reach director Gustaf Husman to see if there will be a part for me in "The Wild Duck." He hasn't responded to my letter or the phone message I left him. Right now, however, I'm a little depressed. It has nothing to do with money or being lonely, which I'm not. I feel terrible knowing that I'm dependent on these good people. Mrs. Åstergard is very nice to me, almost too nice, like she is smothering me. Jens, that lucky guy, living in a cabin, being independent…

It's like I've got two mothers now. Just got a long letter from Mom. I understand she's worried—she doesn't want to lose another child—but giving me advice on how to live my life when I'm over here in Norway just pushes me away. I'm standing outside the nest, but I still can't fly.

I <u>must</u> get a part in either or both "Arturo Ui" and/or "The Wild Duck" so that I can move to Bergen and set up a place of my own. I don't care if I must borrow money—I'll gladly go in debt so that I may have my freedom. I'm grateful to Jens for leaving his guitar and his record player here in his old room. I'd be climbing the walls without them.

Erik booked the Friday night train to Trondheim:

November 24, 1973

Morning. Trondheim. Just arrived. Took a sleeper again. Best way to travel! Right now, it's 8AM and it's still nearly pitch-black outside. What a peculiar feeling. The sky above is black and the sky to my right is bluish and, on the horizon, it turns to green. I'm sitting in the train station café eating some gruel known as "rødgrød med fløde" which means red porridge with crème. My hair is getting long. I shaved my beard while in Demark. Glad I did, but I think I'll keep the mustache for a while.

Looking forward to walking about and seeing the town of Trondheim and the "Trøndelag Teater."

Thrilled that finally I have started my "Norsk" class!

Kjell Sørhegge greeted Erik warmly but had his hands full with a laundry list of details in running a theater. He told Erik he was welcome to stay for as long as he liked and see their current production. Shortly, an assistant to Dr. Sørhegge joined them and offered to take Erik for a tour of the theater.

Both Dr. Sørhegge and his assistant had a reserved air about them, as if they were holding back something. Erik was growing accustomed to this "Norwegian reserve." A picture of the Norwegian psyche was emerging in his mind. "Hold the emotions in check, listen first, speak second, keep your own council, take it on the chin, suffer in silence."

Is this me? Am I like this?

He hadn't noticed this characteristic so much with the Swedes or the Danes. The subtle albeit rigid differences that could exist within these three intertwined and adjacent countries were fascinating.

Erik's knowledge of his Jewish ancestry came from his mother's side of the family and was threadbare at best. The story begins on August 2, 1492, the day before Christopher Columbus set sail for the New World. That was the day when the Jews living in Spain were forcefully expelled from the country.

The slimmest minority of these expelled Jews ended up in Norway, where anti-Semitism was prevalent. It was only through a royal dispensation that these Sephardic Jews, as they were known, were allowed to stay; all other Jewish sects were denied permission to settle.

Apparently, a small group of these Jews settled in the Vestland region near the Sogndal area along the Sognefjord. Any direct knowledge of the lineage ends there. It's assumed that over the centuries, this community of Jews assimilated into the local population.

Erik's rumored Sámi heritage was equally sketchy, but Erik's father's mother swore that the connection was rock solid. She used to hear stories from her grandmother about their Sámi ancestor, who tired of the nomadic life and settled first in Narvik and then in Bodø and eventually in Trondheim, where he became a fisherman, married, and started a family.

Erik asked the administrative assistant how big the Sámi population was in Trondheim. "Sámi?" the assistant seemed surprised with the question. "Well, I suppose we have more Sámi in Trondheim than any other city. At least any city south of here. Why do you ask?"

"Just curious about your indigenous populations. How integrated are the Sámi?" asked Erik.

"I wouldn't know and I don't know of any Sámi here at the theatre. Come on, I'll show you around."

Erik quickly surmised that the assistant had zero interest in the geographic permutations of the Sámi population in Norway and subsequently stuck to asking him questions about the theater.

One interesting fact that Erik learned was that the artistic directors were not wholly free to decide the roster of plays for each season. There was also a board made up of citizens and government officials that had a say. Box office was important, but not to the extent that it's customary in the US.

The Trøndelag Teater was built in 1816, making it the oldest Norwegian theater in continuous use. The World War II occupation of the country by the Nazis was bitterly resented and left deep scars that are still felt to this day. Erik pressed the assistant on how the war had affected the Trøndelag Teater. Evidently it played a symbolically significant role.

Henry Gleditsch, the Trøndelag Teater's artistic director during the occupation, did everything he could to mount productions that ridiculed and satirized the Germans and their *Wehrmacht machine*. Eventually, Josef Terboven, the German commissioner based in Trondheim, had Gleditsch executed for his open defiance.

The fact that the Berliner Ensemble was coming to Bergen to perform *Arturo Ui* was a significant event in the relations between Germany and Norway. After thirty years, many of the Norwegian people still had deep emotional scars and harbored resentment toward the Germans for the years of occupation during the war.

Because it was Saturday, the theater wasn't busy. Many departments were closed. In Erik's experience, the American theater had no respect for weekends. Every theater he had ever worked in had been in full production mode, whether it was a Saturday, Sunday, or Groundhog Day—especially if they were getting ready to premiere a production.

"Our current production is *Oh What a Lovely War*. Are you familiar with the play?" asked the assistant. "We've got a fabulous production. It takes place in England, and it's a satire—a musical satire about the horrors of the First World War. Of course, you can draw parallels to Vietnam. It's quite clever. Kjell said you're welcome to see the play tonight."

After the tour, Erik left the theater and walked back over to the restaurant located at the train station. *I'd like to see the play; it'll be interesting to see how they skewer America for its participation in the war. Still, hanging around the theater over the weekend is pointless—everything is closed and nobody's there.*

For kicks, Erik looked at the train schedules on the big board. A trip up north to Bodø caught his eye. Now there's an interesting thought—a trip up into the Arctic Circle. *It's a nine-and-a-half-hour trip—when will I ever get another opportunity to go this far north?* The train was scheduled to leave that evening and arrive in Bodø early the following morning.

Erik contemplated his options. I'm not going to see anything resembling the inner workings of the theater until Monday. *That means hanging out here all weekend with nothing to do—and paying for two nights at a hotel for the privilege. On the other hand, my rail fare is already paid for. All I have to pay for is a sleeper berth to and from Bodø. I'd be back at the Trøndelag Teater first thing Monday morning, and by then it should be* bustling with activity.

Erik decided to take the train trip to Bodø.

Sleeper berths were so much better than a hotel, and they rocked you to sleep. You woke up refreshed in the morning in a completely new city—it was like a horizontal elevator. Also there was something exotic about meeting and talking to people on trains. Especially in Europe and particularly on sleepers. Something about this combination seemed to inspire conversation in one's fellow travelers.

Erik craved conversation. When he was alone, especially at night, his mind would often wander into hellish swamps where Charlie might have been trapped, unable to extract himself. Feeling Charlie's anguish, Erik would force his mind to engage in fanciful adventures, such as picturing himself as a passenger on the Orient Express, imagining who might be the guilty murderer. Or pretending that he was James Bond in *From Russia with Love*. Robert Shaw could be lurking anywhere, waiting to ambush him for a fight to the death.

November 24, 1973

Evening. Actually, early morning on the twenty fifth. On the night train once again, this time to Bodø! It's inside the Arctic Circle, and it's the furthest north I'll ever have been. And to go there this time of the year! So glad I got this rail pass! This is freedom!

On Monday morning, I'll be back at the Trøndelag in Trondheim. During the day, I'll watch a rehearsal for their next production, and in the evening, I'll see their current production of "Oh What a Lovely War." A British play but will be in Norwegian, of course. Wonder how much I will understand?

Making headway with theater assignment. Have sent several letters to Jack Addison about my progress, but so far—no word back.

As for photography assignment, don't know how I'm going to develop all the pictures I'm taking. I have no idea where I can get access to a darkroom, but I can't wait for the folks to see some of these great shots I'm getting on Dad's old Pentax!

Bodø was different from any place Erik had ever been. Like a frozen ghost town. Cold, somber, windy, and practically deserted. He found a café near one of the docks. He tried ordering a coffee in Norwegian but messed it up when the clerk asked a question he didn't understand.

If anyone thought it strange that he took his coffee outside into the frigid darkness and sat facing the Norwegian Sea by himself, they didn't let on. He put a celebratory pinch of tobacco in his pipe and jotted a few notes in his journal.

> *Bodø is situated just north of the southern arc of the Arctic Circle. With this extreme weather, any lake in Minnesota would have been frozen solid by this time. Instead, here the sea is surging and churning as if it were the confluence of two or more mighty rivers. The warm Atlantic currents and the depth of the ocean in this area keep the waters ice-free year-round.*

Erik spent the day wandering around. It was Sunday, and everything was closed except for a few restaurants. He was trying to stretch his limited budget, so he mostly drank tea and ate day-old bread. Coffee in the morning, tea the rest of the day. A used tea bag may yield up to three or four cups.

The melancholy sky rarely allowed more than a shadow of light to enter its domain. The external darkness seemed to match Erik's internal mood. He burrowed deeper inside his coat as he walked back to the café near the dock. Blue-black clouds traversed the weltering skies, suggesting the coming of a williwaw—a violent squall that frequently blows in these near-polar latitudes.

The majestic site was stimulating and made him feel small and vulnerable, yet excited at the same time. He visualized himself as the subject in a Winslow Homer painting, a solitary fisherman caught in a churning sea, straining against his oars, trying to make land before the storm releases its full fury. Kith and kin still miles and hours away, anxiously awaiting his return with whatever he had been able to pull from the deep—the fruit of his labors. How humbling and inspiring the tempests of these northern climes were. Erik was glad that he would soon be burrowing into the bunk of a southbound train but grateful that he had had this experience.

He could understand how people who lived here might get depressed or moody after a couple of months of perpetual darkness, yet at the same time he challenged himself to look for extraordinary items within the ordinary.

Really isn't survival just a matter of how one looks at life? Folks up here are said to drink a lot. If that's true, why? Why not find a way to enjoy the perpetual night? Was this not balanced on the scales against the perpetual sunlight during the other half of the year?

He made some more entries in his journal.

I wish I had some drawing talent so I could accurately capture this scene and illustrate the power it possesses—like the artists in the National Gallery.

I wish I could compose music that could capture the feelings engendered by these turbulent waters. Like Edvard Grieg.

I wish I could capture the lives of the people who live here and fight to eke out a living. Like Henrik Ibsen. That would be a worthy existence.

They say the Swedes drink more than the Norwegians. Most likely a Norwegian said that. He laughed at the remembrance. The butt of every "Scandinavian" joke told back in Minnesota depended on whether you were hearing it told by a Norwegian or a Swede.

Had someone inside the restaurant been watching Erik through the window, they might have thought he was crazy. Or dismissed him as an eccentric American. Or perhaps they just thought of that old axiom that youth is wasted on the young. To an outside observer, the kid would seem to be enjoying himself a bit too much.

Oh, the "subtle but rigid" differences between the Scandinavians, mused Erik.

The Swedes dress for fashion; the Norwegians dress for the weather. Not sure how the Danes dress. I guess they just dress for work.

He mused awhile on his Swedish and Norwegian lineage, wondering which was more prominent. The more he got to know these quiet, reserved, stubborn, and practical Norwegians, the more he came to understand some of the puzzlement he had over his own dichotomous nature of being both reserved and brash.

Back in Trondheim on Monday, refreshed after a good night's sleep on the train, he checked "visiting the Arctic Circle" off his to-do list. He was getting to know Norway a little better each day.

Erik eagerly showed up for the morning rehearsal. *It feels good to be back in a rehearsal space, even if I'm not one of the actors rehearsing.*

Although polite, the actors basically ignored him. He could have been a set piece. Erik wasn't anywhere near fluent in Norwegian, but he was getting better at picking out words and sentences.

After the rehearsal, he wandered around the theater, trying not to get in anyone's way. As he walked down one corridor, he heard guitar music coming from an open room and he poked his head in. A young man, sitting in the room alone, was playing "Angie," by the Rolling Stones, on an acoustic guitar, and he was doing a damn good job. Every bit as good as Keith Richards.

Erik smiled and waved at him. The man ignored him and just kept playing. *Hmmm, must be the Norwegian way of greeting someone who smiles at you.*

He ran into the assistant from his previous visit. "Oh, there you are," the assistant said. "I heard you were in the building. I can take you to some of the departments that were closed on Saturday."

As they talked, Erik was thinking about how he would structure his theater report. *In Norway*, he would write, *the degree of state sponsorship may have a deleterious effect on the overall condition of the art produced. In the United States, the "survival of the fittest" atmosphere that pervades the art must certainly produce a wilder, edgier product. Theater here seems "safer." In America, there's no safety net and the game is riskier.*

The assistant took him to the costume shop, where several seamstresses were bent over their sewing machines. Erik greeted the ladies with his embryonic Norwegian. They looked up, smiled, and then went back to work. The costume shop visit was a short one.

The assistant then took him to the set design department, which also had been closed on Saturday. There he excused himself and handed Erik off to a man named Alistair, who was a visiting designer, on loan from the Den Norske Opera & Ballett in Oslo.

Erik introduced himself to the man, gave his two-minute spiel about who he was and what he was doing in Norway, and then got ready for the man to excuse himself so he could get back to his design work.

Instead, the man stopped what he was doing and asked Erik questions. "Why Norway? Why theater? Why, in God's name, this theater way out in the hinterlands? Where did you come from? What are your goals?" On and on. He never stopped asking Erik questions.

Alistair was the only person Erik had met in Norway, aside from those with an assumed fiduciary responsibility to him, like the Åstergards or Fru Gullestad, who seemed to truly take an interest in him. Erik was happy that finally someone was not just being polite and waiting for an opportunity to beat a hasty exit.

His name was Alistair Wilderman, born in Scotland, trained as a director, designer, and costumer in England, Germany, and Poland. He was probably in his thirties and had come to Norway in 1967 as an assistant set designer for the Den Norske Opera & Ballett. By 1973, he was the chief designer and was frequently called upon to offer his services to various other theaters around the country, such as this visiting designer position at the Trøndelag Teater.

The man was a tour de force. Fluent in five languages, in demand all over Norway, his set drawings and costume drawings were already hanging in at least one museum. Creativity seemed to pour out of every pore of his body. And he was humble, down to earth, and he sat with Erik for an hour talking to him as if Erik was the most important and talented actor who had ever set foot in the Trøndelag Teater.

Alistair said Erik must come and visit him at the Oslo Opera House, the home for Den Norske Opera & Ballett. Alistair would get Erik in to see the operas and ballets currently in production or in rehearsal. Moreover, Alistair said he had a photographer friend that might be able to loan Erik photo-developing equipment for his photography assignment.

Erik's brain was spinning when he left the Trøndelag Teater that night. He felt as though finally he was starting to get somewhere. Even if he hadn't secured a part in *The Wild Duck* yet, he had a chance to talk with someone about the play. An insider. Someone who understood and seemed to genuinely care.

Erik's spirits were soaring, and he was excited to get back to Oslo and continue learning the language and push forward. He made some notes in his journal.

> It's about 1AM. Am on the night train, heading back to Oslo. Can't sleep. Too excited. I love being on the train at night. I have the room to myself. It's never hard to get a berth on the night train. I have the light on and am writing on my bunk. There's a little "water closet." They don't have stuff like this in America.
>
> I need to develop my mind. I need to gain knowledge. I need to read and study. I'm absorbing this stuff easily now. It's not a chore for me, like it was at St. Cloud College. I had just gotten burned out. Now I'm burning to learn. What does the future hold for me? I don't know what's going to become of the situation at the Åstergards' because it's very difficult for me to live off them, and they expect nothing in return. But if I'm fortunate enough to secure a job, that will change everything.

Back in Oslo, Erik was getting seriously frustrated with not hearing back from Gustaf Husman.

Director Gustaf worked at a TV station. *Maybe my letters never got through?* Erik wrote and called several more times. No luck. Husman's secretary was polite enough, but the man was never available. Erik didn't want to be a nuisance, but he also wanted the job.

Erik poured himself into his Norwegian class. Every evening, when they ate dinner, he encouraged the Åstergards to speak Norwegian so that he could listen and try and understand. They were patient with him. He told Jens's father how badly he wanted to learn the language. Øystein simply said, "You will." His calm reassurance was comforting.

Øystein was the same age as Erik's father, and like his dad, had served his country against the scourge of the Axis powers. During the German occupation of Norway, which began in April 1940 and lasted throughout the war, Øystein was arrested and put in prison, as were many of the Norwegian soldiers. The despised traitor, Vidkun Quisling, who was officially in charge during the occupation years, supported these imprisonments.

Erik's dad spoke little about his time in the service, and Erik didn't ask nearly enough questions. Now he wanted to know everything. One night after dinner, Erik, Øystein, and his wife, Tove, talked long into the night.

Erik learned that the Scandinavian countries struggled to remain neutral as the Nazi menace grew. Norway, however, was in the crosshairs of Grand Admiral Erich Raeder, commander of Germany's Kriegsmarine. Germany desperately needed a continuous supply of the rich iron ore that was mined in neutral Sweden. Since the Baltic route was effectively cut off by ice in the winter months and by the British naval barricades during the rest of the year, the only other way to get the iron ore was through Norway.

The iron ore was carried by rail to the northern port of Narvik—north of Bodø—and then shipped down the western coast of Norway along what was called the Norwegian Corridor, a continuous chain of some fifty thousand glacially formed, small, uninhabited islands running parallel to the shore. Germany hauled the iron ore down this corridor in ships designed specially to navigate shallow waters.

The Nazis were hated in Norway. A bitter pill for a nation that had Viking blood in its veins to submit to the Third Reich. The scars left behind from the Nazis were deep and, for many Norwegians, especially those of Øystein and Tove's generation, deeply personal. Erik came to understand this better as he got more involved in the people, culture, and language of Norway.

Erik's Norwegian class had a mix of students from different countries. There was a guy from Morocco who spoke no English, so their only common language was Norwegian. Other students hailed from France, Pakistan, Germany, Lithuania, England, and Burundi.

The Norwegian classes took place in the evenings on the campus of University of Oslo. Erik felt guilty hanging out at the Åstergards' all day, so he took the morning train to Oslo and spent the days exploring the town and visiting museums, old churches, coffee shops, and theaters and studying at the public library. This became his daily routine.

The library had an entire section of books in English, including translated works of Pär Lagerkvist and Sigrid Undset—the very authors that Dr. Maxwell had recommended that he read. The library also had many plays in English. Now that he was off life's merry-go-round, this was an opportunity to catch up, a chance to read and study without the pressure of having to do so just because of some curriculum.

The first item he read was *The Wild Duck*. At the same time, he checked out other plays by Ibsen, Brecht, Strindberg, and Chekhov, as well as stories by Hemingway, Steinbeck, Fitzgerald, and others. He also started researching the Vietnam War and how America got involved—something he should have done long ago.

Erik felt like he was the recipient of all the attention that the family couldn't give to Jens. Everyone's English was finely tuned because of the year they had spent in the States. Erik begged them to use as much Norwegian as possible around him.

Jens came around more often now that Erik was there. There were more family meals at which Jens was present. By now, Erik was convinced that Jens was not doing drugs anymore, but the schism that had developed between Jens and his family wasn't likely to end quickly or easily.

November became December, and Erik still hadn't heard from Gustaf Husman. *What is it with this guy? It can't be that he doesn't like me—he's never met me. Maybe he doesn't like Americans? Naw, he's probably just busy. After all, he's a friend of Fru Gullestad! I can't let this throw me off. I just have to keep trying to reach him.*

He took out his frustrations at Director Husman's silence by intensifying his daily letter-writing regimen. Erik's list included his sister, parents, Great-Aunt Lucy, an assortment of friends, college professors, Mette in Sweden, Anders Lundström in Sweden, Bob Keefendorf in England, Deuce, and the boys back at St. Cloud—pretty much everyone except Diana. Three or four letters a day, as well as journaling, reading, and studying.

In the middle of one letter to Lucy, as he was trying to explain the "Director Husman" situation to her, he realized that once and for all, he had to put an end to the madness of not knowing whether he had a part in *The Wild Duck*.

The next day, Erik caught the early train into the city, but this time instead of his usual routine, he walked to the TV station where Husman ostensibly worked. *I bet Husman doesn't really work here, it's undoubtedly just a ruse to keep me from finding him.*

The TV station was a large brick-and-concrete building with a busy reception area. The receptionist directed Erik to the executive offices. A secretary acknowledged Erik with a nod as he pushed through the glass doors. He waited for her to finish the phone call before he approached her tidy, crescent-shaped, mahogany desk. The phone never stopped ringing; she efficiently took six or seven calls while Erik waited.

When there was a break in the calls, she asked Erik in English, "How can I help you?"

How did she know to speak English to me? It was annoying. Why does this keep happening? Erik wondered if there was a flashing neon sign that hovered over him telling everyone that he was an American.

Erik said, "I'm here to see Director Husman."

"I see. He's not in now. Did you have an appointment?"

Before he could answer, the phone rang again. She held up a finger for him to wait. She fielded a few more calls. Erik stewed as he thought about the neon sign. Finally there was another break in the calls.

"No, I don't have an appointment, but it's rather urgent that I speak with him."

At that moment, a look of recognition skirted across her face. "Well, since it's urgent, you might find him in the cafeteria. Although," and she said this with a conspiratorial smile, "you didn't hear that from me."

He was prepared to wait all day if he had to, but he much preferred to get this resolved here and now.

He stood in the doorway of the busy cafeteria at the height of lunch hour. As one man was exiting the cafeteria, Erik asked if he knew Gustaf Husman. The man turned and pointed to a table in the center of the room.

"That's him sitting there."

He was eating by himself. Erik walked over to his table. Husman looked up.

"Are you Gustaf Husman?" Erik asked in English.

"Yes?" Husman answered in a way that asked, *And who might you be?*

Erik offered him his hand and a big smile. "I'm Erik Hellberg. It's great to finally meet you."

Director Husman didn't smile back. Erik was pretty sure that he had caught the director off guard. Director Husman recovered and mumbled an apology for being hard to reach. Said he had been busy.

"I'm excited to be in the play," Erik said.

"Well…it would only be a very small part."

"Oh, that doesn't matter. There are no small parts," Erik said smiling, "only small actors."

"Well, we couldn't pay you very much."

"That's fine. I didn't expect the pay would be much."

After a pause, the director said, "The rehearsals won't be starting until February."

"That sounds perfect."

Director Husman appeared to be searching for other excuses as to why Erik wouldn't want to be in the play.

The bird of silence flew over them.

Erik finally broke the silence and said, "I'm studying Norwegian. I'll be fluent by the time we start rehearsals."

Erik debated saying it in Norwegian, but what if Director Husman decided to switch the rest of the conversation to Norwegian and Erik couldn't keep up? *Better not risk it.*

Director Husman stared intently at Erik. His round-framed glasses and thick lenses gave him a Neil Simon-like aura. Was he wondering if this kid would cause him problems, if he would upset the balance of the tightknit family he'd undoubtedly assembled for *The Wild Duck*? Would he be a fly in the ointment? On the other hand, Gullestad had vouched for him, maybe she said the kid was clever. Clearly, whatever he was, he was persistent.

Director Husman looked at him long and hard and finally said, "Well, I suppose that would be all right."

Erik shook his hand again and thanked him. Then he got the hell out of there. He didn't want to give the director an opportunity to change his mind or come up with another excuse for why he couldn't be in the play.

With *The Wild Duck* in the bag, those black clouds that had been hovering over Erik lifted.

There was now an endgame to his stay with the Åstergard family, so he didn't have to worry that they were concerned there was no end in sight. There was a solid job offer on the horizon.

There was a connection, a link between him and Norway and its theater scene. He could now turn his attention to taking care of the things that mattered.

First, he needed to find Christmas gifts for each member of the Åstergard family—he needed to express in some meaningful way how grateful he was for their unselfish generosity.

Second, he had to get back to Sweden. How great it would be to see Anders and his pals in Stockholm and celebrate with them now that he had a job lined up. Then he would be on to Göteborg to see Anders's parents, followed by a rendezvous with Mette. *Ah, Mette.* He hadn't stopped thinking about her since he first laid eyes on her at the disco. *Exchanging letters doesn't cut it. I must see her again.*

Third, he had to take advantage of his Student Rail Pass and visit all the major theaters in Norway.

Fourth, he had to continue to learn Norwegian. He had to be fluent by the time he started rehearsals for *The Wild Duck*.

Finally, where would he live in Bergen? This had always been a vague concern in his mind, but with the shake of Director Husman's hand, the job became a reality, and all details became a priority.

He called Fru Gullestad, told her about his major coup. She was delighted. He was so grateful, and he had to lay every inch of this opportunity at her feet. *She has no idea the kind of impact this has had on my life.* Fru Gullestad agreed that he'd need to find a place where he could stay while in Bergen and offered to do what she could to help.

Erik was simply blown away. None of this could have been possible without the help of so many people. *I'm the luckiest kid in the world. I'm living with the Åstergard family, eating their food, and using their phone, and they haven't asked for a thing in return.*

And Charlie is dead.

It was an automatic reflex. Whenever things were going really great, he thought about how rotten and unjust things had been for Charles

Hellberg. It was inescapable. The bittersweet vicissitudes of life. He realized, in this moment, that Charlie would always be a nanosecond away from his thoughts, no matter where in the world he was. It was as though Charlie was closer to him now in death than he had been in life. As close as his own shadow, whether it was sunlight, moonlight, or no light. And it gnawed at him.

The kindness and friendship of Fru Gullestad and Alistair Wilderman also ate at him—like an unpaid promise. For the prospect of any hope of peace, he had to come up with appropriate gifts that would communicate how much all of them meant to him.

Christmas loomed ahead with all the promise and portent of an approaching iceberg. And with his prospects developing so fortuitously in Bergen, he'd better take his trip to Sweden now before his whole Norwegian adventure kicked into high gear and became a blizzard of activity.

He'd be traveling to Sweden now not as an idealistic dreamer but as one who had achieved a major goal that was recognizable in any society, in any language. He'd landed a job in his chosen field, a profession that was universally understood to be one of the toughest in which to make a mark.

Once Erik arrived in Sweden, he spent several days with Anders at his university in Stockholm. Anders was impressed that Erik had bagged the job in Bergen and said they would have to celebrate. Anders told all his friends about Erik's upcoming job at the theater in Bergen and generally made Erik feel like a superstar. At the same time, Erik was proud and impressed with Anders. He was a force majeure, on his way to becoming a doctor.

Anders was undisputedly the leader of his small group of friends, and he pulled Erik into the nucleus of the group. This was an eclectic bunch of eccentrics, and they readily accepted him as one of them.

There was a tennis player who was rising in the ranks and starting to make a name for himself. There was an SAS Airline steward named Gunnar who was racking up an impressive list of foreign destinations. He had the kind of vulnerable charm that made women want to take care of him. He reminded Erik of David McCallum in *The Man from U.N.C.L.E.*

There were several others, all of whom had the smell of success about them. Erik found it interesting that there seemed to be no homogeneity to the group. They all had diverse backgrounds, professions, and goals.

Anders pulled together a mini-celebration at a pub near the university, and the guys introduced him to the Swedish version of *akvavit*—a powerful spirit distilled from various grains or potatoes and flavored with a variety of spices. These guys seemed to have an unbelievable tolerance for copious amounts of *akvavit*.

"Danes are big drinkers—but not as big as the Swedes." The words of the woman in Århus who gave Erik a place to crash came back to him in this moment. *She was right about Swedes and drinking. And I hope she's forgiven me for eating all her fruit.*

From Stockholm, Erik took the train to Göteborg and stayed again with Anders's parents. They generously offered him Anders's old bedroom and communicated that he was welcome to stay for as long as he wanted. They made him feel like one of their own—a third adopted child.

As much as they put on a show of enjoying him staying with them, it paled in comparison to the way he felt about staying with them. More long walks with Herr Lundström around the city and more meals prepared with love by Fru Lundström.

After one memorable meal, which included *Svenska köttbullar* (Swedish meatballs) with *raggmunk* (potato pancakes fried in butter and mixed with a variety of meats), Colonel Lundström brought out some Schnapps and poured the liqueur into a beautiful set of tall, narrow military glasses. The good colonel said he'd been awarded these glasses after an arduous foreign cavalry campaign, and they drank to the health of the newly crowned King Carl XVI Gustaf.

The Schnapps burned Erik's throat as it slid down into his esophagus. Colonel Lundström refilled the glasses, and they drank to the health of Queen Silvia. Then they drank to Crown Princess Victoria. With every skoal, the good Colonel refilled their glasses. A toast to Sweden itself, followed by a toast to America and its participation in World War II. Finally, they drank to the health of Anders and his sister and then to Erik in his travels and studies.

In the Lundström's newspaper, he found that *The Sunshine Boys* was currently playing at the Göteborg Stadsteater. Erik called Mette to see if she'd like to see a play. He'd never seen the play himself, but Neil Simon was one of the hottest and funniest writers going. How can you go wrong with a Neil Simon comedy? He knew he wouldn't understand much of what was being said, but he also knew that wouldn't matter.

Mette and Erik arrived at the train platform in Göteborg at approximately the same time. Despite the cold, it was an enjoyable, invigorating walk to the Stadsteater. Surprisingly, their seats were good ones, even though the theater was nearly full, and he'd only purchased the tickets yesterday.

He could tell that Mette was enjoying being at a live theatrical event. Maybe it was the first time she had been to a professional play performance. The other patrons all seemed to be in a good mood, and it was fun to listen to preperformance chatter in Swedish.

The Sunshine Boys was a laugh fest. Simon's physical shtick translates well. He could tell Mette genuinely enjoyed it. Much of the humor was broad and no comprehension of language was necessary. He didn't catch every joke, but he got many of them.

It was more important to him that Mette enjoyed herself. Throughout the play, if there was a setup that needed explanation, Mette would whisper it to him. He found it an ironic twist that a Swede was interpreting an American playwright's play to an American.

After the play, they walked the streets of Gothenburg until they found a suitable restaurant. It was cold outside, and it was good to sit down in the warm and cozy atmosphere.

Once their food had been ordered, Erik again found it a challenge to communicate. He recognized that they both were limited in expressing or understanding each other within the confines of their language limitations. Still, they soldiered on. As the conversation lagged, she absentmindedly doodled on her napkin. And there it was, the undeniable expression of her inherent artistic ability. This was a confirmation to him that such things as auras do exist. The aura flowed from her.

"Look at this," he said picking up her napkin. "In less than ten minutes, you were able to draw this, yet you've captured the essence of both of us in this drawing. You didn't even seem to be concentrating while you were drawing."

"It's nothing," she said. "Just doodling."

If I worked at it all night, Erik thought, I could never draw anything that came close to expressing what exists in this doodle.

The drawing was not a caricature—it was a stylized representation of the two of them. There were no wasted lines. Each stroke of her pen was filled with meaning.

"Do you know what a gift this is that you have?" Erik said. "Look, I can tell what these people in your drawing are feeling—even what they're thinking."

Mette shrugged off the compliment, but Erik could tell that she was aware that her gift was central to her purpose in life. Perhaps this is the reason she was sitting here with him now. She must have known that Erik recognized the artist in her that night when they first met at the disco, even amid all the noise and flashing colored lights.

What is it with artists? How is it possible to look at someone and simply know they're talented before they've even said a word? Was it something in their eyes? Was it their appearance when perceiving the world around them?

And why am I drawn to such people? Mette is strikingly beautiful, but that's only part of it. No, the attraction has an internal quality, something that exudes from her. Mette told Erik that she'd been drawing and painting ever since she could remember. She said that drawings and paintings were her way of talking.

That night in the disco, the voice… It was real… I was powerless to ignore it. Maybe our meeting had nothing to do with me and it really had more to do with her. Here was evidence of a force that existed outside of himself that was interested in minute details about not just his life but also the lives of others with whom he came into contact. Just because you love some of the paintings in the National Gallery doesn't mean you have to own them.

It was amazing how art could transcend barriers. Mette could no more have suppressed the art within her than a songbird could have withheld its song. Erik could have sat there all night, but they were out of time. He walked her to the train station. This time he kissed her, and she kissed him back. Then they hugged and held the embrace for a long time. In that moment an internal paradigm shift occurred within Erik.

As he watched the train disappear into the night, Erik admitted that he had wanted her—she was beautiful and fascinating—but at the same time he was overcome with the realization that she was not to have that kind of role in his life. *Fantasy time is over Erik. She lives in Sweden. You are about to move to Bergen. You have a job there. It's going to take everything you've got. You've already made your choice, now you have to go and live it. Looks like saying yes to one thing means saying no to something else.*

Erik's days in Oslo were numbered now, and he wanted to make the most of them. First, he needed to become fluent in Norwegian before the start of rehearsals—an impossible goal, but he had to try. Second, he wanted to show his appreciation to the Åstergard family for taking him in the way they did.

He worried about Jens. Erik had hardly spent any time with him at all, except when Jens was helping him get situated in Norway or stopping in occasionally for dinner. He had to do something for Jens, somehow demonstrate or instill in Jens the knowledge that he mattered, that his life had value and worth.

Erik also had a to-do list of local places he wanted to visit: Vigeland Park, the Munch Museum, the Akershus Fortress, the Viking Ship

Museum, and the Fram Museum, and he especially wanted to take up Alistair Wilderman's offer to visit the Opera House.

Fortunately, Alistair was back in Oslo for his ongoing projects with Den Norske Opera & Ballett. Rehearsals for both opera and ballet were ongoing, and both the opera and ballet companies were frenetically busy. The Oslo Opera House seemed way too small to contain all the activity going on inside.

In his twenty-one years, Erik had seen exactly one opera: *Carmen*. It was an enlightening experience, but when Alistair brought Erik into the Opera House auditorium, he watched an opera being created in front of his very eyes. Rehearsals were early in the creative process, and clearly many aspects of the production were not going well.

Den Stundesløse was a new opera by composer Edvard Fliflet Bræin, based on a play by Ludvig Holberg. This was to be a world premiere, and people were nervous. Even an opera neophyte like Erik knew this one had major issues. Tempers would at times flair on stage, Alistair was in and out of his seat as requests or demands upon his time were made.

"Change of plans," Alistair announced to Erik as he returned from a heated exchange with the director. "Let's go watch the ballet rehearsal. Much more interesting."

Erik had been around enough theatrical productions to know that was a euphemism for "We're in trouble. We need to close ranks and get all visitors the hell out of the house."

The two men walked through an underground hallway and then took stairs up to a third-floor dance hall, where a large group of dancers were having warm-ups. There were about thirty dancers in the room, each of them doing various kinds of warm-ups. Some dancers were stretching, some practicing dance steps in the middle of the floor.

"I'm going to park you here for a while, if you don't mind. I'll be back as soon as I'm able."

It was clear to Erik that Alistair had his hands full. "Don't worry," he said to Alistair. "I'm fine here. Take care of whatever you need to."

Most of the dancers were girls, and some of them were exceedingly attractive.

Erik found an empty metal chair, spun it, and sat in it backward facing the dancers. A woman was playing a piano in one corner of the room, and several dancers were moving to the melody she was playing. Mirrors covered the entire room. Jutting out from the mirrors, about three feet off the floor, ran a wooden railing.

A small, stately woman entered the room, and immediately all talking ceased and the dancers took a position at the railing, which Erik soon learned was called a "barre." The piano player changed melodies, and the stately woman began calling out instructions to the dancers.

The dancers moved as one. Clearly, these were moves each of them had practiced many times—hundreds of times, to judge from their flexibility and commitment to the moves. Erik watched with fascination as each dancer moved with an enviable grace and fluidity. As a gymnast, he could relate to the effort it took to get into the kind of shape that these dancers were in.

It was inspiring to watch. Dancers had such discipline and commitment. Some of the ballerinas seemed so light and petite, yet they had incredible strength. He wanted to be out there with them.

After half an hour or so, the music stopped and the dancers took a break. A few of them left the room, but most of them stayed and continued to stretch or move about, chatting with each other or practicing dance sequences.

One of the female dancers approached Erik. He'd noticed her glancing at him a few times—or maybe it just seemed that way to him because he couldn't stop watching the way she moved. All the dancers were good, but she fairly floated in comparison to the others. Her body was freer, looser, lighter, more agile, and nimble. She possessed an infectious joy about her as she danced.

The young woman spoke to Erik in Norwegian, but she had a foreign accent. Russian, he guessed.

"I'm sorry, I don't understand," he said.

"Ah," she said in English. "You are American, not Norwegian?"

Erik smiled. *Finally, someone who doesn't automatically assume I'm American.* "Yes," he said.

"Ah, then I was correct in thinking it is so. But you are watching dancers? I am asking if you are dancer?"

"'Fraid not. I'm a gymnast, but ballet looks like a lot of fun."

"Ballet needs strong men," she said. "They must have strength to lift female dancers."

Erik noticed that the male dancers in the studio didn't appear to have overly developed upper torsos.

"I see you come into dance room with *scenografen* Alistair Wilderman." This was a statement, but she said it like she was asking him a question.

"He's a friend. I met him at the Trøndelag Teater in Trondheim. He invited me to tour the Opera House."

"Ah, you are singer too?"

He laughed. "I wish. No, I'm an actor. A student, well, I'm here as a student, but I'm also acting."

Nice job, Erik. Way to be clear and concise. Admittedly, he was a little flustered. She had him a little off balance.

"So you are actor and gymnast and you like ballet, yes?"

Her name was Nina, and she was born in Ukraine and then moved to Moscow to continue with her ballet studies. Her body was lithe and whisper thin but incredibly toned. After she sustained an injury, the Soviet Union granted her a visa to teach ballet in Norway. Now she was one of the principal dancers here and continued to teach classes.

The stately woman came back into the room and clapped her hands twice.

"Ah, we are starting now our rehearsals for ballet," said Nina. "You are welcome to watch. Maybe sometimes you come and do warm up at barre with us, yes?"

"Yes, I would like that."

"I think you are strong and will lift the girls."

Erik assured her that he could lift the girls. The rehearsal began in earnest, and Erik sat back in the chair and enjoyed watching the dancers.

Sitting on the commuter train that night, heading back to the Åstergards' in Kolsås, he savored the sweet moments at the dance studio. Speaking with that ballerina, watching the dancers, seeing the strength and control they possessed. It was wonderful. This was something he wanted to incorporate into his acting, a power he wanted to possess. He vowed to do just that, somehow, someway, someday.

Finding just the right Christmas gifts—an opportunity to express his gratitude to the Åstergard family and for friends like Alistair Wilderman and Fru Gullestad weighed heavily...

December 22, 1973

> On train to Lillehammer. Hoping to find unique gifts for the Åstergards, Alistair, and Fru Gullestad. While there, I want to visit the famous Lillehammer tobacco pipe factory.

A short walk from the train station, Erik stepped into the dollhouse town nestled between the toes of soaring mountains freshly covered in sparkling white blankets of snow. In 1844, a woodcarver named Gudbrand Larsen put Lillehammer on the map by starting a business there making tobacco pipes.

After shopping for Christmas gifts in the quaint little town, Erik had time for a meal in one of the local restaurants. He noticed another patron smoking a pipe, and they struck up a conversation. The man's face was weatherworn from a lifetime of eking a living out of the rocky soil in Lillehammer. His name was Hárno Niillas. Erik found him refreshingly friendly.

"Ya, dees are strange times ve living in. Only now are tings yust getting back to normal."

"Getting back to normal?" asked Erik.

"Val, ze Lillehammer Affair, av course."

"The Lillehammer Affair?" asked Erik.

"Ya, yust this summer, Israeli Mossad assassinate ze wrong man here in Lillehammer."

On seeing Erik's blank face, the man continued, "You know ze massacre last year at Olympics in Munich?"

"Of course," Erik said. "Black September."

"Ya," said Hárno. "And Norwegian government granted political asylum to Ali Hassan Salameh, one of ze organizers of Black September. It vas rumor he vas hiding here in Lillehammer."

"Really? And was he?"

"Ya, at least for some time. Israeli Mossad agents got tip of thees and made ze raid. But they assassinate wrong man—a waiter who is Moroccan man. Ze Israeli agents are all arrested, and it brought many people and reporters for television to our small town. Very much big ting."

"Has Salameh been found?"

"Nei, as of this day, nei. He es known as 'Red Prince'—es still at large."

"Why did the Norwegian government grant asylum to Salameh if he was the leader of Black September?"

"Ya, is good question."

Erik had become so caught up in Hárno Niillas's story that he lost track of time. When he realized this, he said, "Yikes, look at the time. I have to hustle, or I'll miss my train." Erik cleared the ashes out of his pipe and hoisted the pack onto his back. He reached out his hand to thank Hárno for the conversation and for enlightening him about the Lillehammer Affair, but then Hárno stopped Erik in his tracks when he asked:

"Are you Sámi?"

Caught completely off guard, Erik said, "What? What prompted that? Why would you ask me if I am Sámi?"

"Because I am Sámi. I see Sámi in you," Hárno explained. "We are a people small in number but living many centuries in northern parts of Norway, Sweden, Finland, and Russian Kola. I am Sør Sámi in Trondheim, but these last years I am living in Lillehammer with wife and family. I see Sámi in your bones, your skin, your eyes, and in your voice. I think in your heart you are Sámi too. Is not so?"

"I can't believe this. I mean, I don't know if I am. I've always heard that we had Sámi ancestors, but I never knew if it was true. What is it in me that makes you think I'm Sámi?"

"I am living many years now. I know my people in some ways by seeing and talking with. The years cannot take all things that make peoples different. I think maybe you are Sámi too."

Erik would have loved to stay and talk with Hárno, but time was not on his side. He caught the last train out of Lillehammer and, once on board, made the following entry in his journal:

December 23, 1973

Norway is full of surprises. First, I just happened to strike up a conversation with some guy because he is smoking a pipe and I learn that a Mossad assassination took place right here in peaceful little Lillehammer. Then, it turns out the guy is a Sámi, and he thinks I'm Sámi too!!!—This cannot just be coincidence. Are you getting all this, Charlie? Dad and Grandma are going to be blown away when they hear this!

Back in Oslo, the Åstergards' Christmas was much like the American Christmases that Erik had encountered all his life. Under their Christmas tree Erik had placed a painstakingly researched present for each family member. The two presents that brought the most enthusiastic joy was the teapot Erik bought in Lillehammer for Tove Åstergard and the harmonica for Morten that Erik purchased in a music store in Oslo. Morten ran around the house blowing into the harmonica and shouting *"tusen takk, tusen takk"* (a thousand thanks, a thousand thanks.)

December 25, 1973

Christmas at the Åstergard house. Today we had a phone call with my family back home. We all shouted, "God Jul og Godt Nytt År!!" It was the first time we've spoken since I left the States.

Tove prepared a magnificent feast that rivaled any Christmas dinner that I have eaten back home. The Åstergards have a tradition of serving a special rice pudding for desert at the Christmas dinner. Whoever has the hidden almond in their pudding gets a special prize. This year it was little Morten. You'd have thought he won a trip to Disneyland!

December 26, 1973

Having Jens there made it feel like the family was complete once again. I think we all recognized it. Jens was relaxed and not in a hurry to leave. He stayed overnight—quite unusual.

The holiday season of 1973, from yuletide to Nytt År, served as a kind of demarcation point in Erik's development as an individual and as an actor.

December 27, 1973

Saw "Pat Garrett & Billy the Kid" with some class friends tonight. I was Disappointed. Sam Peckinpah has lost his touch. Both "The Wild Bunch" and "Straw Dogs" were thrilling and suspenseful, now Peckinpah is stooping to cheap tricks and theatrics. Movies here are subsidized with commercials. Strange, but good for the budget!

Erik was trying to stretch his *kroner* as far as possible, while at the same time getting out and expanding his sphere of influences, friends, and acquaintances as much as possible.

December 28, 1973

Incredible day. Went to see a lighting rehearsal for the ballet version of "Romeo and Juliet" at the Opera House.

Met Alistair's photographer friend, who has a darkroom right here in the Opera House. He said anytime I want to use it to develop pictures, I'm welcome. Good to know for the future when I'm ready to start developing photographs for my photography class.

Opening night of "Romeo and Juliet." No language barrier! Yea! Remarkable to see how the story translates to dance. What a revelation! I'm astounded the way movement and lighting can help tell the story! So inspiring!

Alistair invited me to the cast party afterward at someone's house close by. On stage the dancers exude power and grace. In street clothes, they seem slight in stature by comparison. Yet there's still that "presence" about them. They each seem to possess an inner strength and grace. I envy them. Would like to have that same discipline in my life.

Everyone spoke Norwegian. Mostly, I just listened. Picked up a bit, but the language was filled with art esoterica, so I had to really concentrate hard. Still a long way to go. Alistair is an amazing artist. Everything he touches is artistic, polished, and professional. I'm going to have to raise my game!

Alistair was going back to Trondheim to work on his design for *Måna for Misfarne* (*Moon for the Misbegotten*) by Eugene O'Neill. He was designing not only the set but also the costumes.

He invited Erik to the premiere and then to the annual New Year's Eve celebration at Kjell Sørhegge's house in Trondheim. This celebration had become almost institutional, and many of the major players of the Norwegian theater scene regularly attended.

"This will be a great opportunity for you to meet a lot of important and interesting people," said Alistair.

Erik's Student Rail Pass was still active, so the transportation to and from Trondheim would be free.

At this point, Erik was pretty sure that Alistair was gay. It didn't matter to him whether he was or wasn't. Alistair wasn't the first homosexual he had met. People are the way they are and, for whatever reason, there are a lot of homosexual artists and actors in the theater.

Erik knew that Alistair liked him, but he didn't know whether Alistair was attracted to him physically. Going to this New Year's party in Trondheim would mean Erik would be spending the night at Alistair's house—and this made him a little nervous. Alistair had always been kind, generous, and respectful toward Erik, but he'd never been completely alone with him—let alone staying overnight with him.

Clearly Erik was entering a brand-new world, one where who and what he knew was outweighed by who and what he didn't know. The relative comfort and confines of the college environment were nonexistent here. The safety wheels were off the bike. So far, Alistair was the only person in the world of Norwegian theater except for Fru Gullestad who cared a rip whether Erik even existed.

It wasn't that people were unfriendly, it's just that they were reserved. This often came off as indifference. Add the language barrier to that reserve or perceived indifference, and one starts to feel like they're standing outside looking in. Still, Erik was where he wanted to be, doing what he wanted to be doing. He knew there were challenges ahead; he hoped he was ready for them.

Early on Monday, December 31, Erik took the train to Trondheim. The trip took about six hours, and he arrived in the afternoon. Alistair picked him up at the train station, and the next twenty-four hours were like a bullet train through a cross section of the Norwegian theater scene. They stopped briefly at Alistair's townhouse to pick up a gift he'd left there for Kjell. Then on to the theater, where furious last-minute preparations were being made.

Erik hadn't read O'Neill's *Moon for the Misbegotten*—just one of the billions of things that he hadn't gotten to yet. One of his professors at St. Cloud College said they should read a play a day.

How does one do that? Maybe someone could do that occasionally if they didn't have anything else to do. Maybe someone could set aside one day a week or one day a month to read a play—but every day?

Unfamiliar with the play, and not speaking Norwegian, *Moon for the Misbegotten* made little sense to him. Once again, he felt underprepared for the course he was on. In the conversations during intermission and especially after the play with the assortment of people that Alistair was introducing him to, he felt like an outsider. Like being without a paddle in someone else's canoe on a foreign river, carried along in a rushing current, banging into rocks and debris, spinning, and turning toward an unknown destination.

Eventually, he knew he would find his paddle. Until then, he decided that he just needed to let go and enjoy the ride.

Just be yourself, Erik, and don't try and impress anyone. He had to keep repeating this mantra to himself over and over.

From all appearances, the dress rehearsal was a success. Everyone seemed to be enthusiastic and optimistic that the play would do well with audiences. The director, Sølve Cairn, called the actors into the auditorium for notes. Alistair, who was busy with details, suggested that Erik catch a ride with Kjell Sørhegge to Kjell's house, which Erik was happy to do.

It was snowing when they stepped out of the theater; tiny flakes were lightly dusting the night. Being outside in the brisk fresh air felt good.

Erik and Kjell were the first to arrive at the house. Kjell's house was festively decorated for the season. There were several women bustling about, getting the festal food ready. The house was large, well-lit, and smelled of cinnamon and nutmeg. There was a prodigious amount of food on a large, oak table in the center of a grand dining hall—a tableau worthy of a Viking feast. A separate table held a colossal samovar of spice-livened *gløgg*.

Aside from the main dishes, there were cheeses of every kind, with appropriate *osthøvels* (cheese cutters) for each variety. Norway was a large importer and exporter of *kaviar*, and consequently an assortment of it accented the table. Herring and other types of fish took up any remaining space on the main table, along with stacks of *flatbrød* (paper-thin "flat" bread), slabs of *smør* (butter), and jams from berries unknown outside of the Land of the Midnight Sun.

As he wandered about the dining room, looking at the pictures on the wall and all the evidence of a life spent in the theater, he kept repeating his mantra, *Just be yourself, Erik.*

Just then, Kjell walked up behind him and handed him a cigar and a mug of *gløgg*. In the quiet of this pre-party moment, the two men sat down in large chairs in a small area off the dining room and fired up the stogies.

This wasn't the first cigar Erik had ever smoked, but it was the first one that he smoked with an adult (as opposed to college kids) and the first one that hadn't been purchased in a corner drug store. The two gents set to discussing the wonders of winter, the warming effect of *gløgg*, the universal importance of smoking cigars, and finally the status of theater in Norway versus theater in the United States.

Kjell, who had seemed aloof and reserved when Erik met him back in November, was now freely conversing with Erik as though they were old chums. Maybe Erik had been too quick to judge. Maybe he needed to rethink the "Norwegian reserve" theory that he'd been cultivating.

What if Norwegians aren't reserved at all? What if it's me that's the problem? Maybe I'm just intimidated by these people? Is it possible that I have this all backward? Or maybe it's because I really do have Sámi heritage? Wouldn't that be a mindblower? I'm going to have to do some genealogical research on this.

Erik thought long and hard about this as the *gløgg* unlocked his inhibitions and the cigar smoke loosened his thickened tongue.

Americans in general are outgoing and friendly, quick to thrust out a hand and say "How are you? Great to meet you!" Erik was pretty sure this was a hallmark of his personality and the way he had been behaving throughout this trip. And Hárno Niillas, the Sámi in Lillehammer, had been pretty outgoing.

Stop trying to figure everything out, Erik finally told himself in exasperation. *Just be yourself.*

With that, he smiled at Kjell, raised his mug, and said, "Skoal for the success of *Måna for Misfarne* and for the coming season at the Trøndelag Teater."

It was allaying for Erik to start the evening off slowly like this, one on one with Kjell Sørhegge. As people from the theater began to drift in, Kjell introduced Erik to this person and then that person, and he enjoyed having bits and pieces of conversations here and there.

Document your observations and theories on the Norwegian psyche, Erik. Work it into your report on Norwegian theater. It will certainly be relevant if you can back it up with some academic research.

An endless stream of people began to pour into the house, and the dining room was soon overcapacity. The *gløgg* flowed freely. The language du jour was Norwegian. The topic was everything under the *måna*.

It all became a bit overwhelming, and Erik drifted off to explore the house. He opened a door that led into a den devoid of people. The room featured a large fireplace that was cold and empty.

Odd not to have a roaring fire on a night like this.

There was plenty of wood and kindling stacked on the hearth. Erik set to building a fire. At least this was something useful he could do. After making sure the flue was open; he coaxed a blaze to life, which quickly became ravenous. The once cold den became animated as firelight bounced off the pictures and memorabilia adorning the walls.

I wonder why Kjell closed this room off? Erik figured he had probably just broken some arcane Norwegian taboo as he stared into the fire and drained the last of his *gløgg*. Just then, Alistair walked in.

"Here you are! Kjell wasn't sure where you had disappeared to."

The two men talked about the party, the fire, the production of *Måna for Misfarne*, and other small talk, which dragged on lugubriously for several minutes and then simply dropped altogether like a lead weight off a snapped fishing line. The only sounds were the crackling and hissing of dry wood being consumed by a hungry fire and the muffled outbursts from outside the warmth of this womb-like den.

"I feel a need to tell you that I'm gay," Alistair stated rather abruptly. "But I want you to know that I didn't invite you here because of any designs or intentions or feelings I might have toward you."

Alistair's words articulated precisely the tension that Erik felt had been hovering in the space between them since their first meeting in November. He was glad Alistair had brought the subject up, thankful to be able to address it.

"I appreciate you telling me that." After an awkward pause, Erik said, "I'm not. I'm straight."

Erik immediately regretted saying that, not because it wasn't true but because it felt clumsy and insensitive. But he didn't know what else to say. He couldn't very well apologize for being straight. The moment was an uncomfortable one. Both men stared silently into the fire.

Finally, Erik said, "Alistair, I want you to know that I'm very grateful to you for your friendship. Your kindness has made such a difference in my life here. Both you and Fru Gullestad have been so kind and generous to me. I don't know what I—"

Just then, the door opened and the unabated cacophony from outside was loosed into the den. Sølve Cairn, the director of *Måna for Misfarne*, materialized in the doorway as though seeking sanctuary from the noise. She paused as if to assess the atmosphere in the room and then raised her stein and took a large draft of *gløgg*.

"*Ah, veldig vakker peis i peisen!* (What a beautiful fire in the fireplace!)" she exclaimed.

Alistair spoke in English. "Sølve Cairn, please meet Erik Hellberg, the director of the fire."

Sølve was comfortable in English and warmed immediately to Erik. She was evidently pleased with tonight's performance of *Måna for Misfarne* and in a loquacious mood. As she and Erik fell into an easy conversation, Alistair quietly slipped out of the room. Observing his silent departure, Erik felt a pang of remorse. He'd been honest, but he knew he'd hurt Alistair, and that was the last thing he wanted to do. Here was a man who was admired and loved by people all over Norway, yet the one thing he probably most wanted and needed, Erik was unable to give him.

By now, the house was packed—there were people everywhere, in every room. More people spilled into the den and others joined in on the conversation between Erik and Sølve, which eventually transitioned back into Norwegian.

Then, just as in so many American New Year's celebrations that Erik had participated in, someone announced that it would soon be 1974. Everyone crowded into the main room and the countdown soon began. At the stroke of midnight, horns and noisemakers blasted from every corner of the room. Everyone refilled their glasses and skoals, cheers and hugs reverberated throughout the room.

Erik was feeling the effects of the *gløgg*, and the room felt like it was spinning. He wandered into the garage where there was a spirited game of darts going on. He joined in and was grateful to have something to do that didn't involve discussing dramatic theory in a language he couldn't yet understand.

Erik felt a dichotomy of both wanting and not wanting the night to end. He was tired of trying to fit in as a stranger in a strange land, and at the same time he was concerned about going back alone with Alistair to his townhome.

Alistair had always been a gentleman and respectful toward him. Yet Erik felt outside of his comfort zone and overwhelmed by this foreign world he had stepped into and where he was now completely submerged. That he was nervous to be alone with Alistair in his townhome at night may have been foolish or naïve of him, but that was honestly what he was feeling.

It was after two o'clock in the morning when Kjell Sørhegge announced that he was tired and it was time for everyone to get the hell out of his house. Everyone laughed, and someone proclaimed that called for a final skoal. Many of the guests were still in a partying mood, and one man suggested that everyone head over to his house.

Alistair asked if Erik wanted to go. He didn't, but he said, "Sure, why not?" Erik wished he was back at the Åstergards' house. Still, this was where he was and now he had to deal with the situation at hand and make the most of it.

The partygoers stepped outside and encountered a gentle shower of big, fat snowflakes blanketing the sky and ground. The world resembled a giant, well-shook snow globe. It was so damn beautiful. The party remnant piled into a few cars and caravanned helter-skelter to the new host's house. No one was completely sober.

As they exited the cars and walked toward the house, Erik told Alistair that he needed to go for a short walk in the night air to clear his head. Alistair asked if he was okay. Erik said he was fine, just needed some fresh air after the *gløgg* and cigars and all the noise.

Erik disappeared into the snowy night. He didn't have a clue where he was, nor did he care. He needed to be alone and to stop his head from spinning. It was a magnificent night—morning really. Erik had witnessed hundreds—if not thousands—of snowfalls, and this one was by far the most dazzling one he'd ever experienced. It must have been about three or four o'clock in the morning, without a hint of dawn in the sky. And blissfully quiet.

It was January 1, 1974. He was somewhere in a suburb of Trondheim, Norway. His head was buzzing; the world was slowly spinning. The merry-go-round again. He was happy and sad at the same time. He wanted to get lost, which he most certainly was.

Erik walked for an hour until he became so drowsy that he needed to lie down. *If only I could close my eyes for just a few minutes…* Sleep would be heaven. He wasn't afraid of freezing, but he should have been. His brain was too addled to think clearly.

He came upon a house that had no lights. There was an alcove in front of the door with a bench. He sat down on it and then slumped over, finally curling up on the bench. His eyes were already closed; he didn't care what happened next.

Although his mind had shut down, his body felt as though he was back in the canoe getting pulled down the river. The miles he had traveled over the past months rushed past him as his canoe careened recklessly toward the rapids. He reached for his paddle, but it was gone. The waters around him got rougher and rougher. Huge boulders emerged unannounced, and suddenly a branch came out of thin air and slashed him like a frozen lash.

Erik's eyes popped open, suddenly wide awake. The sky had lightened up a notch and he sensed the night had lost its stranglehold on Trondheim. It felt like he'd broken the night.

How long had he been on the bench? No clue. Minutes? An hour? Couldn't have been too long. He stood up. Felt no frostbite on his fingers or toes, but he was cold to the marrow.

He began walking. His mind was remarkably awake. His headache had dissolved. Erik tried to piece together the last twenty-four hours. He was completely lost, a foreigner adrift in a sparkling universe of snowflakes as big as butterflies.

Erik hadn't been paying attention as they drove through the streets of Trondheim. He remembered Alistair picking him up at the train station, driving to Alistair's place to get the gift for Kjell, and then on to the theater. From the theater, Kjell drove Erik to the party. After the third mug of *gløgg*, Erik's world got hazy. Now he was utterly disoriented.

The sky was a shade lighter. A few dog walkers were out. No one paid any attention to Erik. One or two cars now on the road. Erik didn't have Alistair's address or phone number or anyone's phone number except the Åstergards', and what good would that do even if he could find a phone? Yet he wasn't panicked. He was cold, wet, hungry, tired, and strangely happy. He decided he would just keep walking. Once again, like in Århus, he relinquished the reins of control over his destiny.

Presently, he found himself standing in front of a row of buildings that seemed familiar. A series of townhomes. They looked a lot like the one that Alistair lived in. After scrutinizing them, he concluded that, amazingly, they were.

All the townhomes looked the same. He couldn't very well start knocking on doors. Erik noticed that one of the townhouses had a small candle on the stoop. Who sets a candle out on their stoop on a snowy night?

Erik knocked. A few minutes later Alistair opened the door.

"My God!" Alistair exclaimed. "Are you alright? Where have you been?! We were all worried sick about you!"

The thought that others might have been concerned hadn't occurred to Erik. He knew Alistair would have been, but the others were too drunk and didn't really know him anyway.

"Come in and get warm," implored Alistair. Such was his relief that it appeared he wanted to reach out and hug Erik, but then restrained himself. Instead, he just placed a hand on Erik's shoulder and guided him inside. "You must be completely exhausted. Would you like to lie down?"

"No, I'm fine. Really. I just need to thaw out a bit."

"You have no idea how worried I was. I'm just glad you're safe. My God, you look like the abominable snowman. You must be famished. Take your coat off. Can I make you some breakfast?"

"Food sounds great. Thank you." Erik removed his coat and took a seat at the table while Alistair fired up the coffee maker and started fixing a breakfast.

"Alistair, I'm truly sorry for causing you to worry. I shouldn't have wandered off like that. My head felt like a block of ice, and I couldn't thaw out my thoughts. I got completely lost, but the strange thing is, I didn't care. The sky was beautiful, the air fresh and clean, and it was quiet—like I was walking inside of a snow globe. Have you ever felt like you should be panicking, but instead you're completely calm? That you're happy and sad at the same time?"

"As a matter of fact, yes, I have, repeatedly. It is the reoccurring hazard of my life."

"I knew you could relate. I was… I've been… So much has happened lately. I've been struggling to process it all. I needed to get outdoors into the fresh air and away from everybody. I needed to be alone to clear my head."

Alistair smiled and shook his head. "You are so… Norwegian. There is a phrase they use here, and it fits you perfectly: "typisk Norsk." It means typical Norwegian. The search for your heritage is over my friend."

Maybe not, Erik thought, *I just met a man in Lillehammer who thinks I'm Sámi.*

Alistair brought two eggcups with hardboiled eggs and two plates, each containing a thick slice of dark German bread covered with butter and a dark brown cheese known as ekte geitost (pure goat cheese)—a delicacy available in Norway only during the holiday season. Then he set two cups of steaming coffee on the table and joined Erik.

Alistair said to Erik, "Vær så god" (be so good.)

"Takk" replied Erik, and the two men started eating.

When the food was gone, and they were sipping their coffee Alistair cleared his throat. "You know, Erik, I was afraid that the reason you walked off like that was because of what I told you about myself."

"No. Absolutely not. When I first met you Alistair, you were like a light in a long dark tunnel. Your friendship means the world to me. It's just that… everything is so… I don't know… Sometimes I feel like I've bit off more than I bargained for… No, I don't mean that. I'm thrilled

I'm here in Norway. I'm doing exactly what I want to do. Getting a part in *The Wild Duck*, seeing the dance production of Romeo and Juliet, meeting the dancers, seeing *Måna for Misfarne*, meeting the cast and the director, the New Year's party and sharing a cigar and a mug of gløgg with Kjell…"

"Erik, let me tell you something. You are going to be fine. You're not just some starry-eyed kid taking time off university. You're an artist. I knew it from the moment I first met you. You have an incredible future in front of you. What you are doing right now is exactly what you should be doing. Artists must follow their dreams. It's not easy and it's not supposed to be. Enjoy the process. Being an artist means being happy and sad at the same time—a lot."

The two men segued into a discussion about art, theatre, opera, dance, acting, designing, and especially about how stubborn Norwegians are. Hours ticked away like minutes and soon Alistair was driving Erik to the train station. Erik got his ticket for Oslo, and as he stood on the platform waiting for his train, he felt a renewed sense of purpose in all he was experiencing in Norway. He especially felt grateful to Alistair for his encouragement and his belief in him. Exhausted, Erik collapsed into his seat on the train, and, as always happened before he closed his eyes, his thoughts turned to his brother.

Charlie, I feel you looking out for me, and I want to thank you and tell you I miss you. I was scared up here in Trondheim. It seems foolish now, and I don't mind admitting that to you. Honestly, I don't know how you did what you did in Vietnam. What I'm going through here pales in comparison. Still, I wish it had been me, not you that went over there. Here I am experiencing all of these "life" things—the sweet and the sour—and you can't experience any of this anymore. It's not fair, I know it, I just wish I could talk with you again.

Erik drifted asleep and didn't wake until the train pulled into the Oslo station. A jolt of anxiety hit him as he thought about the role that he had been promised in *The Wild Duck* at Den Nationale Scene in Bergen this spring and everything he needed to do to get ready for the responsibility. Yet, as he walked toward the platform where he would catch the train for Kolsås, Erik thought about what Alistair had said. "You're an artist, I knew it the moment I first met you." As he remembered those words, his heart lightened and a bounce returned to his step.

When Erik originally signed up for Norwegian classes, the government clerk told him that once he had proof of employment, he could be reimbursed for his class. Not only that, but he could also take as many Norwegian language classes as he wanted, and the government would pay for them—so long as he was working. But Erik needed proof.

This meant getting an official document from Den Nationale Scene proving that he had been hired. This was too important a detail to handle over the phone or leave to someone else, so he booked a train to Bergen.

During the train ride, Erik was bedeviled with "what ifs." What if the director has changed his mind? Or what if he has altogether forgotten that he had promised me a job? What if I can't find an affordable place to live? Erik got himself so worked up over everything that could go wrong that he hardly noticed how incredibly stunning the scenery was.

January 4, 1974

Well, getting the contract proved NOT to be an ordeal. Charlie would have laughed at me getting all worked up over nothing. As usual.

I definitely have a part in "Vildanden," as "The Wild Duck" is called here in Norway. I have no idea <u>what</u> that part is, but I will be getting <u>paid</u>. Charlie, I'm a professional actor at last! And I'm going to try and get into another Norsk language class here in Bergen…

Can't stop thinking about my New Year's experience in Trondheim. I keep playing the tape over and over in my mind. Even though I'm in over my head, I'm glad that I'm traveling solo. It's better that I'm alone.

Once Erik arrived at the train station in Oslo, he caught the next commuter train back to Kolsås and resumed his work without delay. Work, which meant studying Norwegian, reading books from the library, working on his project for English class, and writing letters. He also found a letter waiting for him from Mette.

January 6, 1974

Mette's letter was beautiful and made me feel lonely. The feeling snuck up on me and then metastasized. She expresses herself poignantly with so few words. She seems much older than me. She has a beautiful spirit, in addition to this artistic ability that just emanates from her.

I should have told her that I cannot think of her as a girlfriend. I should have told her, but I didn't. I guess I selfishly needed to hold on to her. Just something else for me to feel guilty about. Charlie, Mette, Alistair, the Åstergards, even that ballerina Nina. All the people I've disappointed.

The worst is Charlie. I haven't done a damned thing for him this whole time I've been traveling. I've been pursuing my own interests and haven't come to terms with God over why he let Charlie die. It seems like every time I get close to coming to some sort of a conclusion, something crazy happens in my life that I have to deal with.

Erik picked up some more books and plays at the Oslo library, including *Saint Joan* by Bernard Shaw. At the same time, he felt the need to get some exercise. He hadn't been carrying his heavy pack for a long time, and there had been so much sitting on trains, in the library, theaters, and elsewhere. He'd been cooped up for too long, and he had energy to burn after scoring a part in the Ibsen play.

The Åstergard home was on the highest street in Kolsås. It was the last stop on the train out of Oslo heading west. One side of the Åstergard house looked down into the town below; the other side looked up into the peaks rising above the tree line of Mount Kolsås.

Many Norwegians hiked Kolsås. It's an imposing mountain, with a long, steep trail that culminates in a majestic granite outcropping with breathtaking panoramic views of the Oslo Fjord—or so he'd been told. Erik was itching to make the climb. It was a half-day hike to get to the top. Norwegians of all stripes, from the very young to the impressively old, are forever hiking, walking, skiing, swimming, and in every way imaginable, embracing the outdoors.

The time to make the hike had arrived. He would spend the night at the top of the mountain and give the Åstergards a break from him. It pained him to always be on the receiving end of their generosity. This hike would be a break from his studies, a welcome disruption to his routine. He needed a demanding physical challenge that would pit him against nature in this bracing winter weather.

Moreover, Erik felt his mind yearning to let go of his relentless mental cogitations and to give free rein to his imagination. Honestly, he wanted to simply and languidly pretend that he was Roald Amundsen exploring the uncharted terrain of a newly discovered mountain range.

He wanted to see the view that everyone raved about. He would take the hike a step further by camping out on the edge of the ledge at the top of the mountain, drinking in and inhaling the views. It was now or perhaps never.

Erik gathered the essentials and loaded up his pack. He borrowed a wool blanket from the Åstergards; his sleeping bag alone wouldn't be warm enough. He would leave early the following morning. Naturally, Tove was worried that something terrible might happen to him. She suggested that Erik bring Jens or one of his brothers with him.

But this was a trip Erik wanted to make on his own. There were so many looming prospects to think about. No room in his head for someone else right now. A quick solo trip. Back by midday on Sunday.

One possible exception. Erik would have loved to take Tinka with him. Her broken leg was healing rapidly, and she was full-on walking again. Yet they were not friends. Erik swallowed his pride and gave her wide berth.

Tove insisted on making him *frokost* (breakfast) before he left. Unfortunately, he wasn't feeling particularly well and hadn't planned on eating, but he didn't want to disappoint Tove. Despite the hearty *frokost*, he continued to feel unwell.

Hopefully, I'll be able to just walk this off.

As he began his ascent of Kolsås, Erik had a sensation that he was being followed. Turning, looking back over the trail, he saw a four-legged creature suddenly emerge onto the trail. *Has Tinka decided to come with me after all? What a miracle that would be. She's probably following because I didn't try to coax her. What a contrarian cur!*

Whatever the reason, Tinka made it clear that there was no change in the relationship between them. She didn't let him pet her and she kept her distance. As far as Tinka was concerned, it was sheer coincidence that she and Erik happened to have scheduled a hike to the summit of Kolsås on the same day.

He didn't have a leash for her, but there were no cars in the mountains, so who cares? She could wander around to her heart's content. That was fine with Erik. He couldn't have asked for a better companion.

I'll bet Tove told Tinka to follow me. She is so cussedly protective and motherly. He almost laughed out loud at the thought. It was probably true.

Unfortunately, Erik still was not feeling better. His stomachache and headache weren't bad enough for him to cancel his hike, but dammit, he wished his body would keep up with his high spirits.

Around noon, still not feeling any better, he sat down and took out his lunch. He wasn't hungry, but maybe eating something would help him feel better.

The food did help, but only a bit, as did drinking cold water from his *vannkolbe* (water flask). He continued to hike. The mountain trail became steeper, the higher he went—nearly vertical for short bursts. Every exertion was like a tourniquet tightening around his skull. New muscles seem to emerge and announce their aching presence. When his skin started "crawling," he knew for certain he was sick. *It's probably an influenza, but how bad is it? Best to push on. If I'm going to be sick, it might as well be at the summit. It can't be that much farther...*

When he reached a point where the trail split, he stopped to assess. Continuing straight, forward and upward, involved another nearly vertical climb. Following the trail as it veered westward appeared to offer a level path with a clearing off in the distance. When he arrived at the clearing, he observed a large dead pine laying across the center of it, and it appeared as though previous hikers had used this spot for resting. He would rest too.

He literally had no choice; he couldn't go on. He sat on the fallen tree and was so dizzy that he nearly toppled over. Closing his eyes, he pictured those bullies that confronted Charlie and him when they were children.

"Hey, come here, you little creeps!" they taunted.

The bullies loomed large in his imagination. But the voice he heard now had morphed into something else. Something more sinister. It had a chilling effect. He opened his eyes and stood. The effort made him dizzy, and he sat down again, sweating despite the cold.

His lunch and breakfast fought for expulsion. He resisted the urge.

Tinka kept her distance. *Such an independent husky/wolf—whatever the heck she is.* Much of the time, he couldn't even see her. She was either ahead of him or behind him. At times, he saw her looking down at him from a point high above.

Under his jacket, his shirt was soddened with sweat and stuck to his skin. He wasn't going any farther and he knew it. He threw his ground cloth over the snow, laid his sleeping bag on top, and wrapped the blanket around his bag. The effort to do even these simple tasks exhausted him.

He climbed into the bag and squeezed the world out from his eyes. In the darkness, he had a vision of himself as a cadaver lying in the mountains. Students who looked like trolls wearing white lab coats surrounded him. Greasy hands reached into his mouth and pushed down through his esophagus into his stomach, leaving behind oil and dirt, despoiling his pristine organs. The greasy hands wrapped tightly around his intestines and tugged.

He resisted, yet inch by inch lost the battle. There was no strength to fight. His stomach erupted and he partially caught the effluent in his mouth. Rising and stumbling to the edge of the clearing where there was a ridge which cantilevered over a ravine, he released the full weight of the sally. Thus purged, he weaved and spun back to his sleeping bag, burrowing in as deeply as possible.

Immediately, the demand to vomit returned.

"Come to me," the voices of the boys had coalesced into one sinister whispering voice.

How could there be anything left in my stomach? Like a dog, he returned to the ridge overlooking the ravine he had just befouled.

This time it all came out. Nothing left. He ached from the tips of his toes to the hair on his head. Weak as a kitten, head spinning like a leaf in an ocean eddy, he returned to the refuge of his sleeping bag.

Just lie down, like on the ferry. Don't worry. You know this will be okay. Be still, be calm, breathe…

He tried to ignore the witches brew ulcerating inside his stomach, but his body had a mind of its own. The demand to purge returned with a vengeance. Again, he left his burrow and pulled himself to the ravine. All the forest creatures held their chatter and listened while Erik, prostrated on all fours, loudly disgorged whatever had been left in his depleted stomach.

"You're mine," the voice softly insinuated. Erik instinctively called out to his brother, "Charlie, Charlie, I wish you were here! I'm sorry. I'm sorry, Charlie."

There may have been all manner of eyes witnessing the spectacle, but one mismatched pair of eyes—one blue, one gray—situated high above the scene, kept silent vigil.

Crawling back into his lair, Erik took a sip of water. The cool liquid felt wonderful as it passed over his cracked lips and trickled down his raw throat. He imagined himself as a soldier, risking a drink, with enemies all about. All the research he'd been doing on Vietnam had seeped into his consciousness. He hallucinated that he was in Vietnam, that he'd gotten separated from Charlie and was alone. He imagined he was walking waist-deep in swamps and filthy rice paddies filled with leeches, poisonous snakes, and fire ants.

An icy wind carrying a heavy black cloud rolled down the mountain. The cloud stopped next to his bedding and enveloped him. It changed shape as it hovered around and over him. A helicopter? The blood in his temples pounded, coagulating inside his skull.

The cloud transformed as it swirled around him, eventually morphing from a helicopter into a gigantic jeep sitting just above him. His head felt as though it was going to split in two. Groaning, he followed the pain as it jumped from one side of his head to the other. The pain stabbed like a spike, first into the temple on the right and then into the temple on the left.

He heard a shout. *Was that someone's voice or was that the wind? It must have been a voice.* It was calling his name. "Erik!" The cloud closed around him like a deep freezer. "Erik, you're sinking! We've got to get out of the delta. It's a death trap!"

"Charlie! Charlie, can you see me? Where are you?"

The wind whistled and seemed to scoop the breath right out if his lungs. Was he conscious or unconscious? He'd heard stories of people freezing to death and at a certain point, they're so delirious that they think they're burning up and take off all their clothes, only to be found later, frozen solid and naked.

"I'm sorry, Charlie. Forgive me…"

"Erik! Grab my hand," Charlie was sitting inside the jeep above him and reached down to offer Erik his hand. "C'mon, climb aboard! I'm going to get us out of here."

"Charlie, no. It's not safe. The jeep isn't safe!"

A loud noise cracked through the hissing wind, and the jeep shot up and flew thirty feet higher into the air. The massive vehicle flipped over and came crashing down on top of Charlie, instantly crushing him. Erik lifted his head and peered into the murky blackness, but all he could see of Charlie was his boots. Erik couldn't move. He couldn't speak. He prayed that he could simply cease to exist. His faint whisper was sucked away by the wind. If this was his time to leave the earth, he could accept that. He was at peace with that. He would go with Charlie.

He heard rustling noises and sensed the presence of a wild beast. *Where am I?* A hot breath brushed his neck. *Am I hallucinating? Is this what it feels like to slowly freeze to death?*

Every inch of his body felt frozen, except for his stomach. His stomach was warm. *This is what the body does. It shuts down the extremities and protects the vital organs.* The warmth in his stomach spread. The warmth brought with it a peace. The peace allowed his body to slip into a cocoon, where it lay suspended in a warm embrace.

A scratching, crunching noise woke him. Slowly he opened his crusted eyes. A chipmunk was sitting on the dead pine log, eating crumbs out of the paper bag that had held his lunch. Sunlight was filtering in through the trees. Morning.

Tinka was curled up tightly against his belly, and the warmth was emanating from her. He had survived the night.

"Tinka!"

Tinka opened her eyes but remained where she was.

"You beautiful, crazy, magnificent mutt!"

Erik couldn't fully comprehend how he could go from feeling frozen to feeling...well, actually feeling good. "What a crazy, crazy night that was," he said out loud. As he stood up, weak and unstable, Tinka continued to stay right where she was. She looked up at him as if to say, "Are we good now?"

"*Ja*, Tinka, *vi har det bra nå. Og takk.*" It just came out in Norwegian. It seemed appropriate. "Yes, Tinka, we're good now. And thank you."

"Come on, ol' girl, let's go home. I've had enough of this mountain for one night."

Going to the top was not in the cards for today. Somehow reaching the summit of Kolsås just didn't seem so important to him now after the night he'd just been through. He felt as though something significant had taken place. He wasn't quite sure what it was exactly, but it had to do with Charlie.

As Erik and Tinka walked back down the mountain, Erik felt weak, hungry, light-headed, and strangely rejuvenated. He felt as though he better understood some of the loneliness and fear his brother must have constantly felt. How strange that it should have unfolded like this. Something else that Erik noticed as the two descended the mountain—he and Tinka were walking side by side.

What was it about this mountain hike that altered Tinka's perception of me? How had I proved myself trustworthy? I did nothing. I was weak and helpless. I didn't prove myself to her, she proved herself to me!

Whatever it was, from that moment on, in the gray/blue eyes of Tinka, he was part of her pack.

Back at the Åstergard home, he felt like a new man. Tove noticed it, and she noticed that Tinka's attitude toward Erik had changed. The Åstergard humans had accepted Erik as part of the family a long time ago, but now that Tinka did, that pretty much made it official.

The move to Bergen was now less than a month away. *How could he ever possibly be ready?*

He'd been taking a Norwegian class once a week for less than two months. There simply wasn't enough time for him to keep the promise he had made to the director that he would be fluent by the time rehearsals started. *How are those reports coming, Erik? What about The Wild Duck, have you dissected every aspect of the play?*

These thoughts hounded him every time he climbed aboard the morning commuter train into Oslo.

The end of the second phase of his journey, the "Oslo phase," was fast approaching. The first phase had been England, Denmark, and Sweden, losing Diana, then hitchhiking to Sweden and reconnecting with Anders, and finally, finding Mette. The next phase was Bergen if he found a place to live. Fru Gullestad was making calls, but so far nothing had turned up.

He felt himself changing, adapting to the demands of his goals. What would living on his own and working in Bergen be like? He wanted to squeeze in as much work as possible before he left. He kept notes on the books and plays he was reading…

"St. Joan"

This simple farm girl changed the history of France. Shaw has written about a historical figure. If I take this story, this historical event, at face value, there's no way that this girl, who had no education, could have stood up against all the great powers of France and England and could have accomplished what she did, if she didn't, in fact, hear the voices that she claimed she heard. It's actually a really inspiring story. The fact that she was willing to die for those beliefs, even death by being burned alive, makes me inclined to believe her. She was either crazy or she actually did hear those voices.

Then there was music. It seemed like there was classical music playing everywhere he went—the Trøndelag Teater, the Oslo Opera, cafés, libraries, and the Åstergard home. Beethoven, Bach, Tchaikovsky, Grieg, and other great composers. For a kid that grew up on rock 'n' roll, this was part of an incipient metamorphosis.

The Åstergard routine was to sit in the living room most evenings during the week, discussing the highs and lows of the day over coffee and chocolates. No TV. They had had one when they lived in the United States but didn't feel the need when they returned to Norway. They read the papers every day instead.

Erik went back to the Oslo Opera House to take up the offer from Nina, the Russian dancer.

"I'm afraid I don't have any ballet attire," he told her.

"Es no problem. Here in office, we have many ballet garments for you can borrow and some ballet slippers too. Es fine if you use what you need."

Nina was teaching the class and she had him take a position at the barre. The class lasted for about two hours—the first half at the barre, the second half practicing dance routines along with music. The moves were a lot harder than they looked when Erik had watched the class previously.

"You have natural ability. Not many people have such," she said. "Maybe you become dancer, no? You come again?"

"I'd love to, but I can't. I'm moving to Bergen. I won't forget this though. I'll find another class somewhere, sometime. I'm hooked."

He meant it. Ballet had struck a chord with him, and he knew this wouldn't be his last experience with it. But now wasn't the time or place. Nina seemed genuinely disappointed that he wouldn't be coming back. He was intrigued with Nina, but again, this wasn't the time. Life continually had opportunities, but saying yes to one always seemed to mean saying no to others.

January 20, 1974

Fru Gullestad has found me a place to live in Bergen! It's in the basement of a big house, high in the hills surrounding Bergen. With the money I got back from the state for my Norwegian class, I'll be able to pay the first month's rent. My salary at the theater should be enough to cover the monthly rent.

After spending the morning packing for his move to Bergen, Erik caught the midday commuter train into Oslo. His final Norwegian class was tonight. While at the station, he booked a seat on the train to

Bergen for the following day. As he was coming out of the station, he heard, "Hey, Hellberg!"

Two young men were standing at the opposite side of the station waving at him. Erik recognized the tall one as the acidhead from St. Cloud College who performed those perfect swan dives off the high ledge at the Diving Quarries — Dale Skarsgaard.

"Skarsgaard! What are you doing here?"

"Hellberg! It's great to see you, man," said Dale. "We heard about you, that you've been living in Norway. It's crazy that we ran into you, man!"

"What? How'd you know I was living in Norway?"

"The whole Pro Pace group knows you're here."

"You're with the Pro Pace group? Unbelievable. Is there anyone from St. Cloud who isn't on the Denmark trip?"

"Ha! I don't think so," he said. "So we got in yesterday and we're leaving later today. We're going to work our way back to Fredericia through Sweden."

He wouldn't call Dale a friend. In fact, he doubted he'd ever said anything more than hi to Dale at any point. Still, it was great to see a familiar face and especially someone from the Denmark group. Dale didn't have too much information on Diana, other than she was fine and traveling a lot. Erik wanted to ask if she was traveling with her friend Benny but managed to restrain himself.

"Hey man, can we buy you a beer? Our train doesn't leave for a couple hours."

"Thanks, but I've got a Norwegian class," said Erik.

"That's cool. So you speak the lingo?"

"A little."

"Hey, isn't this European traveling shit just the greatest buzz in the world? We just did the Netherlands and then London, and now we're in Oslo. Crazy!"

These guys were on a whole different wavelength. What they were doing was great and wonderful and all that, but it was just altogether different from what Erik was doing. "Yah, it's crazy," said Erik.

The young men bantered for a while and then said their goodbyes. When they shook hands, Dale slipped a small wad of tinfoil into Erik's palm.

"Just a little present for you, man. We're flush from our stay in Amsterdam. Enjoy!"

It was a gram of hash. It had been a long time since Erik had seen drugs of any kind. Drugs simply were not a factor on this trip—or in his world at this point in his life. He recognized it as a goodwill gesture, and it made him feel good that he was doing a solo trip and not the type of trip where he'd be jostled by a groupthink mentality.

He was sure that everyone on the Denmark trip was having the time of their lives. For most of them, it was undoubtedly an incredible, impactful year that stretched their understanding of the world beyond anything St. Cloud State College could have provided them. But he couldn't help but think that all they were doing—some of them anyway—was carrying on the party they'd begun as freshmen to Europe. Not his scene and not his party.

January 23, 1974

On the train to Bergen at last! This is so incredibly exciting! Booked a sleeper once again. I love this life. It just isn't the same—even remotely—as life in America. I'm ready to start the next phase of my epic journey.

There's only one MAJOR thing bothering me, and it's something that I can't do a damned thing about. That cursed gram of hash the lunatic Skarsgaard gave me, I accidently left in my room back at the Åstergards' house.

Arrrrrrrrrrrgh!

There's zero chance that Tove won't find it. That woman is so fastidious; she doesn't miss a speck of dirt.

What makes my crime particularly heinous is all the problems they have had with Jens over his drug usage. Tove will find it, and she'll think that maybe I've been a bad influence on Jens. That would be terrible—or she'll think it's Jens's! That would be even worse. I hope I haven't been a bad influence on him. I've seen him come out of his shell these past months, and I've seen his relationship with his folks start to mend in many ways.

Ah, this is one of those perplexing situations that one really can't do anything about. Dammit! She won't know that the hash had literally just come into my possession yesterday and that it meant nothing to me and had nothing to do with Jens.

I'll just have to trust that the family will give me and Jens the benefit of the doubt.

Next stop... Bergen!

THREE

BERGEN

Sometimes, and only in the spring, as winter's ice loses its grip and slides from the mountains into the fjords of southwestern Norway, the waters undergo a startling metamorphosis from a dark blue to a milky blue green, lasting for several weeks. This is due to the presence of a tiny, single-celled phytoplankton called *Emiliania huxleyi*. Trillions of these cells, each barely one-tenth the size of a human hair, colonize themselves into shells of calcium carbonate disks. These disks are highly reflective, causing the natural color of the phytoplankton to radiate outward.

Once in a generation, the presence of this phytoplankton is so substantial that it's called a "super bloom," turning the deep, winter-blue fjord waters into an iridescent turquoise color that can be seen even from outer space. The last time this phenomenon occurred, before either Charlie or Erik had been conceived, a certain songbird entered the world in the form of a diminutive baby girl with eyes that uncannily matched the turquoise waters of her home on the eastern bank of Hardangerfjord.

Katarina could sing before she could talk. From the time she was a toddler, her parents' friends and neighbors were stunned when they heard her tiny, pitch-perfect voice soaring effortlessly like a nightingale. When Katarina's father moved the family to the outskirts of Oslo in pursuit of better job opportunities, a world of possibilities opened for young Katarina.

She loved singing, and she happily entertained the neighbors with song and dance routines that she made up on the fly. Aside from her natural singing ability, she was gifted with a graceful, athletic frame and a fierce desire to excel in whatever she undertook. Her parents enrolled her in ballet and figure-skating classes and in piano and violin lessons, and as she grew, she taught herself guitar, mandolin, and the Hardanger fiddle.

At both *ungdomsskole* and *videregående skole* (secondary and high school), Katarina made a name for herself in the community as a standout in the local theatrical productions. After high school, Katarina set her heart on going to Teaterhøgskolen (the National Theater School). As much as she loved singing, she knew that singing, alone, would never suffice.

It was during her second year at the National Theater School that Katarina had a life-changing epiphany. She was in the audience watching a performance of *Hedda Gabler*, starring a talented young professional by the name of Inger Fjeldstor in the title role. Katarina sat spellbound as Inger brought to life the angst and entrapment felt by Hedda Gabler in Ibsen's tightly woven drama.

"That was the moment when I knew what I would be doing for the rest of my life," she explained years later in an *Aftenposten* newpaper article. "The exhilaration of plumbing the depths of a character's inner essence and then revealing those precious and sacred realities upon the stage. I cannot imagine what could be—for me—a worthier or more noble life. Especially when these characters have been so veraciously created and woven into such intricately and achingly real worlds that so artfully depict universal truths."

Teaterhøgskolen is a giant funnel. At the wide end, all the most promising aspirants throughout Norway compete for entrance. Only the most talented gain admittance. At the end of the three-year program, many have been eliminated. Those successful in surviving the winnowing process can usually count on a lifetime of employment in the Norwegian theater scene.

Katarina was a triple threat—equally adept at acting, singing, and dancing. At her core, she was an actress, but if the part called for singing or dancing, she could deliver like an opera singer or a ballerina. After three years of Teaterhøgskolen, she graduated with honors and was as well-qualified as any actor who ever set foot on a stage in Norway.

Her first professional opportunity out of theater school was at the Trøndelag Teater in Trondheim. She spent a few seasons there doing every possible job, from stagecraft to acting. Gradually, her parts got bigger and more consequential until she was offered a position in the Riksteatret, a traveling theater company headquartered in Oslo. Katarina was cast in multiple productions and traveled with Riksteatret, performing in theaters and on stages throughout Scandinavia for several years.

The Riksteatret's roster of performances included an extended tour in Bergen and the surrounding countryside. During this stint, the management of Den Nationale Scene became enamored of her and offered Katarina a role in its upcoming production of *Peer Gynt*. After being on the road for so long, she jumped at the chance to settle into one place, where she could hopefully stay long enough to put down some roots.

Having spent the first five years of her life in the quaint, costal community of Hardangerfjord, Katarina acclimated quickly to the neighboring town of Bergen, and the community soon came to recognize that it had a talented new resident at their beloved theater. A succession of roles followed *Peer Gynt*.

When Den Nationale Scene was planning the 1974 season, the artistic staff and theater management all agreed that they must have an Ibsen play in their repertoire but had difficulty agreeing on which one. They finally settled on *Vildanden* (*The Wild Duck*), with the understanding that they might have difficulty finding an actress capable of convincingly portraying the fourteen-year-old Hedvig.

By then Katarina was in her mid-twenties and many within the management group felt she was too old for the part. She pleaded for a chance to audition for the role, and only upon the insistence of the director, Gustaf Husman, was her request granted.

When Katarina stepped on the stage for her audition, she presented the living embodiment of a fourteen-year-old girl. There seemed to be no vestige of Katarina the actress anywhere on stage. The girl frolicking in front of the auditioners and interacting with the other actors was, for all intents and purposes, Hedvig. At the end of her audition, there was no doubt in the mind of anyone in the audience that the role of Hedvig belonged to Katarina.

Approximately a month after Katarina's audition for *Vildanden*, in another part of Bergen, Erik was greeted by a misty rain as he stepped off the train and into what was to be his new home. He picked up a map at the station and calculated that his apartment was about three and a half miles away as the crow flies. It was easily three times that distance to walk. Erik hoisted his pack and then reached for Jens's guitar, which was covered in plastic.

C'mon little fella. You've been replaced by a sitar, but don't worry. You and I are going to become good friends.

He began the ascent of Mount Fløyen, while droplets of drizzle rolled down his orange pack and green army-surplus poncho. It was a beautiful hike, even in the light shower. The road meandered along a web of switchbacks, pushing its way up Mount Fløyen. For a minute, he had to remind himself that this wasn't a dream. *How could I be so fortunate?* Fru Gullestad had performed another minor miracle. She was responsible for his employment at Den Nationale Scene, and now she was responsible for the apartment.

When Erik arrived at his destination on Starefossvien, he was at the highest point on the highest road of the mountain. He took some time to look down the winding road he had just walked up. *If I walk this route every day, my back and leg muscles will really be in great shape.*

He was surprised at how large the house was—four stories, including the basement. The basement was divided in half to create two apartments.

His home was to be one of those halves.

Erik went to the front door and rang the bell. The owner of the house, Fru Eleanor Menck, greeted him at the door. Clearly, she'd been expecting him, and in perfect British English, she invited him inside.

The interior of her house was immaculately—if not overly—decorated. There were paintings everywhere. There was thick oriental carpeting on the floor, large and small pieces of furniture at every turn—many decorated with framed pictures, glass ornaments, figurines, sculptures, and lace doilies.

A large bay window in the main living room framed a magnificent view of the city of Bergen, which stretched out below. A grand piano sat majestically in the music room next to the living room.

Fru Menck suggested that they walk down to the basement so Erik could see his new home. A stone path wound around the house to the rear, where there was a private entrance to the apartment. After unlocking the door and ushering him in, she handed him the key and gave him a tour, which took all of sixty seconds. Fru Menck then invited him to come and join her for tea after he'd put his belongings away.

The basement had recently been converted from a large storage area to two small apartments. Each had a private entrance, a kitchen, bathroom, hallway, and living/dining room. Construction on the other apartment had been temporarily halted, and it was currently being used for storage.

Erik's apartment was already furnished with a few pieces of furniture: a divan, a wooden table, and two chairs. The divan would serve as his bed and lounge; the table and chairs were all he needed for meals and studying. He would need to buy a desk lamp, a frying pan, two dinner plates (in case he ever had a guest), silverware, a mug, and drinking glasses.

When Erik returned to Fru Menck's section of the house, he half expected that a servant or a maid would pour their tea—such was the magisterial splendor that the old house exuded. But Fru Menck didn't have a maid, and she brewed and served the tea herself.

They sat in a recessed alcove partially formed by the contours of the grand stairway as it thrust out into the main room. A round, marble tabletop held an antique teapot and two delicate cups with matching saucers. They sat down in chairs with blue toile fabric and fancy cartouche-shaped chairbacks.

Fru Gullestad had learned of this place through Fru Menck's daughter, Iris, who was a playwright and lived on the floor between Fru Menck and the basement, but she was currently staying in England where one of her plays was being produced.

Fru Gullestad knew most everyone who was associated with theater in Norway.

The Mencks had been planning on turning their basement into apartments anyway, and when they heard that Fru Gullestad had a young American actor looking for a place to live while working at Den Nationale Scene, they expedited the retrofitting. Erik learned later through Fru Menck's grandson that she had donated the pieces of furniture to Erik's apartment.

He suspected she gave him a break on rent, too, which was NOK85 (Norwegian *kroner*) per month—an amount he might just possibly be able to afford if he could learn to get by without food or tobacco. He was not so sure how he would manage without eating.

Fru Menck spoke English with a slightly aristocratic British accent. In her younger years, she had been a concert pianist and had traveled and performed all over the world. Every square inch in her house seemed to be covered with a painting.

"I've never seen so many pictures mounted in any place outside of a museum." Erik said.

"Many of them are originals. These two, in fact, were painted by Edvard Munch," she said, pointing to two small paintings housed in simple frames and hanging on the curved wall that followed the grand staircase.

"Edvard Munch originals?" Erik was impressed. He took a closer look at the paintings. "I've always been drawn to his paintings," he admitted.

"In fact, I had a print of *The Scream* in my dorm room at school. Right next to a poster of Farrah Fawcett."

"Farrah Fawcett?" Fru Menck said, a puzzled expression on her face.

"Never mind," Erik said. "Not in the same league."

"We are, in fact, related to Edvard Munch," she said. "Although the spellings are different. Some miscreant relation committed an indiscretion, somewhere along the line, significant enough to warrant a name change. No one seems to remember quite what it was or when the indiscretion occurred, but there you are."

Fru Menck was a fascinating mix of contradictions. She was clearly wealthy but frugal. Aristocratic but earthy and easy to talk to. She reminded him a lot of Great-Aunt Lucy, and he couldn't wait to write and let her know about this grande dame.

Fru Menck invited Erik to take in the view of the town of Bergen through the bay window. The view was stunning, and he needed a moment to take it in. It was hard to believe that he'd just walked up from that quaint little town nestled far below, between the mountains and the sea.

As they sat and sipped their tea, he envisioned her background story—a beautiful young prodigy, performing in the storied concert halls of Europe for royalty, who was at the same time being courted by a scion of the Menck family. Erik was guessing that the affair was a whirlwind romance, and undoubtedly, she was quite a catch.

Fru Menck confessed that she would be forever grateful to the Americans for coming into the war and helping to liberate Europe from the Nazis. She said she was indebted to them and that she was proud to have him living under her roof.

That caught Erik by surprise. Hearing these sentiments coming from a foreigner felt wonderful. Although large-scale protests of the Vietnam War had pretty much abated by the time Erik arrived in Europe, there was still a strong anti-American sentiment shared by many people here—especially the young. Once Erik left a pub near

Trafalgar Square rather than engage a couple of loudmouths who were saying that America was an imperialist nation and that American soldiers were murdering innocent Vietnamese people. He wanted to get into their faces, but he knew Charlie would have told him to just let it go. *There's too much fighting as it is.*

Fru Menck was eager for Erik to meet her daughter and her grandson. Her grandson had a standing dinner invitation with her every Thursday. She said that now Erik, too, would be a regular dinner guest on Thursdays and perhaps the two young men could become friends.

As excited as he was to be here, he was nervous when he first saw the apartment where he'd be spending at least the next four or five months, maybe much longer. What would life be like, living completely on his own? How would he measure up? This would be a test for him. He was both excited and a little nervous.

That night, as he lay inside of his sleeping bag on top of the divan, he couldn't stop thinking how lucky he was to be here in Bergen, on the verge of being in his first professional stage production. He kept repeating the Norwegian name of the play out loud: "*Vildanden, Vildanden, Vildanden.*"

On top of everything else, here he was living in the basement of this beautiful house, which was owned by a lady who liked Americans. The house overlooked the picturesque town of Bergen that Erik knew he was going to love. Tomorrow, he would start his exploration of the city and find the location of his next Norwegian class.

Jens had helped Erik sign up for an intermediate Norwegian language course at the University of Bergen, which was located several kilometers from Den Nationale Scene. The start date for the class had already passed, but Erik was able to reserve a seat anyway.

The following morning, he practically floated down Mount Fløyen. His great new life was beginning, and he no longer had to lug his full backpack around. He was fifty-six pounds lighter as he walked about the town of Bergen. He found where his class was, and he found the town library. The building that housed the library was half the size of the one in Oslo, but to his relief, there was a robust English section that included plays.

Erik picked up a copy of *The Empty Space*, by Peter Brook, an anthology of plays by Anton Chekhov, an anthology of Scandinavian literature, and a play by American James Baldwin, called *Blues for Mister Charlie*.

January 27, 1974

After reading Peter Brook's book, I have a name for my abode in Bergen— the "Empty Space." I call it thus, not because it's practically void of furniture, but because it's just me and I need to fill it with the ideas of my life. Brooks says you can take any empty space and walk across it—if someone's watching, then that's theater.

Rehearsals for *Vildanden* started the first week of February. Erik had a lot to do to get ready. The most important tasks were to get to know the play backward and forward and to learn as much Norwegian as possible in the short time left. He had promised Director Husman he would be fluent, but after less than three months of study, he was far from that goal. He would just have to trust that things would work out.

The Bergen Norsk class was more advanced, more conversational. This class was smaller than the Oslo class, which meant more individual attention. Here again was an eclectic group of immigrants and visitors wanting to learn the language. The teacher spoke only in Norwegian unless English was absolutely necessary.

Erik tested himself at every opportunity—at the library, in stores and cafés, and especially with a group of young kids he befriended who lived in a house down the street from Fru Menck. He didn't mind making mistakes—how else do you learn? Many Norwegians seemed as eager to speak English as Erik was to speak Norwegian. Invariably, they were better in English than he was in Norwegian.

The first rehearsal was exciting and confusing. Exciting for obvious reasons. Confusing because he had no lines, nor did he have a clue who his character was and where this unknown character would fit in the play. His name wasn't listed on any call sheet, and the director didn't have the actors introduce themselves, even though Erik was prepared to say a few sentences about himself in Norwegian.

Director Husman gave a speech about his vision of *Vildanden*. Erik listened intently, yet much of what he said was beyond his comprehension. Then Director Husman introduced all the actors except Erik, and they began the read-through. It was hard not to feel snubbed.

As he sat and listened to the play, he was impressed with the casting. In his opinion, each of the principal actors was well-suited to their role. Keeping up with the characters' Norwegian dialogue was not difficult since he was familiar with the play.

Vildanden has five acts. After they read through the first and second acts, the director called for a break. Some of the actors left the theater to get lunch. Others peeled off into small groups and disappeared.

Unfortunately for Erik, he'd neglected to make himself a lunch. He didn't want to leave the theater building to get a bite to eat for fear of returning late and embarrassing himself. He went into the green room where there was a little kitchenette area. He pinched a teabag and made himself a cup of tea while pondering his predicament.

Who is my character, and where does he fit into the play? The only role I could possibly have is as one of the hired waiters/servants in the opening scene in Old Man Werle's house. Each of the dinner guests has a line or two, but all those characters are much older men—they need to be older for their presence within the world of the play to make sense.

After finishing his tea, Erik went back into the empty auditorium, took a seat, and waited. The cast eventually returned and began Act Three. Around four o'clock, they finished the read-through, and the director called for another break.

Erik wanted to talk to Director Husman and find out where he fit into this production, but he was hesitant. After all, Erik had promised that he'd be fluent in Norwegian by the time they started rehearsals. That was a promise he hadn't been able to keep.

Erik was also intimidated. The director hadn't acknowledged him all day. In fact, none of the actors had acknowledged him. No one was being rude or unkind to him; they probably just didn't know who he was or what the hell he was doing there.

I might as well be invisible. What if Gustaf has changed his mind? What if Gustaf has forgotten all about his promise and he's just waiting for an opportunity to say to me that he's sorry, but there just isn't going to be a part for me in the play after all?

One way or the other, Erik had to find out. When the actors came back from break, Director Husman spoke for a short while about the play and what he hoped they'd be able to accomplish. He was excited and said he felt that they had a terrific cast and that this would be a wonderful production.

Then he asked if anyone had any questions. Several actors spoke up, and there was a good bit of discussion over the next hour.

Erik kept silent. How idiotic would it be for him to raise his hand and say, "Excuse me, but what's my part in this play?"

Finally, the director wrapped the rehearsal and thanked everyone for the great read-through. Erik understood him to say: "For those of you who are in the rehearsal tomorrow, go home, get some rest, and come back tomorrow ready for a good day's work."

The actors moved out, chatting among themselves as they exited. Several of the lead actors stayed and talked with the director. Erik bided his time. When the director was finished, he turned and walked toward the door of the auditorium.

Erik caught up with him and spoke to him in Norwegian.

"Excuse me, Director Husman. Where exactly does my character fit into the play?"

The director responded in Norwegian. "Ah. Well, you're one of the *lietjenere* (hired servants) in the opening scene. I'm not yet sure how we'll use you, but we'll figure it out when we block that scene. I may also be able to use your character later in Act One."

Erik understood the gist of what he said. "I see," said Erik in Norwegian.

"Thanks for coming to the read-through. Good night." With that, Director Husman turned and left.

On the long walk back home up Mount Fløyen, Erik had a lot to think about. On the one hand, he was greatly relieved. He just got confirmation that his part in the play was secure. On the other hand, what was his part in the play? He was fine with being a hired servant, but he didn't see a written part for it. The script said *flere lietjenere* (several hired servants), but there were no stage directions for them. They weren't mentioned anywhere else.

So that was it.

Clearly, his position here was that of a *statist* (an extra). That didn't matter to him. Contrary to what Dr. Cervante and some of the other luminaries in the St. Cloud theater department thought of him, Erik didn't think he was above playing small roles. Nor did he think that it was unreasonable for an actor who had one line or no lines to spend as much time rehearsing as did the lead actors. In fact, he intended to do exactly that. He planned to be at every rehearsal for the full eight hours each day.

As he understood it, the director had said that there would be rehearsals for different sets of actors at various times throughout the week but not on weekends until they got closer to the opening. There would be a daily posting on the bulletin board of who would be needed for rehearsals the following day.

Erik looked in the green room for a call sheet but didn't see one. He was pretty sure that Director Husman had said rehearsals began at nine o'clock sharp. Well, regardless of whether his character was needed for the rehearsal tomorrow, he was going to be there.

Vildanden was an example of the style of theater known as "realism," of which Ibsen was considered a pioneer. Moreover, he was considered the "Father of Modern Drama." This was due in large part to the dearth of realistic and naturalistic theater throughout the Western world during the nineteenth century.

It was Ibsen's genius to combine psychologically driven drama—where plot was secondary to the interior lives of the play's characters—with tightly woven storylines that an ordinary citizen could relate to.

The Wild Duck is deceptively well-written. Filled with symbolism, the play depicts the clash between the "claim of the ideal" (idealism) and the "harsh reality of everyday life" (realism).

Old Man Werle is the ultimate realist. His son, Gregers Werle, is the ultimate idealist. When Gregers returns home after being gone for many years, their world views clash, with tragic consequences. Gregers observes that his father has set up Hjalmar Ekdal, Gregers's old school friend, in a modest photography business. Upon further investigation, Gregers realizes that this was not an act of altruism.

Old Man Werle had introduced his maid, Gina, to Hjalmar and encouraged a friendship. When the friendship blossomed, the old man advocated for a quick wedding between the two. In a surprising act of generosity, he paid for the wedding and financed Hjalmar's photography business. Less than nine months later, a daughter, Hedvig, was born to the young couple.

Another long-buried secret was that in a government swindle scheme, Old Man Werle orchestrated circumstances so that Lieutenant Ekdal, Hjalmar's father, wrongfully took the fall when the swindle was discovered, resulting in the lieutenant's bankruptcy and societal ruin.

Now, for the last fourteen years, Hjalmar and Gina, along with "their" daughter, Hedvig, have been living a relatively happy life, albeit one that, according to Gregers, was built upon "deception and lies." Hjalmar's father lives with them and has managed to find a "sliver of happiness" in tending a menagerie of wounded animals, including a wild duck, adopted by Hedvig, in their rooftop garret.

When Gregers arrives on the scene, he learns the truth of what his father has done and informs Hjalmar, thinking this will give Hjalmar the opportunity to see his life for what it really is and not some fantasy existence. Gregers believes that like the wild duck, Hjalmar needs to be set free from the deception that has been perpetrated on him. Gregers believes that once Hjalmar knows the truth, he'll be free to rebuild his life with his wife and daughter—without the deceptions and lies.

Instead, Hjalmar is in agony at learning the truth. He rejects his wife and especially his daughter Hedvig, thinking that she couldn't possibly love him since he now knows that he's not her biological father. Gregers, oblivious to the fact that he has ruined the lives of Hjalmar and Gina, turns his attention toward Hedvig. Thinking that he's being helpful, Gregers encourages Hedvig to sacrifice her beloved wild duck as an offering to her father to prove her love for him. In an ironic and cruel twist of fate, rather than sacrificing the wild duck, Hedvig takes her own life.

The first rehearsal was a limited cast, consisting of the actors playing Old Man Werle, Gregers, Hjalmar Ekdal, and Fru Sørby (Old Man Werle's female companion). Erik was the first one to show up, and he took a seat in the back of the theater. When the others arrived, they seemed curious about Erik's presence, but no one said anything. Director Husman would glance at him from time to time, but since Erik wasn't being disruptive, everyone eventually forgot he was there.

Erik kept an English copy of *The Wild Duck* on one knee and a Norwegian copy of *Vildanden* on the other. This proved to be an effective exercise in language comprehension. At lunch, the actors broke and either left the theater or went into the green room to eat. Erik remained alone in the theater and ate the sandwich that he'd remembered to prepare that morning.

After lunch, when the actors filed back in, Erik made of point of greeting each one. Again, no one was unfriendly, but somehow they each managed to project an air of disinterest. The actors, following the example of the director, effectively created an invisible barrier between themselves and Erik.

Perhaps there was an unwritten rule that *skuespillere* (actors) must not speak with *statister*. Reflexively, Erik began to adjust to his status as someone less than a full-fledged member of the cast. Nevertheless, he was optimistic that he'd eventually break through and make friends here.

There was a small group of elderly men who were cast as *kammerherre*r (chamberlains)—officials in charge of managing Mr. Werle's estate. Erik felt a kinship with these men. Most of them were retired. All had been professional actors, to varying degrees, for at least a portion of their lives. These men took a liking to Erik as immediately as he did to them.

Erik consoled himself with the knowledge that he was getting paid to be part of this production—a brilliant play, written by a certified genius—and that the play was being performed on this most hallowed of all stages in Norway. Even if he didn't have any lines, his character as a hired servant still had to understand the language of the realm, so he could respond to his cues. He resolved to be the best damned *lietjenere* that Old Man Werle ever hired.

Each day, Erik checked the bulletin board to see who would be needed the following day. Director Husman didn't work linearly through the play but focused on his main characters, which was fine and, frankly, what Erik expected. This wasn't Dr. Cervante's all-hands-on-deck directorial style, where there would be two weeks of exploration and discovery, imitating animals and staring at each other until someone blinked or had an epiphany.

If he left his apartment at six thirty in the morning, he could be at the theater by around eight thirty, without having to walk too fast. He vowed never to walk in after a rehearsal had already begun. Rain or shine, it was a majestic walk down the mountain each morning to the theater.

His daily routine was to arrive at the theater early, take a seat, and watch all rehearsals until they ended, usually at five o'clock. He took copious notes in the margins of the play and listened intently to the delivery of each line. When rehearsal was over, he'd walk back up to his apartment, unless he had Norsk class or errands to run. His evenings were free to read plays and literature, write letters, or play the guitar. He kept notes on most of the plays and books that he read:

"Uncle Vanya" by Anton Chekhov

Chekhov's characters are accessible, real, and multidimensional. They raise the questions: What is the purpose of hard work? Must we not work to survive? What is the purpose of life?
Chekhov is asking the same questions I am!

The first weeks in the Empty Space, Erik wrapped himself in the solitude like a blanket. The experience was deeply soothing. Without interruptions, he found he could read, write, and study for long periods of time.

He never heard a peep out of Fru Menck, never saw any neighbors or even any foot traffic on their street. There was no one living in the other half of the basement, since it was being used as storage, and with Fru Menck's daughter off in England, his home life, it seemed, consisted of himself, his books, and his pipe.

"Towards A Poor Theater," by Jerzy Grotowski

Interesting, but not sure I buy all of it. Among other things Grotowski wants to get rid of are all the nonessential elements of theater (like lighting, costumes, makeup, sets, etc.) and break theater down to the essentials—the play, the actors, the audience—an interesting idea and probably popular with elitists and theater snobs, but I think it takes a lot of the fun, entertainment, and magic out of theater.

Fru Menck was as good as her word—the next Thursday night, Erik got a knock on his door by a young man who introduced himself as Asher, Fru Menck's grandson. Together, the boys went up to Fru Menck's quarters, where she had a dinner prepared. "Tonight," Fru Menck announced, "I propose to join you two handsome young men for dinner."

Fru Menck was a seasoned conversationalist and adept at bringing out salient aspects from each of their lives. Although Fru Menck abstained from joining them in subsequent weekly dinners, the young men found common interests and enjoyed each other's company. Asher's English was excellent, but Erik never stopped attempting to improve his Norwegian.

Asher was three or four years younger than Erik and a bit of a raconteur. He had traveled a lot for someone his age and enjoyed both telling stories—usually bordering on the bawdy side—and listening to stories. After dinner, Fru Menck left the two of them alone to get better acquainted. They sat in her smoking room, the grandson with cigarettes and Erik with a bowl of his Mac Baren Mixture. The generosity of Fru Menck even extended to an after-dinner snifter of brandy.

Erik no longer harbored any trepidation about living alone. That fear had dissolved immediately. The solitude and the lack of interruptions was in stark contrast to his life up to this point.

In college, even his interruptions were interrupted. The desire to study may have been there, but so were the usual sophomoric temptations. Here, like an egg beneath a bird, Erik felt a nurturing that allowed him to probe into an array of writings offered over the centuries by scholars, poets, philosophers, moralists, and others who grappled with the common questions of humanity.

He wrote in his journal:

This is what I've always wanted. To see what would happen if left to fend for myself, without curriculum or arbiters. To have only what I can create with my own hands and gray matter. What are the true distractions—those which are thrust upon us or those which we create for ourselves?

Ole, one of the kammerherrer who lived not too far from Erik's apartment, invited Erik to join him and his wife for dinner one night. He introduced Erik by saying to his wife, "This is the American I have been telling you about." Apparently, everyone in the theater referred to Erik as "The American." His wife spoke no English, so here was another opportunity for Erik to practice his Norwegian.

After dinner, the three of them sat down to watch Norwegian TV. It was a Monday night, and that meant *Columbo* was on. It seems Peter Falk, as the indefatigable detective, was quite popular in Norway. Monday dinner and TV at the *kammerherre*'s house became a standing invitation.

As a member of Den Nationale Scene, Erik was able to see all its productions gratis. The first production he went to see was the musical *Jomfruburet (The Virgin's Cage)*, about the life and music of Franz Schubert.

Set in Vienna, the shy, young composer Franz writes a beautiful love song to his beloved Hanne. He asks his best friend, Baron Schober, to sing it to her, and she promptly falls in love with him instead of Franz. Hilarious subplots concerning Hanne's two beautiful sisters and their boyfriends develop, and the show explodes with brilliant singing, dancing, and wonderfully fun Schubert music.

If this is the level of productions at this theater, I'm in for an amazing experience. How in the world could I have been so lucky as to land at this theater, with this level of talent?

The dazzling production inspired Erik to work that much harder on educating himself and studying.

"The Three Sisters" by Chekhov

Depressing to witness the Prozorov family disintegrating from both internal and external forces. Is Chekhov making the statement that this is a normal condition in society? That people are becoming course and sordid? Depressing, but engaging and realistic.

One day, while engrossed in his studies, Erik heard voices outside of his window. *Who can that be? No one ever comes here…*

A voice called out, "Hellberg?"

Erik opened the door to find two old friends—Jeff Nelson and Eddie Henson from Pro Pace.

"What are you guys doing here? And how the hell did you find me?"

The guys had been traveling since early morning and were amazed to be standing with Erik, in front of his Bergen abode. He invited them in. Since he only had one beer, he divided it among his one glass, his one coffee mug, and the single cereal bowl he owned. The guys talked until late into the night.

The next morning, Erik blew off rehearsal—the only one he had missed, and his presence wasn't required anyway—and walked his visitors down into town, where he showed them some of the sites. He took them to the university where his classes were, then to Korskirken (Holy Cross Church), an old church dating back to the late twelfth century. Then they walked to the Tyskebryggen (the German Wharf), where they watched the fish vendors selling their catch, and had a great lunch at one of the neighborhood eateries. The guys bought a small bucket of fresh shrimp and carried it up to Erik's apartment, where he fried the shrimp in butter and they savored the delicacies with a bottle of wine.

"I can't believe you speak Norwegian," said Jeff. "You've only been here, what, three months?"

"Four months now, and believe me, I've got a long way to go."

"Don't you get lonely up on this mountain?" asked Eddie.

"No, I'm too busy. Besides, I enjoy the quiet."

The next day was Saturday. Jeff and Eddie were taking the afternoon train to Oslo and then on to Stockholm. Early in the morning, Erik took them on a short hike farther up the mountain, where there was a spectacular view of the city below and the fjord surrounding it.

"This view is mind-blowing," Eddie said. "You're a lucky man."

That's when Erik asked, "How's Diana doing?" He immediately regretted asking the question. He'd told himself that he wasn't going to, but it just came out.

"She's good. Traveling whenever she gets a chance."

"Good. I'm happy for her." That was mostly true. The only girl he thought about now was Mette. Beautiful, beguiling Mette—although he knew there was no future for them.

"Are you still playing?" Erik asked Eddie, eager to change the subject.

"Yeah, we have a small nucleus of musicians who get together every couple of weeks, depending on who's around. Most of us are from Pro Pace, but sometimes a few Danes will join us. We sometimes play stock sets, but a lot of times we just jam."

They walked down the mountain, and Erik took them to Den Nationale Scene so they could see where he worked. "This is where you work? How incredible," said Jeff. "You're doing it, Erik. I mean, you're pursuing your career, doing what you want to do."

"You know, it's not really me. I mean, I didn't do this on my own. I had a lot of help and got some lucky breaks. I'm grateful though, and I think I'm right where I'm supposed to be."

Erik walked his two friends to the train station and wished them happy trails and smooth rails. When the train pulled out of the station, for the first time since arriving in Bergen, Erik felt lonely.

He also felt like he was discovering who he was when left to his own devices and as master of his own time. With every book or play he read, he felt like he got a bit closer to…what? That's what he didn't know. He needed to understand. He was missing too many pieces of the puzzle. It just wasn't clear.

"The Cherry Orchard"
A Comedy in Four Acts

I don't understand why Chekhov called this play a comedy. Aside from the occasional comic relief of Firs, the mumbling old valet, and of "Two-and-Twenty Troubles" (Yepikhodov), this play is as somber as any of his other plays. Gradually, the victims are stripped of their possessions and the trees in the cherry orchard are chopped down, symbolizing the losses of the Lyubov and Gayev clans. What's comic about that??

Chekhov's characters are preoccupied with love and industry. I can relate to that. I need an object of love in my life, even if the object is beyond my reach. I also need industry. Sleep is scant without industry and sweet with it. Discipline is like a muscle—it grows stronger with exercise.

Like Chekhov and Ibsen, Erik was discovering that industry is one of the sustaining virtues of life.

Notes on "Brand"

"Brand" was a turning point in the life of Ibsen. After "Brand," he was accepted as a major author of importance throughout Europe—not just Norway. After its publication, Ibsen became a new man. He discarded his role as disheveled artist and relished his role as an important voice in the conscience of society.

"Brand" affirmed a moral standard which Ibsen felt was necessary for Norway to maintain. Ibsen was ashamed of his country when it failed to come to the defense of Denmark during the Prussian Invasion of 1864.

Somehow Ibsen was able to see with moral clarity far beyond his own circumstances and milieu and to articulate his insights in stage plays in a way that communicated with the public at large. That was his gift, his genius.

What do I bring to the world? Nothing! I don't even know who I am or what I believe about the world. What is truth? Are we just random atoms swirling around in primordial dust clouds, eventually coalescing into an order that permits habitation? Is there an intelligent force with some purpose behind it all?

I understand why we fought in World War II. Hitler was evil, and his National Socialists were committing atrocities on a massive scale. I understand why the Civil War was fought. Slavery was evil, and war was the only way to end it and preserve the union. I understand why we got into the Vietnam War, but I don't understand how things went so terribly wrong. And I don't understand why Charlie had to die.

Erik didn't have the answers to so many questions, but felt he had to have them to continue down the path he had chosen. *Acting is about honesty and transparency. The audience knows if an actor is being honest or just faking it. If the actor doesn't understand, then how the hell can the audience understand?*

Now, sitting in this tiny basement apartment at the highest habitable place on Mount Fløyen, overlooking the town of Bergen, completely off the merry-go-round, Erik felt as though he was starting to obtain some perspective.

February 13, 1974

I am so inspired by Ibsen. I've started thinking about a modern-day Ibsen and what his take on the Vietnam war would be. I don't see it as an epic poem though, more like a stage play. Rehearsals going well. Have been on stage several times now with the entire cast for Act One. It's unbelievably exciting. When Director Husman gives me stage directions, they're always in Norwegian. Clearly, Husman took it literally when I said I'd be fluent. I may not be as far along as I'd like, but I'm fluent enough at least to follow his stage directions.

Good thing I'm not playing Gregers or Hjalmar!

Other than the *kammerherrer,* Erik hadn't been able to mix with any of the actors at Den Nationale Scene. And not for lack of trying. He made a point to greet every actor that he met throughout the days of rehearsal. Again, no one was overtly rude, but none of his greetings resulted in a substantive conversation.

Normally, this pervasive snubbing would have depressed him and sent him into a tailspin. However, he was determined to overcome any obstacle he might face during this great odyssey he'd undertaken. He was discovering a resilience that he didn't know he had.

Vildanden was his favorite of all the plays at Den Nationale Scene. He came to respect the genius of Ibsen more and more with each rehearsal. The cast was remarkable. Sitting in the back of the theater, observing the actors as they went through the process of bringing their characters to life, was exhilarating. This is the way Erik wanted to spend his life. Doing exactly what these actors were doing. That would be a good life, a worthy life. He was here to learn, and that was exactly what he was doing.

February 15, 1974

Tonight I went to see the Jack Lemmon movie "Save the Tiger." Husman was also at the movie. I said hi to him, but he barely acknowledged me.

This isn't "Norwegian reserve." Director Husman doesn't like me for some reason. He doesn't know me, so it's simple prejudice. Maybe he doesn't like Americans.

As I walked back up Mount Fløyen, I thought about what Henry David Thoreau said about self-reliance—that one must have unfailing trust in oneself and confidence in one's faculties. Choosing individuality over conformity to society allows a person to "follow the bent of his genius."

There was a side of Erik that wanted to take all this personally, but he suppressed that urge. He tried to be analytical about it. *I'm a visitor.*

Not part of their world. And I'm an American. Seems like most Norwegians under the age of forty or so don't have a high opinion of Americans.

Erik was there by the good graces of Fru Gullestad and, before her, by those of Dr. Walter Van Langenhove.

I can't let them down. It's an honor to be on this stage. I fought hard for this role. If I didn't previously understand, truly understand, that there are no such thing as small parts, only small actors, I do understand this now.

February 17, 1974

This has been a good day. Got a lot done with Norsk. Finished reading "Brand." Spent some time with the neighborhood kids, and I played the guitar for them. Also was finally able to channel a lot of what's been going on in my mind into the play I'm writing.

A letter from Diana arrived. It might as well have been blank, but Erik immediately started writing a response:

After so long without hearing from you, your letter caught me by surprise. Glad you're having an AMAZING growth year. Good to know you've been able to visit a dozen cities—including Bergen—

Erik paused. *Wait, why am I writing her back? Why did she even bother to send me a letter? She said nothing, except that she came to Bergen. Obviously, she made no effort to get in touch with me. This is just a letter she's writing to basically let me know how over me she is. What could I possibly say that wouldn't sound foolish? If the end wasn't official before, and it was, it's now officially official.*

His head was over her, and now it appeared his heart was too. Seems the heart has a mind of its own. What would have happened if he'd gotten involved with Mette? Clearly, realistically, any relationship with Mette that went beyond friendship wasn't possible. That became obvious after their meeting in December. They continued to write each other. The letters weren't love letters, but they seemed to be more than just simple friendship letters.

Seems the human heart is always longing to love and to be loved.

February 19, 1974

Finished reading "Diary of Anne Frank" today. Moving. Sad. Profound. Especially painful to witness such childlike optimism in the face of such hatred and evil.

Erik needed a good day at the theater. He'd been feeling a little depressed. He thought the cause was a combination of the rain, the reserved nature of the Norwegians, his invisibility at the theater, a lack of letters from home, and the lack of an intimate friend here. Instead of going home after rehearsal, he noticed that there was a Marx Brothers movie at one of the cinemas and he couldn't resist.

Right now, it's the wee hours of Saturday morning, 23rd of February. I'm celebrating with a cup of my world-famous tea. The day started early at the theater, which is abuzz with talk of "Arturo Ui." Hoping I haven't lost my chance to have a part in it. Went to see "Duck Soup." There's a zany quality about Americans, perfectly embodied by the Marx Bros, that I haven't witnessed in any other culture.

I'm in love with a thousand things!

Weekends were the best because he didn't have to make the long walk into town. He could stay in the Empty Space and relax, drink tea, write, and read. The solitude was like heaven.

As much as he loved being a part of Den Nationale Scene, his job wasn't easy. Since he wasn't fluent in Norwegian, he had to be hyper focused during rehearsals to follow what the director and actors were saying. If Erik didn't understand his staging and blocking notes, he was obliged to ask for clarification in Norwegian. His role was that of a waiter during the dinner party scene in the play's opening act. The directions called for him to be interacting with the other waiters and chamberlains, so comprehension was essential.

Moreover, Erik wanted to be there every minute of every rehearsal. He sensed that the actors were uncomfortable with him being there, but he came anyway. He felt it was his duty, part of his assignment—his assignment in life, more so than for any school assignment.

February 25, 1974

Today I went to visit one of my friends from Norsk class—Randy, a Brit, who has a Swedish girlfriend. They live near the German Wharf. It was raining as usual while I walked to their place. On the way, I noticed a lugubrious old woman, bent with pain and age. She walked slowly, as if each step might be her last. My attention was diverted temporarily by a movement on the steps below an alcove—it was a cat trying to stay out of the rain. I stooped and extended my finger to the miserable creature. That damned cat walked right up my arm and perched on my shoulder! I felt a little foolish crouching there in the rain with a cat on my shoulder. That old woman stared disgustedly at me as she passed. Her look suggested that I might have been a deranged imbecile.

It was truly an Ingmar Bergman moment.

As March closed in, Erik fleshed out his life with Monday dinners/ *Columbo* TV shows at his *kammerherre* friend's house, Thursday dinners at Fru Menck's with Asher. He genuinely enjoyed both events but was nevertheless frustrated because it was two entire evenings in which he couldn't get any reading or writing done. Finally, there were Norsk classes, and rehearsals. Aside from these staples, there were two looming events constantly on his mind—whether he was going to get a part in *Arturo Ui* and the work that still needed to be done on his school assignments.

February 27, 1973

Not too worried about Theater History, been keeping detailed notes about Den Nationale Scene and "The Wild Duck," plus all my notes and photos from all the theaters I've visited.

The English assignment was proving to be much tougher.

The damned crafty instructor is really making me work. Picked up an anthology of Pär Lagerkvist's short stories, got three books by Sigrid Undset and two by Knut Hamsun. The bonus in reading all these stories is that it is helping me with the modern-day Brand play. It's just hard to find the time to write. Just going to have to slug it out. Anyway, beats being at St. Cloud...

As for photography... If I was in Oslo, this would be no problem, but no one I know out here in Bergen has a darkroom.

Not knowing what else to do, he wrote to Alistair. He got a response almost immediately.

Dear Erik,

I talked with Stephan (my photographer friend here at the Opera House, whom you met). He knows a photographer who lives in Bergen. I believe he's out of the country at present but am sure he'll do whatever he can for you when he returns...

What a good friend Alistair has been and continues to be. Erik tried contacting the Bergen photographer but got no reply. *Will just have* to keep trying until I reach him. Late assignments will be considered a fail.

Would Erik be hand-delivering his assignments, or would he be mailing them in? The answer to that question depended on whether he got a position in *Arturo Ui*.

It's weird. I haven't seen any postings about auditions for Arturo Ui, yet everyone at the theater is talking about the play. Maybe casting is being done without auditions? If I don't get a part, what does that mean for my future here? How will I pay for my room and board? I need work.

Erik reached out again to Fru Gullestad. She confirmed that most of the casting was being done through back channels. But he shouldn't give up hope—she was doing what she could.

That was somewhat reassuring, but he needed a backup plan. There was the summer theater program at Theater L'Homme Dieu in Minnesota. He wouldn't have been ready last summer, but he was now. Yet committing to Theater L'Homme Dieu would mean an end to his sojourn in Norway.

I'm not ready to go back. I haven't yet done what I set out to do. I'm not there yet. When he left the United States, he'd purposely bought a one-way ticket; he didn't want the safety net of a return ticket beckoning him.

To start with, he hadn't broken in. He wasn't accepted or even recognized by the other cast members. Except for the *kammerherre*r, the cast basically ignored him.

Maybe I just don't belong here? I know I have an introverted side, but that side is generally recessive. Most of the time, and for most of this trip, I've been an extrovert. I've visited eight major Norwegian theaters now— no one can say I lack assertiveness. The toughest theater to crack has been this one, with Director Husman as the gatekeeper.

It felt like he was on the outside looking in. Erik reasoned it was the "Norwegian reserve," coupled with the bias against him as established by the director and by his own introverted response to the prejudice.

It's almost like being blackballed all over again, except in a foreign culture. They must be thinking, who the hell is this guy? There's no reason for him to be in rehearsals at all until his character is needed on stage. He can't be getting paid enough to come and sit in the back of the theater every day.

The premiere of *Vildanden* took place on March 5. The theater was full, and by all accounts the production was a success. Even though this wasn't a play that the audience would leave dancing, every conversation he overheard was filled with excitement. The ending was shocking, even if you've seen multiple productions, as most Norwegians have.

Ibsen was a master at pathos. *Vildanden* was a thought-provoking, deeply moving— even disturbing—play. One gets angry at the injustice, stupidity, and ignorance of people and society. Most of the theatergoers were visibly moved by the production. How could they not be? This was an excellent play—the cast was terrific, and Erik had to admit that Director Husman had done a remarkably good job as director.

More than that, Erik was personally deeply touched by the play. Because he watched the play develop day by day and saw the genius of Ibsen's intricately created world slowly weave the strands of its web into an ultimately and inevitably tragic ending, he may have appreciated its accomplishment more than anyone.

The cast was superb, and none more so than the actress who played fourteen-year-old Hedvig. He knew she was older than fourteen; he guessed she might have been mid-twenties. On stage, however, he believed she was fourteen. Even though he hadn't had a conversation with her or any of the other lead actors, language was not a barrier in recognizing talent. He made a silent pledge to always be as truthful as these actors in whatever role he might take on in his future career.

There were only two people that he wished he could share this moment with—his debut as a professional actor—and unfortunately one of them was dead. It grieved him to no end to think that Charlie would never again share in any aspect of his life or the life of anyone in the family—of anyone on the planet, for that matter. It was just a hard, rotten, fact of life, and there wasn't a damned thing he or anyone else could do about it.

The other person was his great-aunt Lucy. She was his inspiration and guiding angel. More than anyone, Lucy knew what Norway was like. She'd been to Oslo. She'd been to Bergen. She would have loved being here at Den Nationale Scene and seeing *The Wild Duck*.

Following the premiere, there was a cast party in the green room. All the actors were there and talking excitedly among themselves. He sat down in a corner and enjoyed the ebullient atmosphere in the room. To make it look like he had important stuff to do and wasn't just sitting in a corner like a dunce with no one to talk to, he pulled out a blank postcard and wrote...

Dear Lucy,

The Wild Duck just had its premiere. It was wonderful. My performance was singled out in all the papers as a real tour de force.

Ha ha! Just kidding! I have a small part, but it's an honor to be on the stage with talented actors in a brilliant play. I only wish you could have seen it. My favorite part of the—

Just then, one of the *kammerherrer* tapped him on the shoulder and Erik put down the postcard to talk with his friend. Thank goodness he had at least a few friends in the cast. Walking home that night, he felt elated. He'd just completed his first professional performance as an actor. True, he was only a *statist*, but who cared? Technically, he was now a professional actor. His actor friends back in Minnesota were all slugging it out as students or acting in community theater productions and not getting paid.

Who knows where it will lead? I might get a part in Arturo Ui—that would be a huge step up. I'd be working with an international cast of Germans and Norwegians.

The stars were out in a dazzling display. Raindrops from earlier this evening clung to leaves and shimmered in the starlight.

He heard an owl hooting. He stopped dead in his tracks and looked to see where it came from. Owls were his favorite bird, and they're usually hard to spot.

Then he saw it. The owl was calmly sitting no more than twenty feet away from him. It was surprisingly small, most likely a short-eared owl. Amazingly, this little fellow didn't seem frightened of Erik in the slightest. A magic moment to cap a magic day.

A few days later, Fru Menck greeted Erik at her door when he arrived for his weekly dinner with Asher.

"We have a special guest tonight, Erik. My daughter, Iris, has just returned from London where her play is currently being performed. Come, I'll introduce you."

Asher and his mother were in the sunroom laughing uproariously when Erik and Fru Menck entered. Immediately Erik recognized the family resemblance in Iris. She was an intriguing mixture of both her mother and Asher. Apparently, mother and son were sharing a laugh over something that had occurred at one of the performances of her play. Asher had been present for the premier in London and no doubt had some interesting and funny stories to recount.

Erik had a sneaking suspicion that this was going to be a spectacular night, and he was not disappointed. Iris and Fru Menck joined them at the dinner table (she usually just fixed the young men dinner and then abstained from joining them.) Tonight, she brought out an impressively old Bordeaux.

"I've been saving this wine for a special occasion. My father acquired a case following the war, of which this is the last bottle. It is from the Chateau Mouton Rothschild, a 1929 vintage, an especially dry year that produced a bumper crop of superb wines. You are all too young to know, but 1929 was two years after Norway regained their senses and ended prohibition. Which, I will have you know, Erik, was four years prior to the United States ending that misguided practice."

The Menck family were all well-traveled and active in the theater community. They discussed *Vildanden* and Ibsen and Brecht and the state of theater worldwide. They talked about Iris's play, which was being performed at a theater in London, and about an offer she'd received to bring her play to America. The conversation veered to a discussion of other productions at Den Nationale Scene, like *Jomfruburet*.

The music of Franz Schubert was a favorite in the Menck household, and after dinner Fru Menck treated them to an impromptu concert on her magnificent grand piano. Her playing was superb. Honestly, Erik had never heard anything like it. He was astounded at how her fingers just danced over the keys. He was literally moved to tears.

The capper of the evening for him, however, was when Iris mentioned that she was concerned about how her play would fare in America. The current version had been translated from Norwegian by a British Norwegian for the British theater. Would the subtleties and nuances of language translate for an American audience? She worried that her play might sound too British.

As they discussed that situation, Asher told his mother that Erik was also writing a play. When Iris heard that, she wondered whether Erik would look at her play and see if it could be Americanized. She gave him a copy. He said he would read it and would offer his impressions about its suitability for an American audience.

The next day, he showed up at her lodgings upstairs. "I love your play," he said. "And I think Americans will love it. However, I agree with you that there are a lot of British idioms used in the translation and they'll stick out when the play is performed in America."

"Oh dear," she said. "That's what I was afraid of. Do you think that you would have the time to go through the play and Americanize it for me? I could pay you for your time."

"I have the time, and I'd be happy to do it."

Erik was over the moon. This was right up his alley. A professional assignment that he felt he was particularly well-qualified for. They agreed he would start immediately, and he would bring his results to her the following week.

It felt like circumstances were starting to change. He didn't know whether this was because the long winter was finally ending or if he was coming out of his own personal deep freeze. Now that the play had opened and performances were in the evenings, his days were suddenly free.

That same week, Fru Gullestad sought Erik out and found him in the green room at the theater.

"Erik, I'm sorry to tell you this, but they've made final casting decisions on *Arturo Ui*, and I'm afraid there will be no part for you," she said. "I tried my best, but with this being a foreign director and a foreign company, it just wasn't possible."

Erik was disappointed but not surprised. Getting a part was an improbable situation at best. He didn't speak German, his Norwegian was not yet sufficient, and he'd never personally auditioned or gotten to the point where he was even offered an audition.

Besides, *Arturo Ui* had already accomplished a great deal in the life of Erik Hellberg. Had there not been the specter of the possibility of getting a role in *Arturo Ui*, he might never have come to Norway in the first place or lasted more than a few months.

"I have another opportunity which may be of interest to you," she said. "The Norwegian government is eager to provide entertainment to the families of the workers on our oil platforms. These families have come to Norway from all over the world and most of them speak English. We want to put together some educational entertainment for them, and we're thinking of creating a kind of "reader's theater" project based on world literature. Might this be something that you would be interested in developing?"

"Are you kidding? Where do I sign up?" he said.

"Splendid. I've spoken with another American student who happens to be majoring in English and taking a year abroad here in Norway. Perhaps the two of you could work together? She's quite clever."

Fru Gullestad said she would set up a meeting in her office, and Erik and the American student together could create the Literature Tour.

Now that Erik hadn't been cast in *Arturo Ui*, that meant that as soon as *Vildanden* finished its run, he would no longer be employed and wouldn't be able to afford his apartment. The Literature Tour gig was nice, but it would be over soon and wouldn't pay much. Same situation with the translation—a quick job and a small paycheck.

The reality was, unless he got a more permanent job, his days in Bergen were numbered. His mom had been wondering when he'd be returning and he knew she was worried about him, so he let her know it could possibly be sometime after the run of the play if he couldn't find other work. But he was careful not to make any commitments.

Fru Gullestad shared office space with her husband in an old section of Bergen next to the Bergen Maritime Museum and overlooking the park at Nygårdshøden. Erik thought he was arriving early to this initial meeting of the Literature Tour committee only to discover Fru Gullestad already engaged in a robust conversation with a young woman about the author, Joyce Carol Oates.

The young woman was Heather Sandvik, recently graduated from the University of Illinois and was now taking some time off before going to graduate school to earn her master's degree in English. It seems Fru Gullestad and Heather shared a passion for the writing of Ms. Oates, who no doubt would be featured in the eventual Literature Tour program.

Heather was engaging, bright, and enthusiastic about the Literature Tour. She was staying with her relatives who lived in Bergen and had known Fru Gullestad for many years. While Erik and Heather's taste in literature differed, Fru Gullestad saw this as an asset for the program rather than a liability.

The syllabus for the program would be entirely up to Heather and Erik. The funding and itinerary would be Fru Gullestad's responsibility. Their first meeting lasted for over three hours with Heather and Erik kicking around many ideas of the authors they would like to include in the program. Their future meetings wouldn't include Fru Gullestad, although they would keep her informed of their progress.

It was right around this time when one of the actors in *Vildanden* had a birthday and the cast threw him a party in the greenroom following the evening's performance. The events of that night were a turning point in Erik's life, as he noted in his journal.

March 13, 1974

> I cannot believe how incredibly dense I am! How have I managed to survive for twenty-one years with such a total lack of awareness? All I can say is that someone up there's looking out for me, because if not for that, I wouldn't stand a chance in this life. I made a colossal mistake tonight, and I'm thoroughly embarrassed—but this was the most wonderful mistake I've ever made. They say God looks out for drunks and children. Tonight I feel like both.

During the gathering in the green room, the actress who played Hedvig walked over to Erik and said something. He didn't hear what she said because he was so startled that she was speaking to him. She was addressing him in English, and she wasn't smiling. In fact, she seemed upset.

Erik said, "*Unnskyld meg?* (Excuse me?)" and asked her in Norwegian to repeat what she said. She held up a postcard—the one he had started writing to Lucy some days ago but had lost.

The actress said to him in English, "I found this. Is it yours?"

Erik's face turned red. *My God, she found my postcard! She read what I wrote to my great-aunt. How embarrassing!*

Erik was at a loss for words. He finally found his voice and answered. He probably should have spoken in English, since she was addressing him in English, and the damned card was in English, and everyone in the theater referred to him as "The American." But he was stubborn, and he wanted her to know he could hold his own in Norwegian.

"Yes," he said in Norwegian. "It's a postcard to my great-aunt. I thought I had lost it."

He admired this actress. She wasn't a prima donna like so many of the actors he had encountered throughout his career up to that point. Her performance as Hedvig was perfect. In his humble opinion, she was the finest actor in the cast.

She switched to Norwegian and asked, "Why are you here?"

With searing pithiness, she asked what must have been on the mind of many of the actors at Den Nationale Scene. Her tone was almost accusatory, like he was somehow besieging their country and had no business being here.

Still, it was a fair question and frankly one he was glad she was asking. He would have been delighted had some of the other actors asked him that when he first arrived at the theater.

Erik answered her, and she peppered him with a dozen more questions. For him, it was wonderful. Finally, a conversation with one of the cast members. He liked the attention, and they had a spirited exchange. All his Norsk classes and studying were finally starting to pay off where it really counted.

She asked how he came to be at this theater and how he managed to get a part in this play. He understood most of what she was saying and he responded in Norwegian, but she was speaking so rapidly it was hard to keep up.

"*Du er ganske flink på Norsk,*" she said. ("You're quite clever to have learned so much Norwegian.")

Finally, as the conversation went beyond the small talk and got layered, he had to switch to English. He was afraid his limited Norwegian made him sound stupid and shallow. He didn't want to confirm her suspicions that he must be a rube. Surely this was what the main cast must have thought of him. Still, she said she was impressed that he'd learned so much in such a short time.

This was the first time that he'd spoken to her or that she'd spoken with him. He knew she was older than the fourteen-year-old Hedvig, but now he could see she might have been ten years older than that. He was even more impressed at how well she was able to convey the innocence of such a young girl. To him, the part of Hedvig was what makes the play tragic. Innocence was what must be sacrificed.

If the part wasn't handled with sensitivity and deftness, if the audience doesn't relate to her, doesn't come to love her and empathize with her, then the play misses the mark. In his mind, this actress playing Hedvig was one of the primary reasons that this production of *The Wild Duck* was such a deeply felt and powerful success.

Of course, he didn't tell her that. But this was exactly what he'd come to believe during all those rehearsals he watched. Being invisible has its advantages. A quiet and attentive observer sees all the subtle interpersonal exchanges between people. She was focused, intelligent, talented, and respectful of others. The other principal actors were talented, too, and he had to admit that the director was good at his craft and had earned the respect of his cast.

Yet there was something about this actress that was unique. Even in a crowd of stellar performers, she stood out. Her performance was subtle and understated. Never pushy or showy. Her presence on stage was like that of a kitten who had inadvertently wandered into the scene. The eyes of the audience were riveted on her to see what she would do next, because her movements and reactions were always authentic, organic, and unpredictable.

Her tone had softened considerably since they first started talking. Maybe she realized that Erik wasn't the ogre that some had perhaps thought him to be. At least she could see that even though he was an American, he wasn't the enemy and he wasn't a threat.

She asked him if he'd seen any of the other plays at the theater.

"Yes, of course. I've seen all of them."

"Oh, did you like any of them?"

She asked the question in such a way that he sensed the scuttlebutt at the theater was that some of the plays were terrible. He needed to be careful the way he answered.

"Yes, I did. I was impressed."

"Really?" she said with a surprised tone. "Which ones impressed you?"

Uh oh, he thought. *Why is she surprised?* He had to be careful here. He knew the ways of theater people. Everyone has an opinion about everything. There was always groupthink going on. The collective wisdom was usually that some plays are great and some are awful. He had no idea what anyone around here thinks about anything, because no one talks to him.

Still, he'd already committed himself and he had to say something.

"Well, aside from *Vildanden*, I'd have to say that my favorite play was *Jomfruburet*."

"Really?" Clearly, she hadn't expected that answer. "What did you like about it?"

She asked in such a way as to give the impression that it was a thoroughly unwatchable play and that no one of any refinement or sophistication could possible like it.

Crap, now I've stepped in it. This is probably the dud of the season, and the theater scuttlebutt is that everyone hates it. What do I know about musicals anyway?

Still, it was the truth. He did like the production. In fact, he thought it was wonderful.

"Well, it was very well done. I love Schubert's music, and I loved the choreography and the exuberant dancing, and it was just such a fun, light play. And the acting was great."

Erik was pretty sure he had fumbled and had crawled out on thin ice. Now he was managing to sound stupid and shallow in two languages.

"Honestly? You're joking, right?" She said this with doubt and incredulity in her voice.

He was committed to this tack, and he couldn't backtrack now. He knew he'd gone too far and had exposed his ignorance. This American clearly had no taste and couldn't recognize a good play from a bad play. This conversation would be ending soon. Still, since he'd started down this path, he had to continue. So he pushed on.

"Yes," he admitted, "the acting was great. Didn't you think so?"

"Which actors?" she demanded.

She would know all the dirt and the inner gossip, so he had to pick his words carefully.

"Well, all the actors were talented. Especially the three sisters. And that one sister, what an amazing singing voice she had!"

"Which sister?"

His inner voice was practically shouting. *Erik, be careful what you say! She knows everyone at this theater. Maybe she hates that actress. You simply don't know. Keep your mouth shut.* He never thought he was going to get grilled on this—least of all by the actress playing Hedvig.

"Uh, it was the one called Hanne."

"Now you're joking!" She laughed.

Erik wanted to change the subject so badly. He had painted himself into a corner. He clearly had picked the lemon of the season. The actress who played Hanne was probably the president of prima donnas club, and no one at the theater liked her. He would have had no clue about this.

He decided to push through his embarrassment and naivete and simply said, "No. Didn't you think she was amazing? Her singing was incredible. Honestly, I was very impressed."

"But that was me," she said.

There was a very long moment when he said nothing. He just stood as still as stone, while what she said sunk in. His face slowly got redder and redder until it must have resembled a tomato.

How could I have been so obtuse? How could I have had no idea? What an absolute idiot I am! How could I not have known? How could I sit in rehearsals day after day, watching this actress play Hedvig in Vildanden and not know it was the same person who I'd seen acting the role of Hanne in Jomfruburet?

She laughed and thought it was funny and seemed to enjoy Erik's anguished embarrassment. He supposed it was a high compliment for an actress to have been so successful in transforming herself from one role to the next that she could even confound someone who watched her every day.

In his own defense—and admittedly it was a poor one—Erik was so self-absorbed with his own insignificance within this troupe of actors that he had difficulty getting outside of himself. He was unable to break out of his own shell. He'd allowed his perception of the director's disdain for him to dictate his persona at the theater.

Because he hadn't made any friends at the theater, he had no idea what was going on outside of his own miniscule world. He'd only seen *Jomfruburet* once, when he first arrived at Den Nationale Scene, and clearly, he hadn't read the program notes.

No kidding, I wouldn't have been ready for Theater L'Homme Dieu last summer! Let's face it, technically I'm no longer a minor, but I have a lot of growing up to do.

Hedvig handed him the postcard to Lucy. She was smiling now. They continued talking for a while, and he felt that her attitude toward him had changed. Even though he'd displayed an appalling lack of awareness, he was relieved that he'd stuck to his guns and called it like he saw it.

Erik had a lot to think about on his walk home that night. He felt as though he'd just been through his baptismal moment at Den Nationale Scene.

Katarina. She was maybe twenty-five or twenty-six years old. She'd been acting since she was quite young and had been through Teaterhøgskolen. All the lead actors in the cast had been through Teaterhøgskolen. The unwritten rules were really very simple: if you didn't go through the national school, your chances of having a theatrical career in Norway were next to nil. (One glaring exception was Liv Ullman. She managed to become an internationally known stage, film, and TV actress, author, and director, without having qualified for Teaterhøgskolen).

Erik got up before the sun the next day so that he could start work on translating Iris's play from British to American English. He enjoyed this work immensely. Spotting the British slants wasn't difficult, and thinking of colloquial alternatives was fun.

In the meantime, he hadn't stopped thinking about the conversation he'd had with Katarina and how dense he'd been in not recognizing that she was the same actress who played Hedvig in *Vildanden* and Hanne in *Jomfruburet*. *How could I not have recognized her? Her eyes are unmistakable.* He was feeling a mixture of embarrassment over his faux pas, gratitude for her confronting him, and awe at her talent.

Their conversation may have registered only as a simple blip on her radar—a single conversation on a single day in a calendar of 365 days—but she had touched him. For Erik, that blip represented a mountain peak on his radar. He wanted to express this to her somehow.

A few days later Katarina asked Erik if he wanted to go with her to a party after the performance on the following night. She usually went home after performances, but some close friends had invited her to a special event, and she felt obligated to go.

What? Erik thought. *She's inviting me? The American?* Erik was excited and intrigued, but he didn't want to let it go to his head. *She's being nice to me. She probably knows that the rest of the cast has had the wrong idea about me all along and this is her way of showing it.* Erik was touched. Deeply. He immediately thanked her and said that he would love to go.

The party was held on the upper floor of Sigurd's Verft, a restaurant in the center of town. They walked up the long, narrow stairway leading to the second floor. When they came to the landing at the top, they encountered a larger-than-life poster of Katarina that covered the entire wall.

The poster evidently caught Katarina by surprise. She appeared slightly embarrassed but took the honorific in stride as she and Erik entered the room where the party was underway. The room was packed, and Katarina introduced him to various people as they moved about the room.

What Katarina hadn't told him—what he figured out on his own as the evening progressed—was that this party was thrown in her honor. It was a celebration of her contribution to the Bergen theater community.

Erik immediately noticed a difference in the way people regarded him. The difference was that they *were* regarding him. He wasn't used to this reaction, especially around the theater people who somehow hadn't previously noticed him at Den Nationale Scene.

He spoke Norwegian with everyone he met, even though English would have been wiser since everyone's English was better than his Norwegian. But, like his Norwegian antecedents, he was stubborn, and he felt a need to prove how *flink* (smart) he was.

Erik was conflicted. On the one hand, someone had shown an interest in him and had gone out on a limb for him—and not just anyone but someone whose position in the world of Norwegian theater was secure. She had nothing to gain by being kind toward him. He was struggling to enjoy the moment.

It brought back the discomfort he felt at Kjell's New Year's Eve party when he was preoccupied with the thought that the people might assume he was Alistair's partner. Had he been more self-secure, he wouldn't have been concerned.

Erik met and had conversations with a lot of people that night. When he tried to speak in Norwegian, the conversation could only go so far. When he dropped his Norwegian front, the conversations flowed naturally to English.

One especially enjoyable English conversation Erik had was with an actress who was there with her son. She had lived and acted in several different countries, including the United States, and she had even spent time in Minneapolis. When Erik asked if her son was also an actor, she looked a bit embarrassed and told him that he wasn't her son, but that he was "her man."

Ouch. Erik kicked himself for assuming that the person with her was her son. True, the kid was half her age and there was an overriding familial resemblance, but still, Erik knew he had been imprudent.

The harsh reality was that sooner or later, everyone must grow up. Erik was off to a slow start, and this was an embarrassing lesson to learn. There was no tactful way to recover from such an indiscretion, but fortunately Katarina's friend was gracious.

When Katarina and Erik left the party, he told her that he wished he was further along in Norwegian; she said not to worry about it.

"Just speak English," she said. "You've already come a long way, and you'll get there. Be patient."

But he wasn't patient. He wanted to conquer this language, and he wanted to do it yesterday.

Katarina was surprised when she learned how far Erik had to walk to get home. He said the walk was no big deal. He was used to it. She asked if he walked to and from the theater every day. He told her that he did. She got thoughtfully quiet, as though she was processing what he'd just said.

"*Typisk Norsk*," she murmured.

There's that phrase again: "Typical Norwegian." Maybe he wasn't Sámi at all, or maybe he was, and the Sámi were just as stubborn as the Norwegians. Was Erik's true heritage identity finally revealing itself? Whatever the case, he wasn't sure if she meant that as a compliment or as a character flaw.

The winding road up Mount Fløyen appeared quite different from previous treks home. Most obviously, it wasn't raining. The moon was out, and the stars danced enticingly in and out of patchy white and gray clouds made up of rows of fluffy ripples. Yes, it had been a special evening. It was late, but he wasn't tired. He felt alive.

Have I been incubating all these months in Bergen? Am I finally out of the incubator? Katarina. Who is she? What's going on? Does she like me? Do I like her? What's happening? Is there some mystic power she has that has caused the clouds to part and allowed me to see the moon and stars as though for the first time? Has the door of acceptance finally been opened a crack for me?

The clear weather held, and the next day he basked in the rays of a resplendent sun all the way to the theater. He was excited but nervous to be back at Den Nationale Scene. *Would things be different at the theater? Would the dynamics have changed, and if so, what would that look like?*

What will it be like to see Katarina? Will she be playing it cool and only acknowledge me as a statist, or will she break ranks with her fellow actors and treat me as nicely as she did last night at the party?

He didn't need to wait long to find out. He ran into her in the green room, and she was genuinely happy to see him again. Amazingly, she seemed devoid of any awareness that there might even be the slightest hint from the other actors of anything resembling disrespect for Erik as a human being.

Either this woman is secure in who she is and doesn't give a damn what anyone else thinks, or I'm just being paranoid and making it all up about what the other actors think of me.

There can be no doubt that Katarina was intimately aware of what the other actors thought about Erik. She must have known they didn't like the fact that he was here, that he didn't fit in. And there was was no reason to think that Katarina had felt any differently than her coworkers. There must have been a few inner-circle conversations about the young misfit, the American.

Clearly, no one openly disliked him. He wasn't brash or arrogant like many of the Americans who had ventured into the Land of the Midnight Sun, but he was an American. It was best to simply keep him at a distance, to not get acquainted, and let whatever arrangement he had with management just play itself out.

Perhaps it was that postcard that gave Katarina pause. "My performance in particular got great reviews in all of the local papers…" She undoubtedly saw that he had a sense of humor. Maybe she thought it was quaint that he was writing to his great aunt. Maybe she had been wrong about him. Maybe they all had been wrong. Anyone could see that he was polite and respectful, that he was sensitive. Sure, he's quiet, but that doesn't mean there's not a lot going on inside his head…

Erik made up his mind that he had to do something to let her know that she'd touched him, that she'd made a difference in his world, and that it meant a lot to him. That night, after the performance and during his long walk home, he let his mind wander and gave his imagination free reign.

By the time Erik arrived at the Empty Space that night, he knew what he wanted to say to her. He sat down and pulled out his journal.

The Gift

> When the lights go down and the curtain rises
> There is a gift which lies in wait, backstage
> Softly, in subtle surmises.
> Like a flower in the morning,
> Scarce a hint of the fragrance yet to rage,
> It bewitches and sends us aromatic warning.
> Yet were I skilled in thought or deft of tongue
> I could not express this gift, O flower of the stage.
> For 'tis more than flower, with immobile blossom brung,
> she wings the air, as a butterfly, in dominion breeze.
> And we, like children of the wonderment age,
> Lie on the hill, our bed of grass
> To watch our gift feather the sky with masterful ease,
> While dainty feet emulate the stars.
> Then forth her rhapsody sweet, a gift of the gift,
> Which storms and sooths, but quietly is ours.
> Sending us twilight upon the wake of this gentle thunder.
> Higher we ride, with enraptured safety
> Until at last, by divider red and velvet, we are brought asunder.
> Retaining our gift, though not within our mindful sage.
> We consult our soul, whose heart has awoken now to wonder.

Erik arrived at the theater early the next day and placed the poem in her dressing room next to her mirror. Then he went to the dressing room that he shared with the *kammerherrer*.

Most of these gents were former pros. Several of them had been to the theater school years ago and had spent a lifetime in the theater. They were all retired and now were just having fun. They could care less about the social status of anyone at the theater, and they helped Erik to not take himself so seriously all the time. They liked Erik for who he was and didn't give a damn which role he had in the play.

Erik didn't get a chance to talk with Katarina until the next day. She stopped him in the foyer of the theater and thanked him for the poem. She said it was beautiful.

That was it. She went off to get ready for the performance. He didn't know what else he'd expected. But still he was glad that he'd written the poem and had given it to her. He felt like it was the least he could do. He wanted her to know the impact she'd had on him.

Katarina treated him the same way she treated everyone at the theater, with kindness and respect. It's not that she'd been unkind before the postcard, but it was more that he went unnoticed, like a phantom.

Erik observed something else in Katarina. It appeared that her attitude toward him had shifted since he gave her the poem. It was subtle but detectible. The way she looked at him, the way she lingered a little longer in conversation. There was an openness, a brightness in her smile. Yet she was not overtly forward, and it dawned on him that the ball was in his court to reciprocate the attention. Or was it just her natural kindness that she'd shown him?

She invited you to that party… What have you done for her? What can you do to show Katarina how much her reaching out has meant to you? A poem won't cut it Erik.

You could take her out to a restaurant? No, that's a dumb idea; You can't afford it. Besides, you don't know if that would be appropriate anyway. You and Katarina are just friends.

Even if he could afford a restaurant, taking her to dinner would be pushing the boundaries. He didn't feel like it was his call to push boundaries.

Maybe you could give her a gift, but what would be appropriate? The more he thought about it, the worse the idea seemed. In the first place, anything he could afford wouldn't be good enough.

Even if you could scrape together the money for something nice, what kind of a message would that send? It had to be something special but not expensive; it had to be intimate without pushing the boundaries of friendship.

It's too bad you can't make dinner for her at the Empty Space. That would solve the money issue.

But there were major problems with that idea. *To begin with, neither of us have a car and my apartment is a two-hour uphill walk. It doesn't matter how "Nordic" she is, that idea would bomb before it left your lips.*

Another problem was that he had never cooked a meal for anyone in his entire life. And finally, how would it look? He was proud of his little apartment, and he wouldn't be ashamed for her to see it, but bringing her there would really be crossing the barriers.

Barriers. Why are you concerned about breaking boundaries and crossing barriers, Erik? I thought you were done with all the morality baggage that you had when you left the States.

Having her come to the apartment would solve the money problem, and as much as he didn't want to be hung up on morality issues, somehow the setup just didn't seem right.

Okay, this would feel different if there were other people involved. It would be less like a date. Yeah, the situation would be better if the evening was more like a dinner party with a few good friends.

The more he thought about the situation, the more a dinner party at his apartment seemed to be a good solution. *How difficult could it be to find some friends and make a dinner? And as for cooking for others, you've got to start somewhere, right? How difficult could it be?*

Erik was sure that Fru Menck would loan him a table and a few chairs for the occasion, maybe some plates and silverware. He could make a vegetable soup and fry some steaks, bake some potatoes, and serve a bottle of wine.

What could go wrong?

So he told Katarina that he was planning on having some friends from his Norwegian class over for dinner and asked if she wanted to join them.

"When?" she asked.

"I haven't set a date yet. I wanted to check with you first."

She pulled out her planner. Erik was confronted with an intimidatingly full schedule.

They managed to find a free night and made plans. Randy, Erik's friend from Norsk class, would bring Maren, his Swedish girlfriend. Randy said they'd take a taxi and offered to bring Katarina. That worked out astoundingly well for Erik and left him free to prep his apartment and make the dinner.

Erik wished he could say that the evening was an unqualified success.

On the plus side, everyone got along great. All three of Erik's guests brought bottles of wine. Randy didn't travel in theatrical circles but was articulate on a variety of subjects. Likewise, Maren proved to be a good conversationalist on just about any topic. Erik was impressed with how effortlessly Katarina adapted herself to his other guests and eloquently spoke on many subjects that had nothing whatsoever to do with theater.

The one topic that everyone agreed on was what a lousy cook Erik was. The soup was passable, but the steaks were a tad leathery. Erik's lack of skills in the kitchen became the brunt of much good-humored ribbing. Erik didn't mind. In fact, the more they ribbed him, the more relaxed he became. He was happy that they were genuinely enjoying themselves, even if it was at his expense. He opened the third bottle of wine and filled everyone's glass.

"A skoal to all of you for enduring my cooking and a prayer that none of us come down with ptomaine poisoning."

Everyone laughed as they skoaled each other, but Erik caught a glint of concern in Maren's eyes as she exchanged a glance with Randy. Randy saw that Erik had seen Maren's concern, and he quickly changed the subject.

"Erik, I see you have a guitar. Do you play?

"What? No, not really. I mostly just pick."

"C'mon man, play something for us," said Randy.

Maren jumped in. "Yes, you must play for us, I would love to hear you play."

Truthfully, Erik was intimidated to play in front of Katarina. He'd heard her sing, and she was in a different league, a different universe. Not that it was a competition, but she was a pro and he was, well, he was mostly just a picker. He liked music, loved it actually, but it wasn't his strong suit. Some actors are great players and singers, some aren't.

Erik shot a glance at Katarina. She wasn't saying anything, but those sparkling eyes were speaking volumes. He knew instantly that this was a challenge and that she was very curious to see how he would respond. He'd had just enough wine to overcome his apprehensions, so he stood and walked over to the guitar. He hesitated a moment before he picked up the instrument, but once it was in his hand, he felt confident. He strummed and tuned for bit as he thought about which song he should play.

When he was waiting for rides while hitchhiking across Europe, he'd often sung to himself lines from Graham Nash's song, "Teach Your Children." He loved the idea that "you, who are on the road, must have a code that you can live by." He knew the chords and words, so he let the wine take over and began playing.

After all the good-natured ribbing his guests had given him about his cooking, they were surprised to hear that he could play and carry a tune. When he got to the chorus, Katarina quietly joined in and took the harmony. She sang softly. Her voice was clear, gentle, and effortless. When the second verse came, she gave Erik the solo and then joined in again for the chorus.

Was this a watershed moment for Erik and Katarina? So much of the vast space between their worlds seemed insurmountable. Yet there was something mystical in their harmonizing. Perhaps the evening served to put this budding friendship between Katarina and Erik on new footing.

This small, intimate gathering at the Empty Space served to reveal that Erik was exactly who he'd presented himself to be—a young man with lots of questions and serious intentions about a career in the theater. At the same time, Erik was convinced that this dedicated, talented artist was truly the humble and kind person that she projected herself to be.

Erik's long winter of solitude outside of rehearsals and classes had afforded him the luxury of indulging in reading, writing, and thinking. But the solitude gave him few opportunities to discuss the theories and questions that he'd accumulated about the plays, authors, and concepts he'd been studying. These concepts found a learned and willing debate companion in Katarina, who displayed an intense curiosity about what might be found inside this hitherto silent and enigmatic cast member.

Several days after the dinner in his apartment, Katarina invited Erik to watch her in a rehearsal at a neighboring venue. She had a part in one of the many activities surrounding the upcoming Festspillene i Bergen, the international festival of the arts that the city of Bergen hosted every spring. She asked for his feedback on a transitional segment she was to perform with some others during the festival.

Erik watched Katarina's rehearsal of a segment from *Jomfruburet* that she was to perform with the other two "sisters" from the musical. Although Erik's facility with the language was improving; he didn't understand all the details, but he got the gist of it. Still, he found himself hard-pressed to offer Katarina any constructive criticism that would be of value to her. More than anything, he understood that she was honoring him by opening herself to his evaluation.

In turn, Erik asked Katarina to watch a rehearsal of the Literature Tour that he was putting together with Heather, the other American with whom Fru Gullestad had paired him. Not having a director, they were on their own for creating a performance that would be both substantive and entertaining for the oil platform community.

Their piece was just over an hour in length. Ten minutes in, Katarina stopped them.

"You've chosen some interesting poems and pieces of literature, but you're presenting them in the straightforward manner that one might expect," she said. "How about if you change the staging and the tempo a bit and present them in a way that the audience might not be expecting?

"For example, right now, you're alternating so that when one of you finishes a poem, the other one reads the next one. Predictable. What if you broke the poems and stories up and each read a line here and a line there—both of you within the same poem? Try to keep the audience engaged by keeping them guessing what might be coming next."

Good point, thought Erik.

"And your staging is predictable," she said. "You're both just sitting on stools reading to the audience. You'll lose them if you don't get up and move around, always be motivated by and reflecting the prose or the poetry. You can't just be narrators—you must be characters, jumping into and out of the literature like it was burning hot or freezing cold."

She's right.

"And Erik, I notice that when you read, your face falls into predictable patterns. You lift your eyebrows constantly. Always be aware of even small details like that. You might want to try putting scotch tape on your eyebrows during rehearsal, so you're aware of every time they rise and fall."

Erik didn't immediately respond. It was hard to accept her constructive criticism, and he wanted to get defensive. But he had enough sense to keep his mouth shut. After all, he'd invited her to come and watch them rehearse. He'd asked for her opinion. That's all she was doing. And most of what she said was good advice. Then he thought about the impressive performances that he'd witnessed from her, time and again. Katarina subordinated herself to whatever role she was playing, which itself was subordinated to the play.

Even though he didn't feel like it, he said, "Okay, that's good. I'll have to try that. Thanks." He sensed that Katarina was curious to see how he would take criticism. Heather was in total agreement with everything that Katarina said. This was not a moment to let his pride get in the way.

Katarina and Erik had a lot in common. Their commonalities were likely greater than their differences. Both were committed to pursuing truth within this peculiar art form. Both were *typisk Norsk*.

People talk of the beauty of the Swedish people and the industry of the Danes. When they talk about the Norwegians, they mention exploration, innovation, and creativity. It was an undeniable fact that a country with such a relatively small population had produced an impressive number of explorers and artists, including "Erik the Red," Leif Erikson, Roald Amundsen, Thor Heyerdahl, and Fridtjof Nansen, not to mention the towering figures of Henrik Ibsen, Edvard Grieg, and Edvard Munch.

Katarina had dared to look beyond the director's prejudicial disdain for Erik and see something in him that others had not. In doing so, she stood to lose much by displaying an interest in this unheralded American student who seemingly walked in through the back door unannounced and into Den Nationale Scene.

She questioned Erik about everything, including the reports he was preparing for college. He was happy to talk with someone about his projects, even if she didn't always agree with his concepts. Their discussions often led to disagreement, yet her feedback caused him to rethink some of the assumptions he'd made about his subjects.

Katarina shared with Erik how she got started acting and how she knew from her earliest memories that she loved performing. Teaterhøgskolen had been a revelation to her—to see so many talented people, all working to be the best they could be at their craft. She especially loved the art of acting, delving into the marrow of a character and then transporting it onto the stage. She knew this was her calling in life and appreciated how much Norway supported the arts.

Erik related completely. He shared with her his respect for their profession. He viewed it as a calling. He told her about the best-actor award he'd won in a statewide competition while still in high school. Despite this and his other acting accomplishments, he sensed that she viewed his development as an actor to still be in the nascent phases.

Regardless of where Erik stood in the timeline of his career, what mattered more to him was the potential that he had to offer as an actor. He believed in himself and felt he could make his mark in the profession.

Katarina displayed a genuine interest and continued to probe into other aspects of his life. He hadn't initially planned to, but he told her about Charlie and how he'd been killed in the war. He even told her that he wished he'd gone in Charlie's place. She listened quietly and with empathy, but he sensed that she wasn't sympathetic with America's involvement in the war and that she restrained herself from making any judgements.

Everything that had preoccupied Erik a month ago was now undergoing a transformation—a whole new set of preoccupations was taking shape.

What's happening between Katarina and me? Clearly, we've developed a friendship. Is this something more? Where's this heading?

Shortly after *Vildanden* closed, Katarina had a little gathering at her flat for some of the actors in the play and she invited Erik. This wasn't a wrap party—that had already taken place at the theater. This was a small gathering with her close friends. Everyone was relaxed and in great spirits.

Her flat was on the top floor of a small building in an especially old and quaint part of the city. Narrow cobblestone streets led to the building. She had gabled windows looking out over the streets of Bergen, with a view of both city and mountains.

The flat was neat and tidy and not overly decorated. He was greeted with the delicate scent of her perfume the moment he stepped inside. Her various pieces of furniture seemed to embody different styles, yet somehow they all worked together beautifully. One would never have guessed that this flat belonged to an actor.

The dinner she served was a far cry from what Erik's friends were forced to endure at the Empty Space. First, she had matching tableware, linens, and an abundance of flowers throughout the apartment. And, in contrast to Erik's offering, her food was delicious.

This was Erik's first opportunity to have deeper interactions with several of the other actors from the theater. Katarina's acceptance of him had been a groundbreaker, shattering the fourth wall, as it were, between him and other cast members. Surprisingly, he didn't sense any attitude other than parity coming from her other guests.

Without Katarina's abiding acceptance of him, which permeated the room, he could have been intimidated by the language barrier or the professional experience level of the others in the room. Instead, he found himself comfortable in their presences. Erik looked at them anew—as people, not just actors.

He felt for the first time that he was no longer viewed as "The American" but instead as a promising young actor from America. Although the play had ended, he felt that he was now part of this mosaic known as Den Nationale Scene. Perhaps not so much that they viewed him differently; this was more about climbing out of the shell where he'd entombed himself.

The dinner started early, as several of the guests had other obligations at Festspillene i Bergen that evening. When those guests departed, only Erik, Katarina, and Katarina's friend Svana remained.

The three of them were in excellent spirits and giddy from the wine. Both women were teasing and making fun of Erik—his accent, his being an American, the fact that he was still in college. It was all good fun, and he didn't mind the teasing.

They also knew that he'd been a gymnast, so they were teasing him about that, too, saying he wasn't all that strong and that two girls together could easily take him down. That led to some wrestling and roughhousing. Even though it was two against one, he was pretty sure he could have overpowered them if he tried, but he also recognized that this was a game, and it wasn't about who was the strongest.

Katarina and Svana managed to pin him down. Katarina sat straddling his chest, holding his hands to the floor while her friend sat on his legs just below his knees, making any amount of movement for him nearly impossible. They were all laughing, but at the same time Erik was experiencing both frustration and excitement at having been physically overpowered by the women.

Erik gathered his strength and tried throwing them off, but he failed. *Are you really trying your hardest, Erik? Have you truly released your full strength?* He wasn't sure. He wasn't sure he wanted to throw them off. *This is a game, right? You have to be careful; you don't want to hurt them.*

Katarina was facing forward and couldn't see what her friend was doing as she sat on his legs. Svana had leaned forward, unbuckled Erik's belt, and was slowly unzipping his pants. Erik had been laughing along with Katarina and her friend, but his face must have registered that the nature of the game had morphed into something other than what it had started out to be. Or had it?

What was going on? Was this planned? Had Katarina and her friend been scheming this? He was aware that in this insular world of Norwegian theater, the options for a young actress were limited, even for one as attractive and accomplished as Katarina. Many of the male actors were already either married or in relationships or simply not romantically interested in women.

As much as Erik had been enjoying and was excited by the teasing of the girls, he was also confused. Katarina noticed the change in his face; she turned around and saw Svana pulling Erik's pants down. Both girls started laughing and giggling uncontrollably. The laughter sapped their strength and made it possible for Erik to roll out from under them and escape.

Once he was on his feet, he felt the dynamics change. They were all still laughing, but clearly game time was over. This was more than just a change in dynamics—there was a sexual current loose in the room.

Katarina's friend suddenly mentioned an engagement for early the following morning and begged leave. Katarina walked her out into the hallway where Erik could hear them quietly giggling. When her friend left, Katarina locked the door and after a moment, she walked through the apartment turning off lights.

Up to this moment, their relationship had been…well, a friendship. They'd never defined or even discussed the nature of their friendship. His relationship with Diana, by contrast, had been a romantic one out of the gate. And with Mette, circumstances had prevented anything beyond a friendship from developing.

Katarina was a whole different ball game. She was complex, alluring, enticing, mercurial, challenging, intelligent, thoughtful, mature, focused, courageous, wise, and…a little dangerous.

They stood in the darkened room, now lit solely by moonlight coming in through the gabled windows. Neither spoke. They both just looked at each other from across the room. Erik knew what the moment called for. He knew he could walk over to Katarina, take her hand, and gently hold it while they looked in each other's eyes. He knew that she would wordlessly tell him the extent of what he would be welcome to do.

Yet he didn't move. Perhaps had he been older or more experienced or more fluent in Norwegian or had drunk more wine… *No, it's not any of those things. How do you honestly feel about her, Erik? Do you like her, or are you just overwhelmed with her? Is it that you're grateful to her for her acceptance and attention? Or do you truly have feelings for her? Can you define your feelings? Where is this relationship heading?*

He had many questions, but what he did know was that she wanted honesty. She was not interested in infatuations. She wanted the real deal and nothing less. This was not anything they'd ever discussed, but he knew this about her. He knew that if he held her hand, if he kissed those eyes and lips, he knew what would be expected of him—not just tonight, but tomorrow and every day thereafter.

He felt her acceptance and had seen her kindness, but he also saw something else. He saw a hunger, a need. Erik was certain that she could read his thoughts, and he felt naked in her gaze.

The moonlight that splashed across the floor seemed to amplify every thought in the silent room. Volumes passed between them. In such moments, truth is often sacrificed for emotions. But this was not to be one of those times. It was as if she saw both who he was and who he was becoming. She must have divined that this was someone who was capable of giving and accepting commitment, but that the cost to her would come in the form of long, patient forbearance.

Her voice cut through the silence that stood like an invisible barrier between them. "It would be crazy for you to walk home now. You can spend the night, but you'll have to sleep on the couch."

She went to the closet and pulled out sheets and a blanket and set them down on the couch. She then took a pillow off her bed and handing it to Erik, she said softly in Norwegian, "Good night and sweet dreams."

He didn't move for a long time after she left the room. Eventually, he sat on the couch. *What else could she do, Erik? You left her no choice. She's in motion, Erik; you're not. You're standing still. She's giving you space. Where are you at, Erik? Where's your heart? And where's your head?*

The following morning, she entered the room like the sun itself. She was kind and happy and immediately began making coffee. He folded the sheets and blankets and helped her clear the table and wash the dishes from the party last night. An organic adjustment began to emerge, a new paradigm in the friendship. He helped Katarina prepare breakfast, and they discussed their separate duties for the day ahead.

As he walked up Mount Fløyen, he wondered what a relationship with her would be like. Would they be consumed with living and breathing theater twenty-four hours a day, seven days a week? Would acting be more important than the relationship? He envisioned what the demands of a full-time acting career were and how difficult these demands could be on a relationship.

Yet Katarina was different. Erik had had the opportunity to study her during the many weeks of rehearsal, when his presence was indistinguishable from the theater seats. What attracted him to her was more her genuine goodness and kindness than her talent and beauty or any accolades she may have received for her work.

In the days and weeks following, they spent more and more time together, which often served to highlight their differences. Age, cultures, life experiences, maturity levels—everything seemed to be a challenge. She was usually ten steps ahead of him. Whenever he reached a destination or a conclusion, she seemed to already be there waiting for him.

She took him to task, for example, if he tried carrying on conversations with her friends in Norwegian. "Why do you persist in speaking Norwegian? They speak to you in English, and you answer in Norwegian. That kills the conversation because you aren't yet fluent enough to carry on in-depth discussions, and you're missing out on many opportunities."

She was right. Yet Erik wanted to be fully conversant in Norsk. He wanted to be able to discuss the issues of the day in their lingo. Not being fluent enough to do so was so damn frustrating and so he forced himself into the arena. He should get an *A* for effort. *Couldn't she see that?*

In the days that followed, Katarina challenged him on other fronts, as well. The questions Erik wrestled with regarding God and his purpose in life didn't pose the same quandary for her. They'd grown up with different belief systems and faith traditions—or at least had drawn different conclusions about the ultimate laws that govern the universe.

Erik was deep into his journey of challenging his own beliefs about these laws and deciding what was true and what wasn't. Katarina challenged him even further. Erik couldn't throw out the existence of a creator nor the personal involvement of such a being. He'd been protected and guided too many times at too many critical junctures in his life.

"But Kat," Erik said. "Don't you see that every aspect of spring exploding all around us speaks of a creator with intelligence, understanding, and purpose? The faculty of the human mind, of man's ability to reason, and the existence of a spiritual as well as a physical nature are undeniable realities."

This belief of Erik's was foolishness to Katarina. How could he be so naïve to believe in something as simplistic and unrealistic as a God who took personal interest in them or their jobs or careers and any of the minute decisions that they made day to day?

"What about the insane cruelty of mankind? How could a creator allow for a Hitler or a Stalin or a Chairman Mao? No, if God existed, He or She is absent." In her opinion, Erik was foolish to believe in such things.

She clearly had thought through the big questions of the universe and had reached settled conclusions. Her career was firmly on track, and she had the major aspects of her life figured out. She knew what she wanted. From her perspective, Erik's acceptance of a metaphysical entity playing a role in the creation, or the governance of the universe could be chalked up to his youth. He simply hadn't lived long enough or thought through these concepts the way she had. She could help guide him in this regard. He was a good man. He was worth investing her energies in. His good qualities far outweighed his bad.

The long walks up Mount Fløyen that were part and parcel of Erik's daily regimen were becoming increasingly inconvenient not just to Erik but also to Katarina. She often insisted that he stay at her flat for the night. During these sleepover nights, by unspoken mutual agreement, Erik slept on the couch. This platonic arrangement, while eliciting restraint on both of their parts, also provided some benefits.

Of all the questions that hung unanswered in the air, the biggest one was where their relationship was heading. Every other question hinged upon the answer to that one. The fact that their relationship had not crossed the Rubicon allowed for greater expression of friendship without the complications that sex inevitably brings.

They spent more time together now that their schedules were freed up. As their relationship developed, they revealed more of themselves to each other. Katarina clearly saw Erik as an artist, but he was young and had to develop his talent. He also had some archaic American ideas that she believed would eventually fall by the wayside. She believed in him; she was willing to take a chance on him. In fact, she wanted to take a chance on him. She had grown to care for him, and she made herself vulnerable to him.

Erik knew he had a decision to make. The die had been cast the day he learned he hadn't landed a part in *Arturo Ui*. He would have to make some big changes in his life if he were to stay. Katarina's course was firmly established; Erik was the one up on the high wire.

All winter long, it had been rainy, cold, and dreary. Now, along with the warm sun, majestic flowers began erupting everywhere. The mountains surrounding Bergen quite literally exploded in color and fragrance all around them. Even the Norwegian name for flowers—*blomster*—reflects this explosion.

When the sun shines in Bergen, young and old alike make up for all the time they've been forced to spend indoors during the winter months. The local expression was *sitter på solen* (sitting in the sun). Even the normally austere and gothic Den Nationale Scene building underwent a colorful floral upgrade. As the spring flowers opened all around them, Katarina and Erik did the best they could to let the sun shine on their relationship too.

Not having to be in rehearsals during the day or performing in the evening was a blessing. Bergen was an adopted city for Katarina, and there was much she hadn't yet seen. They explored parts of the city together.

One especially beautiful day, they went on an excursion into the countryside. Katarina had packed a picnic lunch, and together they discovered a grassy outcropping on the edge of Sognefjord—the deepest and longest fjord in Norway. While Katarina served the picnic, Erik stood transfixed as he stared across the ancient waters that once were the launching grounds of Viking warriors.

Returning to Katarina, Erik stopped dead in his tracks when he saw that she had removed her top. She was naked from the waist up except for her belt, which she had wrapped semi-discreetly across her chest. Upon seeing Erik, she laughed and stretched out her arms as she spun around, letting the warm sun embrace her.

Erik was spellbound. His entire body tingled with excitement, and he yearned to enter this world she was dancing in. He, too, removed his shirt. She laughed as she danced and reached out her hands for him to join her. Together they danced like two woodland sprites, free from inhibitions in their celebration of the sun.

Oh my God! Who is this woman who is so free and full of life?

Erik was spellbound by this enchanting creature. Life with Katarina could be magnificent and fascinating. Norway itself seemed slowly to be subsuming him. That evening, Erik built a small fire on the outcropping, and they roasted *pølse* (sausage) over the coals and drank wine.

"Oh, look Erik. A søstermarihand. My favorite flower. It's an orchid. How unusual to find one here in the west. Normally they grow only on the eastern side of the country. How wonderful! I dare not pick it—it's too rare and too beautiful."

At this time of the year, Norway stays light until at least midnight. As embers from the fire slowly died, they lay together on the blanket watching the sun flirt with the horizon, trying to make up its mind whether to submerge. The waters of Sognefjord appeared markedly different tonight. At first, Erik thought it was the midnight sun playing games with him; but no, he could see clearly the waters were now a vibrant iridescent turquoise. *What is that color? Why is it so arresting and familiar?*

While Erik was pondering the color of the waters and the nocturnal light show, Katarina could no longer suppress commenting on an aspect of Erik that had been troubling her for many weeks, something she'd never fully confronted him with before.

"Why do I never hear you talk about your brother?"

Erik struggled to find the right answer to her question. Finally, he said, "I suppose because it's painful."

"All the more reason to talk about him," she said. "It's good to talk about the things that hurt. It helps."

"Well, talking about him is not going to bring him back."

Katarina sat up. "That's an idiotic statement. It's not about bringing him back; it's about learning to live without him. It's about facing life in his absence. We all need to talk about the things that hurt us; otherwise the pain just festers and never goes away, never gets resolved."

He knew it was idiotic the second he said it. But it was painful, and he didn't like talking about Charlie's death. Doesn't she know that he blamed himself. That was another thing that he didn't like talking about. People would think that was idiotic. Yet it was true.

"Look, I was drafted, and I fought those bastards at the draft board. They didn't believe that my birth certificate was wrong, or if they did, they didn't care. But I kept arguing with them. I wore them down. Yet, I didn't lift a finger for Charlie. He never should have been drafted. What was God thinking?"

"God?" exclaimed Katarina. "What has God got to do with it? My God, Erik, you're always talking about how reserved the Norwegians are, how 'stubborn' they are, but you're the same way. *Kjære Gud*! (Dear God!) You're more Norwegian than I am!"

She doesn't understand. Charlie was a good man, much better than I'll ever be. Charlie was honest; he always told the truth, even if it made him look bad. I'm not like that. I lie. I cheat, I've stolen stuff. I've probably broken all ten of the Commandments. No, my life is destined to be tormented by Charlie's death. Katarina is the last person who would understand this. How could I explain to her that Charlie's death is God's punishment against me, when she doesn't even believe that there's a God?

"Yes," Erik said. "I know it's idiotic. I should talk about it. It's just that Charlie was such a good man. He was gentle and honest. He didn't deserve to die. He wasn't a fighter, like me. Even though he was my older brother, I kind of looked out for him."

Katarina didn't respond. Perhaps she felt that Erik was on the verge of unburdening himself. And, after a moment of silence, he did.

"One time, when we were really little—Charlie was probably about seven and I would have been five—there were these bullies who lived down the street from us. They stopped Charlie and me once when we were walking home. They wouldn't let us pass. They said we had to take our clothes off if we wanted to pass. I was scared and started crying and when I did, the bullies let me go, but they said Charlie had to stay. So I left. I left and Charlie stayed.

    I abandoned him. I was more concerned about myself. I should have stayed and helped my brother. I should have fought those bullies, even though I was afraid of them. Eventually, Charlie made it home. He didn't end up fighting them, and he didn't have to take his clothes off. I'm not sure what happened; Charlie never gave me a complete answer. I think he just talked his way out of it."

    "So you're saying that Charlie wasn't a fighter, and that he should not have been sent to Vietnam. What could he or you possibly have done to keep him out of the war?"

    "You don't understand. Charlie got a draft lottery number of fifteen. I got a five. A five! They should have sent me to Vietnam. But I wouldn't let them. I went to the draft board and told them they made a mistake. I told them I was born on September 26, not September 28. They didn't believe me, of course, but I showed them my birth certificate and showed them how the six looked like an eight. They still didn't believe me, but I kept arguing with them. I wouldn't shut up. Maybe they ended up believing me, or maybe they were worn out by the anti-war movement and all the deaths of young men that they'd been sending to Vietnam. In the end, I just never reported for duty, and they never came after me."

    Katarina listened intently but didn't respond. They both stared out into the limitless fjord, which was majestic in this twilight hour. Another campfire burned on the opposite bank of the fjord. Several sailboats could still be seen moving silently across the water. The wind picked up and Katarina leaned into Erik. He gently lay back down, cradling her in his arms. They both looked up into the sky and watched the stars peek through the orange-red remnants of the sun's final ode to the day, as the turquoise waters of Sognefjord lapped upon the shore.

    Then it hit him. He turned and faced Katarina. *The turquoise waters of the fjord. Her eyes. They're the same color as the fjord.* He'd never identified the unique color before. But then, he'd never seen the waters appear this color before. *What kind of enchantment is this?* It was as though Katarina was being revealed to him for the first time. Staring into her eyes, which seemed to be the very embodiment of the waters surrounding them, he said, "Kat, you are so beautiful."

Their carefree days were short-lived. Katarina's Festspillene i Bergen project started its run, which kept her busy in the evenings. She'd also landed a role in *Arturo Ui*, and rehearsals for that had begun. Erik's Literature Tour project was in final preparations. The tour would consist of multiple performances in different coastal communities. Fru Gullestad was still finalizing the itinerary. Once the tour was over and Erik was paid, that was it. No more income.

He had nothing else lined up, and he wasn't what anyone would consider to be a man with great prospects in Norway. Not at present anyway. This was a major obstacle. He'd been lucky thus far. Sooner or later, he'd have to find a way to make a living if he wanted to stay.

This relationship with Katarina—whatever it was—had blossomed like a wildflower. Prior to getting to know her, he'd anticipated that he would probably leave sometime after *Vildanden*. He'd even written to family and friends, hinting that before long, he might be leaving Norway and heading back to the States. Now he wasn't sure. He was off-balance, confused. He was having trouble thinking clearly.

You're just going to have to accept that you don't have clarity right now. You can't stop living just because you don't have all the answers. This is what Erik had to keep telling himself over and over. *You need to trust that the right answer will come. Enjoy what's in front of you and stop worrying.*

Erik believed that there was no place on earth more beautiful than Bergen in the springtime. This little *byen om syv fjell* (town among seven mountains) was transformed during May and June. Of course, he hadn't been everywhere, but this little seaside hamlet had to be up there with the other natural wonders of the world.

The pinnacle of springtime in Bergen was Syttende Mai—otherwise known as the Seventeenth of May or National Constitution Day—Norway's equivalent of Independence Day in the United States. Every nation has a national day, but few of them are so enthusiastically and uniquely celebrated as the Seventeenth of May, which usually lasts for days.

There are flags everywhere—literally everywhere. People dress up in the traditional gowns, known as *bunads*, each one representing the region or county of their birth within Norway. Nordland, Hardanger, Telemark, Hallingdal, Trøndelag, and more—each *bunad* is proudly worn and beautifully accessorized with regional jewelry and accoutrements. Syttende Mai was a remarkable celebration—a genuine national outpouring of pride in the country.

Katarina was in performances most of that first day, leaving Erik free to wander about town experiencing this Nordic celebration. That evening, Erik and Katarina had dinner in her flat and watched from her balcony window as the celebrations continued into the night. It was impossible to watch such a spectacle and not be moved with a sense of patriotism. Emotions run high on the Seventeenth of May.

The emotionality of the day and the specter of the celebrations outside Katarina's garret window must have triggered a frustration within her. Their relationship had not developed to the extent that she wanted it to—that she needed it to. Erik wasn't making any decisions about the future. His indecision wasn't fair to her. She had a life too.

Her frustrations must have been like a voice in her head that kept repeating, "I've been patient, I've been understanding, I've been supportive…" Then her words came tumbling out. "You've missed so many opportunities by your stubborn refusal to engage with the people I've introduced you to," she said. "You continue to try and impress people with your Norwegian language, and instead you're hindering yourself because your language isn't yet good enough. Why do you do that?"

"I'm getting better every day. How can I grow if I don't practice?"

"That's an excuse. You don't want to grow. You've been given every opportunity. You're scared. You're hiding."

"I'm not hiding. I'm out engaging every day. You just can't see it."

The argument grew heated, and Katarina closed the windows. What she said hurt because it was the truth. He *was* scared. He *was* hiding. But rather than admit it to her, he kept arguing and defending himself. They both became angry and continued to fight.

She hit him with a barrage of examples where he hadn't asserted himself and had failed to turn this or that situation into an opportunity, or how he clung to antiquated ideas that had no place in this modern world.

"And you need to face the truth about your brother. It's asinine that you blame yourself or God for your brother's death. What nonsense to think God was involved just because your brother's number was fifteen and yours was five and then you got it changed to three hundred and forty-four or whatever. Only a cruel God would do that. He had nothing to do with it."

"My brother didn't—"

"And it's idiotic for you to feel guilty for going to the draft board to tell them what your actual birth date was. Anyone would have done that. That wasn't being dishonest, that was being truthful."

"My brother didn't deserve to die. He never should have been drafted. He was way too sensitive and honest."

"That's the problem with war. War doesn't care how sensitive or honest people are. War just wants to kill and destroy."

"There are things worth dying for—"

"And you think you should have died instead of your brother?"

"Yes."

"Neither of you should die. You both should be able to live out your natural lives."

"Kat, this is crazy. I'm not going to debate the justification of the war with you. What's done is done. I can't bring him back."

"No, you can't. Do you think Charlie would have wanted you to die so that he could live?"

"No. I don't think that. Just the opposite. Charlie would have wanted it this way."

"Did you hear what you just said? If this is the way Charlie would have wanted it, who are you to judge him or judge God?"

Erik opened his mouth to speak but couldn't think of an answer to her charge. He was no match for her. She was throwing truth bombs at him left and right, and he couldn't keep up with her. She'd been holding too much inside herself for too long.

Besides, she had a point. Charlie would never have wanted Erik to have taken his place. Why had he never seen that before? And what she said about God is probably true too. God isn't vindictive. Whatever her belief system was, she was probably right that he had been unfairly blaming God for Charlie's death.

The harangue ended, and the room became quiet. Erik couldn't say a word. He was guilty of the charges she made about him not asserting himself, and what she said about him blaming himself and God for Charlie's death stopped him in his tracks.

He disagreed with her about his "antiquated" ideas about faith and the existence of a creator. Without that connection, he feared he'd feel lost, cut loose, adrift in the world. But the other things she said...

He sat on the edge of the bed while her words ran around and around inside his brain… "Did you hear what you just said? If this is the way Charlie would have wanted it, who are you to judge him or judge God?"

He couldn't think anymore. He was exhausted and didn't want to argue anymore. The fight had left the room.

He sat silently for a long time. They'd never had an argument that had escalated to this level. The room was overly hot and stuffy. Katarina got up and opened the windows. The streets below were empty now. The celebrations were over. A cool breeze came into the room and washed over the bed.

"You're right," Erik was hoarse. His words came out as a whisper. "I am scared. I don't want to be, but I am."

He sat very still for the longest time before he spoke again.

"Charlie wouldn't have wanted me to die in his place. I know he didn't want to die; he didn't want to go to war. And I'm sure that he would have preferred that if someone had to die, it would be him and not me. That was Charlie. I was wrong, Kat. I've been wrong all along."

Charlie was gone. Erik was here. If it was the other way around, Erik would have wanted Charlie to be building a radio station or broadcasting or doing whatever the heck it was that he wanted to be doing. He would have gladly given his life for Charlie, and he knew then that Charlie felt the same way. He knew it. He knew that Charlie was happy. Right now, in this moment, wherever Charlie was, he was happy.

Seeing him sitting there, hearing his full-hearted admission of being scared and being wrong about blaming himself for Charlie's death, how could she not be moved? Yes, he was young and inexperienced. Yes, he was having to adjust to life in a different culture and a new language. But in that moment, it was plain for anyone to see that the truth was he was just a man, a man with a broken heart. She showed compassion.

"I'm sorry for yelling at you. I know I've been hard on you." She put her arms over his shoulders and pulled him close.

After a moment, he turned and looked at her. The woman he saw was not Hedvig or the young maiden in *Jomfruburet*. This was a woman who saw him. A woman who cared enough to see what others hadn't. A woman willing to confront him, to challenge him, to contradict him, to fight him, and to fight for him.

He moved his face closer to hers until his lips touched hers. It was the first time their lips had touched. The touch became a kiss. It was a slow, gentle kiss at first; it had been a long time in coming. It unleashed a suppressed passion in both of them. The kiss became long and deep and hard, like two thirsty souls drinking from the same fountain.

He leaned his body into hers and brought his hand up onto her breast, igniting an electrical current that coursed through his entire body. He gently pushed her backward. She resisted and stayed sitting up straight. Then she pivoted and placed her fingertips on his chest and slowly pushed him down onto the bed.

He tried to rise, but she held him down. She wouldn't allow him to sit up. He reached up to hold her, and she gently but firmly put his arms down. She leaned over him and then unbuttoned and removed his shirt. He attempted to resist, but she ignored him and continued to take off his clothing.

When she had stripped Erik down to his boxer shorts, she said, "I'm not going to have intercourse with you. You'll have to get those experiences from your American girls." Then Katarina pulled his shorts down the length of his legs and tossed them onto the floor.

She stood up, fully clothed, and looked down at the naked man lying on her bed. He felt raw vulnerability, but at the same time his body surged with excitement. Erik shivered as the cool night breeze from the open window flowed over the bed, enticing goosebumps to rise over every inch of his skin. She calmly raised her hands to her head and pulled out the few pins that held her hair up. She shook free her light brown locks, which came tumbling down across her face and onto her shoulders.

Katarina crawled onto the bed and knelt next to Erik. She leaned over him and let her hair cascade down onto his bare chest. Slowly and methodically, she swept her hair lightly over his skin. His arms reached out to stop her, vainly trying to arrest the sensations rising through every fiber of his body. Her hair, like a wildfire, continued to sweep mercilessly across the entirety of his body.

Erik closed his eyes and groaned. His body was on fire. He held his breath, arched his back, and pushed his shoulders and head deep into the mattress. Every muscle in his body was taut. Her hair kept sweeping back and forth relentlessly, until finally he could no longer contain the fire inside of him and the flames erupted. Only then did she cease the torturous ecstasy she was inflicting upon him with the sweeping of her hair. Slowly Erik's body relaxed, and his breathing returned to normal.

After a moment, Katarina stood, left the room, and returned shortly with a large towel that she draped across Erik's body. She crawled onto the bed and snuggled next to him, laying her head and hand on his chest.

He embraced her and kissed the top of her head. They lay still for the longest time. He watched as her eyes slowly closed, and her breathing became regular and steady. Eventually, she fell asleep. He was tired, but he wasn't sleepy. There was a part of him, deep inside his heart, that had been aching ever since Charlie left this world. Suddenly, it wasn't aching. Instead, that spot felt warm. It pumped warm blood with every beat. The warm blood coursed through his body, and he felt a sense of peace. He drifted off to sleep.

A week later—on a southbound train out of Bergen—Erik and Heather, his Literature Tour partner, headed toward Ekofisk, the oldest and largest oil field in the North Sea. Norway had a growing number of communities supporting its burgeoning oil industry. The workers in these communities came from all over the world. There were Americans, Norwegians, Canadians, Russians, Saudis, and others. Often, the only common denominator besides oil was the English language.

Fru Gullestad met Erik and Heather at the train station in Haugesund, a small community south of Bergen. The Gullestads owned a cottage in the mountains not too far from Haugesund and she and her husband were vacationing there. She drove them to the scheduled performances at two separate communities for the first day of the tour. Other than *Columbo* on Monday nights, Erik doubted there was much entertainment available for these workers—many of whom had their families with them.

The discovery of oil in the North Sea was changing far more than just the demography of Norway—it was causing an economic shift within the Scandinavian countries. Norway was rapidly becoming a dominant player in the geopolitics of the region. Following the OPEC (Organization of the Petroleum Exporting Countries) oil embargo in

October of the previous year, many nations, including the United States, were brought to their knees. This was not going to be Norway's fate.

The Literature Tour performances were well received, but for Erik, meeting the families afterward was the most interesting part. Hearing the stories of several families and their journeys resonated with him. He found himself reexamining his own journey in the context of the impact it had on those around him. Some of these workers had met their spouses in the communities in which they were now working. Some had put down roots and had started a family here.

These encounters provided an opportunity for Erik to look down the road further into the future. A man comes to a place, looking for work, looking to define himself, to make a name for himself. He makes friends, opens doors, meets someone special, starts a relationship, starts a family…

The more time he spent here, the deeper the roots would grow. The intimacy they'd recently shared was investing more sunshine and sustenance into those roots. Not deciding was deciding. This wasn't something that he could allow to happen by default.

The Literature Tour took six days and in that time, they performed at five different communities. Erik and Heather spent several nights with Fru Gullestad and her husband at their cottage, the other nights Fru Gullestad was able to find them other accommodations. Erik and Heather worked well together; they developed a kind of brother/sister relationship with neither one taking the lead. It worked out to be a mutually respectful partnership.

The Gullestad cottage was everything that Erik imagined and hoped a Norwegian cottage would be. Old and rustic with rich, age-blackened oak wood floors and thick knotty-pine walls. Floor to ceiling bookcases framed each side of the stone fireplace. Interestingly, the cottage boasted a door on the second floor for when those Norwegian mountain drifts blocked the first-floor doors. The Gullestad's spent a lot of time in their cottage. Hiking and boating in the summer months, skiing in the winter months. They often took extended family members and friends with them.

When the tour ended and it was time for Fru Gullestad to drive Erik and Heather back to Haugesund to catch the train to Bergen, Erik was reluctant to leave. These small communities with the billion-dollar views called to him. He envied the workers and the uncluttered lives they seemed to live. If one could carve out a life in Norway as an actor and do good, challenging work throughout the year, and then, whenever possible, retreat to one's cottage in the mountains and be near the fjords, that would be a good life.

On the train ride back to Bergen and during his hike up Mt. Fløyen to his apartment, Erik listened intently for the voice that would tell him what the true and right choice in his heart was. He needed to know. This wasn't something one decided, this was something one knew. And he didn't know. Yet.

When he arrived at his apartment, there was a letter waiting for him. It was from Alistair. The letter said his Bergen photographer friend had returned to town and was available to loan Erik the photography equipment.

Oh my God! I forgot about my photography assignment. I must develop those photos and get them in the mail immediately or they won't get back in time to be graded. That would mean a failing grade.

Erik turned right around and walked back down the mountain and went to the photographer's house. Fortunately, this time, the photographer was there when Erik knocked on his door. He let Erik in and showed him the equipment. There were lights, developer fluid, fixer, stop baths, basins, tongs, gloves, squeegees—everything he needed to develop negatives.

The only item he didn't have was a darkroom.

"Sorry, I can't help you there," the photographer said.

Erik had to move quickly. His only option was to turn the bathroom in the Empty Space into a darkroom. He called a taxi and took all the equipment up to his apartment. It took all night and most of the following day for him to develop the pictures.

When he'd finished, he called the taxi back and then returned all the equipment to Alistair's friend. Shelling out for two taxi rides was a lot, but the deed had to be done.

Erik had worked nonstop from the moment he'd read Alistair's letter until this exact moment when he returned the equipment. And that entire time, he'd thought unceasingly of Katarina and his decision. He had to see her now. The future was now the present.

Vildanden was over, he hadn't secured a part in *Arturo Ui*, and he had no other work lined up. He'd already been paid for the translation on Iris Menck's play, and the Literature Tour was finished. How would he make a living?

As he walked to her apartment, he went over everything in his mind again. *Kat has opened her entire world to you. She's been truthful and honest with you ever since she found the postcard. She wants you to stay. If you want to stay, you know that you and Kat can work everything out. She'll help you get started. Isn't that what she's been doing all along?*

Had he never met Katarina, this would have been an easy decision. Hell, it wouldn't have even been a decision. He would have taken his stage credit and experience from Den Nationale Scene back to the United States, finished school, and started his career.

Yet they did meet, and their hearts had touched. There were no painless options here. Not that he was afraid to face the pain, but he had to make the right decision. And the decision needed to be made now. He couldn't base this decision on just feelings, and right now he was having difficulty seeing the situation clearly.

As he walked up the stairs to her apartment, he prayed for clarity. He owed her the truth. He knocked. No answer. He waited, yet no one came to the door. He was exhausted. He sat down on the steps, closed his eyes, and fell into a deep sleep.

A taint from the darkroom chemicals clung to him as he descended into a grim dream that had him barefoot on the ledge overlooking the Diving Quarries. As he struggled to make up his mind whether to dive, he heard footsteps behind him.

"Are you really going through with this?" said the voice. Erik spun around.

"Charlie! You're here!"

"Of course. You don't think I'd let you do this alone? You may be bigger than me, but you're still my little brother."

"Charlie, I'm so glad you're here. I—I don't really know what I'm doing. To tell you the truth, I'm scared."

"'Erik the Auburn' scared? No way."

"It's true. Charlie, I've missed you. There's so much I've wanted to talk to you about."

"Go ahead. I've got all the time in the world."

"I didn't expect to see you here. Now I can't think of what I wanted to ask you. I'm so confused."

"I don't think you're confused. You know exactly what you're going to do. When you don't have a choice, the decision is easy. You just make the dive."

"Is that what you did? You didn't have a choice, so you just dove? Is that right Charlie? Charlie? Where are you, Charlie?

"Erik! There you are!"

Katarina's voice yanked him from the dream. He opened his eyes with a gasp of confusion and disbelief.

Katarina came up the stairs with a bag of groceries in her arms.

"It's maddening that you don't have a phone in your flat! Come on in. Are you hungry? Who were you talking to? It sounded like you were talking with someone."

Erik's mind was spinning as he extricated himself from the powerful dream. He traveled a thousand miles in seconds as he struggled to put two sentences together.

Yes, he was hungry. He realized that he'd eaten little since picking up the photography equipment.

Katarina made dinner while chatting about what she'd been doing for the last few days. As they ate, she asked about his Literature Tour.

Revived from the food, his brain started working again and he told her about the communities he saw, the men who worked on the rigs, their families, the beauty of the countryside, the Gullestads' mountain cabin, and the train ride along the fjords and through the mountains. It was an amazing experience, and he was grateful for having had the opportunity.

She smiled at Erik as she handed him a bottle of pinot noir. He opened the bottle and poured two glasses. They moved out onto the balcony and sat in her white wicker balcony chairs. The sound of a ship's deep bass horn drifted up from the harbor. Mountains in the distance appeared purple under the scarlet sky. This was the Land of the Midnight Sun, and the view was indescribably majestic.

For a moment, they sat there without talking, just taking in the beauty of what lay stretched out in front of them for miles. In that moment, Erik realized that he knew what was in his heart and mind…and in his soul. He was on the edge of the cliff, with his toes over the edge…

"I've fallen in love with Norway," he said. "I think I've loved it from the first second I arrived here, and I keep falling in love with it more every day." He took a long pause. "I've fallen in love with you too, Kat, but I can't stay. This isn't my home."

She was silent.

He continued, "I was trapped. I thought I was lost and that I came here to find myself, but no, I've always known who I am and what I needed to do. I wasn't lost; I was trapped in a prison of my own making—a prison of guilt, handcuffed with doubt. You helped me see that when you said I had to face the truth about Charlie's death."

There was a long silence. He wanted to fill the silence with words, but the words he had inside him were too heavy. He couldn't lift them. Besides, the hardest words had already been spoken.

"You can do whatever you want. I don't care anymore."

She had every right to say that. He deserved whatever was coming next. He braced himself for a torrent of anger. Instead, she stood up and walked into the kitchen. She busied herself with putting away the dinner things.

He stood, turned away from the boundless twilight, and stepped into the apartment. For a moment, the urge to take back everything he'd just said fought to be released. But that was impossible, and it wouldn't be the truth.

Eventually, she came out of the kitchen. Her body language had changed. She appeared stronger, resolved. She spoke and her voice was calm.

"When are you leaving?"

He should have expected that question but, as always, she was ten steps ahead of him.

"In a few days, I guess."

"I see," she said. She stepped past him and out onto the balcony, looking toward the mountains. Her back was to him. He wanted to reach out and embrace her. He wanted to comfort her. Then she said, "I don't think you should stay here tonight."

Erik winced inwardly. Yet he understood and he couldn't blame her. He felt foolish standing there with a glass of wine in his hand. He crossed into the kitchen and placed the glass in the sink.

He walked back in the room and looked at her as she stared out at the mountains. He wanted some reaction, some instructions from her, some response. She turned and faced him.

"Let me know when you're leaving."

"Okay," he said.

For a long time, no one spoke. Finally, he said, "Well, good night."

"Good night."

Her tone wasn't harsh—just the voice of one who was trying to control her emotions.

His heart ached for her. He turned and left the apartment.

The famed Bergen spring weather continued for the waning days of Festspillene i Bergen, showering the various performances and venues scattered around the city and countryside with its sunshine and beauty. Grieg music filled the air in a dozen different arenas. The harbor disgorged passengers from foreign ports of call.

Alone in the Empty Space, Erik packed the few belongings he had left after shipping several boxes home to his parents' house and giving away anything else of value. He said goodbye to a life that had come to mean so much to him. He struggled against the realization that this life not only in Bergen but also in Norway was all about to be over.

The next afternoon, Erik walked up to Fru Menck's portion of the house for a final cup of tea. While he was there, he used her phone to call Katarina to let her know when his train was leaving. She told him that she wouldn't be going to the train station to see him off.

Fru Menck had just returned from a European vacation and was filled with stories of meeting old friends and musical peers in Vienna. He had grown so fond of her, and here was yet another person he'd never be able to repay for the kindness shown him.

"Erik, we couldn't have asked for a better tenant. We'll miss you terribly. Please remember to thank your father personally from me for his valiant service during the war."

Katarina was all he could think about, and he couldn't shut his mind off. During his final night at the Empty Space, he wondered how his life might have been different had Katarina not found the postcard that he had half-written to Lucy. *What if she hadn't had the curiosity and the courage to reach across the invisible barrier and talk to him? What if she hadn't pushed and challenged him in nearly every facet of his life? What if she hadn't confronted him on his personal guilt over Charlie's death?*

Yet fate had dealt them a different hand. She did find the postcard. They did connect. She had challenged and confronted him, and they had touched each other's lives. And now they were each dealing with their separate realities. He couldn't speak for her, but his life had been forever altered, infinitely more meaningful, wonderful, and painful.

The brief Bergen sunshine season had come and gone, and now a light rain accompanied Erik on his walk to the train station. He should have been elated to start his journey home—he'd achieved his goal. He could honestly say that he'd found what he was looking for.

Instead, he was miserable. He'd hurt someone who didn't deserve it. Someone who had been kind to him, whose attentions had permitted others to view him as something other than an outsider. She'd been open and vulnerable with him. She'd been honest with him. She'd invested herself in him. *Could he say the same?*

Erik was no longer a boy, but he didn't feel like a man either. He felt like the shell of a man. He took off his pack and leaned it against one of the platform pillars and looked through empty eyes down the tracks.

A woman's hand reached around from behind him and pressed against his chest. He tried to turn but the hand would countenance no movement. A soft body pulled insistently into his back and a warm whisper penetrated his inner ear, triggering tingling sensations throughout his body.

"Don't turn around."

A familiar perfume ignited silken memories. The two figures stood there for a frozen moment. Erik staring stupidly ahead, unable to move, while the woman hugged him as if he was the only living person on earth.

Her delicate fingers slowly unbuttoned his raincoat, then reached up under his sweater and shirt. Erik inhaled a quick breath at the cool touch of her hand against his skin. Her fingernails lightly scratched him as they slid down his chest, leaving something moist and fragile in its wake. A søstermarihand—her favorite. The fragrant yellow orchid appears only when the sun shines during the short spring season. Except today there was only rain in Bergen.

She whispered again in his ear. "Don't turn around, and don't look." He felt her hands leave him and her body pull away. He stood for a moment, stunned and dumb—finally turning and looking out into the rain.

She was gone. Not a trace of her anywhere. *Was she just a figment of my beleaguered imagination?* He reached inside his shirt and pulled out the yellow orchid. The flower's aroma conjugated with the scent of her perfume and clung stubbornly to him, refusing to be washed away by the rain.

Sometime later that night, as the sun's rays evaporated on western peaks that turned purple in the night air, his eastbound train burrowed its way through and around mountains en route to Oslo.

Lit by a table lamp in the dining car, Erik opened his journal to the first page. He read what a boy had written in September of the previous year. An eager and optimistic lad, but one who was also idealistic and naïve. Clearly, the author was frustrated and dying to leave the United States, hell-bent to figure out who he was and to make some sense out of a senseless world.

Erik ordered a coffee. It was useless to try and sleep.

Normally, he would have been bunked down by now and the sounds of the rails would be lulling him to sleep. But he didn't want to sleep. He could still feel a burning sensation where the *søstermarihand* had touched his skin. He didn't want the stinging to stop. He needed the pain at that moment.

Erik closed the journal and pulled out his briar. Scratching a *fyrstikk* to life, he held the flame against his perfectly packed plug of Mac Baren Mixture. The rich, aromatic tobacco always had an ataractic effect on him.

His mind, like the smoke that dissipated throughout the dining car, wandered. Each click of every wheel as it rolled from rail to rail sent a signal up through the layers of the train until it reached the seat upon which Erik sat.

The train lurched and yanked him out of the unsettling torpor embracing him. His neck and back were stiff. An outer murkiness had crept inside the dining car, and an oxygen paucity signified they were high in the mountains. Erik was alone in the dining car.

The overwhelming aroma of Katarina's orchid penetrated his heart. He fought tears as a wave of loneliness engulfed him more intensely than he'd ever experienced before. The train surged steadily, inexorably eastward, further and further from Bergen.

She hadn't wanted him to go. She'd opened her world and invited him in. She'd been kind, generous, loving, and truthful toward him, and he'd walked away. She said she wouldn't see him off, and yet she came anyway. She came incognito, with great stealth and tenderness and, with a single parting gesture, she wounded him as surely and as deeply as if she'd held a knife in her hand instead of a flower.

The trip to Oslo takes seven hours. He needed to be wise about how he spent these hours. Right now, he needed to concentrate on this cauldron of emotions that was churning inside him. He needed to dive into the pain and let it burn to whatever extent it was going to. He had to give it free rein. He was wide awake, with synapses firing like a Roman candle.

Erik knew leaving Katarina was the right thing to do—it never would have worked. He wasn't worried about competing careers; they would have been mutually supportive of each other. Philosophically though, he sensed a tear in the fabric between them which would only grow worse in time. He didn't want a death of a thousand cuts. He preferred one bullet to the heart.

He'd known it would be painful, but he didn't anticipate that it would be like this. Not this painful. He didn't realize how much anguish was created by the simple act of her showing up at the train station—unanticipated and unannounced. He almost wished there had been an outdoor amphitheater where he could shout out his rage and anguish at the top of his lungs.

Erik turned to a blank page in his journal and mentally left the dining car. He went back to the green room where Katarina first confronted him with Lucy's postcard. He remembered her laughter at his embarrassment when he realized that she was the maiden in *Jomfruburet*. He mentally traversed the miles and the moments until he was standing at the Bergen train station being enveloped in the aroma of her flowered presence…

The Flower of Bergen

A cold Bergen rain dancing on the rails,
the final leg of my journey at last unveils
burning eyes and a tomb for a heart,
that she will remain, and I will depart.
Her terse eloquence echoes in my ears:
"I will not see you off;
you will not see my tears."

Amidst the crowds at the station
I cannot escape the sensation
that I am not alone
and being called to atone
for the hours my heart has spent
and from which I'll soon be rent
of this hamlet by the sea.

I try to lose this hollow feeling
as though from some promise I am stealing,
or as if a ghost has refused me leave
and to my backside has somehow cleaved.
A warm breath now finds my flesh,
"Do not turn around, do not make a sound,"
while a slender hand presses a flower to my chest.

And for a moment, the fragrant shadow clings
against my skin
like rain-soaked wool that stings
as though it were sin.
My face blushes a crimson hue,
singling me out to the platform crew,

and I know not what to say or do.

I walk forward, toward my train.
I try to turn, but it is in vain.
She will not let me see
the one who is left in this hamlet by the sea.
If I could change, I would do so now
and say that I lied, that everything is the same,
that I needn't go, that I may here remain.

But I cannot speak, no words from me depart,
as though the rain has struck dumb my heart.
And when the ghostly shadow disappears,
the rain rolls down my back like icicle tears,
taking nothing, stripping me bare,
leaving me freshly empty with only a fare
and the flower of Bergen branded on my heart.

And the Flower of Bergen branded on my heart.

The sun crept in through the windows of the dining car as Erik finished the eulogy or lamentation or whatever it may be called. He was exhausted and spent. All he could think about was sleep.

Sunlight began to contour the mountains that streamed by as he made his way toward the sleeper car. He forced himself not to look because he knew that if he did, he wouldn't be able to stop looking and he needed sleep. As Erik fell into his bunk, the rhythmic clicking of metal on metal lured him into a deep and heavy slumber.

The train lurched to a stop in Oslo. Erik clambered out onto the platform, groggy from all that had transpired in the last fortnight—the night he spent with Katarina after their fight, the trip into the countryside for the Literature Tour, staying at the Gullestads' cabin, getting home, finding out about the photography equipment, rushing to pick it up, spending the entire night developing the pictures, returning the equipment, and then going to Kat's, having dinner, and telling her that he had decided to return to America and would be leaving her. Finally, the coup de grâce, having Kat show up at the train station and giving him that flower.

There was a bank of phone booths in one section of the terminal. He called Jens and told him that he was at the train station and that he'd catch the local train to Kolsås.

Jens spoke to Erik in Norwegian, *"Nei. Jeg er i Oslo nå og har bilen til faren min. Jeg kommer og henter deg. Jeg vil være der om en halv time."*

Pleased that Jens knew Erik would understand what he said, Erik responded back in Norwegian that it was fantastic that Jens was already in Oslo with his dad's car. He said that he'd look for him in half an hour.

Jens was standing in the parking lot, leaning against his car, when Erik walked out, backpack on his shoulders and carrying Jens's guitar. Jens was smiling. He looked different. He looked older, happier, more confident. His hair was still long, but the Fu Manchu mustache was gone.

During the first part of the ride to Åstergard house in Bærum, the young men conversed a great deal in Norwegian. Jens was impressed by how much of the language Erik had learned, yet he had to laugh at the Bergen accent Erik had assimilated.

Before they arrived at his parents' house, Jens told Erik what had been going on in his life. This year, he said, had been an important one for him. He had truly needed the "year of solitude" that his little *hytte* in the mountains had afforded him. This had been a year of reflection, spiritual awakening, growth and reckoning.

He had experienced deep depression and some gut-wrenching lows; he had nearly lost his life at one point as he tried to escape the pain he was feeling. Yet he'd survived, and he was now ready to "rejoin" life. His days in the *hytte* were numbered, as he had plans to sell it and move back into civilization.

Erik hurt for his friend and wished that he'd been more available to him over this past year. Jens had been through hell ever since he and his family returned to Norway from living in America during his father's sabbatical. Erik was dealing with his own challenges and obstacles, of course, but his weren't life-threatening. This Norwegian brother had been fighting for his survival.

Erik was stunned as he listened to the depths of his friend's despair but thankful that he was sharing and speaking of these things as events that had happened rather than as events that were currently happening. At the same time, it was good for Erik to take his mind off his own dramas. He preferred to bury the mysteries of his painful, albeit wonderful, relationships deep inside him and lose the key.

"You played a role, Erik, a significant role." Jens was speaking as a man who had escaped a horrible fate, perhaps even death itself. "When I saw how you faced your challenges, it struck a chord in me. You never tried to advise me or interfere with any of my problems, but what you did do was ask me for help. You needed help in getting a foothold here in Norway. That may have been the best thing for me. Everyone else was pointing out my failures; you needed my help."

The joie de vivre which Jens was experiencing had an influence on his family, as well. It felt as though a new spring had bloomed in the Åstergard house. Jens was now a regular guest at his parents' home. His eyes were clear, and his mind as sharp as ever.

Seeing his friend emerge from the grip of this consuming stigma was like a soothing balm to Erik's soul. It gave him a sense of peace during these hectic final days in Oslo. There was so much to do before he left.

During his first night back in the Åstergard home, Erik went through Jens's room with a fine-tooth comb, looking in vain for that damned gram of hash that Dale Skarsgaard had gifted him. If Tove Åstergard ever found it, she never mentioned it.

He no longer had to worry about his school projects for St. Cloud State College, since he'd mailed them all to the States. Only his professors knew whether he'd be getting *As* or *Fs*, but at least he wouldn't be getting incompletes.

After purchasing his return airline ticket to Minneapolis, he visited a few tourist destinations he hadn't previously been to—the three extant Viking longships, Fridtjof Nansen's famous ice-breaking ship; Fram; and Thor Heyerdahl's Kon-Tiki, a 45 foot long raft made of balsa wood, which he used in an attempt to prove his theory that Polynesia and Easter Island were originally populated by people from South America and not Asia.

The last few days and nights at the Åstergard home in Bærum were bittersweet. He'd grown to love this family and felt as close to them as he did his own in Minnesota. He knew that the Åstergards had given him a gift that he'd never be able to repay. This was going to be one of those gifts that he'd be paying forward over a lifetime, as place and circumstance gave opportunity.

It wasn't just that he was saying goodbye to the Åstergards—it was also the end of his Norwegian odyssey. Erik had developed a profound love and respect for the people and the country of Norway. He understood now, in a way he never had before, the extent to which this cultural imprint had marked him. This journey had added immeasurably to the colors in the palette of his soul through the places and lives he had encountered.

Among the places and events he knew he could never forget were the days in London that he shared with the students from Philadelphia and the plays he saw there. Then there was his trip to Durham where he commiserated with his lonely friend Bob Keefendorf, only to go out for the evening and have a magical encounter on the stone bridge over the River Wear with the beautiful green-eyed coed. Finally, before leaving England, he spent a beautiful, heartwarming night in the Harwich B&B owned by Harriet and Aiden.

In Fredericia, Denmark he had his heart broken, but in the end, he came to understand that it was simply one chapter ending so that another chapter could begin. Erik running into Jim Coleman in

Copenhagen seemed providential and provided a rare opportunity to share his grief with someone who understood the breadth of what Charlie had been through.

In Gothenburg, Sweden, Erik chanced into a discotheque where a surreal voice orchestrated a fateful meeting with an enchanting young artist who would inspire and fill his imagination for many lonely months. Later, in Stockholm, he forged a lasting friendship with the charismatic and irrepressible Anders Lundström.

Finally, arriving in Norway, he was embraced by the Åstergards family who put him up for several months in their beautiful little community of Bærum. His night in Jens's *hytte* provided the two friends with a spectacular sunrise experience in the snow blanketed mountains. Erik's first trip to Bergen and Den Nationale Scene is imprinted indelibly in his memory. His visit to Trondheim and then on up into Bodø, gave Erik a rare perspective of life inside the polar circle.

His visit to the Trøndelag Teater facilitated an introduction to the multi-talented Alistair Wilderman who befriended Erik and opened many doors for him including witnessing the inner workings of the Oslo Opera House. On a quick side trip to Lillehammer Erik encountered a Sámi gentleman who provided him with an unexpected potential clue in his quest for the heraldic origins of Erik Torsen Hellberg.

Of all the experiences and encounters made during his travels, perhaps the place where they all coalesced most comprehensively was in the seaside hamlet of Bergen, Norway, where a piece of his heart is destined to remain. It was here, at Den Nationale Scene where he made his professional acting debut, an experience no actor will ever forget. It was here too, where a young man had to shed the final cloak of boyhood and take his place as a citizen of the world where he could measure his mettle against the teeming masses in the great unknown of life.

More than the places were the people. Erik would never forget the four students from Philadelphia, Bob Keefendorf, the green-eyed coed, Harriet and Aiden, Diana, Jim Coleman, Anders Lundström,

Mette, Colonel and Fru Lundström, Jens Åstergard and his family, Fru Gullestad, Kjell Sørhegge, Alistair Wilderman, Director Husman, Fru Menck and her grandson, Asher Menck, the kammerherrer, Katarina, and Iris Menck. God willing, he would soon return to reconnect with these good people and hopefully while the waters of the fjords surrounding Bergen were experiencing the next super bloom, turning their colors to an indescribably iridescent turquoise.

AFTERWORD

This is where Erik must end his tale—not because his story ends here, but because all the triumphs and tragedies that lay before him belong to a new tale, a new story.

Erik left his small town in the Midwest carrying the insuperable burden of guilt over the death of his beloved brother. He sought relief in the answers to questions he asked in the land of his ancestors. The kinds of answers he sought weren't contained in any geographical location, of course. The truths he found were uncovered in the choices he made—both the wise and the foolish ones. Knowledge, and certainly wisdom, come at a cost.

Katarina continued to light up stages across Norway, with both starring and subordinate roles. She chose her roles based on content and challenge—not on size or salary.

After her year abroad in Denmark and traveling all over Europe, Diana returned to Minnesota, where she earned her bachelor's degree in fine arts. Shortly after her return, Benny and Diana started a family together. As much as Diana LOVED her year abroad, she said that having her daughter was the BEST thing she ever did.

Alistair continued to design sets and costumes for the Opera House and other theaters throughout Norway for the next several years. Later, he was recruited by the Royal Opera House in London, where he spent several seasons before lending his considerable talents to various opera companies in Scotland, Belgium, and the Netherlands.

Fru Gullestad was offered and accepted the artistic directorship at Den National Scene, followed by similar positions at Det Norske Teatret and Den Nationaltheatret.

Mette went on to teach art at both the University of Gothenburg and at Lund University. Many of her works have been exhibited at Mollbrinks Gallery, No Limit Street Art Borås, and the Färgfabriken gallery.

Anders Lundström settled down and opened a private gynecological practice in Gothenburg, where he lives with his wife and three daughters.

Jens moved to Denmark, where he built a home and became a husband, a father, a life coach, and mentor.

Immediately upon returning from Norway, Erik became part of the acting company at Theater L'Homme Dieu in Alexandria, Minnesota. Following that, he met with director and former drill sergeant Dr. Cervante at St. Cloud State College, where he confessed to having learned the lesson of "no small parts, only small actors."

Erik earned two *A*s and one *B* on his Norwegian projects for school. The *B* was for photography. In his notes, the professor wrote, "Occasional brilliance in composition and range of subject matter, with apparent 'rushed' darkroom development technique…"

St. Cloud State College became too stifling for Erik, and he transferred to the University of Minnesota, where he earned his bachelor's degree in theater with a minor in Norwegian language studies. Following graduation, he spent the first two years of his American acting career in Minneapolis. During those two years, he also took ballet classes with the Andahazy Ballet Company. Eventually, the company offered him a dance scholarship and made him part of the corps de ballet. Apparently, he could "lift the girls."

The Hellberg family had buried their beloved son and brother in the family plot behind United Methodist Church in Madelia, Minnesota.

It seemed to be the perfect spot for Charlie. It was quiet, away from the metropolis of Minneapolis, yet not so far that they couldn't visit on weekends. Charlie's plot lay next to a giant old willow tree on the banks of a wide creek that wound leisurely through the church's property.

The family bequeathed to Erik the old VW bug that Charlie had owned before he was drafted. Erik set his sights on Los Angeles, but before leaving, he spent a few days alone with Charlie in Madelia. In the solitude of those moments, Erik recognized the eternality of the bond he shared with Charlie. They'd always been together and would always be together—as if Charlie reflected an omnipresent and inextinguishable light. Erik invested those days in planting dozens of perennials around the final resting place of Charlie's earthly remains and wondered why it is that we rarely recognize how much we love someone until they are gone.

The flowers reminded Erik of a certain seaside hamlet on the western coast of Norway. It was in this hamlet that a young man discovered an aspect of the truth he had been seeking. It is like a flower when it blooms and releases all the secret gifts contained within its petals, showering sustenance, life, and love on all who encounter it. These secret gifts can be discovered only by those who seek them with a pure and adventurous heart. Once found, they cannot be lost. They are like a flower that has been forever branded on the heart.

ACKNOWLEDGMENTS

I am indebted to the following early draft readers: Robert Pierce, Maureen McCormick, Jens Aagenæs, Reinhard Denke, Tom Shuck, Troy Schulze, Doug Stebleton, Bill MacLean, Jeff Nevin, Laurie Anderson, Ralph Weinstock, Cullen Douglas, Ted Hollis, Kimball Cummings, Jr., Terence Michos, John Ellefson, Gordon Harrison, Scott MacCloy, Coleman Luck, Michael Titus, Julia Thompson, Greg Campbell, Eileen Black, Ann Nyberg, Libby Sweiger, Art Mortell, Dom & Kae Oliver, and Deanne McLaughlin.

My gratitude also goes to Virginia Underwood and her extraordinary team at Shadelandhouse Modern Press.

Finally, without the encouragement and support of Maureen McCormick, Natalie Cleary, Robert Pierce, Reinhard Denke, Laurie Anderson, and Anthony Barton, this book would never have crossed the finish line.

ABOUT THE AUTHOR

Originally from Minnesota, Michael Cummings currently lives in Los Angeles, California, where he works as an actor, writer, producer and filmmaker. *Bergen Spring* is his first novel.